Diamond Boy
in the Rough

Helen Faul

Paperback ISBN – 978-1-910667-27-9
.epub ISBN – 978-1-910667-28-6
.mobi ISBN – 978-1-910667-29-3

For My Mum, Elaine Rothery.

Mum is no longer with us but she was with me during the infancy of writing this first book. I still feel her energy encouraging me, watching over my shoulder as I write, nudging me on. Thanks for sowing the seeds of my imagination as a little girl, making the world of books and storytelling such an exciting and adventurous place to escape to with no boundaries no limitations.

For Mark My Soulmate.

This has been a long time coming but you have held my hand with love and strength, been my rock and kept me sane, for that I will be forever eternally grateful, you never doubted I would get this book done and kicked my butt when I needed it. Thank you, thank you, thank you.

Meet the Family – Chapter 1

The Diamond family were on the move, leaving the hustle and bustle of Leytonstone, East London, many miles down the motorway to take up residence in a sleepy hollow of a village called Haddenham in the county of Buckinghamshire.

An entourage of removal vans, family cars and even a couple of motorbikes swept expectantly down the endless miles of elephant-grey tarmac. Alfie Diamond, youngest of the brood stared intently out of the window of the family car, he had tried to count the number of overhead lamp posts but soon lost interest.

After 47, you've seen one lamp post you've seen them all, he thought and anyway he was beginning to feel like the repetition would send him off to sleep and he wanted to be awake at the other end.

He changed his interest to the other members of his party, his mother was driving the car he was in, his father driving a hired minivan with two of his sisters Tallulah and Mollie in the front and the family cats, Tonka, Buffy, Angel and Cordelia, safely tucked up in the back with an assortment of bedding, towels, curtains and kitchen equipment because his mother didn't trust the removal men to not damage her highly-prized black gloss accessories and general household items that a family of eight would require to set up home.

Alfie was glad that he wasn't in the van listening to the girls gossiping about Zac and JLS, cooing over how lush they were, whatever that meant. He was also hoping his new room would have a respectable distance from them so that his Xbox wouldn't be drowned out by their caterwauling as his father called it. Best-case scenario, the room right at the top of the house; it was almost like a lighthouse, with 360-degree windows and a small balcony, just what a young man like him needed, at least that would be his argument should he have the chance to plead his case.

He could hope as much as he liked, deep down he knew it would never happen, no one not even his older brothers would get a look-in. Their mother Nellie had a deep-rooted fear of the room, in all the time they had visited their grandma they were never allowed up the entrance stairs leading up to the rooftop room let alone go inside. Once Charlie, Georgie and Jodie had tried to sneak the key and get themselves into this most secretive and elusive room. All they had needed to do was turn the rickety lock but the lock fought back and refused to budge.

"Damn it we need someWD-40. Dad says it works on everything."

Without thinking it through they sent Mollie on an errand to go and retrieve the WD-40 from Grandma's shed.

Whilst rummaging in amongst hand shovels, packets of seeds and pots of compost, she had drawn the attention of both her mother and grandmother who were spreading bark around the swing set up for the little ones, Alfie's younger cousins.

"What you up to in there Molls?" called Grandma rubbing her hands free of the mulch and beginning to walk towards the shed. Bang, crash, wallop! Mollie was now losing her balance and tripping over the various pieces of garden equipment.

"Ow!" she cried out as she fell and scuffed up her knee on the roughened floor.

Nellie's head appeared, "Are you OK? What have you done, anyway what you after?" Mollie blushed up which was an instant giveaway and stuttered a garbled reply. Sternly Nellie said, "Mollie what are you doing?" to which Mollie in a heartbeat gave up her two brothers and sister and told her mother exactly what her siblings were up to.

To say that Nellie was angry was an understatement and it was made perfectly clear that none of them was ever to attempt to get into the rooftop room. She had insisted that the floors were rotten and therefore very dangerous but not one of the Diamond children believed that, not even youngest son Alfie. There was something more to Nellie Diamond and her fear of that room.

Alfie made a mental note to himself as he sat in the back of his mother's car chewing on a Peperami. *Make a plan – get into room, get out without discovery!*

Looking to the other side of his mother's car he could just see in the distance his brother Charlie manoeuvring his way through the traffic on his motorbike with his girlfriend Emily perched behind him.

Alfie really liked Em as he called her, she was kind to him and stuck up for him when his older siblings tried to remind him of the family pecking order – he was rock bottom of the list a mere speck on the horizon, fit only for hand-me-downs – fortunately this kind of tomfoolery was just bravado as they all had a special affection for their baby brother.

As the motorbike drew level with the rear passenger's window, the devil took over Alfie and he decided to moon at his eldest brother, quickly checking that his mother could not see him in her rear-view mirror.

He switched himself around in his seat and dropping his joggers and boxer shorts proceeded to waggle his bare butt cheeks from side to side snorting and giggling to himself.

There that should do it, he thought to himself as he settled back into his seat returning his clothing to its correct position still grinning to himself. He turned to look at his startled big brother's face only it wasn't Charlie or even Em staring back at him it was a rather annoyed policeman, who then proceeded to indicate to his mother that she should pull over.

"Oh god what do they want I wasn't speeding?" Dutifully she pulled over and wound down her window as the officer approached.

In the meantime Jodie who was sitting in the front with his mother turned and said to her little brother, "You OK little man? You look a bit peaky. Perhaps you shouldn't have eaten an entire family packet of Peperami. Oink! Oink!" she smiled using her thumb to push up her nose.

Without lifting his head he muttered, "Yeah fine."

This puzzled Jodie. *No comeback. What's going on here?* she thought.

By this time his mother had vacated the car and was engaged in a conversation with the officer at the side of the road. Barely lifting his head up Alfie could see the officer gesturing and pointing back at the car.

Jodie meanwhile, who was still unaware of her little brother's crime, kept saying, "I wonder what she did?" as his mother now standing with her arms folded tightly across her chest looked back at the car as the policeman indicated to her to remain at the side of the road whilst he turned back in the direction of the parked car.

Alfie's face was burning crimson, "Oh crap, oh crap!"

Jodie turning to him said, "Oh, what's with the language? Mum will go mad if she hears you."

Letting out a big sigh Alfie said in reply, "That is the least of my worries."

By now the officer was level with Alfie in the back, he seemed to stand there for an eternity before bending to bring his face level with Alfie's who in the meantime was staring with a fixed gaze straight ahead whilst also avoiding his mother's laser beam eyes.

There was a tapping noise on the glass.

"Alfie I think he wants you to open the window," said Jodie unbuckling her seat belt and turning to stare at her brother.

"Do you think so!" said Alfie sarcastically just as he saw his other brother Georgie pull over on to the hard shoulder and get out approaching his mother who was now wildly and dramatically relaying what the policeman had told her. Georgie at this point was now nearly crying with laughter and the window was not slow enough for Alfie, who obviously wanted to avoid the impending conversation with the miffed policeman.

"Well young man I think you know what this conversation is going to be about," said the rather stern-faced officer.

Alfie then just blurted into panic mode. "I didn't know it was you, I thought it was my brother Charlie, he was on a motorbike with his girlfriend, I wouldn't have done it if I thought it was some one else."

"What did he do?" interrupted Jodie.

"I believe the term is 'moon'," said the officer.

Desperately trying not to giggle Jodie quickly turned away just as the hands-free car phone started to ring and 'DAD' came up on the screen.

Without thinking Alfie shouted, "Don't answer it!"

Jodie pressed answer. "Hi Dad."

"What has he done now? I just had a garbled call from Georgie. Where's your Mother?"

"Er Dad the officer is dealing with Alfie now. Call you back in a minute."

"Right young man, how old are you?"

"I'm 11 sir," he said throwing a look at Jodie who was taking great delight at watching her brother squirm.

"OK well you're too young to be arrested."

"Arrested! Arrested? What for?"

"Exposing your bottom young man and causing a disturbance on the road, this is very serious. You're very lucky not to be up before a judge," he said winking at Jodie. "I've had a conversation with your mother and we have decided that the best course of action would be to not set up your PlayStation or Xbox for a week once you get to your new house and that you must load and unload the dishwasher without complaining for a week and…"

"And!" said Alfie forgetting himself for a minute.

"Here, your mother drives a hard bargain. She wanted to make it two weeks. I had to do some negotiations. You also got one…"

Alfie knew what was coming next; feed the cats. As much as he loved the cats he hated the smell of cat food.

"You also got one week of feeding the cats and washing out their bowls."

Hanging his head he almost wished the officer would put him in chains now as he saw his mother make her way back to the car.

"OK Alfie do we have an understanding? Your mother has my number. I hope she doesn't have to use it."

Spluttering and stifled laughter came from the front seat.

"Yes sir," replied Alfie.

Alfie's mother got into the car. All she said was, "Consequences.".

By the time they pulled up outside everyone else had arrived and were already busy unloading, dragging huge items of furniture back and forth; organized chaos really. Of course as soon as Mother was spotted every man and his dog descended upon her with a million questions. Alfie was relieved, mistakenly he thought that a window of opportunity would open up and his great plan to escape the boredom of un packing, being helpful and generally get his hands dirty could be avoided, only he hadn't planned on his Dad waiting for his Mum to arrive and do the ceremonial unlocking off the door "Damn it" he cursed under his breath, no chance to slope off, A quick rethink was required he thought to himself, as he manoeuvred himself skilfully around the back of the largest removal van.

"Er, where do you think you're going sunshine?" It was Georgie. God knows where he came from but he was standing looming over his absconding little brother. "Mum thought you might try 'The Great Escape' so she has put me on guard duty, so you are not to move more than one foot away. Understand Tiny Pickled Onion?" That was Georgie's nickname for his youngest sibling and to be honest Alfie couldn't really complain about it, as in reality the name was perfect for his pongy feet.

Most of the time Georgie and Alfie got on well – they had common ground – both of them loved gaming. Whether it be PlayStation or

Xbox, both eagerly awaited new games with such enthusiasm that no one else in the family quite got apart from their uncle. Uncle Knobhead they affectionately called him but secretly they actually liked the fact that he was so geeky and was always so eager to update them on the latest reviews or releases with such intense enjoyment.

When all three got together Charlie would enter the room, turn on his heels and announce to the world, "Do not enter, there is a nerd-fest going on in there."

However, the minute the game talk stopped so did the temporary lull in hostilities, it was everyone for himself.

"You're not the boss of me," said Alfie as tried to sidestep his captor. Cue fake laughing like a mad scientist.

Georgie hugged his brother and said, "Oh but I am. Don't fight it. You are my butt wipe for the day. Come along Tiny Pickled Onion, first job of the day" watching as his Mother clumsily fell through the unwilling front door" Pausing he tapped his chin with his finger in a mocking manner of consideration, squinting out of the corner of his eye to get a sneaky look at Alfie. "Hum, what to do, what to do… I know! To the library my good man," he said forging ahead with an umbrella held high as if leading a legion of sightseeing Japanese tourists behind him.

Tutting and muttering under his breath Alfie dutifully, if reluctantly, followed behind dragging his feet as if they were entombed in lead boots as he passed by his Mother and Father hugging in the entrance way.

"We haven't even got a bloody library," he called to Georgie, who wasn't listening and had set off at a ridiculously fast pace. Alfie knew what his brother's plan was, the oh so predictable, 'go and hide from Alfie, jump out on Alfie and make Alfie crap his pants' plan. Well this time he wasn't getting his way.

Alfie allowed his brother to get far enough ahead and then he spotted one of the furniture removers in what was to be the sitting room.

"Excuse me mister, could you give me a hand? I just need to move some boxes for my Mum in the other room," asked Alfie with the sweetest smile he could muster.

"Yeah course I can little man. My name's Joe, you don't have to call me mister," he said ruffling Alfie's hair with his huge shovel-like hand.

Alfie allowed Joe to step ahead of him and said, "Just up here, I haven't got big enough muscles, those books are well heavy."

As the heavy oak door swung slowly back into the room a sense of anticipation swept through Alfie; somewhere in that room his brother was waiting in ambush.

He didn't have long to wait as out from behind the door a ghostly white figure swept into view screeching like a wailing banshee, wildly waving unseen arms. "Give me your soul. Let me eat your brains!"

Jumping back at least three feet Joe the removal man coloured the air with a few well-chosen swear words and staggered back into a tall vase standing on the floor. As if someone had pressed the pause button all the occupants of the room froze with hanging mouths, eyes wide, as the vase now took on the guise of spinning top, whirling round and round by unseen hands.

As if with superstrength, Joe the removal man dived with all the skill of a Premiership goalkeeper into the path of the whirling dervish, outstretching his palms, guiding them to cup and enclose the vase.

"Thank god for those shovel hands!" shouted Alfie triumphantly punching the air, ignorant of the flashing eyes of both his brother and Joe who now was panting heavily both with relief and annoyance.

"Let's have no more shenanigans today, eh lads."

Georgie hurriedly rushed to help Joe to his feet brushing him down, apologizing profusely, meanwhile Alfie snuck out of the door and up the corridor to freedom.

The only reason Alfie hadn't yet been missed was completely down to the fact that so many family, friends, cousins, sisters, aunties, uncles, brothers, fathers-in-law, old and new neighbours and even the local fire brigade, had amassed in the large area at the front of the house in amongst vans, one lorry, at least four cars, two motorbikes and, of course, the one obligatory nosey kid from up the road on his BMX.

A babble of conversations rang around the entire property, some folk catching up, others relaying instructions along a chain of assorted people; old, tall, small, short, young, girl, boy and to top it all six members of the local fire brigade who had all grown up with Nellie and Mark. All of them welcomed and appreciated into the mishmash of pushing, pulling and shoving that comes with house moving.

The hum of spoken word through the air was occasionally splintered by the crash of china smashing to the ground and "What the hell was that?" followed by a less than reassuring, "Nothing. Don't worry about it."

But that was the point, there was no point worrying there was too much to do and not a lot of time to do it in, well that's what Nellie thought as she looked up to the threatening skyline.

Looks like it might snow, she thought to herself. *Christ that's all we bloody need.* She made a mental note to put 50p in the swear jar whenever and wherever she found it. *Hope that smash was the bloody jar. Oh blast another 50p.*

Nellie Diamond was mum to six drains on her resources, as she liked to teasingly call them; three girls and three boys. People often asked her which were easier and of course she could have arguments for girls or boys, but in her mind it didn't matter she loved them all equally, but now as they were growing up she and Mark had decide that living in a city was probably not the best place for them. Well actually, if the truth be told, she hadn't really had any say in the matter. Mark was one of the most laid-back people she had ever met in her life, to the point of annoyance, but it was entirely his decision and he had been uncharacteristically and defiantly steadfast that there was no other option. His usual 'go with the flow' mentality was straight out of the window and this time he wasn't prepared to take no for an answer. A year to the day; totally coincidental by the way.

***

Nellie was rudely awoken by a massive banging.

BANG, BANG! The noise crashed through her brain ripping her from her slumber.

"Jesus Christ Mark, how many times have I got to tell you to turn off the bloody telly?" Instinctively she was patting the duvet in search of the TV remote. She suddenly realized the usual flickering screen wasn't present the bedroom was in total darkness. BANG, BANG! Gathering her thoughts Nellie listened and quickly jumped from the bed grabbing her dressing gown as she went.

"Mark! Mark! Get up, it's coming from downstairs," she cried flicking the light switch on as she ran from the room. By now other members of the family had also crawled from their beds.

"Mum, someone is outside the front. I can see blue lights," said Mollie. Nellie's heart began to thump furiously in her chest so much so she could no longer distinguish between the pounding on the door and her own heartbeat both ringing in her ears.

Running down to the hall she called out, "I'm coming. I'm coming." Her fingers fumbling with the lock and chain, frozen with fear at what lay beyond the door. Suddenly calm but purposeful hands took over from her trembling attempts, it was Mark. As he slid the final chain across and released the latch the door flew open with such force it sent him crashing to the floor as a figure sprang through it.

"Mum! Mum!" It was Georgie their second son. He was absolutely sobbing and babbling so much so no one could understand a word he was saying but to all and sundry it was obvious that something terrible had occurred. As Nellie cupped his face in her hands to make him focus on her she became aware that he had something sticky on the surface of his skin and the same strange substance down the front of his T-shirt, then she smelt an aroma that seemed so familiar. She questioned in her mind what was it then it suddenly dawned on her.

"Put the light on, put the light on," she barked. Drawing deep breaths she dared to look at her son's face, it was what she had dismissed in her mind. Blood!

Blood all over Georgie, over his face, all down his front, even soaking his trainers. Motherly instinct took over as she frantically patted her son, tugging and pulling at his T-shirt whilst everyone else stood in a circle stunned at the scene before them.

"Madam. Madam." It was a police officer who had now stepped into the hallway. "Madam he's OK," as he tried to gently lift her hands from Georgie. "Please calm down he's OK. It was his friend that was attacked, please calm down," he said looking to Mark to intervene. A female officer also entered and asked Jodie to get some blankets.

"Who was attacked? Who?" asked Jodie.

"Please just get the blankets; your brother he is in shock." She did as she was told.

"I think you should call your own doctor. Georgie wouldn't let us take him to the hospital, he probably needs something to calm him down," said the officer to Mark. "He has some minor injuries he sustained whilst protecting his friend."

Mark pulled the officer to the side. "Who was it and what state is he in?" asked Mark.

He was almost scared to ask judging by the mess Georgie was in, but before he could answer Georgie blurted out from behind him, "It was Lucas. Dad they stabbed him, they stabbed him really bad. He's dead I know it, I know it," and he fell sobbing in a heap on the floor with his mother rocking him.

"No son he's not dead," replied the officer. "He's in bad way but he is out of danger. You saved his life son when you gave him first aid, you did a good thing and you saved him, you gave him more time till the medic got to him."

Patting his son on the back and helping him to his feet Mark took charge. "Come on son let's get you out of these clothes." Mark steered his son towards the stairs. "Do you need any of the clothes?" he called back to the police officers.

"Best we take them just in case, just place them in a bag. Don't worry Georgie you will probably get them back."

In a steely cold voice Georgie answered without even turning round, "I don't want them!" Nellie steered her son gently up the stairs to the familiar safety of his room.

Later on placing the soiled clothes into a paper bag and without even turning to look round at her, Mark said in a calm, soft but firmly stated tone, "We are moving to your mother's house. I've got an estate agent's number. I'm asking them to come round today, OK?" He wasn't really asking her opinion and Nellie knew there was no argument to be had, for as much as the thought of returning to the house sent an unsettling tingle up her spine, the vision of her son covered in blood and his poor friend Lucas's impending long, hard recovery would be forever burned into her mind's eye. So with a troubled soul she smiled impassively in agreement.

It had not come as a surprise to any of the children. They had never known any other place than the scruffy old Victorian house they lived in, which seemed to be becoming more of a fortress against the harsh reality of changing life in a modern suburb than their home. You didn't have to travel too far from the front doorstep to witness the gang culture and seedy shadowy figures in the dark, swapping cold hard cash for little unassuming packets of white paper hiding the latest street drugs and of course their brother Georgie's brush with violence that nearly claimed the life of his best friend, had made the move a welcome one, perhaps even expected.

***

Nellie looked up at the old stone house as she slowly made her way down the shabby overgrown driveway; it hadn't weathered well since her last visit six months ago. That final day had been difficult to say the least, once the hustle and bustle of packing away keepsakes and delicate china, and making decisions as to what should go to charity had been made. Having thrown dust sheets over furniture and pulled closed the heavy curtains that hung like a comforting old favourite jumper around the weary sash windows, it finally dawned on Nellie that never again would she see the familiar form of her mother standing in the upper landing window, waving and smiling as they made their way towards the house with the children just as enthusiastically returning her wave back to her. Nellie's emotions had well and truly run the gauntlet that day from grief, anger, disbelief and even a weird sense of euphoria, probably down to her stress hormones kicking in. After all she and her sisters were exhausted, their journey with their mother whilst her illness had progressed had taken them on many lows but also surprisingly some unexpected highs, and dare she think it, a shift in the dynamics of her relationship with her mother over those two years of caring for her. From beginning to end nothing had been predictable about the cancer that had eventually consumed her mother, riding high on the hope that it had been contained and that she had been given a second chance, to in no time later, cruelly having those glimmers smashed, that this disease was going to beat her and surely and inevitably it did.

Nellie shook her head as if to dismiss these creeping thoughts picking their way from the dark recesses of her mind, she didn't want to deal with them today. Inhaling an enormous breath and forcibly blowing it out again, desperate to rid herself of the emotions gathering momentum within her, she silenced the engine, turning the key slowly as the menagerie of eager and willing family, friends and removal men all turned and stood in silence like expectant statues, she stared back at them, temporarily frozen as she absorbed the scene before her, stacks of boxes, assortments of furniture neatly but obstructively now building up around the entrance to the house. A sense of expectation on all of the faces before her "Oh my god!, we really are moving in" she thought to her self, swallowing hard "She really has gone!" her hands gripped the steering wheel as her knuckles whitened it was all she could to stop herself from firing up the engine, slamming the gears into reverse and high tailing it out of there but then a softening of her anguish .

A sense of sadness crept over her replacing the ones of anger and irritation that she knew would like to rear their ugly heads, an image of the black funeral car sliding away so gracefully like it was propelled on ice carrying her mother, the children's grandmother, to her final resting place, burned brightly in her mind's eye. She could feel the tears well up and fought them to make them stay on the tip of her lower lids to hopefully evaporate into mist, not roll down her cheek giving her away. She felt a small warm hand gently rest upon her own, she smiled a reassuring smile to her eldest daughter. Tap! Tap! on the window next to her, making her jump out of her skin, it was Mark grinning at her cheekily and winking at Jodie who was now clutching her chest "Christ Dad you scared the crap out of me" he laughed and waved the chunky rusting key at Nellie, "We waited for you, didn't seem right to go in before you got here". Undoing her, she secretly wished that they had just piled in taken the responsibility from her as she closed the car door behind tentatively, standing outside of the old worn oak door, quickly scanning the faces looking for her youngest son, she couldn't spot him so made a mental note to herself to get Georgie to keep an eye on Alfie.

As she looked up at the ominous brooding house, she noticed the curtains were all pulled shut making the house look as though it was sleeping, waiting for someone to come and wake it up.

As Nellie firmly placed her hand against the door for a tiniest second she felt a moment of dread, no in fact it was fear, the lock strained against her force, as though it was resisting her. Shoving her hip into the gnarled wood, Nellie knocked the wind from her lungs as she clattered against the stubborn door, an imaginary battle of wills prevailed, she gave it all she could. At last the heavy door swung away from her, everyone cheered. Although she had been the last car to arrive it was decided to wait for her, she had to be the first person to enter the empty house; she had wanted to ask the house to be kind to her family as they would surely be kind to the it. The battle at the front door didn't really convince her that her request had been duly noted. Stepping over the threshold leaving footprints in inch-thick dust, Nellie strode towards the centre of the hallway. Standing with her hands on her hips she looked up to the galleried landing slowly surveying the area, straining her eyes to see into the shadows.

"What can you see?" a voice whispered in her ear. Nellie spun round so fast she nearly lost her balance, laughing Mark caught her under her arm and pulled her close to hug her.

In mock anger she punched him on the chest. "You idiot you nearly gave me a heart attack."

Lifting her chin gently with a bent finger he said, "Seriously there is nothing to worry about it is just a house," as he planted an affectionate kiss on her forehead, the kids all piling in behind.

"Err get a room," squealed Alfie as Mark guided her towards the army of people awaiting their orders. In the distance a loud bang came from one of the rooms.

"Must be a window ajar somewhere," said Mark firmly directing Nellie towards the front door preventing her from looking back over her shoulder all the while not allowing her to make eye contact with him.

For now she would have to be content just to get everything in and hopefully in one piece as the first flurries of snow began to fall; thoughts of rotting window frames, peeling blistered paint and rattling downpipes were pushed to the back of her mind to form an orderly queue along with the feelings conjured up from her childhood. She purposely put a thought into her head, *I must check on Alfie*, trying to con herself that she wasn't disturbed by the house and the feelings that were beginning to gain momentum.

Whether the house liked it or not Nellie, Mark and the Diamond children were here to stay, she defiantly told herself, catching a glimpse of herself in a dust-laden mirror. The face looking back was not one of confidence or even excited anticipation at their new beginnings, more like that of a lost child.

Awakening – Chapter 2

Crisp dark curls sparkling like perfectly crafted black glass already had begun to stick to his pale forehead and temples as if purposely placed and arranged by unseen fingers, putting his hand up to ruffle his hair Alfie was firstly surprised at how wet the mane of wild curls had become and that there was a hint of stiffening from ice crystals. He half expected them to snap off into his hand much in the same manner that icicles would do. His clothing, which was completely unsuited to this environment not least to a beach holiday in the Bahamas, was also succumbing to the snow, sticking unpleasantly to his rapidly cooling body. There was no relief, no matter how he picked and pulled at his sweatshirt, the fabric just sucked straight back to his skin; the T-shirt underneath offering no barrier against the rawness of the cold. His shorts made out of tatty cut-down jeans seemed to be taking on the weight of a small toddler hanging on to his leg, as they absorbed the melted residue of the once delightfully powdery snow. His trainers, there was nothing to say about them, just that they were neither use nor ornament. They looked as if they had been mauled by a bear, then passed on to a pack of hyenas and the possibility that they had gone through a sausage-making machine would not have seemed unrealistic. The only thing keeping them together was good old duct tape, Alfie's staple for all DIY jobs; that tape had saved him from many a telling-off, well at least postponing the Spanish Inquisition that inevitably followed a mishap along the way, giving him some breathing space, time to concoct a cover story and had for a while earned him some dosh. It was surprising how many other kids at school seemed to court an unhealthy interest in how things worked and like him also enjoyed poking and prodding, usually with a bit too much enthusiasm, the end result being a snapped catch or a collapsed shelf, wobbly door handle or hands falling off a clock face. In one week he had managed to make a fiver just by selling a ruler's length of the sticky metallic tape at 25p a time, his selling point being that they used it on the space shuttle so therefore it followed that if this stuff was strong enough to survive having been into space and back, it could easily hold up a shelf with Mr Porter's family photos and a framed certificate and a small trophy for the longest drive in the county schools' golf tournament. The tape did its job but only for two days. Alfie's best mate Harry had a habit of slamming doors behind him to make a spectacular entrance into a room, down came the shelf for a second time crashing to the floor sending the highly prized possessions bouncing and dismantling as they slid across the surface of the lino, coming to a mishmash pile-up at the feet of a crimson-faced Mr Porter, who picked at the now flimsy flapping strip of duct tape pathetically just hanging on.

"Alfie Diamond hand it over now," he bellowed without even turning to look as he flapped his hand up and down trying to release himself from the leech-like grip of the tape. "Didn't stick this bloody well to the wall," he muttered under his breath.

Giggling and whispering bubbled up in the rear of the classroom. "What sir?" called Alfie doing his best impression of innocence.

"That bloody tape boy, you know exactly what I mean, get it up here or you're going to be the next thing I tape up." The class of 32 all gasped in mock shock at the use of a swear word from a teacher. "Like you've never heard me swear before. Shut the racket up or you're all getting detention." The class quickly fell silent and Alfie was made to donate his ill-gotten fiver to the school allotment fund. He chuckled to himself as he remembered that incident prodding at the soggy tape as he sat ankle-deep in snow.

He had no socks and at least two holes big enough to get his little finger in, generally caused by the excessive use of his feet as brakes whilst on his bike. Burning rubber he called it.

His father called it burning money. His lack of sock wearing drove his mother mental, she would bang on and on about how not wearing socks on his sweaty little feet would cause them to stink. A pungent eye-watering odour she called it; rotting the very fabric of the trainers and costing her a fortune to replace them for new non-smelly ones, that didn't look like they belonged to the local tramp.

He didn't know if it was the cold getting to him but he got the giggles, he had reminded himself about one occasion when he had managed to somehow bypass his mother's scrutinizing eye and slip under the radar to sit halfway through his cousin Luke's wedding before the occupants of the two pews in front and three behind began to shuffle, whisper amongst themselves, hold fingers tightly to noses or use the order of service pamphlets as makeshift fans, culminating in Uncle Felix booming, "What is that GODAWFUL smell?" Slowly all eyes turned on him as he felt a hand on the collar of his shirt, it was his mother.

How he wished his mother's hand was feeling the back of his sweatshirt now, at least he wouldn't be alone and for once in his life he wished for a pair of comfy warm socks. Huge fat tears welled up.

He shuddered as his teeth began to chatter, using all his energy and strength, he pulled himself upright to stand and survey the land around him, jumping up and down as if doing an Irish jig. Whichever way he twisted and turned there was nothing, not a footprint, memorable tree, thrown down sweet wrapper, not a single trace to lead him home. He looked up at the sky which was now heaving with a new snowfall, determined to wipe all trace of his size four feet. The flakes, softly falling gracefully on to his eyelashes, cheeks and lips caused him to lick them away. Erk! What a weird taste sensation; snot from his runny nose mixed with sour salty tears and cold icy powder from the flakes. If he hadn't had known for a fact that he had no longer than 20 minutes ago walked through this part of the wood, he could have easily believed that he had grown wings and flown through the forest leaving no trace of his journey, for as far as he could see there was virgin snow. By now the notion stuck that he was well and truly up to his neck in the brown stuff as his mother would say, only she used the proper word. Well he thought I'm gonna use the proper word, *SHIT, SHIT, SHIT*. Shit if she thought no one was around, quickly switching it to sugar if she realized people were in earshot. When would he be in such a position to shout out loud a forbidden word at home without fear of reprisal? But if he was honest he would have given anything to hear his father booming from the hall or kitchen, "ALFIE GO TO YOUR ROOM AND LOOK UP AN ALTERNATIVE TO THE WORD YOU HAVE JUST USED THAT DOES NOT OFFEND POLITE COMPANY!" In fact nothing would have given him more pleasure than to be sent to find out some fact or nugget of information that would improve his education or knowledge of life at this very moment of peril. He questioned whether somewhere stored in his 'useless information imposed by Dad' section of his brain there was in fact an answer to his current predicament. Try as he might he wasn't bombarded with solutions, the only thing that popped in to his head was how to build an igloo, but that was no good because he didn't have a spade which was a crucial piece of equipment. And his hands were by now next to useless with the biting cold. How indeed had he come to be in such a state of jeopardy? This kind of thing didn't happen to boys like him, there should have been a responsible adult to supervise him, pulling him back from the brink of danger, he shouldn't have to make any decisions regarding his welfare, he did not need to consider his choices because someone else should be there to point him in the right direction and wag a disapproving finger in his face. His downfalls were nothing to do with him it was always the fault of the poor bugger who got the short straw. After all he was the baby of the family who obviously could come go as he pleased, wasn't he?

23

Over and over in his head he could hear his mother's voice, *Consequences young man, consequences.*

Consequences indeed. He and he alone was the architect of his own downfall and for the first time in his 11 short years he considered that maybe it was time to be his own keeper, forge his own future and face up to the fact that he was no longer the cute little five-year-old bumbling along from one mishap to the next with big brothers and sisters ready to jump to his defence and sort out his mess. He should take on that role, it was only right to do so... But where to begin he thought as he spun around in all directions.

"Mum, Dad, someone!" he shouted sinking back to his knees hunching over himself. He knew they couldn't hear him, they didn't know he was even outside because he had taken every measure to sneak off undetected; how stupid, how dangerous now, stranded in the woods in his stupid Aussie surfer dude outfit.

The biting cold stiffened up his joints and the muscles in his jaw tightened as if to burst, his lashes clumped together and the cold raw air froze his lungs from within. It dawned on him that he was seriously in danger; he had pushed the button too far this time. His bare calf muscles purple with white blotches tightened with cramp.

He was desperate and desolate and more importantly completely alone. What should he do? Should he just keep walking in the hopes that he would eventually bump back into civilization or should he bed down in a makeshift shelter in the snow until someone came looking? Who would though? Sensible people had drawn their curtains against Jack Frost nipping at their windows, stacked up the logs for the fire and probably were munching down on toasted cheese whilst sipping hot chocolate. Alfie's stomach rumbled. His mouth watered at the thought of the melting salty cheese not sure which he craved more the food or the warmth it brought.

For the first time in a long time he began to sob, not just with a slight discomfort but with real genuine fear for his life, his cry became primal, surging deep from within his core sounding full of rage and anger.

His yells of pain from the gripping cold causing spasms within his leg muscles echoed and bounced around the surrounding trees. The caustic pain in his chest ground its way to the surface. This must be what a heart attack feels like he thought as he clenched at his ribcage with his gnarled and twisted fingers that no longer looked or felt like they belonged to him.

The sensation of sea sickness swam in his head, he was shocked to feel a circle of heat where he had laid his hand on his chest exactly in the spot covered by his birthmark. It must be down to his brain playing tricks perhaps, he couldn't define the difference between hot and cold, his nerve endings were beginning to shut down.

As panic set in deeper the source of the weird feeling felt like it was taking on a pulsing vibration all the time now, getting hotter and hotter, more and more powerful. Alfie fearfully looked down at his chest to be stunned at what he saw.

A glowing blue white light, instinctively he tried to brush away the object with his hand but it just continued to build and swell, his hand forcing against an unseen band of pure power. He could feel his eyelids being dragged back tight against his eye sockets like he was on a twisting turning roller coaster, G-force wrenching at his skin, sucking his flesh flat to his bone, an immense pressure bearing down on his body.

His ears now boomed with the crescendo of whirling waves of sound, absolutely battering him further into the ground all the time washing over his body intense heat from his head to his toes.

Is this what it is like to die? he thought as his body involuntarily began to shake violently, the light now so bright he couldn't bear to look but he knew it was surrounding him. Should he fight to survive or give in to the inevitable? The pressure was now bearing down on him making every cell in his body cry out for release again, he roared in defiance at what was happening to him as though competing with the sounds all around him. A massive wave of energy circled out away from him flattening everything within a three metre radius, his own heartbeat thumped in his head as he hyperventilated gasping for breath. The pressure lifted from him.

As quickly as it all began there was a sudden silence, as though time had stood still, he lay there staring straight up his chest heaving to suck in oxygen, his mouth bitterly dry and his throat raw from the terrifying experience he had gone through.

Then he heard a voice soft and comforting and felt the gentle movement of fingers tenderly stroking his brow and curls from his sweaty forehead.

"Calm yourself little one it has passed."

His eyes, still adjusting to the brightness, couldn't see where the voice came from and indeed to whom it belonged. His logical mind was telling him that he must be in hospital because they had obviously found him in the woods and now a kindly nurse was whispering in his ear that he was safe and any minute now his anxious mother would come bundling through a door to chastise him closely followed by his father and siblings. Only she didn't come. He could still feel the wet damp sodden ground beneath him, the snowflakes were still landing on his upturned face and now he was aware of a shape taking form. Like looking into a deep pool as a fish swims closer to the surface, he began to make out a face with long, really long hair falling gracefully either side of the cheeks, he could see the mouth moving forming unheard words. He put his hand to his ears to cup them as his hearing seemed to float in and out, muffled and baffling. Gentle hands eased him up into a sitting position as he stared straight into the eyes of the most beautiful face he had ever seen.

"We must be quickly on the move little one, they will be aware. I must get you to safety." Tugging him up on to his unsteady feet the beautiful stranger pulled a large woven shrug around his shoulders and then let out a whistle. Alfie flinched slightly at the noise but was still in shock as he surveyed the site before him. The ground around him was scorched as though it had been burned and within a small circumference encircling him, some of the trees looked as if something had torn and lashed at them sending broken branches and foliage flying in all directions, as if a bad tempered giant had stomped in amongst them wreaking havoc along his way, but more disturbingly a shadow of his humanly form was etched on the ground right in the centre of the carnage.

"Did I do this?" Alfie asked as he turned his face up to his presumed rescuer.

"Yes," she replied. "But do not worry you didn't hurt anyone. I will explain everything but not right now."

Again she let out the whistle and scanned the area watching and seemingly searching.

In the distance Alfie could hear what sounded like a bark but it was like no bark he had ever heard in his life before, deep rumbling and throaty almost monstrous, the thud of something pounding the ground could be heard drawing nearer and nearer. He turned to where he thought it was coming from, whatever it was it was coming fast and furious, crashing through the undergrowth.

It was all too much for Alfie, his own heart pounded in his chest, rivalling the pounding of the thing, whatever it was. Again he began to feel faint as he felt the strong hands holding him up. As his eyes slowly closed a huge dog burst forth out of the woods. He slipped gently into unconsciousness managing to hear parts of a conversation, as the welcomed warmth of slumber took him deeper.

"Risla aid me with the boy. Why did you take so long?"

"Lolah got caught in the briars; I had to cut her fur free, I am sorry Seraphina. Quickly we must get the boy mounted; there are already signs that the Gorans are making moves."

Seraphina caught his hand. "What do you mean Risla? What did you see?"

Hauling Alfie across the large hairy dog's back he replied, "Silver ravens, a whole flock of them, circling the boy's house. Do not fear we took measures to make sure they did not see us."

Seraphina's lilac eyes darted back and forth in contemplation. "We cannot take him back there now, they obviously know of him. Take him to the cavern. I will meet with you. First I must cover up the sight of the Awakening, they will try to recover his essence. At least we can keep that from them for the time being. Go quickly and protect him with your life."

Risla nodded, he knew better than to argue with her. As Alfie grumbled and stirred slightly Risla whispered to Alfie, "Do not worry little one I will not let you fall," as he jumped astride the huge dog grabbing handfuls of long shaggy grey hair. "Onwards Lolah, fast. Good dog."

Seraphina stood a few seconds and watched them disappear into the woods, then turned her attention to the site; the scorching was the biggest giveaway that had to be dealt with. Bending down on one knee she began to utter under her breath, placing her hand upon the blackened soil. Soon the surface of the ground took on a life of its own, bubbling and bouncing. From nowhere tiny black beetles appeared like water dancing across pebbles in a stream, they chewed up the soil and churned it till the form of the young boy vanished before Seraphina's eyes. Next she turned her attention to the trees. They were broken and ripped and she had to make it look as if humans had been at the sight chopping wood, with that she took out her blade and slashed at the gnarled ragged wood giving clean-cut edges and hauling logs into a makeshift pile. She purposely set a small fire then set herself down to wait pulling her hood over her flaxen hair warming her hands over the flickering flames, all the while listening for the telltale calls of the birds as they grew closer. Her eyes flicked from side to side but she was careful to keep head down as their colour would truly give her away. She spotted the first bird to be followed quite quickly by another four or five, their raucous calls sounding out around the woods, screeching at each other seemingly in frustration, as more and more congregated their calls become ear-piercing. She had to be patient as she felt the burning red eyes of the silver ravens watching her every move, she just gently prodded the fire turning the embers. She began to hum to herself to appear to be unaware of the birds like any human might be, hoping that they were taken in by her act. For the longest time the birds sat and she sat, no one party wanting to give way. No further birds came, no further bird calls, Seraphina had got away with it. All she had to do was wait for them to leave, probably to return to their roost at the boy's house. A little time later they left as did she. Eager to come face to face, up close with Alfie Diamond of the Delaney clan she took off at great speed.

In the meantime Alfie snored amongst the comforting fur of his rescuer, oblivious to how his life was about to change.

Time for a Faerie Tale – Chapter 3

As Alfie sat amongst the logs and animal skins with his hands outstretched towards the welcoming flames, he could feel his clothes, although not completely dry, were in a far better condition than when he had been in the open air. They no longer dragged down with the weight of cold dripping water and they gave off a slight whiff of damp dog but he didn't care, at least he was out of that terrible weather, sort of in a safer place, he didn't dwell on that thought though.

He sneakily looked out of the corner of his eye following Risla moving around the cavern as he prepared some food contentedly whistling as he busied himself with his task.

Risla was a funny looking one; well that's what Alfie's initial impression was. His hair was jet black, long down the back but shaved almost to the skin on the sides and there seemed to be drawings on the side of his head but the light was quite low so it was difficult to be sure and anyway Risla didn't stand still long enough to see properly.

They were more than likely tattoos thought Alfie as he breathed in the warm earthy smoke. He continued to study the long gangly youth, he had the look of a Native American about him, his Mohawk hair, and leather bindings strapped up his forearms more for adornment rather than practical use. Well at least that what Alfie thought. He didn't have the skin tone of an

Indian though, he was so pale he was almost luminous. Even his sister Tallulah wasn't that white and the family called her the Moon Child in reference to her pale but interesting skin, a term she used a lot during the summer months. Risla might be about the same age as his brother Charlie. He could certainly eat like Charlie, shoving food into his mouth whilst carrying out his chores and not averse to talking with his mouth full.

"You want some?" said Risla holding out a grubby looking morsel splattering Alfie's face with half chewed food. Scrubbing at his face with his hands and resisting the urge to gag Alfie backed himself into the damp cavern walls.

Risla laid out what looked like a lump of fur on to a large wooden board and unceremoniously chopped it in two, it was rabbit. Risla ripped back the skin with such skill he obviously had carried this act out many a time. Alfie's stomached rolled at the sight of the pinky-toned flesh separating from the silvery fur jacket. Risla grinned and then set it upon a rock sitting in the centre of the fire. It sizzled and spat as the moist meat adhered to the hot surface of the stone and the smell was intoxicating, but even though his mouth had begun to water Alfie shook his head in refusal at the food.

"Ah go on, it's only hopper. It's fresh killed. Build you up it will."

Alfie pulled a quizzical face as he looked Risla up and down, he was as thin as a rake, so much so his hands and feet seemed far too big for his body and yet he was still stuffing his face with nibbles and titbits he was pulling from a pouch tied to his belt. *Where did the food go?* thought Alfie. As Risla lent in and out of the fire to tend the food, Alfie could see that he had the same beautifully strange eyes that the blonde lady had only his were more prominent because he had dark eyelashes and eyebrows. His face in general, although seemingly human, also had an elfin element to it. Alfie half expected that Risla's ears would be pointed though in fact they weren't but they did seem to be larger than normal, probably to match his overly large hands and feet, and they were adorned with silver and gemstone spheres. His teeth were exactly how Alfie expected, yellow and pitted with leftover rabbit, with one front tooth missing from his piratey grin.

"Gots to keep your strength up little man, you're gonna need it," beamed Risla. Alfie's eyes widened. What could he mean and did he need to breathe quite so closely to his face?

Surely he would just be taken home to his family and that would be the end of his adventure. The furs around him seem to take on a life of their own as they began to move, Alfie must have jumped up six foot and embarrassingly screamed out like a girl. Risla roared with laughter clutching at his belly and kicking his oversized feet into the air.

Instinctively Alfie searched out an exit, running in all directions whilst being completely unaware that the furs were in fact Lolah, the Old English sheepdog, she who had carried him safely away from danger and who Alfie had inadvertently fallen asleep on. She had been stirred from her slumber by the delicious aromas now wafting around the cavern.

Lolah sat bolt upright surveying the scene before her, her pink floppy tongue hanging from her mouth as she panted and then let out a huge yawn exposing her teeth and red gums. Alfie froze as that is what his mother had told him to do if ever he came across a bad tempered dog and this dog was huge, with a huge mouth and huge teeth, he chanted repeatedly in a thick heavy whisper, "Don't bite me, don't bite me!" Risla in the meantime was crying with laughter at the strange shape taken on by Alfie as he stood in his frozen pose, he knew he should reassure the boy that he was completely safe but he just couldn't string the words together as his stomach muscles painfully cramped with the effort of laughter.

Lolah by this stage had wandered over to Alfie as he started to hyperventilate at the prospect of being eaten alive by such a vicious animal. She nudged him with her muzzle on his hand, hot warm breath brushing against his skin. He winced in preparation of gnarly teeth clamping down on his thigh or calf whichever was the most accessible. He had once been bitten on the finger by an irritated hamster and that bloody well hurt big time, Christ only knew how unbearable a dog bite would be, but he needn't have panicked as Lolah licked his face in a friendly nice to meet you way, not a I'm gonna chew you up way. Her tongue looked like a slab of ham which she slapped across his cheek all wet and slobbery. It had a weirdly pleasant roughness to its surface.

"Ooh yuk," said Alfie as he quickly rubbed his face with his T-shirt. The odour of dog breath mixed with soil and chewed up rabbit bones wasn't particularly nice and even less so when it was pasted on to his face but he did think her breath was mildly less offensive than Risla's.

Wiping away his tears of merriment, Risla composed himself. "She will not harm you little man, she is sent to protect you," he said patting the hairy angel on the head. "See, look when I lift the hair from her eyes, are these not the kindest eyes you ever seen?" Tentatively Alfie stepped forward towards the dog and in the dim light of the cavern he could see Risla was right as two warm chocolate brown eyes stared back at him without even the slightest hint of menace about them.

He moved closer. "Can I pat her?" he asked Risla.

Chuckling Risla said, "Yes, she is yours to command. She is your dog and mark my words little man, she will protect you to the ends of the two worlds."

Alfie screwed his face up at the last comment. 'Two worlds'? What was Risla going on about? He chose not to question him as he was rather chuffed at the fact that he was the proud owner of this fine specimen of a dog. However, he wasn't so sure his mother would be as enthusiastic once she got a look at the gigantic paws which were now heavily resting on the boy's shoulders. Alfie could feel his knees buckling with the weight of this very large dog.

"Get down Lolah you will surely squish the boy," ordered Risla.

"My Mother is going to go mental when she see's Lolah," said Alfie turning to hug the dog affectionately around the neck.

"What is mental?" questioned Risla. Either Risla was messing with Alfie or he genuinely didn't have a clue. Alfie was inclined to believe the latter.

"You know, throw a wobbly, have a fit, do one, lose the plot." Risla's blank expression confirmed that he didn't understand a word of what Alfie said. "OK then the lady with the long blonde hair seems to be the boss of you, what would she do if you displeased her?" still no sign of acknowledgement.

"I am sorry little man I do not understand human ways." Alfie began to feel his head for bumps because that had to be the logical explanation to all this madness. He obviously must have fallen and hit his head on a rock or something similar, his concussion was distorting his mind and pretty soon all of the hallucinations would stop.

"Will you stop calling me Little Man, that isn't my name. Why do you keep calling it me?"

Risla rose up and strode over to stand next to Alfie, he towered above the boy. Alfie tipped his head back to stare up at Risla.

"OK fair enough, point taken, but you could just call me Alfie."

Risla chuckled and ruffled the boy's hair. "OK little man." Alfie beamed back at his tall new friend.

Risla's attention was turned back to Lolah who was standing on all fours now facing the covered entrance to the cavern, a low throaty grumble vibrating deep within her chest, her head lowered in aggression.

Quickly he grabbed Alfie protectively pulling him behind him, putting his finger to his mouth indicating silently for Alfie to be quiet.

Goose pimples rippled up Alfie's arms and the hair on his neck began to stand on end, the dog's growling becoming more solid and full of intent. Alfie held his mouth firmly shut with both hands just in case a single muffled cry might sneak its way involuntarily past his lips giving them all away.

But then Lolah changed her stance tipping her head comically from side to side as if listening in anticipation of something good. She didn't have a tail so it seemed like her whole rear wobbled and wiggled to make up for the lack of a long bony wand coated in hair.

Risla knew who was coming through the tunnel leading to the cavern, his mood completely lightened. "It's OK little man, it's Seraphina, see how pleased Lolah is for her return."

"Who is Seraphina?" asked Alfie just as the beautiful blonde lady ducked through the opening.

"Did you fool them, have the silver ravens gone?" asked an excited Risla.

"Yes for now but we must get the boy back to the Lair it's the only place to keep him safe from the Gorans. They will be aware of his presence; his essence carries on the winds."

She walked towards Alfie and tipped his face up with her fingers, they were cold. She looked directly into his eyes. "You have your mother's colour."

Alfie was stunned. How did she know his mother or even what she looked like?

"Colour? What do you mean?" he stammered.

"Her eyes, the curl of her hair and the mark on your chest are the same as hers."

He was now utterly confused. His mother didn't have a mark. She had always referred to Alfie's birthmark as his 'Angel's Kisses' and she had certainly never shown him the same mark on her.

Seraphina could see his confusion, "Come sit." She patted the furs beneath her. He obediently dropped to the floor. "Your mother has the same mark as you, only as she has grown and she has forgotten. She also wears a pendant does she not, which she never takes off? Under this pendant is her mark, be it all faded from time, it is still there. She has been made to forget over many years, she pushes the pain away to the back of her mind telling herself she has memories made of dreams. Has she ever spoken of her Gemini?"

Alfie just sat with his mouth hanging. In his head he asked, *What the hell is a Gemini?*

Lifting his jaw back to its normal position Seraphina said, "I will tell you what a Gemini is."

Crap she can read my mind, thought Alfie.

"Yes I can and I believe that your mother does not like you to use such words."

Double crap this is some well weird... he was about to use the brown stuff word and then remembered Seraphina would hear his thoughts. Sheepishly he looked at her and said out loud, "Sorry."

"Never mind. Now listen very carefully to me Alfie we don't have much time and there is much to tell. Did your mother ever speak of her sisters?"

"Yeah all the time. She has two and a brother, they are my uncle and aunties, I've seen them loads of times, although one lives in America," and he proceeded to ramble on about the joys of driving across the US of A in a huge Winnebago with all his brothers and sisters.

Seraphina gently placed her hand on his mouth to passively silence his tales of travel. She looked him directly in the eyes and said, "No, another sister born at the same time, her twin, her Gemini."

The young boy looked confused. "You must be wrong, she is the eldest girl, then there is my Uncle Tom and then my Auntie Bella and then Auntie Nesa who is the youngest, there are no others. I'm sorry but you must be mistaken." He started to get quite worked up in his insistence of the facts. "Do you know something I think I would like to go home now I'm sure that my parents will be worried, I have been out a long time now so if you could just take me back that would be good."

Risla and Seraphina exchanged glances. Alfie began to feel agitated and could feel the panic well up in his chest like before in the woods.

"What are you a couple of weirdos who snatch kids? Is that what you are, is that why you won't take me back?" He was looking for a path across the cavern to get to the exit and out of all this freaky weirdness. *Any minute now I'm gonna wake up from this nightmare*, he thought to himself.

Seraphina knelt down before him. "Alfie you must calm down you are fully awake, this is all very real, you must learn to control the Awakening."

There she goes again with all mind reading crap.

"Really, please try or you will give us away and the Gorans will come for you." She tentatively placed her hand on his shoulder. "Slow your breathing down it will calm you." Whistling she called Lolah over. "Lay Lolah, here," she ordered the dog.

By now Alfie was breaking into a sweat across his brow. *Not again please not again*, he thought as the waves of terror began to wash over him as the pain in his chest gained momentum. He could barely hear Seraphina over the pounding in his head, her voice seemed so distant and faint.

"Lay down against the dog." She was ordering him, he instinctively struggled.

Risla bounded over and tried to reason with the very scared boy. "Little man hear me, hear me please. We mean no harm to you. Please lay upon Lolah listen to her heart. It will calm you, please follow her beat with your breath, you must calm down."

Alfie felt Lolah lick his hand; it snapped him back to consciousness as he began to listening to the voices.

"Follow her beat" that was the instruction, so he listened for the softened boom and the regular pattern as his face turned into the fur against her ribcage.

Boom, pause. Boom, pause. Boom, pause. Boom. The tension began to release in his taut muscles.

The heaviness of release allowed his body to seemingly melt into the soft fur of Lolah. His breath synchronized with her heartbeat, the pain diminishing in his chest and his eyes began to focus on the faces in front of him.

He could see the relief on their faces as they watched him recover. "Risla bring me the water and food."

She brushed the dampened curls from his face and softly held his hand in comfort not restraint, like a mother would a sickly child.

"Now you must try to eat," as she helped him sip from the wooden goblet. "The food will give you strength, your life force has been drained and sorely tested. We need you up on your feet, we must travel."

Alfie still was not willing to eat the rabbit although he accepted the water as his throat was parched.

"He be a stubborn one!" said Risla munching on the morsel that was meant to be for Alfie.

Tutting Seraphina snatched the meat back from her companion and turned to Alfie once again. "If you were able to have anything you could to eat right now what would it be?"

In a half dazed tone Alfie replied, "Oh that's easy my mother's roast dinner."

Risla leant forward. "Ooh is it lovely? Does it make your belly jump for joy?" he eagerly enquired.

God, thought Alfie, *that boy has an unhealthy attitude to food.*

Seraphina chuckled as she moved back over to the fire busying herself with her back to Alfie.

Whilst Risla continued to question Alfie about his favourite foods and treats demanding to know in detail about the smells, colours and tastes. Alfie came to the conclusion that Risla would probably be a sugar junky if the occasion ever arose, his excitement at the imagined sweet taste of a doughnut had him mesmerized, clapping his hands together and licking his lips.

"How wondrous these things sound." Punching the air in celebration, Risla lay down next to Alfie upon Lolah.

Alfie giggled at Risla's childlike joy as a waft of something familiar tickled his nose. He sat up on his elbows, if he hadn't known better he would have thought he had been transported back to his mother's kitchen on a Sunday afternoon. The smell of roast chicken was intoxicating and delicious with a subtle hint of lemon stuffing; hmm, his favourite smell in the world. He lifted his head and nose higher into the air and greedily snorted in the heady fragrance as Seraphina walked towards him carrying a wooden platter.

"First you must drink some water before your food," she said as she offered him the goblet again.

He eagerly knocked back the drink stretching to see what offering was awaiting his attention. For about a second he felt a slight judder skip up and down his body, a bit like the relief he felt when he was absolutely bursting for a wee and one of his brothers was pretending that the lock was stuck on the loo door.

After crashing his way in he would experience a euphoric bliss of release and that was the exact same feeling.

Oh crap! I hope I didn't pee myself. He quickly patted himself down to check for a telltale sign down the front of his shorts, they were bone dry. The water had left a strangely smokey taste in his mouth but he just put that down to the wooden goblet that it came from.

Seraphina was now gently waving her hand back and forth across the food encouraging the smells to venture in Alfie's direction.

He almost sent the platter flying in his haste to snatch it from her, he couldn't believe his eyes when he looked upon the feast presented to him. How could this be, it just wasn't possible; it was his mother's roast chicken dinner with all the trimmings.

Bloody hell, he thought as he shovelled the food in at a rate of knots, not caring that Seraphina was probably frowning at his language.

He had never wanted to taste this dish as badly as he did now, it was divine, each and every morsel burst with flavour as he happily aimed spoonful after spoonful into his eager mouth. He didn't question where it came from or how it came to be on an old wooden platter in the middle of a dark, damp, smelly cavern. His belly was groaning gratefully with the feeling of fullness and Alfie had a strange air of contentment.

"Was that good?" ask Seraphina as she surveyed the empty dish, winking at Risla whilst he grinned back.

She scraped the rabbit bones from the platter into the glowing embers of the fire, they didn't sizzle much as Alfie had all but chewed them clean. Chewing on chicken bones was a fitting end to a grand dinner, or so he thought. Seraphina replaced all the herbs she had used to prepare Alfie's 'chicken' dinner back into her leather pouch and tied it securely, she didn't want to risk losing her precious potions and tinctures.

"I should like a nap after such a good meal." He was mimicking his father, patting his belly and licking his fingers clean.

"There is no time for napping, we must be away before nightfall, the Gorans will be at full strength once the skies darken.

No we must on our way," insisted Seraphina.

"There you go again. Who and what are Gorans, and why should I be so afraid of them?" asked Alfie now standing, stretching out his legs.

Risla piped up from behind him. "You must show him Seraphina to make him understand. Show him the Orb."

Seraphina threw Risla a look of annoyance. "Do not speak of the Orb, he is too young to see."

Risla went to speak again but her intense stare shut him up immediately. Alfie could see her once light lilac eyes were now burning deep purple and actually made her look quite menacing. Risla had bowed his head in submission of her anger at him speaking out.

"Well, this is awkward," said Alfie. "What's an orb then?" Again she threw a look at Risla who was pretending not to notice whilst he used his knife to pick out the soil from under his toenails all the time aware of her burning eyes boring deep into his skull.

"I said, what's an orb?" Nothing, no one spoke. "OK if you don't tell me then I'm not bloody going anywhere," he stared defiantly at Seraphina.

It was all that Risla could do not to give in to the raucous belly laugh that was surely set to burst forth at the petulance of this young boy.

"Do not use…" She was interrupted.

"What? Do not use language that my mother wouldn't approve of? Well she's bloody well not here and so I can say what I bloody well like, you're not my mother!" he shouted.

She grabbed him by his arm and started to drag him towards the exit and the tunnel beyond.

"By the Elders you have tried my patience too long now, you will do as you are bid and for once in your short life be less stubborn." She shouted at Risla to put out the fire and gather up their things.

Lolah was at this stage jumping about in a kind of excitement but also with concern for her human charge. Risla tried to calm the dog down as her loud bark would definitely draw attention.

He set off down the tunnel after Seraphina and the boy who was still trying to dig his heels in.

"I'm not going! I'm not going!" he shouted.

"Seraphina see reason you cannot drag him through the briars hollering, he will surely bring silver ravens or worse, the Gorans, down upon us."

"If you want me to come you have to show me the Orb," shouted Alfie defiantly.

Risla nodded in agreement. "It is the only way Seraphina."

She came to a standstill, letting go of Alfie, putting her hands up into her hair and running her fingers down through the layers. She drew in a deep breath whilst contemplating her next move.

"OK, quickly back to the cavern," she ordered them.

Alfie almost squealed with excitement and anticipation, he was going to see an orb, whatever that was, but it sounded mysterious and dare he think, even a little dangerous. After all Seraphina was so keen not to show him so he steeled himself, completely at a loss as to what to expect.

"Whatever happens you must not break the surface of the Orb," said Risla.

"Yeah, yeah. Ooh isn't it spooky," Alfie nervously giggled.

Taking a seriously adult tone Risla took hold of Alfie and said, "Really little man you must respect and honour the Orb. You will witness things that will scare you and above all else you cannot move until the ceremony is complete, do you swear you will do this for me as my friend?"

Wow, this was beginning to get a bit heavy. Alfie was secretly wishing he had kept his big mouth shut. "Yeah of course I swear with my little pinkie."

Risla's face was blank. Alfie held up his little finger on his right hand and grabbed Risla's right hand pushing up Risla's little finger.

"Now we hook them see like this," and he wrapped his finger around Risla's much longer bony finger. "I swear," shouted out Alfie.

Risla seemed inquisitive and played with both their fingers twisting and bending them.

"OK that's enough that is actually attached you're gonna wrench it off in a minute," he said as he pulled his hand away to a safer distance.

"So it is like a pledge to honour then. Ah yes, it is like ours only we use a blade to slice the thumb, squeeze blood which we then bind together, a solemn promise to each other, we could do that also," said Risla smiling whilst holding out his small hunting knife.

"No you're alright mate I think we've done enough honouring with the pinkie thing OK."

Alfie was not a fan of blood especially his own. He quickly turned his attention to Seraphina.

She was now sitting with her legs crossed with a large bowl of water directly in front of her.

"Sit directly behind me and no matter what happens do not move, Risla sit behind the boy but first tether Lolah good and strong."

Risla nodded and called Lolah to the back of the cavern. He placed a leather bind around the neck of the dog and tied the other end to some exposed tree roots that had broken through the rock.

"It will not be for long stay down Lolah." The dog whimpered nervously as she bed herself down into the mulch and soil floor.

Alfie was trying to stretch and see round Seraphina bobbing from left to right of her body.

"Alfie stop being so fidgety you must remain behind me at all times," ordered Seraphina.

She was starting to get on Alfie's nerves, it was like he was being told what to do by an overbearing

headmistress. He pulled mocking faces behind her back, sticking out his tongue and pretending to be a monkey.

"For the love of the Elders, when will it become clear in your mind? I see everything you do and I hear everything you do, I have done so from the day you came into the two worlds born of your mother." scolded Seraphina as she spun on her backside with a firm determined look on her face.

"Jeez Louise someone needs to take a chill pill," retorted Alfie rolling his eyes at Risla, who was seriously biting down on his own lip to prevent himself from laughing at this most infectious little boy. Risla thought to himself that he had never experienced such amusement in his whole life as he had had in the few short hours he had known the little man. This was surely going to be an adventure and he swore to himself that he would teach Alfie everything he could to keep him safe and help him along his journey.

In the meantime Alfie had gently and politely leant forward to tap Seraphina on the back and coughed as if to let her know he was still sitting directly behind her as ordered.

"Now what?" she asked impatiently.

The young boy looked at her. "I was just wondering when in fact you said you see and hear everything I do…"

"Yes?" she barked.

"Well does that include when I am sitting on the loo doing a number two or perhaps even when I fart in Mrs McConnell's cooking class because to be honest I don't feel comfortable with that amount of intrusion."

Seraphina let out a huge sigh, muttered under her breath, shook her head and clasped her hands together tightly as if to prevent herself from lunging at him.

Risla grabbed him from behind clapping his hand over Alfie's mouth.

"Shush," he whispered into Alfie's ear. He could see that Seraphina was pushed to her limit, she might even lose her rational thought and transform Alfie into a small creature with her Magiks, he had seen her do it before and the little man was setting himself on dodgy path if he didn't hold his tongue.

"What's a number two?" he quietly whispered.

"SILENCE!" shouted Seraphina. "We will begin."

The candles all extinguished, the cavern was now in total darkness and Seraphina began to chant in a language Alfie didn't understand. At first nothing seemed to happen, she repeated the chant with more force and passion in her voice. Alfie could hear what sounded like water bubbling in a pan although it was much louder. A source of light began to grow in front of Seraphina and all the while the bubbling got louder and louder. Her dark silhouette set against the glowing globe of light; still the bubbling and steam swirled around them. Alfie could swear the ground underneath him was vibrating, the leaves and loose debris began to spin like mini tornadoes. Seraphina's long hair whipping like tentacles caught up in the energy of the growing globe.

Tiny particles of shale began to drop from the cavern ceiling along with clumps of moss that carpeted the surface of the rock. Alfie felt that he needed to screw up his eyes as so many bits were flashing past him catching on his lips and hair. Then suddenly there was a whoosh of air and then total silence.

From behind him Alfie heard Risla say, "The Orb!"

Alfie stared in amazement at the large silvery bubble-like structure gently bobbing suspended in mid air. It slowly rotated, glinting luminous colours as it went; lilacs, silver, emerald green, really beautiful.

Seraphina reached behind her and guided him next to her, Risla followed suit so all three sat in line with Alfie safely between the two Faerians.

"Ask of the Orb what you will but do not touch it," instructed Seraphina to Alfie.

Alfie was caught off guard, he wasn't expecting to participate. "Er, um. Does my Mother have a Gemini?" The Orb continued to spin no change. Nothing.

"You must name her," said Risla.

"Is Nellie Diamond a Gemini?" he asked. There was a slight jolt then again back to the regular slow spin.

Alfie looked questioningly at Seraphina, she too had an expression of confusion. It was as though the Orb had reacted then changed its mind.

Risla coughed drawing attention to himself. "Perhaps the Orb does not recognize the name you are giving it."

Alfie looked at Risla. "I knows me own mother's name, God!" Tutting he looked at Seraphina to confirm what a twit Risla was.

"Ah yes, that is right, well done Risla," praised Seraphina.

"What?" said Alfie.

"The name given to her at her pledging day is that not the name of your father?"

"Pledging day? What the hell is that? Christ I'm getting a headache with all this performance. Can't you just speak plain English?"

"Surely by now you can accept we do not speak clearly in your mother tongue because in fact we are not of the human race, we are Faerians. Whilst time has changed our language to enable some of us to walk amongst you, there will be occasion where we will differ in choice of words and a little patience would be gracious would it not?" Seraphina stared sternly at him. Alfie felt kind of embarrassed at his ignorance.

"OK I'm sorry but I don't understand what you mean by pledge."

"When your mother became pledged to your father did she not take his family name Diamond? She was not born with that name was she?"

"Oh, you mean married. We call it married. No, oh crikey what was Grandma's name?" He had to rack his brains for a good few minutes.

"I do not wish to rush you but we must give the Orb a question soon or it will disintegrate."

Excitedly Alfie threw his arm into the air, a reaction always brought on by question time at school in response to the teacher at the front of the class.

"I know! I know!" he cried as he bobbed up and down on the spot on his bottom. "Delaney, that's what it is," he shouted with such exuberance you would have thought he was going to win a medal.

With a big cheesy grin he asked out to the Orb, "Is my mother, Nellie Delaney, a Gemini?" In actual fact he had clearly forgotten that the most likely response was probably going to rock him to his core.

The Orb began to spin rapidly, all the colours blending into one as the spherical shape whipped around at lightning speed, generating a wave of heat not that dissimilar to a heat haze on a summer's day, only this was a turquoise blue undulating in and out, whilst a high-pitched squeal not unlike an old enamel kettle whistling for attention having been left too long on the hob, filled the air. Its piercing decibels forced Alfie to poke his fingers in his ears to protect them from the din.

Alfie stared expectantly into the Orb as the colours now completely disappeared to show a translucent ball, crystal ball-like in appearance.

He squinted his eyes and rubbed at them with his hands, as an image began to form in the centre. Mesmerized he slightly leant forward to get a better look.

Risla's hand immediately shot across the front of his chest acting as a barrier. "Do not touch."

"I know," came Alfie's somewhat irritated reply.

His attention now turned back to the Orb as the image became crystal clear. *Just like HDTV*, thought Alfie.

Two very young children, in fact babies filled the Orb, they both had dark curly hair and were obviously in some kind of crib facing each other, babbling away as if in deep conversation, their little chubby arms and legs waving excitedly in their play. They were both obviously girls as they wore pink romper suits and small white booties on their feet. Alfie could hear the sound of a woman humming and the rhythmic sound of a creaking floorboard as something tipped back and forth, it was more than likely a rocking chair. A small lamp on a table gave a limited light towards the crib but the remainder of the room seemed to be in darkness. The rocking stopped and then came the sound of light footsteps as a woman came into view, her hands reaching in to lift one of the girls from the crib. "Come along Mimi," she said.

Alfie's heart skipped a beat, he was watching his mother as a child with her sister Mimi. That must mean that the woman in the vision was his grandmother.

"Here we are Nellie, play with teddy for a bit whilst I feed Mimi."

Alfie gasped out loud, it was true his mother had been a twin, a Gemini, the two babies were identical. There could be no other explanation Seraphina had spoken the truth.

He turned to ask her a question but she stopped him. "There is more to come we must continue to watch," she ordered him turning his face back to the Orb.

He could still hear the soft humming of his grandmother and the creaking of the chair but there seemed to be a change in the baby Nellie, she was sitting up in the crib as though she was looking at something in the darkened perimeters of the room through the safety bars. She had discarded her bear and showed no interest in her other toys. Alfie also to tried to scrutinize the shadows, he thought he could see flitting shapes, nothing specific just varying shades of pitch black through to greys seemingly darting across and around the room, never staying still long enough to come into proper focus.

Nellie was beginning to become distressed, her eyes widened with fear as she pulled herself up into a standing position against the bars and precariously edged round the frame to get closer to her mother all the while checking over her shoulder as her cry became more urgent, more demanding.

"It's OK Nellie, nearly done, your turn next," came the calm voice of her mother. "Shh, shh little one," but Nellie wasn't having it, something was absolutely petrifying her. She was climbing at the rail but her little legs weren't long enough to reach to the top of the rail and she fell back to the mattress several times, but each time she jumped straight up to make another escape attempt. Even though Alfie knew it was a memory he was watching he couldn't help but feel peril for this little girl, his Mother, there was something or someone in that room and Nellie was painfully aware of the fact. He wanted to shout at his grandmother, "PUT ON THE LIGHT, LOOK!" The shadows were drawing nearer and nearer as the darkness began to swallow up the little amount of light from the pathetic lamp.

Risla let out a gasp which made Seraphina and Alfie both jump out of their skins.

"What is it Risla what do you see?" implored Seraphina.

Whispering he replied, as though he might be heard by the things in the vision, "Look! Eyes, burning deep in the dark, many sets of them. Can you not see them?"

"Oh my god yes, yes I can," replied Alfie.

"And I," said Seraphina. It was all that Alfie could do to stop himself from jump up into the Orb to crash into it and save the babies from this terrible evil he could so unbearably feel deep in his heart.

Nellie was frantic, hysterically crying, she couldn't have made it clearer that something very bad was about to happen, her cries unnerving her sibling Mimi she too joined in.

Out of the shadows, creatures came sliding across the floor keeping low as possible so that the human adult would not see them until it was too late. There were at least eight that Alfie counted and who knew how many more lurked in the shadows? As they came nearer into the light he could see their cruel claw-like fingers, reaching out and gripping into the wooden floorboards to drag themselves closer to their quarry.

Alfie was beside himself with outrage, how could his grandmother not be aware that she was not alone with her baby girls? The room was now swarming with the odious creatures with cruel intent on their minds. They had got close enough now it didn't matter if they were seen, they could easily overpower this weak human woman. They began to chatter, there was an evil malicious giggle, they lashed out at each other as they bumped into one another, each one wanting to be the one who completed their mission and grab the glory.

Maggie Delaney had never been so scared in all her life at the vision before her, the floor seemed to be undulating, moving with a life of it's own, as unrecognizable creatures writhed and clambered over each other, drawing in closer and closer to her and her precious babies. As if in union, they rose up on their hind legs and began trying to grab at Nellie in the crib and Maggie and Mimi in the chair. The stench of these dirty foul creatures filled the air, Maggie gagged from the smell and the fear as she lunged from the rocking chair with Mimi shoved under her arm towards the crib. The creatures swiped at her lashing at her face in an attempt to prevent her reuniting with her baby, they were trying to isolate the group and separate them but she wasn't having any of it. She kicked out with her feet at them, screeching with rage they were sent flying across the room as she made a path through these monstrous beings. Her legs were strong she was used to dealing with boisterous pigs in pens on her father's farm.

Standing at full height they only just reached her hip but they were quite squat and muscular, their leathered dark skin with wiry hair across and down their backs showed signs of many battles or beatings. Deep scars and even new lashings fresh with blood seemed to affect each and every one of them.

Alfie simply couldn't believe his eyes he kept saying over and over again, "Is this real?" The ugliness of the creatures was unbearable, they had long pinkish snouts, rat-like in appearance with yellowed tusks protruding from their gums, salivating copious amounts of slime from their snarling jaws underfoot it was becoming dangerously slippy. All Alfie could think was that these most depraved creatures were going to try and eat the babies as they seemed to be their focus.

Maggie knew she needed to get back to the door with both babies strapped around her waist, they were clinging on for dear life so tightly in fact they were almost choking her with their grip around her neck.

They were screaming, Maggie was screaming for help but they were at the very top of the house, who knew if anyone downstairs could even hear their calls? Then she suddenly thought, *The dogs* so she whistled as loud as her lungs would allow, they were down in the kitchen she prayed that for once her husband Jono had left the door open.

Seraphina spoke, "She is losing her strength." Both Alfie and Risla nodded in agreement, all seemingly forgetting that it wasn't the present but images from time past. Alfie sniffed as tears welled up in his eyes and Seraphina placed a comforting arm around him. Into the image burst two dogs, one small and the other exactly the same as Lolah, they came snapping with vengeance, with fierce protection of their beloved owner and her children, in all the confusion Maggie slipped and fell to the floor still holding both girls.

Alfie wanted to cheer with passion as the dogs set about destroying the intruders. He couldn't believe that Lolah was part of this drama playing out in front of him. "They're going to be OK aren't they?" he searched Seraphina's face but she didn't make eye contact with him.

"It isn't Lolah," said Seraphina, "But it is one of her ancestors." Alfie watched in amazement as the small terrier lunged with no care for its own welfare making short work of its enemy, driven by pure fury that such a creature would dare to set foot into this house let alone attack his beloved owner.

The lamp got sent flying and the room was plunged into total darkness, still Maggie screamed out for her family down below to come to her aid. The dogs were fighting back but they couldn't take on all of the creatures they were just too many. Maggie had backed herself into the fireplace alcove pulling both children with her. Trying to curl around them both to shield them from the creatures, she could feel her strength ebbing, the adrenaline beginning to leave her body as she felt one of the children ripped from her arms. Screaming, "No, no not my baby!" her legs failed her as she tried to stand. They were like jelly as she searched blindly in the dark with her hands, hoping against all hope that her baby daughter may have rolled close by.

Suddenly the main light flooded the room as the dark forms appeared to vaporize into the open fireplace. Maggie couldn't have chosen a worse place to try and shelter the babies, the creatures had come into the house through the fireplace and had left the same way only this time taking her baby with them.

Alfie sat stunned as he watched his grandfather, his grandmother's brother and his wife burst into the room trying to make sense of the carnage and attempting to console Maggie who was a babbling wreck.

Jono walked to the corner of the room and moved blankets, clothing, tipped up feed bottles to discover his baby daughter safely cocooned amongst the fur of Esta the Old English sheepdog.

It was Nellie, he turned to Maggie. "Where is Mimi?" he gently asked his wife.

"They took her, they stole my baby!"

The Orb began to spin rapidly distorting into a slender cone shape then dissolving into a sparkling mist of fine particles that softly floated down on to the three stunned faces that had been tipped towards the Orb, filling Alfie's open upturned palms resting on his knees.

All three sat in silence for a good few minutes absorbing what they had seen, only snapping out of their own personal thoughts by the sound of Lolah whimpering in the back of the cavern, where she had quietly laid throughout the whole saga.

"Oh forgive me, forgive me precious hairy one," said Risla jumping up from his position, he had completely forgotten about her. His nimble fingers quickly unpicking the binds that had secured the dog, she licked a single lone tear from his cheek as Risla hugged her neck. He felt so sad for what he had witnessed and also for Alfie, what must his little friend be feeling, to watch and not be able to lift a single finger to help, it must have been torture for him.

"Now you know the truth. There is still more to be told but my gut is telling me to get you back to the Lair, it is the only place I can keep you safe," said Seraphina as she gently pulled him up on to his feet brushing him down with her hand to remove the mulch from his clothing.

Rather surprisingly he nodded and threw his arms around her waist. She comforted him back as Risla walked over with Lolah trotting behind.

Alfie lifted his dirty tear-stained face towards Seraphina, "Were they Gorans? Did they take Mimi?" questioned Alfie in a broken croaky voice.

"The creatures are called familiar, they carry out the bidding of the Gorans, I believe that somewhere outside your grandmother's house they would have been waiting. Someone in your grandparents' family carried out Magiks to prevent them entering, or at least to prevent evil entering the house."

Alfie looked puzzled. "How did the familiars get in then, surely they are as evil as they come?"

"Both worlds hold the key to many Magiks, I have knowledge of some but I am not a master. We need the skills of Arksanza, he is the most knowledgeable Elder of our tribe, however I do know your ancestors descended from the tribes of The Emerald Isles and they of all the human tribes practised the most powerful Magiks, so strong was their belief in the unquestionable presence of evil. There are many legends of your kind fighting long and bloody battles against the Gorans and it is said that your kin in particular were directly responsible for driving them deep under ground where to this day they still are kept captive, that is at least till the night-time falls, they cannot walk above the ground in daylight.

"Wow!" cried Alfie. "Really, really? No messing?" He looked to Risla for reassurance.

He smiled his toothless grin, "Yes little man if Seraphina says it is so then so it must be." He scooped up Alfie and swung him around on his back to give him a piggyback.

Alfie was grateful that he didn't have to walk, he was absolutely shattered. He wearily let his head flop forward on to Risla's shoulder as Seraphina placed a fur across him tucking it underneath and around him with just a tuft of dark curly hair poking out of the top, he easily passed for a hunter's pack.

As Risla strode off down the tunnel with his precious cargo, Seraphina turned to look back at the now empty cavern checking that they had cleared all signs of the Orb, their fire and food and importantly she spilled out the entrails of the gutted rabbits on the ground hoping that as they rotted they would mask essence of Alfie. That was why she had asked Risla to carry the boy so that the Gorans couldn't follow them back to the Lair. If he didn't place his feet upon the ground then he couldn't leave tracks for them to follow him with, their Gorja hounds would be next to useless and the leftover rabbit guts would be a definite distraction for them if they did somehow find the cavern.

She was satisfied that she had done everything she could, blowing out the candle and wetting the wick with spit on her hands, she placed it into her pouch turned on her heels and ran down the tunnel to catch up with Risla and a snoring Alfie. She couldn't wait to be in the relative safety of the Lair she thought as she turned her eyes to the darkening skies, the birds' evening song heralding the beginning of night. She took that as a sign that for the moment at least they were alone, no spying eyes to tittle-tattle upon them. The songbirds would not have been so vocal if there had been even a hint of a tainted one lurking in the woods.

"Come Risla we must make haste," she said as she ran ahead clearing a path for him with Lolah scouting ahead for any signs of danger.

There was a slight grumble of discontentment from Alfie as his body jolted as Risla upped the speed and stride of his gait, then he turned back to a his reassuring snoring. Risla could only hope the little man's dreams were of the wondrous foodstuffs he had described and not of the visions delivered by the Orb.

Welcome To The Lair –
Chapter 4

Alfie had no idea how long he had been fast asleep tucked up on Risla's back but surely it wasn't enough.

"What ya waking me for? I'm cream-crackered," he asked Risla who was tugging at his arm quite impatiently.

"I have been trying to waken you for the last five minutes. I began by gently tickling your face, then I tried with my hair sweeping it across the top of your lip, I tried tickling you feet and then I resorted to my most smelly and pungent feet which I then realized would not affect you in the slightest as yours I believe stink worst than mine!" Lolah barked as if in agreement with Risla.

"Well even so, you didn't need to pull me arm out of its blooming socket," Alfie grumbled.

"Would you rather I dragged you through the freezing waters of the fall without waking you then?" scold Risla as he turned the boy's head to look at the splendour of the crashing mountain of water, cascading down over the rocks falling into a rocky pool of frothing bubbles.

"What? We ain't gotta go in there have we? Are you nuts?" he said to Risla.

Seraphina was standing to the side of the rocks. She had removed her heavy outer garments and was left in just her bare feet, leggings and a sleeveless tunic that was pulled in at the middle by a twisted leather belt to which her precious pouch was hooked, she had plaited her long white blonde hair and pulled it to the side; it stretched down to rest just at the top of her hip. Now that her arms were bare he could see she too had tattoos on both arms, beautiful bright coloured stories drawn with great skill no doubt but also he spotted scars, they didn't look like they belonged there, in parts they had interrupted the flow of the inked images, slightly breaking the crisp edges of the art.

Alfie felt Risla come close to him. "Do not stare at the scars and do not ask of them," he whispered into the boy's ear.

Seraphina gathered her belongings into a tight ball. "Come along, hurry. We must get to the other side. Alfie strip down to your shorts and tie your clothes as I have done, hold them high above your head, like so," she demonstrated how to keep the water from the bundle. "Use one arm to swim into the face of the fall but do not go through until I say, and the other to hold up the bundle." Alfie tested the water with his toe, its spine-chilling cold shot up his leg, he grimaced.

Seraphina spotted him. "There is no other way. I am sorry little one this must be done. Risla climb the rock and place the fixing stone, it is the safest way to get him through the water." Dumping his bundle of clothing next to Seraphina's, Risla clambered up the rocks with great dexterity hauling himself up with ease until he reached a ledge protruding out from the rest. A large boulder with a talisman carved into it was sitting precariously close to the edge it took all of Risla's strength to roll it across the ledge towards the source of the water. All the while Risla was muttering an incantation which Alfie didn't attempt to understand. It was becoming clearer as time passed that there were many strange things he would see, hear and feel, and he knew he would have to accept that for now, he must just take it all in his stride and see where the journey took him.

As Risla shoved with all his might the boulder gave into his demands and trundled over the opening shutting off the water, slowing it down to a gentle pour. Down below Seraphina and Alfie had edged their way into the rocky pool, Alfie desperately trying to kick with his legs and hold his clothes above the water.

The biting raw cold was eating into his bones as they waited below for Risla to give the signal to cross the threshold.

At last he called out, "The stone is in place." Alfie had got to the point of thinking that he couldn't hold his arm up any longer. Lolah launched herself into the pool with such great enthusiasm as she swam circles around the boy.

"Stop it Lolah you're making waves!" He could see under the crystal-clear water as she dove down deep with all the grace of a hairy hippo as she tried to catch up with the darting fish as they slipped in and out of the rocks, her long grey white hair trailing behind her.

"Quick, quick the stone will not be still for long swim behind me true and fast," Seraphina ordered Alfie.

Seraphina surged ahead, her strong athletic build propelling her easily through the water as she disappeared through the waterfall, Alfie panicked a little and nearly dropped his clothing into the pool.

Seraphina's face reappeared in the stream of falling water. "Come quick, what ails you?" she called.

"Can't I just drop the clothes? They're gonna get wet in the waterfall anyway. My bloody arm is killing," whined Alfie, spluttering and coughing.

"NO!" came the most definite reply. "You will be in the fall for all of a second, the clothes will be damp not wet, there is a difference now, stop moaning and hurry yourself across."

He kept thinking of a brick wall and not the fire-breathing dragon he would liked to have pictured although he wasn't entirely sure that Seraphina would have read it as an insult in her Faerian mind, it would probably be considered an honour.

The pouring water knocked his breath out of him. Christ knew what the full force of the rampaging fall would have done. He felt Seraphina grab him under his arm and haul him on the bank, he lay there flopping and heaving his breath into his lungs like a landed fish, whilst Lolah licked his face and then soaked him again, shaking her huge hairy coat to loosen the water from it. Seraphina sat serenely next to him, hardly breaking a sweat, unplaiting her hair, raking it through with her fingers, shaking out her clothes and checking the contents of her pouch.

"Did it get wet?" asked Alfie.

"No it has been waxed and tied tight with cord, it is fine."

Alfie tried to see if he could see through the fall but the waters were too strong, they were pounding and crashing so loudly as the flow returned to its former glory, he had to raise his voice above the din.

"Did the stone fail? How will Risla get through it?"

Seraphina laughed. It was the first time he had heard her, laughter lit up her face.

"Watch," as she pointed back to the fall. It seemed like an eternity that the fidgety boy had to wait when suddenly with no warning Risla came somersaulting through the thrashing water and landed elegantly on to the bank like an Olympic gymnast showering them both with water. He turned and bowed to an imaginary audience accepting noiseless admiration. Alfie giggled whilst he pulled on his clothes.

"What happened to the stone? Did it fall down?"

"No it rolled back to its rightful place, the chant will only work for moments, it is a guarded secret amongst our kin, it is the entrance to the Lair," said Risla as he pulled on his boots. "I shall arrange you with proper clothing once we get to the Lair," said Risla as he picked up Alfie's half rotten trainer. "These will be gracing the fire."

Alfie jumped up and down trying to climb up Risla's leg to snatch back his trainer. "Get off there's nothing wrong with them!" shouted Alfie whilst Risla dangled them just out of reach of his grasping fingers and pinching on to his own nose.

"The smell, the smell," said Risla mockingly grabbing at his throat and pretending to choke on toxic fumes.

"Settle down now, you will be waking the entire Set. I want to slip in gently under cover of dark," said Seraphina.

"What's a Set?" whispered Alfie to Risla.

"Well," said Risla. "The Lair is made up of many Sets, each one linking to the next. Some lead down under ground and other's lift high up into the trees but they are all connected by passageways. It would be very easy to get lost in them and that is the point of them, if ever we were invaded by the Gorans it is believed that they wouldn't be able to find their way into our sacred book rooms and most importantly the Honour Room."

"Wow, what's in the Honour Room?"

"Risla," snapped Seraphina, "that's enough of your tales. Come Alfie stay close by me hold tight to my gown, you will not be able to see as it is so very dark in the passageway, just trust in me."

"Haven't you got a light or something?" He didn't care much for walking about in the dark.

"Ooh what's the matter little man are you afraid of the night-time beasties?" teased Risla.

"I bloody well am not," insisted Alfie, "I just don't wanna hurt meself falling over."

"Why are we going in without light Seraphina?" quizzed Risla.

Seraphina was becoming impatient with Risla. He knew better than to question her and he seemed to have completely forgotten that the Faerian ways would be completely unknown to Alfie and also were meant to be secret and sacred. This small boy was going to need their help to understand and believe the life-changing knowledge that would be bestowed upon him in the next few days.

She turned and stared full on into Risla's eyes, the same menacing purple hue as Alfie had seen before, she did not speak nor did she brake away her glare, Risla appeared to attempt to turn his head but an unseen force seem to fix him in position, his own eyes flaring with silver flashes and gold.

Instinctively Alfie knew that she was doing the freaky mind-reading tricks only this time she was telling Risla off, not reading his thoughts. Risla bowed down his head in submission before her as she turned and grabbed Alfie's hand. Lolah had already bound off ahead, totally unfazed by the dark.

"Come, stay close and do not let go." Risla fell in place behind them as Seraphina took off at lightning speed, it was all that Alfie could do to keep up. He was totally disorientated, his feet catching on every uneven lump or bump, his free hand scratched against the rough surfaces of the passage walls, he really had no sense of how large or small it was. He occasionally stepped into a small puddle which seeped into his weather-battered trainers and several times Seraphina had stabilized his balance preventing him from clattering to the ground. He could feel a stitch gathering momentum under his ribcage but he didn't dare complain, he might have got the purple eye thingy from Seraphina. She must have sensed his discomfort he thought but she was a woman on a mission determined to get somewhere pretty damn quick.

Just as he thought he couldn't continue at the mental pace and would have to admit defeat, they came to a sudden stop. It was still solid black darkness all around but the air had changed, it was cooler and fresher as though they were out in the open but there was no starlight or welcoming greeting party with torches to guide their way. Alfie became aware of Risla standing next to him and reached out in the dark to find his tall skinny friend's hand. Risla allowed him to hang on to his index finger for comfort, he could sense the boy was unnerved. They all three seemed to stand for an eternity when suddenly in front of them a chink of light formed on the ground, like a glowing white slit on an inky blanket. It grew longer and wider and then a gnarled ancient hand came up through the entrance followed by an arm, a set of shoulders and a hooded head, huffing and grunting with effort. Alfie just wanted to bolt, what was this apparition before him? It was almost out of the hole that had been created in the ground, surely they should run.

Risla loosened Alfie's vice-like grip on his finger and stepped forward to help the faceless form step out of the confines of the ground. Out of nowhere Lolah came bounding at full speed crashing into the figure emerging.

"Oof, my goodness," an unknown voice cried as both dog and what Alfie thought looked like a life-size garden gnome bundled around on the ground, Alfie was confused. Why wasn't Lolah growling and snapping at this attacker? Risla was trying to catch hold of Lolah as she charged around in circles jumping up at the 'gnome' wagging her butt like a mischievous puppy.

The stranger didn't seem at all distressed at the unprovoked act of affection and let out a booming belly laugh which then quickly turned into a coughing fit.

"Lolah enough be still," ordered Seraphina as she stepped forward and gently stroked down the front of the stranger's face with the flat of her hand from forehead to chin greeting him, he returning the greeting back to her. "My Lord Arksanza." Helping the Elder to his feet she straightened up his robe and replaced his cap upon his balding head, while he pulled his plait around over the front of his shoulder tucking the end into a pocket. It was long and white with coloured ribbons twisted in amongst it. The plait came from the back of his skull and neatly sat under a small skullcap. Arksanza patted and checked everything was in place and then pulled his hood up over his head. Lolah was still nudging at his hand, snuffling at his pocket then sitting like she was begging for some kind of titbit. He obliged and pulled a small pouch from which he picked out what looked like a sweet of some kind.

"There are not many things of man's world that I care for but these little nuggets of pleasure and sweetness are one I can make exception for, eh Lolah?" Arksanza balanced the sweet on her black tarry nose holding his finger up then flicking his hand, she was given the freedom to gobble down the treasure. Gone in a second but she obviously enjoyed it as she smacked her lips as though she had devoured a large rib-eye steak.

"Now where is the boy?" said Arksanza bobbing his head side to side to look behind Seraphina for Alfie.

He had tucked himself tight into her side and was gripping on to her clothing for dear life, he felt like he was five again on the first day of school hiding behind his mother's skirt with a nervous gurgling stomach churning away as this strange-looking elderly face came closer and closer. Alfie couldn't see clearly as the only light source came from the entrance in the ground which was behind Arksanza so his features for now were shadowy, hidden from Alfie. This unnerved him, he wasn't comfortable being spoken to by a faceless voice.

From being a small child he had always studied the faces of people whilst they spoke to him. If they seemed open, had smiling eyes, making eye contact with him he generally found that he liked them but if they aimed to cover their mouths, look above him or down to the floor then more often than not they weren't trustworthy. This was proved when Alfie had come across the lad who was meant to be helping the milkman on their local round. He had been distinctly shifty, fidgeting from one foot to the next, asking Alfie through the open kitchen window if his mother had left the money out for the milk bill that week, all the while looking back over his shoulder and not actually speaking directly at Alfie or even turning in his direction.

He's a bad one," that's what Alfie had thought to himself so he had climbed up on a stool and slammed the window shut slipping down the latch pulling his mother's jumbo-size handbag with him which took a great deal of effort as she obviously kept bricks in there. Next he'd scuttled across to the back door to make sure it was locked and snatched up the key to wave triumphantly at 'The Robber' as Alfie had labelled him.

"You ain't coming in 'ere sunshine!" Fuming and tapping noisily, the wannabe thief tried to coax the small boy to come back to the window.

Stubbornly he had stared up at the irate teenager through the pane of glass and yelled the loudest yell he could.

"MUM!" He just saw the tartan-coloured shirt tails disappear through the bushes as his mother came running into the kitchen.

"What on earth is the matter?" she had said.

"It's alright don't worry sorted it out meself," he'd commented as he strode off like the man of the house with his bewildered mother scratching her head.

Now as Alfie stood before the Faerians, he felt a slight pang for home and his mother. It seemed to him that the further he went into this adventure the more weird it was going to become. He had already decided that he didn't need to keep pinching himself or that he had been injured or he was going to wake up from a cheese-induced nightmare.

"Come, step down into the light then my face will become clearer," said the elderly stranger.

Oh no, not another one, a bloody mind reader, he thought. *Is there anyone who can't actual read my mind?* he thought to himself.

In unison both Seraphina and Arksanza said, "Risla." Each one of them thinking perhaps they should have waited for the boy to verbally ask as it was becoming a bone of contention.

Alfie stared at them and then turned to Risla who was kind of giggling at the situation, then Alfie sighed and jumped down into the illuminated hole, he had got nothing to lose and part of him was curious to see what the Elder Faerian looked like.

He need not have worried, the eyes staring back at him were kindly and true, they were a washed-out lilac like Seraphina's but time and age had worn the brilliance of colour from them. Alfie wasn't sure but he could even have been blind in one as there seemed to be an opaque silver sheen to his left eye with an uneven puckering of skin on the outer lid. His skin was pale but papery with deep lines of life etched into his face. Alfie didn't think he had ever seen anyone as old-looking as Arksanza.

His nose was the same as his other two companions, slightly tipped, but his showed signs of wear and tear; maybe past battles. This was a face of someone who had many tales of high adventure to tell if you took the time to sit awhile and listen. The tattoos that once stood out bold and firm in his youth were now mere faded images as though softly painted on with a feather's edge, worn away by the winds of time. What little hair he had left was grey and wispy and was tied back into a long plait, so long in fact it seemed impractical. Maybe that was why Arksanza tucked it into his pocket else it would easily catch and be caught against trees and the like.

"Why do you have such long hair, bit long for a bloke ain't it?" he reached over to tug at Risla's which on the younger Faerian was thick and strong.

Risla instinctively grabbed at the hand of the boy. "You should not touch my hair without first asking of my permission."

Alfie was taken aback with the tone of Risla's voice it was very defensive. "I'm sorry, I didn't know," he said pulling back his hand rubbing at his wrist where the skin had been pinched.

Risla softened his voice. "I know little man, all is well. You did not mean harm. I am forgetting that there are many of our ways that you know not of. In our beliefs our hair is our strength, we do not cut it from our first breath until our last days in the two worlds, when we have drawn our last breath, then it is cut from us."

"May I touch it?" Risla reached round and passed the rope-like plait to the small boy, a weird sense of energy passed through Alfie's hands. "Ooh," he said, the sensation was unexpected Risla grinned.

"That is nothing, watch. Hold tight," he told the boy. Risla rubbed his hands together vigorously as a crackling wave of blue energy began to build all along the length of the plait, snaking out and arcing a luminous discharge of electricity sliding it's way up Alfie's arms, head and shoulders, making his curly wild hair stand on end; everyone giggled at the sight. Risla stopped rubbing his hands and the power began to fade, just popping sporadically, eventually fizzing away to nothing.

"God that is so cool. Why can't I have electric hair?"

"It is not a mere plaything Alfie. We use it to protect us in battle or ambush. Risla was just teasing at its full power, the Lockan is a mighty powerful weapon capable of killing foe."

"Oh my god really? What's it called again?"

"Lockan."

"Do you think if I grew my hair long I could have a Lockan?" said Alfie excitedly.

Ruffling Alfie's hair with both hands Risla laughed. "If you grew it anymore it would be as a huge great bush, under which you could hide."

"Now enough of this amusement, back to the task of bringing Alfie into the Set. It would be best to conceal him until lights dawn, no need to be bringing out the Set Dwellers, let them slumber."

"Yes I am in agreement with you Arksanza. We shall tuck him again like a hunter's pack and Risla can carry him forth," said Seraphina.

The tunnel ahead was well lit with flaming torches. Alfie could see various darkened areas leading off from the tunnel; they must be the other passageways Risla spoke of.

"Come quick little man jump upon my back as before, once we leave the tunnel we do not have far to go but be as quiet as you can, tonight we do not wish to draw attention." Seraphina and Arksanza wrapped the animal skins as firmly as they could around his body and feet attempting to make him look as least like a small human boy as possible.

"OK now we go. Lolah bind to my side and do not bark any greetings," said Arksanza pulling the huge dog to him talking directly to her. She seemed to comply pulling in close to the Elder. Alfie tucked his head down tight into Risla's shoulders as they set off with determined speed.

Alfie took a sneaky look expecting Arksanza to be behind the younger Faerians but he wasn't there. Alfie lifted his head above the shoulder line of Risla to see Arksanza matching Seraphina pace for pace with Lolah obediently trotting alongside.

Crikey, they must 'ave some bloomin' good vitamin supplements or maybe he eats all his greens, thought Alfie to himself.

They had now left the shelter of the tunnel and had come out into a clearing, there were little dots of light, similar to street lights back at home, subtle but equally gave enough light to see a path ahead. Alfie was meant to be keeping his head covered but he couldn't resist peaking out, he was desperate to get a look at the Set, what the houses looked like.

With one eye he could make out hut-like structures in the trees just silhouetted against the partial moonlight, down on the ground the same huts were there but longer and wider. It was very difficult to see with one eye whilst bouncing up and down on Risla's back which seemed all the more bony as this trip he wasn't dog tired.

Risla suddenly darted in close to a hut wall. "Shush keep quiet," he whispered to Alfie. Ahead Arksanza was greeted by a watchman as he patrolled around the Set. Seraphina distracted him engaging him in conversation whilst Risla nimbly slipped past and into the entrance of Arksanza's dwelling, dumping Alfie unceremoniously on to the floor collapsing in a heap next to the boy.

"All this sneaking around is very hunger causing," said Risla jumping up to ransack the store cupboards.

"I can't see anything, can't we get a light or summat?" asked Alfie.

"No, not till Arksanza returns. We must be quiet."

"Says you banging around like a bull in a china shop. You could wake the dead, the racket you're making."

Risla froze. "It is being true. Truly could I be waking the dead." Even in the inky darkness Alfie just knew that Risla's face would be mortified with horror at the thought that somehow he had brought about the awakening of souls passed over. He just couldn't help himself; he slinked along the floor like a serpent easing his way closer and closer to the unsuspecting Risla. Clamping his own hands over his mouth to silence the laughter building, he slowly rose up behind the petrified Faerian and oh so gently poked him in the back saying in his best James Cagney voice, "Put 'em up you dirty rat!"

All hell broke lose. Risla smashed and banged from one side of the room to the other, sending his gangly arms and legs knocking into Arksanza's possessions, crashing into cupboards, a crescendo of noise all around.

Alfie was in the middle of it all shouting, "Risla stop it, stop it! It was only me messing with ya. Crap we're gonna get in so much trouble. Stop it, stop it." Still there were the rumbles of falling pots and clay smashing, then suddenly the door flung open with torches flickering filling the room with light.

"What is this unearthly noise?" demanded a voice. It was Bevanelle, leader of the Set tree dwellers. She swung her torch around the room to come across Risla partially buried under the debris with his arms and legs poking out in all directions and his head and face covered in powders and potions tipped from their containers. Groaning as a large jar fell off a shelf and landed on his head spilling its contents all over him, Alfie could see hundreds of stripy small balls, rolling all over the place like marbles. They were black and white, he knew exactly what they were; humbugs! Lolah pounced in and about, disregarding the fact that Risla was being trampled by her huge paws. It was Arksanza's precious stash of human sweets. Holy crap, they were going to be in so much trouble.

The room was now filling up with the shaken residents of the Set all eager to see what the rumpus was about.

As Bevanelle's torch swung around the room a great gasp went up as the light picked up the face of curly-haired human boy... "Er hello."

More and more of the room filled with Faerians eager to get a glimpse, as the whispers drifted down the chain of eager sets of eyes, disbelieving their ears and wanting physical proof of the human boy.

"Make way, make way for Lord Arksanza," ordered Seraphina, physically barging herself through the jam of bodies, preventing them closing in behind her to allow space for the Elder to pick his path. She bundled out into the centre of the room. "Make way there is nothing to see. Please go back about your slumber." The whole room was stunned into silence.

"Nothing to see?" spoke out Bevanelle. "Then who pray tell is that sitting there amongst the pots and pans?" So many faces to look at, Alfie didn't know where to begin, all of them staring straight back at him, some male, some female, small, tall, blonde, dark, just too much to take in.

A unified whisper waved around the room. "He's the one."

He wasn't quite sure what to think about the attention he was receiving and so decided to try to shrink back into the darker corners of the room, whilst his travelling companions sorted out the mess.

Seraphina raised her eyes to the roof and then turned to look for Risla, he had in the meantime snuck down low into the crowd and was trying to ease his way out of the room unnoticed; too late she had spotted him. Reaching in amongst the various

Faerians still squabbling amongst themselves to get a look she grabbed hold of his disappearing plait snaking in and out of the carnage, for a fleeting second he did think about giving her a zap but he knew he was already in a lot of trouble so he gave up on that idea and just accepted his fate.

With all her might she yanked him out and on to his feet hissing into his ear, "What part of enter the Set under cover of night, in silence, fits into all this pandemonium?" She was absolutely furious with Risla, who was protesting his innocence.

Arksanza had to intervene, "Seraphina this is not helping to calm the situation." Slapping his hands hard together he ordered everyone to leave his home and told them that when morning light came then they would have a gathering in the Book Room when all would be explained.

"Where are you going?" Risla was still trying to sneak out. He was very tired, very hungry and just wanted his bed. "Sit over there with the boy," barked Seraphina.

"How you expect anyone of us to sleep now beggars belief," moaned Bevanelle as she too was ushered out of the door, firmly but politely by Arksanza.

He let out a huge sigh of relief as he slammed the old wooden door shut, double-checking that he had fixed the bolt over. Turning to survey the ramshackle room he tried to pick free crushed confectionary from the sole of his shoe, muttering to himself, "What a waste tut-tut."

Alfie jumped up. "Well that was a bit of ado weren't it?" He grinned an extremely fake over-the-top grin as though it would take the edge off the high tension in the room.

Seraphina was still fuming, the purple flashes of her eyes flaring out in the direction of both Alfie and Risla. The young Faerian knew not to make eye contact dragging Alfie back down to the floor.

"Just sit and let her anger pass. Believe me it is the best way," he said keeping his head down whilst trying to shake the dust and debris from his hair. "Now I will be having to wash my Lockan in the river, that will be a chore," said Risla.

"You're lucky I have not sliced it from your head young Faerian," called Seraphina.

"Enough, enough. This is not the time to apportion blame, what's done is done. They would soon enough have known of the boy. Perhaps a little less theatre may have been called for though," said Arksanza winking at the boy as he rubbed his sticky hand against his tunic. "Let us leave this mess till the morning light, I am sure we could all do with some sleep. Risla go home to your bed, you too Seraphina."

"But My Lord, the broken mess. Is it not right that Risla should clean it away?"

"Ah, it was not just my fault. I cannot carry all the blame," said Risla turning to Alfie expecting him to pipe up and take responsibility.

"What? It weren't my fault. You shouldn't be such a chicken."

"You said I would wake the dead, you let me think the dead were here with us in the room."

Alfie put his hands to his face and pretended to cry. "Wawa, get me a wambulance."

Risla's blank face made Alfie think that it was pointless trying to goad him as most of his human terminology was irrelevant, he wouldn't get the same reaction as he would from his brothers because he didn't understand.

"I take it from your impish expression that somehow I must be offended by your actions," said Risla with more than a tone of sarcasm.

"Risla to your bed," said Arksanza pointing to the door. Reluctantly he sloped off into the night air, followed by Seraphina.

She left Arksanza as she had greeted, him stroked her hand softly down his face. "Sleep well My Lord. Rest yourself and regain your strength for the coming days." He waved them off.

"Now young Alfie you can sleep upon the rugs with Lolah. She will keep you safe and warm through the night till morning's light. I shall retire to my chamber to ease my weary bones," he said as he picked his way precariously across the scattered remains of his belongings.

Alfie nodded. He was still a little intimidated by Arksanza although he felt safe enough. He lay down and cuddled up close to the dog, twiddling her fur around his finger as he lay in silence listening to her heartbeat and to the sounds of night-time outside the door.

The Book Room – Chapter 5

The waft of something sweet and wholesome, tantalizingly urged him from his sleep. The gurgling of his stomach and the tacky dryness of his mouth were all signals that it was time to awaken. Turning from his back to his side he slowly opened his eyes, the lashes gripping to each other like Velcro, as tiny chinks of light fought their way to the back of his eyes forming an image of a big fluffy face, dark moist nose and that floppy pink tongue hanging directly above him glistening with frothy dribble poised precariously on the tip of Lola's tongue.

For 30 seconds or so Alfie lay in a kind of limbo whilst his mind adjusted the picture in front of him. There was a lot of wood like being in a log cabin, but there didn't seem to be modern equipment like he would expect in his own room, no TV, no radio, no fish tank. Mind you, he thought to himself, he didn't actually know what his room at home looked like as he hadn't yet managed to spend the night in his new house before he had found himself smack bang in the middle of this adventure.

His mother must now be frantic with worry he had been out all night, they must surely have sent out everyone looking for him, he was beginning to feel troubled and guilty that they were being put through such an ordeal.

He sat bolt upright, making Lolah jump up in anticipation. He looked all around the room to see if he was alone, obviously someone had been there whilst he slept as there was evidence of food having been prepared but what troubled him all the more was the fact that the room had been returned to some state of tidiness.

There were the odd hints of the previous night's antics. Someone had attempted to tie back together a stool with twine and there was a jug with a missing handle in the centre of the table. A pile of very old battered books was stacked neatly in the corner of the room with the shelf they should have been resting on propped against them.

Again that lovely enticing smell just caught under Alfie's nostrils. Where was it coming from? He searched eagerly with his eyes, stretching his spine to see over the table without getting up from the rugs.

Looking towards what looked like a small stove, he spied them; a platter of pancakes still with steam rising from the top of the stack, the gorgeous aroma of hot honey that he could almost taste. His mouth watering, he quickly scanned around the room, apart from himself and Lolah, who was now showing a disturbing interest also in the pancakes, it seemed he was alone.

Jumping to his feet he stepped forward towards the stove, Lolah mirroring his movements with dribble dripping from her mouth, catching in her fur as she swung her paws one after the other closer and closer to the hot delicious prize. Both boy and dog, with eyes as big as saucers, sniffed great gulps of scrumptiousness as Alfie raised his hand to touch the runny honey dripping and oozing down the sides. Placing his finger into his mouth it was magical, Lolah whined.

"Oh sorry girl," said Alfie as he picked up the first pancake from the top. It was pleasantly warm but still he blew it a little before he made Lolah sit, her wagging behind in danger of bashing against the stove. He remembered how Arksanza had flicked his hand when giving the dog a sweet so he repeated the same action, she swallowed it down in one without so much as a thought of chewing.

"Blimey, you must have been hungry," he said with his mouth full of half-chewed pancake. "You can have one more cos I don't really know if we're meant to be eating them." She devoured that one in seconds as well.

"You can have as many as you like, I baked them for you," came a young female voice. Alfie nearly choked on the food, spluttering and coughing trying to get his breath whilst searching the room for the owner of the voice, at the same time slamming down his half-chewed pancake as if he had been caught stealing it.

She stepped out of the shadows from where she had been watching him. "I'm sorry. Did I cause you fear?" Alfie tried to compose himself and rub away the damp chewed morsels stuck to his chin.

Forcing a fake chuckle he replied, "Oh, of course not. No, please do not worry. I just swallowed it down the wrong hole." He tried to sound as manly as he could, well as manly as any 11-year-old boy could do in front of a very pretty girl, even if she was Faerian.

"What is the wrong hole?" she questioned, her beautiful large eyes sparkling and twinkling. He couldn't really hear what she was saying he just watched her pretty rosebud lips form the words but they didn't register, she held a bouquet of flowers in her hand ready to put into the jug on the table, they gave her a gentle floral fragrance mixed in with the intoxicating pancakes. Alfie thought he had died and gone to heaven.

Think of something cool to say, he thought to himself. "Do you come here often?" He winced as the words fell out of his mouth, she giggled as she picked up the platter and moved it to the table.

"I come often to help My Lord Arksanza, he is not so sprightly as a young man and I am happy to carry out his chores. Come sit, eat, you must have great hunger after your journey," she patted the bench. Lolah charged around and jumped up resting her front paws on the bench as if to ask where do I sit?

"Lolah take your bones and lay down by the fire, no more pancakes for you hairy one."

Alfie sat and watched the young Faerian girl move around the room. "Did you tidy all the mess?" he asked her, she nodded and he felt a pang of guilt. As she placed a pitcher of water next to him, he reached out for a goblet at the same time that she did; their hands made contact. Alfie jumped back with shock at the energy that passed between them, sending the pitcher tumbling over, spilling water across the table pouring down on to the floor. Inside his stomach tiny butterflies flipped over with excitement and he could feel his face burning crimson red.

"God I'm so sorry. It was my fault, it was all my fault. Last night too. I'm really sorry you that had to clean it all up. Please let me help." He tried to take the rag she grabbed from the cabinet from her hand but all he did was crash into the flower jug sending it in the same direction as the water pitcher.

Behind him there was laughter and he knew instantly it was Risla; he knew that belly laugh.

"So you're deciding to be sorry now are you? Pity you did not feel so last evening, when all and sundry were placing the blame upon me. When Seraphina was wishing to detach my Lockan from my scalp."

Alfie continued to mop up the water. "Yes thank you very much mate but I think we can manage 'ere. Everything is under control, everything is cool," he smiled at the pretty Faerian girl.

Risla strode around the table and took the rag from Alfie wringing it over his head. "You need to cool down little man, and to be rather honest you stink to the highest heavens. Perhaps a dip in the river is required."

Alfie was getting annoyed with Risla. He pulled him aside and whispered, "You're cramping my style. Even my mother don't embarrass me this much, just chill man, I got everything under control."

"Oh really?" said Risla grabbing hold of the boy, picking him up and throwing him over his shoulder. "It's off to the river with you my little friend."

Alfie wriggled and struggled. "Put me down you nitwit. Don't you dare chuck me in."

Risla wasn't listening. He set off with a sense of purpose, striding straight through the middle of the square, drawing the attention of all of the gathered Faerians all waiting to see the main event. News had travelled fast of the previous night's goings on. Risla strode straight into the waters and flung Alfie unceremoniously into the slow-flowing river.

"When you have scrubbed your grubby pits with this," throwing a bar of what looked like a lump of lard at the boy, "then you can get out and my sister will give you clean clothing. We have to go to the Book Room."

Alfie slapped at the water in temper launching the soap at Risla's head as he climbed back up the bank which was now lined with laughing smiling faces.

"Which one is your bloody sister anyway?" he asked as he studied the many female faces in the crowd. There was a slight shuffling and then a parting of bodies as a young Faerian stepped forward holding a bundle of folded up clothing with a pair of boots sitting neatly on the top.

"Behold little man, my sister, Eisiam," shouted back Risla. "What's the matter little man nothing to say?" he called laughing out loud with the others.

It was the pretty girl from the hut, she held out her hand to assist him from the water. "Come, dry yourself by the fire and put on these."

He shivered a bit but he wasn't cold. She looked all the more beautiful in the full sunlight as her auburn locks caught the breeze, glimmering like ribbons of silk. Her skin, perfectly pale, luminous but for the tiny copper flecks freckling across her nose. She was so delicate and fragile in appearance.

"Please take these," she said as she passed him the bundle. She stomped over to the river's edge shoved her hand deep into the glorious gooey brown mud drawing it up, forming it into a ball and without warning lashed her arm back at great speed unleashing the fastest moving missile Alfie had ever seen in his life, straight at the back of her brother's head. Time seemed to stop as all and sundry watched almost in slow motion as the trailing dripping ball flew through the air towards Risla who was completely unaware of the impending attack.

Alfie was in two minds. Should he call out to his friend or should he let him take his medicine as dished out by his sister? Beauty won out to friendship.

The splashing noise was nuclear, a sound wave rippled outwards to the audience watching with their hands over their mouths. "Wooow," a collective call went up.

Eisiam skipped past her brother and in the sweetest of voices said, "You better wash your Lockan again, hog brother of mine. Alfie is our guest and you should mind your manners." Beckoning to Alfie to follow, she turned on her heels and set off back for Arksanza's dwelling.

Alfie scuttled past Risla, as he stood with mud sliding down his hair and back, winking as he sped past the stunned Faerian.

"See you in the Book Room then," he cheekily called behind him. His thoughts of his family and their thoughts of his disappearance seemed for now to have been washed away in the river along with his smelly rotten trainers, he sprinted after Eisiam.

The entrance to the Book Room was not how Alfie had anticipated it to be in fact it was quite unassuming, if he hadn't been led there by Seraphina and Arksanza, he could easily have missed it.

There were no oversized ornately carved doors, no booming, crashing locks to undo, no armed guardians and certainly no drawbridge with portcullis ready to impale intruders. Just overgrown flowering vines, intricately woven in and out of the aged wooden planks pitted with the odd rusting iron nail.

Alfie was confused. They all seemed to have put great importance on this room and yet there was nothing about it to show it the reverence they bestowed upon it. That was until an Elder, even more bent over with age than Arksanza, shuffled forward and stood before the doors.

"I, Exsarmon, command the nature to open to your chosen ones." Everyone patiently waited then the vines began to rustle and come to life, drawing back from the wooden doors weaving in and out, releasing their grasp from one another, the petals falling from the flowers only to be gathered up by the very young Faerians collected into woven baskets. Drawn right back now and laid out flat the vines looking like coiled serpents set free. The doors swung open and back, as the Faerian Elders, followed by their kin, entered the room, splitting into two, going either left or right in a circle close to the walls, an endless stream of bodies.

It was Alfie's turn to cross the threshold, he had Eisiam and Risla either side of him but as he approached the vines jumped into life, whipping up in a frenzy, sliding straight at him, entrapping him cocoon-like, in a matter of seconds he was completely entombed.

Eisiam screamed and tried to rip at the vines with her bare hands, her brother pulled her back. "Help him, help him." She could hear the muffled cries of the young boy. "They will strangle him. Arksanza come to his aid."

Seraphina appeared next to her restraining her, Risla telling her to be quiet. "They will not harm him, have trust in me Eisiam."

The vines seemed to speak amongst themselves, rustles, snapping, shaking, individual finger-like vines probed into the cocoon, all the time a terrified Alfie silently screamed for help, just his eyes showing through the small gaps in the bindings. Eisiam couldn't bear to watch the fear grow in the green of his eyes, so wide now they looked as though they would pop from their sockets, she buried her face into Seraphina crying like she had never in her life cried before.

"Have faith, have faith, he is the chosen one. I believe that in my heart, but he must prove himself to the Nature." There was a rising pounding as the vines drew in tighter and tighter, the sound thumping louder and louder and louder. It was the boy's heart fighting to subdue the vines, his inner Awakening gathering strength; this was a battle of two forces. The sheer power of the vines lifted Alfie from his feet and propelled him still tightly packaged, slamming into the roof of the room, sending foliage and debris crashing down on to the heads of the gathered Faerians below. Arksanza swapped anxious glances with Seraphina as the roar of defiance sung out from above, Alfie was fighting back, he was finding his inner strength.

"Lay down low everyone, protect your young ones," called out Arksanza as some of the youngest Faerians begin to whimper at the seriousness of this occasion, they had never before in their young lives witnessed anything like this. Seraphina pulled Eisiam to the ground shielding her from exploding vines and the sap splattering across the room, a powerful vortex gyrated from its point of origin. Alfie was the origin, his essence rising up from deep within, no longer frightened by this primal rage as he had been in the woods, he embraced the sense of energy, he could feel the vines connect with his soul, surge after surge of images, knowledge of times past and some things to come from the future, at this very moment he had never felt so alive, his whole body zinging with pure energy. The vines had become one with him and he with them. They had willingly shared their ancient knowledge, as they had with Alfie's ancestors before him. If he didn't realize it before, he knew now that this episode wasn't an act of chance, a random encounter. It was his destiny, his preordained journey, circumstance and events all played to one end, to bring him to the aid of the Faerian race, who in turn would aid the humans, a fusion of the two worlds. Eisiam's crying slowed to a subtle whimper as she turned her head to look again at the scene before her. The vines had grown still their supple soft green tendrils now hardened, dry, brittle and dead looking; a rigid cage of capture around the boy from which he burst forward, free-falling to his feet, gasping for breath, sinking to his knees, dripping from head to toe in sap. Eisiam wriggled trying to break free to help her friend up.

"No Eisiam let him be," said Arksanza. "He must take his place under his own strength. Move back and let him enter." All the Faerians made space for him parting to the sides as he stood up tall, his tunic was torn and shredded exposing his chest.

There for all to see was the mark burning brightly like liquid larva erupting up from the earth's ripped crust, embers glowing out from the skin of this special boy, a tearing sound was heard as the skin puckered and distorted like cheese melting on a hot grill. Like a parasitic worm just present under the surface it formed a symbol, the slight blemish of his birthmark dispersed forever to make way for this strong and bold talisman.

Eisiam studied his face. He showed no grimace, no indication that this scene the whole room was witnessing was even mildly painful and yet as a bystander it could not have looked more horrific. He should have been on his knees in agony writhing in pain but no, Alfie stood straight and strong, staring straight ahead, almost just waiting patiently for the procedure to finish.

Even Risla seemed confused. For all intents and purposes Alfie looked like he was being branded but by who or what he didn't know. He knew the symbol from somewhere but in all the confusion he just couldn't recall it. He looked to Arksanza for reassurance. The Elder placed his finger to his mouth, Risla took this to mean that maybe it would be explained later. He turned back to his friend, the little man, just a boy. How could he have brought him here to suffer this experience and what more was to come? He stared intently into Alfie's eyes. There seemed to be change, the green was sharper, acidic, a whole new brightness like you would expect to see in a newborn baby, but with the knowing of an ancient Elder. Risla was definitely intrigued, he hugged his sister close to him to give her reassurance that Alfie was going to be OK.

Poor Eisiam he thought to himself. She of all his siblings had a natural nurturing trait. If ever an injured animal or creature was found everyone brought them straight to the House of Aspenola, tapping at the door and asking their mother if Eisiam was there, she genuinely felt their pain but she also knew what to do best for them.

Their whole house was littered with hidey-holes plugged up with recovering or ailing patients, it wasn't uncommon to retire to bed and find a hopper tucked neatly up along with your feet, apparently the warmth did them good, or find a mouse secreted in a pocket of a tunic with a note pinned to it 'Do not wear this day'. When she wasn't fixing up all creatures great and small, she carried out many tasks for the Elders in the village. Her mother would proudly speak of her to her neighbouring Faerians, "That young one is destined for great things," and they would nod in agreement as they watched her busy herself about the Set.

Risla wiped the tears away from Eisiam's cheeks with his thumb. "Is it over?" she asked her older brother.

He looked to Seraphina and Arksanza, the Elder shook his head. "There is one more trial, he must be attuned with the Ulla. If they do not accept him then there is no future for us or him and his race."

Eisiam shuddered. "Will it hurt?"

Exsarmon walked to centre of the hall picking his way through the coiled vines and avoiding the pools of sap that had accumulated on the ground.

Taking his pendant from his neck and twisting the leather thong around his fingers, he began to swing it around in an arc, faster and faster until it began to sing out a high-pitched whistle the vibrant green stone in the centre glowing, throwing out sparkling glitter dust all over the crowd. The vines sprang back into life, new shoots twisting and curling out of the shrivelled remains of the old, sucking up the sustenance of the life-giving sap, climbing quickly up the legs of Alfie as he stood knee-high in foliage. This time they were not tight or binding they just gently cleansed away the gooey white remains of the event. Now restored to their full strength, the stronger base vines sent out seeker vines, purposeful and full of intent, delving deep into the soil below the hall, searching down into the ground, accepting no barriers, forcibly forging their way like relentless battering rams until they discovered their targets.

"What are they doing?" whispered Alfie to Seraphina.

"Stand still and listen, you are connected to them now. What they feel you feel, what they see you see, you must work hard to develop your skills and intuition. Now what do you see?" she said.

Alfie looked a little confused. "I can see the same as you. What you on about? Look at all this mess, which by the way, I didn't cause."

"Now is not the time for your childish jokes. Close your eyes and allow the vines to show you."

Alfie could see Seraphina was becoming impatient and he already knew that things had changed for him. As soon as he had walked through the entrance to the Book Room, he knew he had a great responsibility upon his shoulders, only the trouble was he didn't know if he could do what they wanted of him or even if he wanted to do it. The Alfie of old was battling with the new improved version, in his mind was a battle of turmoil. Old Alfie would quite like to go back home to his safe mundane life where everything was done for him, handed to him on a plate, where he didn't have to say he was sorry or take responsibility. However, this new world he was being shown had opened up all kinds of possibilities. All his young life he had craved the freedom to roam as he pleased, no bossy parents, brothers and sisters, teachers all telling him what's best for him, restricting him with rules and regulations. Now here today he could have an adventure, well that was at least what he thought.

He had made new friends, they weren't judging him, calling him tubby or scolding him for not doing homework; they needed him, really needed him. His chest swelled with pride at that last thought, and so he shut his eyes tight, he could feel Seraphina's hand on his shoulder.

"Breathe deep and relax the visions will come to you."

Breathe in, breathe out, breathe in. Each breath lifted his anxiety away from him, there was a tingling in his hands and feet, warm surging blood through his veins, and there in his mind's eye a crystal-clear image of pots, terracotta pots, hundreds of them.

"Pots," he said out loud, frightening himself, shocked that he could see them clear as day in his mind's eye.

"They have found them," called out Exsarmon as the very ground beneath him and the other Faerians began to rumble.

Seraphina spoke softly into Alfie's ear telling him just to concentrate on the vines and their images, as the rumbling grew louder.

"They're coming, they're coming. Stand back, stand back!" ordered Alfie, his eyes snapping open, pushing Seraphina to the side as the earth exploded outwards and upwards, showering everyone in a five-foot radius.

The vines burst out from the ground carrying their targets, the pots, tightly wrapped, safe and secure. The shower of soil had coated some of the Faerians that hadn't be able to comprehend Alfie's order quick enough and they stood like they had been coated with drinking chocolate trying to brush away the soil from their eyes and faces, spitting and spluttering, as the seeker vines swayed hypnotically in front of Alfie, holding the pots a good six or seven foot in the air as if awaiting further instructions.

Exsarmon walked towards Alfie and held out his hand. Alfie first looked to Arksanza, Seraphina and Risla as if to ask what he should do and then he turned to Eisiam. She no longer looked distressed as she had remembered something Arksanza had taught her years before. He had told her always to trust her instincts and listen to her inner voice, the same skills she used when helping her animals, in all the noise and confusion she had forgotten this teaching and was making judgements on only the visual images. "Do not judge a book by its cover, look deeper within," he had told her. This was one of Arksanza's favourite human sayings, he strongly believed that one day the human race would find a way back to their ancient teachings, give less importance to material things and care more for their fellow man.

He was right she had not seen the situation for what it was. She felt protective of Alfie and had allowed his distress to colour her mind, logically she should have told herself that these three Faerians who she held dear would not have willingly put Alfie in harm's way, there was a purpose to it all even if it wasn't yet clear. He obviously had stronger qualities which she had not given him credit for. So she smiled, a serene calming effect on Alfie, who it had to be said had taken a real shine to Eisiam, he turned and placed his hand into that of Exsarmon's and allowed him to lead him to a huge wall of vines. They were pulsating at the same beat of his heart, the seeker vines snaked behind him still carrying their precious cargo of pots then sliding around the side of Alfie and Exsarmon they laid them down.

Exsarmon held up both his and Alfie's hands towards the vines and called out, "Accept this soul or send us away." There was a moment of total silence, a pin dropping would have been heard, then the vines began to shudder sounding as though they were whispering amongst themselves and then they began to part.

The wall of vines drew back like a great velvety curtain to reveal a carved wooden tablet. Risla's eyes widened; there was the symbol that he had seen on Alfie's chest. The carving was done by his father, Arman, when Risla was but a child. It was a huge circular design with seven points cut out from it, each with a small ledge ornately decorated. The vines were depicted in the carving as they were in life, twisted and binding. Small wooden channels chipped into the solid oak linked each ledge to the next, all leading to a cavity in the centre of the symbol.

Exsarmon called out, "Nature do your bidding bring forth the Ulla." As he turned to hold both of Alfie's hands, the seeker vines snatched up the pots raising them high into the air and shifting forward towards the talisman placed them precisely on to the ledges, sliding them back into the alcove that had been carved out. One vine slid back with a pot to Exsarmon balancing it in front of him. The Elder placed his hand inside the pot and scooped out a rich green paste-like substance. With his thumb Exsarmon drew the same symbol on to Alfie's forehead and then ordered the vine to return the pot to join the others. The vines now turned back to Alfie, as Exsarmon, still holding his hands asked, "Do you willingly give yourself to the Ulla, Alfie, child of the Delaney clan?"

Alfie hesitated for a second then glimpsed across to Eisiam, who was watching him intently with her beautiful, beautiful face. Showing no signs of fear, he replied "Yes!"

"Then so be it," called out Exsarmon as he let go of the boy's hands. The vines lifted him up high into the air bobbing him in a wave-like motion into the remaining empty cavity, placing him with care and precision in amongst the cobwebs, they tickled across his cheeks making him sneeze. He could see that the carved hole was just plain and unassuming although it looked as though a slug or snail had passed through at some time, the silvery trails they had left behind giving them away. He looked down on the gathering below him, so many faces expectantly looking back up at him. For all intents and purposes he could have been attending one of those 'hippy do's' as his father like to call them, full of the 'great unwashed with their long tangled hair braids' also another less than complimentary view. Alfie was beginning to see how they could pass so easily into the human world, they did actually seem to fit in, in a kind of weird way, just different enough to be left alone but not so different that they would immediately stand out and draw attention.

I'm gonna get me a tattoo, he thought to himself as he scanned the pictures inked on so many bodies. *Yeah, a bloody great dragon, that'll be cool.* He caught Seraphina's eye. She was having a little chuckle to herself. He flushed pink a little with embarrassment, but then in his mind deliberately asked, *Will I be OK?*

The beautiful Seraphina with her long, pale blonde hair nodded in acknowledgement. Yes!

The whole room had turned to face the talisman and the young human boy so many had heard of in legends told and retold through the generations. Elders who believed their days in the two worlds would be all but used before the legend came to fruition, watched in awe as did the younger Faerians who had not believed for a second that tales their parents had told were based on truths, and were not just a way to get them to settle to their night-time slumber after all.

"Summon the vine keepers," called out Exsarmon as a side entrance swung open and out flew several small figures. Alfie first thought that they looked rather like cherubs but as they flew closer to him he realized that they were in fact cute chubby babies, they were grinning from ear to ear, swooping in and out of each other, babbling away like they were having a lot of fun, tiny little paper-thin wings fluttered furiously on their shoulders unlike those of a cherub. Their sparse hair was pulled into topknots, each one wearing a mini version of the tunic that the older Faerians wore. On their little feet were leather bindings with just a peek of small toes poking out, they must have flown everywhere as the soles of their feet seemed impossibly clean.

Exsarmon swooshed at them with his arms. "How did they get in there again? Some Faerian has not taken their duties properly!" he said as he quickly eyed the guards who were showing immense interest in their feet for some reason.

***

The rowdy babies soon spotted Alfie and were very curious hovering just in front of him, their big bright green eyes scanning him from top to bottom, his curly hair particularly causing a stir. One slightly bolder baby ventured close enough to carefully pick at a curl, winding it around his finger and giggling loudly as it sprung back to shape, they all joined in completely enthralled in their game with the curly-haired human. It seemed the more excited they became by the presence of Alfie the more they glowed, just like baby fireflies thought Alfie. He grinned at them fascinated by them as much as they were of him.

Exsarmon was becoming impatient clapping his hands together to draw their attention but they were so wrapped up in their enjoyment they simply couldn't hear him. He shuffled over to a table upon which was a large metal platter, shaking his head and muttering, he tipped the fruit from it, picked up a long wooden spoon and proceeded to bash it as hard as he could. A crashing almighty sound rang out making all and sundry jump from their skins including the preoccupied babies. They were stunned into submission for about two seconds then Alfie knew what was coming next, he had enough experience of his little cousins, first their doe-like eyes began to brim with big fat tears then their rosebud lips began to tremble. 'Pet lip' his mother called it, a true sign that these babies were going to yell the place down. He quickly plunged his fingers in his ears as one after the other let out an eardrum-shredding scream.

Exsarmon flapped his arms pointlessly. "Shush little ones I needed to get your attention." They neither listened nor cared much about what Exsarmon had to say as they all tried to gather at the feet of Alfie, a big bundle of babies all vying to get a position on the precarious ledge with Alfie doing his best to calm them.

Exsarmon was now bossing some of the male Faerians about, ordering them to drag the table nearer to the talisman and then insisting that he could climb upon it without their assistance. The Elder ravaged with age stubbornly trying to haul himself up with his wobbly strength-drained arms was causing quite some concern.

"Please My Lord allow me to assist you." It was Risla. The Elder flicked his hand as if in acknowledgement of the request, holding out his hand for Risla to take. Risla wasn't a hundred per cent sure how to approach this task as it wasn't the done thing to manhandle one of such esteem, he couldn't shove him from behind nor just yank on his frail arms.

"Perhaps My Lord you should just rest against the edge and then we could swing your legs around and up?"

"What? Speak up youngster."

Risla repeated his request but it fell on deaf ears.

Risla looked up at Alfie who was now beginning to smile, Risla rolled his eyes. "I said," said Risla shouting loudly, the elderly Exsarmon cuffed Risla across his ear.

"There's no need for you to be raising your voice, I can hear perfectly well. I swear that you are as annoying as those pesky youngsters with wings."

Alfie couldn't hold it in, he burst out laughing gripping at his belly, stamping his feet up and down on the spot avoiding trampling any babies underfoot who by now had stopped crying and were smiling and clapping their chubby little hands at the merriment of Alfie chuckling uncontrollably, they joined in the giggling as a ripple of disbelief waved around the Book Room. This was meant to be a ceremony, a most serious ceremony and it was fast becoming a comedy of errors. Each time Alfie looked down he was met by the image of the Elder bashing Risla as he clumsily tried to assist the increasingly irate Exsarmon in his monstrous climb upon the table.

Tears of laughter were now pouring down Alfie's face. "Stop it, stop it! I'm gonna be sick in a minute."

From the back of the room voices and conversations were floating to the front. "What is occurring? Does the boy cry? Is he in pain?"

"No, it be laughter. What is the Aspenola youngster doing to Exsarmon?"

"He does not look happy."

"Who? The youngster or Exsarmon?"

"Both," came the reply.

The human boy's laughter rang out all across the room, it was infectious. The Faerians were a highly ceremonial race, in particular the Band of Elders, but something about this young boy touched them as it had Risla, without wanting to small groups began to snigger and nudge each other, pretty soon the small ripple became a tidal wave of raucous laughter.

Even Exsarmon in all his pomp and ceremony found himself raising a smile, a very rare occurrence. The babies buzzed around the room, their little wings sending them swooping up amongst the rafters, lapping up the warmth of the laughter.

Arksanza stepped forward. "There is no need to climb upon the table Exsarmon I shall deal with the infants." Taking his pouch from his hip he took out a small drum-like object. It was made of tightly drawn animal hide over a wooden base and on each side were small plaits knotted with beads. A piece of hazel was tied to the centre which Arksanza was vigorously spinning between his palms making the knots rattle against the hide. It did the trick the babies all turned their attention to the musical toy and followed Arksanza from the room like the Pied Piper.

"Ah, what a relief. I really must speak to the vine keepers, those infants are becoming a real problem. Now, where was I?" said Exsarmon turning his attention back to Alfie who was now sitting with his legs dangling from the ledge of the cavity. "Young man you must return to your feet and stand back into the cavity, do you see there is a channel either side of your body?"

Alfie turned his face left then right, although it was a bit overgrown with the vines he could see what Exsarmon was talking about. "Yes," he called back down to the Elder.

"Excellent, now we can begin. Place your arms into the channels, like so," as he stood with his arms out from his side.

"Er My Lord, are we not forgetting something?" said Arksanza who had now returned to his place, tutting.

An exasperated Exsarmon turned. "What? What is it now?"

Arksanza pointed to a slightly raised platform to the side of the vines which had a stone altar on it.

"Yes, yes Arksanza, it is the vine keepers' altar. What of it? Really, my patience is being tested this day."

"Should not the vine keepers be present My Lord, as it is they who shall carry out the ceremony?"

A blank expression upon his face Exsarmon turned to face the altar and scratching his head mulled over the suggestion. A look of acknowledgement quickly swept across his wrinkled brow. "Oh my goodness! Yes, yes you are correct Arksanza. Those winged infants have put me in a tizzy, summon the vine keepers please," he said screwing his face up and throwing Alfie a side glance as if to dare him to start giggling again.

Once again the side door was swung back by guardians and the vine keepers called for. Through the door walked three maidens their hair was loose flowing behind them as they swept towards the altar, their skin had been smeared with some kind of green paste, and they were wearing flowing gowns made from silk. They like the rest of their kin also had tattoos but theirs were much darker almost black and they twisted up their arms like vines. Around their heads they wore a leather band with the same symbol as the talisman carved into it. Each one carried a pot similar to those that had been recovered by the vines from beneath the earth. As they walked towards the altar Alfie could see that they had were in fact identical. *Cool*, he thought to himself, *triplets*. The vine keepers placed their pots upon the altar and then strode across to stand directly in front of Alfie.

"You must listen carefully to our instructions Alfie of the Delaney clan." They all spoke in unison, in a lilting musical tone, not quite song but not just speech either, their tone was very soothing and calming. "Place your arms into the channels. Do not be afraid, no harm will come to you. The vines and the creatures within are your friends not your enemy. Do you understand Alfie of the Delaney clan?"

Alfie nodded, now a bit self-conscious that the whole room was completely focused on him.

The vine keepers climbed up on to the platform and encircled the stone altar. Linking their hands they began to sing, the song was beautiful. Alfie didn't understand the words but he thought it sounded very similar to the Irish folk music his grandmother used to play on her old record player when he was a very young child. They sang for a good few minutes, it seemed to have a relaxing effect on everyone in the entire room then Alfie noticed a tiny wisp of something spiral out from the pots that were on the altar.

Smokey little trails climbed higher and higher above the pots, white and green intertwined, locked together as the depth of the wisps began to build and thicken, the singing grew stronger and louder building to a crescendo as the sweet-smelling smoke began to waft across, filling the room.

"It is done. Now we must awaken the Ulla," said all three maidens.

They walked back to Alfie and then without warning they jumped, one after the other, up on to each other's shoulders with the greatest of ease, until the final triplet came level with Alfie's face, she looked directly into his eye's. Alfie was shocked she didn't have a mouth, there was just smooth skin, no lips, no opening at all, and yet she was speaking to him and they were all singing and it appeared that all the Faerians present could also hear the lyrics as they had responded to it. Seraphina had told him that only Faerians of a certain age could speak with their mind, he was now very confused. Perhaps the smoke was affecting him; he did feel a little woozy.

The vine keeper atop of the stack asked him, "Are you prepared Alfie of the Delaney clan?" She tipped the contents of the first pot into one of the seven in the cavities and placed her hand directly inside swirling it around like she was mixing a cooking pot, then she placed the contents from the second pot into the same one and then the third until the pot in the cavity was full. The vines had snaked across the floor and were spiralling up the bodies and legs of the three vine keepers holding them steady whilst they sang out their song again. The pot that had been filled now too was smoking and spluttering. Alfie was trying to see inside but couldn't lean forward for fear of falling. Something was beginning to appear at the rim but the drifting smoke was masking his view, if he didn't know better he would have said it was a huge fat worm-like creature.

The worm was a creamy glistening colour, slightly translucent. It oozed its way over the edge of the rim plopping to the soil on the ledge, as it wriggled along it left a trail of silver behind it. Forcing itself into one of the channels leading off from the centre, the worm set off on its journey making its way around to the next pot.

Alfie was getting a crick in his neck trying to stretch to see what was happening as now a second worm joined the first, doing as before, climbing from its home and tracing its way around the network of channels until all of the seven pots had been abandoned by the worms as they relentlessly carried on with their mission set on a determined path.

Flicking his head around Alfie had worked out that the channels all seemed to lead to one place. Him! They were migrating to various points on the talisman which lead to Alfie's hands and his head.

"You must be still Alfie of the Delaney clan for fear you will damage the Ulla. Be assured they mean you no harm," called out the triplets.

Alfie thought to himself, *That's alright for them they haven't got worm goo all over them*, as the first of the worms got to the cavity he was standing in. They wriggled and undulated first up his feet and legs, some came from the side up the other channels until all seven were resting along the length of his outstretched arms. Alfie tried to stare straight ahead as the first of the worms began to slide up the side of his neck, his breath became a little laboured as he purposely blew his cheeks out to prevent himself from instinctively flapping the oozing invader away off his body, taking only marginal comfort that these bad boys were way too fat to slip into his ear! As it continued its journey up the side of his face, he glanced down at Eisiam, she was still smiling at him willing him to be able to complete this task. He told himself that as long as they didn't go near his eyes or mouth he could get through this ordeal, just as the first worm appeared over the back of his curly head forcing its way through the mass of hair. Alfie tipped his head slightly back as the worm arched itself into a crescent shape and attached itself to the symbol on his forehead, it felt very much like someone had shot him with an arrow with a sucker on the end of it. The worm seemed to stay motionless for 30 seconds whilst the remaining worms followed the same path, as the second appeared at the back of his head, the first detached and dropped into the hands of the triplet still standing at the top of the stack, she passed it gently down to her sisters and then Exsarmon carried it to the stone altar.

Alfie was beginning to feel relaxed as it was obvious now that no harm would come to him as one after another of the worms dropped and were reunited on the stone altar.

"Moondavna, did the Ulla accept the offering?" called up Exsarmon to the vine keeper. She indicated to her sisters to bring her closer to Alfie, the vines around the base released their hold freeing the legs of the triplets to walk forward.

She stared intently at the boy turning his face gently, first left then right. She was checking that all of the paste that had been used by Exsarmon to make the talisman on his brow had been devoured by the Ulla.

She nodded yes to her sisters and in one voice they all answered, "It is all gone My Lord." Alfie could still not get his head around the fact that these three beautiful Faerians did not possess mouths and if he was honest it kind of freaked him out a little.

Seraphina's voice came into his mind. *Do not worry so young one, you have much to learn and little time to do it in, we will do our best to answer your many questions but now is not the time.* He smiled in acknowledgement at her.

Exsarmon shuffled over to the stone altar where upon he produced a small knife as he laid the Ulla out one by one. The triplets had now returned to the ground and stood watching the Elder perform a chant over the Ulla. Alfie couldn't quite hear what he was saying but nearly jumped out of his skin when suddenly without warning Exsarmon plunge the knife into the worms. Unexpectedly for Alfie a plume of glittery dust shot up, and not the creamy goo he was expecting, rising high up into the air showering the Elder, the vine keepers and the altar. As it fell and settled Exsarmon gathered the dust, scooping it with his hands into one of the pots.

"Now all that is needed is the blood of the boy," called out Exsarmon.

"What?" stammered Alfie. He knew it was too good to be true. The Faerians he thought were his friends were going to sacrifice him. Instant panic set in as he searched frantically for a way down, he twisted and turned, sat down on the ledge and tried to gauge how far the drop would be, stood back up and looked above his head to see if he could climb up the vines into the rafters and make his bid for freedom through the roof. By this point he was hyperventilating, the thought of anyone taking his blood let alone a gang of boy-eating Faerians was enough to make him faint and that is exactly what he did.

He must have hit the ground with some force as it was a fair way up, no one not even Risla had been able to move quick enough to try and catch him or break his fall. As his eyes flickered open a mass of faces surrounded him, they looked like bobbing bodiless heads, with one familiar one closer to him, it was Eisiam.

She cradled his head upon her lap. "Be still Alfie you had a very bad fall, let Arksanza check your bones."

He winced slightly as Arksanza patted along his legs and right arm. "He will survive but he will be sore."

Alfie sat bolt upright. "What? Survive long enough for ya to put me in the cooking pot?" His head was still swimming. "No way mate." He tried to stagger to his feet only to fall back into a group of outstretched hands willing to catch and prevent him from hurting himself further.

"What does he say?" asked one bystander.

"Something about cooking I believe," said one.

"He must have bashed his head good," came another.

"It's my blood and you ain't having it!" he cried still struggling to get to his feet and shoving Risla away from him.

"Calm yourself little man you must rest."

"You're not my friend. You brought me here so they can cook me. Get off me!" he shouted.

Seraphina stood in front of the boy and firmly held him at the shoulders. "Enough. You must listen and listen good young man. You have fainted. I believe that is what your mother calls it, and in doing so you fell from the ledge and hit your head. Shush," as Alfie attempted to protest. "Your blood has been taken already, see." She held up his hand and showed him a tiny prick on the tip of his finger. "No one here wishes to cook you, or eat you, or bring any harm to you in any way. Now sit and recover then let us bring this ceremony to its end."

She forcibly plonked him down on the ground and ordered everyone to go and sit in their places.

"I'm sorry I shouted at you," he said to Risla who was sitting next to him.

Risla grinned and tweaked his cheek. "At least your colour returns. Cooking pots!" he let out a belly laugh as he to returned to the bench he had been sitting on.

Alfie smiled sheepishly as Exsarmon clapped his hands to conclude the ceremony.

"The blood of the boy is mixed with the Ulla. We shall feed it to the Nature and pray that he is accepted."

The Elder walked to stand at the foot of a huge wall of vines, stooping he tipped the contents of the pot into the roots and then stood back. Expectantly the room fell silent. Alfie studied the faces as they all fixed upon the wall of vines all standing in anticipation, gradual mutterings filtered their way down through the crowd, whispers carried doubt.

"Is it working?"

"Does not the book vine accept him?"

"He is too human in his ways."

"Perhaps he is not the chosen one."

Arksanza put up his hand to silence the tittle-tattle as he could see that the boy was becoming upset by the mindless gossiping. He looked to Seraphina who steadfastly stared with such intensity straight ahead, strong in her belief that the young boy before her, the infant she had watch grow, her charge she had sworn to protect with her life if need be, was indeed the chosen one. She knew it with every fibre in her body surging with such conviction, it was all that she could do to contain herself and not snap back at these doubters and misbelievers. She both could feel and hear Alfie's anxiety as the seconds ticked away followed by minutes; he was finding the waiting unbearable.

"Hold true Alfie. I believe in my heart that this is your rightful destiny, the vines are testing you."

Alfie turned to look back at Seraphina, a slight tip of the corner of his mouth, a half smile, his eyes welled up with tears. She placed her hand upon her heart turning it into a fist then tapping quite firmly to underline her trust in this young human boy, as she did so a faint crackling noise could be heard.

Alfie turned to face the front again as the sound became stronger. At the base of the vines the soil had began to pop and bubble as though boiling hot oil had mixed with water. Frothing and spluttering the ancient gnarled vines thick with age began to show signs of life, a green hue growing and developing along their lengths bursting into life, exquisite flowers magically springing from wizened dried up buds, all the way up to the very rafters brilliant colours flashing from all over, the rustling of the vines loud like muffled conversations amongst excited friends. Each time a new flower appeared the same glittery dust that had come from the Ulla cascaded out into the crowd, heralding its arrival.

Alfie felt like he was at some kind of weird floral fireworks display without the ear-shattering bangs and booms. He couldn't turn his head fast enough to keep up with the new flowers appearing right, left and centre, until the entire huge wall was covered from top to bottom and the smell was simply intoxicating as the perfume of the flowers weaved in and amongst the Faerians.

Out of the corner of his eye Alfie could see to his left the small group of very, very old looking Elders. They were the Band of Elders as Alfie recalled, each one was either pulling up their own hood or helping their companion so that their faces were completely covered, they now looked like a band of monks hunched over with age, thought Alfie to himself. He was puzzled and had lost interest with the flowers and was concentrating more on what the Elders were doing. Arksanza spotted him and twisted his fingers in a twirling motion indicating that Alfie should turn back around as he then also pulled his hood over his head.

What are they up to? Alfie thought to himself just as the reason became apparent. Without warning the entire wall of vines and flowers exploded outwards, splattering each and every one in the room, the Elders knew what was coming and had protected their wispy thin white Lockans with their hoods. A wave of energy boomed out across the room sending smaller, less physically able Faerians tumbling back, they lay in crumpled piles of bodies. No one was hurt just shocked at the intensity of the event and all were stunned to see that all the plant life had be eradicated leaving a intricate carving over the entire wall, the Band of Elders knew of it but no one else did, they all gasped in amazement at the wonder before them.

Exsarmon beckoned Alfie forward towards him. "Come Alfie of the Delaney clan." He took Alfie to the foot of the wall and placed the boy's hand into a carved hollow, it was a perfect fit for him just like a glove.

As the weight of his hand settled against the solid wood, Alfie felt his chest tingle, it was the mark, his new mark not his birthmark any longer, it burned brightly like liquid gold spreading out across his chest and down his arm spilling from his fingers into the hollow containing his hand, his whole body now surged with a powerful energy.

"Look," said Exsarmon tipping Alfie's chin up. "See what you have done," he said smiling the biggest smile ever.

Racing above Alfie was the gold liquid filling every crevice of the pattern, pouring into all the nooks and crannies bubbling away like larva escaping a volcano. The audience behind him was in awe as the dull lifeless carving became a majestic and wondrous artwork with a life all of its own.

Alfie gasped. "I really did didn't I?"

Exsarmon hugged him. "Yes my brave young boy you did. You can take your hand from the hole now."

Alfie pulled his hand free, it was spotless and clean no gold anywhere. He waved it at Risla grinning like a Cheshire cat and mouthed the words 'I did it'. Risla smiled at his friend with pride and then pointed up to the wall. Alfie turned back to see thousand upon thousand of Ulla crawl from their suspended sleep, all driven to reach the centre of the carving to release their queen from her cocoon. Some closer had already begun to nibble at the tough exterior. They would all have to work as an army to free her from her prison. Thousands and thousands of munching mouths chewed away the leathery mottled brown casing to eventually allow her to emerge into the light, she was larger than her rescuers shining gold, with red spiked hairs down her spine.

"My Queen we honour your Ulla as we honour you," said Exsarmon bowing low as did the entire room.

Alfie remained standing straight, mesmerized by the giant worm and to his amazement she spoke to him in a language he did not understand. For a second he wasn't quite sure how to respond, in his confusion he looked to Arksanza and Seraphina.

Seraphina told him to greet the queen as Exsarmon had done so he repeated the words and to his amazement she spoke back to him in English. "As we too are blessed to join with you Alfie of the Delaney clan. You young human have claimed your birthright. Our knowledge is your knowledge. We shall strive together as one; Faerians, Ulla and you, Child of the Vines. Ask of us any question and we shall come together with all the combined wisdoms of vines, human clans and Faerians, no secrets shall be lost to the Gorans. Myself and my Ulla are just links in the chain of knowledge. You, Alfie of the Delaney clan, are the final piece in our war against the evil that prevails within the clans of the Gorans. Come, step forward and allow me to show you a glimpse of the wondrous legends and tales as passed on down the generations; the vicious battles fought with great bravery against the Tyrants of the Gorans, the Magiks that will strengthen you and prepare you to steel yourself to come face to face with the malevolent Triamena princess and daughter of Traska, king of the Goran Empire." She extended out her red spikes and softly wrapped them around the boy, they tickled against his skin as Queen Betina of the Ulla, infused herself with the energy of her soldiers. One after another they lit up with sparkling light and energy each one connecting to its neighbour running a physical link of knowledge around the wall like an electrical circuit board. Alfie thought his head would explode with the sheer volume of images, spoken words and chants, some he understood, some completely foreign, all kinds of different beings, it was as if he had his own private science fiction film going on in his brain. The speed at which the pictures flashed by was phenomenal, they occasionally stopped momentarily at those he was suppose to take note of but if Alfie was honest with himself, he was utterly overwhelmed. The physical strain on him was becoming apparent to both Arksanza and Seraphina.

"We should bring the ceremony to an end for this day," said Arksanza to Exsarmon, he nodded his head in agreement; the boy was showing signs of exhaustion.

"My Queen, Wonder of The Ulla, we should call an end to the proceedings and go celebrate this day with a feast in honour of the Awakening do you not think?" He spoke in a passive manner so as not to offend the queen.

She turned to face the Faerian considering his request, slowly beginning to untwine her spikes from the boy. "He does not know his enemy or our enemy. Should he at least look upon the face of his foe?"

Seraphina was becoming agitated. She wasn't completely sure that it would be a good idea to bring the face of the dreaded Triamena forward from the visions at this present time. Alfie was absolutely shattered, he had travelled an emotional roller coaster, how were they to know if such an image might push him over the edge and send him scuttling back to his mother and family, his safe haven away from this world they were trying to educate him in? She took a step forward. Arksanza placed a soft but restraining hand upon her arm, she looked to him.

"My beloved you have watched this boy from birth, from the shadows his whole life, keeping guard, keeping him safe. You have love for him as would his mother but now is the time to let him go and allow him to grow into his destiny. After all is this not what you have worked to? He is in no danger whilst here amongst us, but Betina is correct, he must know his enemy and the choices made now must be his and his alone. If he turns and runs then so be it." A single lone tear gently glided from her eye. Seraphina turned and returned back to her seat, tipping her head down slightly allowing her hair to fall forward shielding her dewy eyes from those surrounding her.

Alfie felt the spikes return back to his body, the whole wall behind the queen flashed like the finale to a massive fireworks display, something big was coming Alfie could feel it in his blood. The images were so fast now their colours blurred into one, no longer discernable, then just as quick as they warped up the speed, it all came to a sudden stop. At first all Alfie could see was a tiny dot way off in the back of his mind, growing larger as it grew nearer and nearer to his mind's eye. Blurred features out of focus strained to refine and define themselves. Initially he saw a figure not that dissimilar to the female Faerians he had come into contact with, an athletic build, tall and purposeful but there was something different about the picture before him.

She, Triamena, was more muscular, her skin was darker, more tanned. If she had tattoos they were far less obvious against her espresso skin tone but what was blatantly obvious were vicious deep scars all along her forearms, they couldn't have been battle scars they were too regimented.

No thought Alfie to himself, these were deliberate. He winced at this last thought. "What kind of person could be capable of such self-harm?" he asked out loud. No one replied they did not wish to disturb him in his vision.

Triamena's face surprised him. He expected her to be similar to Seraphina and Eisiam but he couldn't have been more wrong. Her skull and forehead were distorted almost as though she may have had horns growing at some point, she had piercings through her lips and nose and brandings of some kind across her cheeks, spirals that raised in welts rested on the surface leading back towards her ears and although she had quite a masculine jaw she had painted her mouth with a pitch black paste a bit like Alfie's sister Jodie used to wear when she went through her Goth phase. That was it. He suddenly realized why he wasn't quite so freaked out by the image of Triamena. She just looked like an extreme version of a Goth with body modifications; he had seen countless magazines in Jodie's room. Triamena could easily walk into an underground club in the middle of London and mingle with the club goers and no one would bat an eye, she would simply disappear into the crowd.

As the image grew closer Alfie could see that the demon princess had a strange belt wrapped around her waist, shrivelled up dried objects seemed to dangle from it. He looked left to right trying to decide what the wasted prune-like items were as his eyes tipped back to the left he could see one object different from the rest. There was blood dripping from it and then to his horror he realized he was looking at an ear freshly removed from its owner piercing still intact. She was displaying them like trophies.

"Oh god how gross," he said out loud.

Queen Betina sighed. "This is just a taster. She, Triamena, is evil personified. Even her own kin cannot abide her, she rules with an iron rod and rotten heart."

Alfie shuddered even though it was an image, he could feel her cruel eyes burning straight back at him as though she was really standing there in front of him, at any moment capable of snatching out her razor-sharp nails dragging them across his face whilst watching in pleasure as his pain-stricken voice called out for help.

"Enough now," said Arksanza. "The boy has had a gruelling few days. He must rest and we must celebrate this great occasion," he said still trying to keep a pacifying tone, Queen Betina had a reputation for being obstinate.

When it suited she could be rather demanding as she knew her powers and gifts were held with great esteem amongst the Faerian race. She and her Ulla were the equivalent of a modern-day supercomputer in the human world. They stored centuries of information, a biological library passed down to the larva of the Ulla, they could raid the archives of the most influential books of history, munching their way through page after page, eagerly searching their way through secret legends to the most seemingly unimportant facts all secreted away ready to pass from one to the next suspended in time awaiting the call.

Arksanza and not to mention Seraphina were anxious to not offend Betina, an uncomfortable two or three seconds passed.

"I agree the boy does look drained, he must be in need of nourishment. Call forward the vine keepers, feed the Ulla the petals and feed the Faerians. Now is the time for merriment for tomorrow begins a new chapter in the war against the Gorans," and with that she retreated back into her cocoon as the vine keepers sprang into action like acrobats tumbling from a circus gathering up the abundant coloured petals ready to be distributed to the Ulla singing out an upbeat song gathering up the party spirit.

Alfie lay flat on his back as all around him young and old joined to dance together as others ran off in different directions to prepare food for this spontaneous party.

Eisiam stood in front of the tired boy holding out her hand, she invited him to come and dance with her. He didn't need to be asked twice, giggling with joy at the sight of gangly Risla whooping it up with some pretty Faerian girls. *Tonight is going to be a good night*, thought Alfie. *Tomorrow can wait.*

The Listening Tree – Chapter 6

Standing at the base of the massive tree, Alfie placed his face against the bark and tried to look up the disappearing trunk to see to the top, he couldn't, it was swallowed up by the clouds.

"Let me get this right. You want me to climb up to the very top and as you put it 'listen for voices.'" said Alfie to his friend Risla.

"Well I do not possess the gifts that you have so it will have to be you but I will accompany you so do not be fearful that you will be alone," replied Risla as he sorted out his twine rope.

"Oh I'm not fearful cos I ain't going up there sunshine. No way. Not on your nelly."

"But we must, it is the best way to hear the voices," protested Risla.

"Look, where I come from if I told someone I was gonna climb a bloody great tree to listen to voices then they would lock me up in the nearest loony bin." Alfie plonked himself down as if to make the point.

"The voices carry high into the air. It is a great opportunity to get some good information especially from the Gorans."

"I thought you said that they can only come out at night. So what we doing here in the day?"

"That is most true, however it will take us some time to climb and as you are not yet at your fittest that will cause a delay."

Alfie spun around. "What you saying? Just cos I'm a bit burly?" prodding into his ribcage looking for a rib or two.

Seeing that Alfie was offended Risla tried to backtrack. "No, no little man. You have not had to grow amongst these woods as I have done. It would not be natural for you to climb such trees or run everywhere, you have metal boxes to take you do you not?"

"Well if you put it like that, I can see ya point," replied Alfie, eyeing his companion suspiciously but still patting at his adequate padding.

Risla threw a pair of leather gloves across to Alfie. "It would probably be best that you put these on, the twine can be less than kind to soft hands."

Alfie tutted to himself. *He must think I'm a right mummy's boy*, he thought tugging at the stitched leather sniffing them. "What is that godawful smell?"

Risla laughed. "It is rather pungent but I have to say not as bad as your feet little man. Now watch me and follow what I do. I shall do it first to give you an idea and then I will come up behind you just in case you…" Risla paused perhaps he shouldn't finish his sentence he thought to himself.

"What? Fall? Bloody marvellous! Give me some encouragement why don't ya," retorted Alfie snatching at the huge rope-like twine, he was shocked at the weight of it. Risla threw it around the base of the tree like it was a feather. Alfie heaved and puffed, sweat breaking on his forehead as the twine pathetically flopped to the ground. Risla shook his head and pondered his next move. Alfie was too inexperienced to even contemplate climbing the tree the traditional way.

"No, this is no good. You require much training and we do not have time enough before daylight runs out. No there is only one thing to be done. Come, jump upon my back, I shall carry you to the top."

Alfie's head dropped in defeat there was no arguing with Risla, the young boy who had spent so little time with his gangly companion already knew how determined and stubborn the Faerian was. Resigning himself to his fate Alfie hopped up straddling his legs across and around Risla's hips, checking into the woodland that there was no audience to watch the agile athletic Faerian ascend the tree with a giant baby upon his back!

Risla exhaled his breath and with phenomenal strength hauled both himself and Alfie and the huge twine rope up the beginning of the base.

"Would it be possible for you to loosen your grip around my throat? It would be good to draw breath," rasped Risla.

"Oh sorry. It's just that I'm not good with heights," he said softening his grip slightly.

"We have only gone up a few feet once we get to the top branches you will easily be able to climb the rest of the way."

Alfie stared straight up at the endless miles of roughened tree bark disappearing into the lush green canopy of the leaves, his head began to swim a little and he felt a slight tremble in his leg muscles. 'Jelly legs' is what his mother called it. He closed his eyes tight and pressed his head into Risla's back as his stomach flipped over and over. He hummed in his head to distract himself. *Always look on the bright side of life.* He gave a nervous giggle to himself at the irony of the lyrics. There was no bright side to falling to your death from the top of a monster tree and more than likely being doubly killed by the nutter who carted you up there in the first place, when the said nutter landed on you seconds after impact.

"I think Alfie you should try to calm yourself. I can feel your heartbeat through my back. Now would not be a good time for an Awakening to occur."

"Oh really? No shit Sherlock! I am bloody calm, this is me being calm, I am as calm as can be 100ft up a tree with no bloody parachute," he screamed his knuckles whitening with the intensity of his grip. "If I was much bloody calmer I'd be asleep," he shouted in Risla's ear.

"Seriously Alfie I think we need to do some work with your anger issues, all these emotions are not good for the soul."

"I will tell ya what's not good for me; being stuck up here with you, you loony, dragging me to the top of this tree to listen to voices. How's any of that gonna be good for my soul? If an Awakening happens it won't be my fault, you shouldn't be dragging me up here, Seraphina is gonna go bonkers when she finds out."

Risla laughed. "I do love your funny ideas and sayings. 'Bonkers' that is a funny word."

"You won't think it so funny when she tries to cut off your Lockan."

"She is not going to because she will not find out because you will not tell her and we will be down and back at the Lair before we are even missed." In all the back and forth arguing Alfie had not noticed that they had made it to the canopy, so preoccupied was he at getting his point over that he hadn't registered the final 15ft and was now nestling in the bushy green foliage. "There that was not so difficult." Plonking his irate passenger unceremoniously on to his bottom Risla moved across to a thickened bough of the tree. "Here you can rest and recover yourself before we climb the final stage."

Alfie was emotionally exhausted as he slumped into the comforting crevice that felt almost purpose built for the occasion. The leaves rustled and whispered and he felt a weird calmness roll over him, his breathing slowing to a softer less panicked rhythm. He would be quite content to rest there indefinitely but he knew his companion would have other ideas, even the hypnotic sway of the treetops didn't seem to hold fear for him any longer. No he was completely happy to stay put and absorb the clean fresh air so high up.

"Come," said Risla tapping at the young boy's knee. "Not far now." Alfie hoped he could con Risla into believing that he had fallen asleep and although Risla's tapping became more urgent Alfie persisted in the pretence, trying his hardest not to giggle at the impatient huffing and mutterings. "First of all he does not wish to come up the tree because he is so fearful, now he is so content he can slumber with no problem." Risla pushed his face closer to Alfie and blew at his eyes, not a movement not a flutter. "Tut!" Then he gently pinched his lashes between his fingers and softly lifted the eyelid. Alfie let his eyeball fall to the side as though he was deeply asleep. "I seriously cannot understand this boy," Risla ranted to himself plonking himself down opposite Alfie, "I will just have to await him." Alfie sneaked a crafty look out of one eye. Risla looked like he was getting comfy for a quick nap himself. Alfie smugly hugged his knees closer to his chest and settled down to a legitimate snooze.

The next thing he became aware of were voices as he stirred, conversations between more than one person, unrecognized voices gruff and rasping. He instinctively looked down to the ground expecting to see figures below them but as his eyes adjusted he realized it had become darker, the natural daylight was diminishing and a damp chill was descending through the treetops. He was confused, even in the waning light he could not make out any telltale shapes of people, he strained to listen but the words were not clear and whoever they were they were speaking over each other. Still Alfie felt the voices didn't come from below, it felt like they were all around, a stirring of panic began to well up, this was not good.

Alfie turned as quietly as possible to where Risla lay snoring, happily oblivious to his surroundings. Alfie carefully stretched out his leg and prodded Risla in the thigh with his foot, he kind of grunted and shuffled himself into a more comfortable position. Alfie shoved harder and again didn't get the response he wanted so he kicked harder causing Risla to let out a yelp. Alfie leapt across to his friend slapping his hand across his mouth to stop Risla ranting and raving. Pulling the Faerian close to his chest he whispered into his ear, "Shush, we have slept too long my friend the dark is coming." Risla's eyes widened and instantly Alfie knew they were in serious peril and those unknown voices would be the bearers of such peril. "I can hear voices but I'm not sure where they are coming from."

Risla gently prised away Alfie's fingers from his mouth and pointed upwards. "We must climb above the canopy, you will get a better idea where they come from," he whispered squeezing Alfie's hand reassuringly. The young boy gulped so loud with fear that Risla heard it. "It's OK little man I will help you. Come, follow me. There is plenty to grab on to."

Alfie nodded in acknowledgement but really his fear was not for the height of the tree or the long drop down it was the voices, they sounded menacing and aggressive. They had appeared garbled at first but his powers were strengthening as he began to decode this new unknown language. They were searching for something, barking orders out to other companions to go off in different directions. He could also hear the throat growls of hounds, snarling and snuffling amongst the undergrowth, teeth gnashing impatiently in pursuit of their prey.

"What is it Alfie? What do you hear?" asked Risla grabbing the young boy by the arms seeing the distress in his face.

"I'm not sure but I think they are looking for something. I can't make out all of the words."

"Let us get higher it will help you hear better."

Alfie scrambled up through the branches unaffected by the sharp barbs of the leaves against his face and arms, he was desperate to piece the conversation together, deeply disturbed by his gut feelings that some how he and Risla were involved in it.

Alfie burst through the canopy to emerge out into the twilight sky, the last swathes of the sunlight just dancing across the horizon as the deeper oranges and pinks signalled the passing of day into night.

"Shit, it's bloody night-time! Don't you dare tell me not to swear," he said pointing an accusing finger at Risla.

"Calm yourself and tell me what you hear."

Alfie scanned across the distance ahead of him. He screwed his face up in confusion, straining to hear the words but also stunned to be able to see them lift up through the canopy like words appearing on a laptop, like a story being typed out in front of him.

Risla tugged at his arm. "What? What is it you hear?" he whispered, waiting with baited breath, Risla staring straight at his young friend desperate to know.

"I can see the words as well as hear them. This is some messed up..." Risla slammed his hand across the young boy's mouth instinctively knowing some kind of cuss would follow, he glared intently, his face only millimetres away from Alfie's.

"Focus, it is good that you are able to see the spoken word, it shows your powers are developing."

"Us," came the reply. "They're searching for us."

Risla clasped his hands to his head. "I'm sorry. I should never have brought you here."

The two friends stared into each other's eyes in the rapidly fading light.

"Do you know who they are?" asked Risla.

"Doh, I can't see them can I dummy?"

"I am aware of that. If you could see them then so could I and I would not require your assistance to determine who is searching for us."

"Oh don't get shirty with me sunshine. It wasn't my bloody idea to come up here in the first place."

"Yes, I apologise for my air but do you remember the ceremony with Queen Betina and the Ulla? Can you remember the surge of knowledge from the vines?"

Alfie looked puzzled. "Er yeah, but it was loads of stuff. I don't know what you're getting at."

"Concentrate. Try to match the sounds of the voices to the images in your mind. See if you can recall them. Listen hard."

All the while Risla was becoming aware that there seemed to be movement in the treetops ahead of them, some way off in the distance but nevertheless they, whoever they were, had climbed the trees and for the moment did not seem to be aware of their quarry but Risla did not believe for one minute that this situation would remain the same for long.

Without wanting to panic the boy, Risla became more insistent that he should think and think quickly. The images flashed before Alfie whilst he tuned his ears to pick out the words and saw them in the night sky, still in disbelief that the words formed against an unseen blackboard, silvery and sparkling.

"Human, a scent." That had to be referral to him. "Tracks of a Faerian. Let loose the Gorja hounds." Alfie recited them out loud, whilst Risla drew in his breath with absolute disbelief at their predicament and his own stupid ego. What was he thinking to bring such a young inexperienced boy to such a place of danger in the hopes that somehow they might steal away some nugget of information from the Gorans? Risla didn't need Alfie to confirm who they were, he already knew. What he needed was to find out whether they were scouts out hunting on the off chance or whether they were lurking in wait with a deliberate mission to recover the boy for themselves.

"Traska King of The Gorans," blurted out Alfie the voice matching the face in his head. "Is that bad Risla? Is it?"

Traska was the one name he didn't wish to hear. The Gorans for the most were a bunch of undisciplined rabble but Traska their leader although old was a different kettle of fish, he was intelligent and a master of the arts of battle and he possessed a steely nerve that drove him on to claim his prize.

Grabbing the boy firmly by his shoulders Risla spoke coldly but definitely. "I will call out the alarm with my Lockan, it will be heard by the Set and they will send out the warriors but once I do this it will give us away so we must move quickly through the trees back towards the Set."

Alfie interrupted, "Wouldn't it be quicker to climb down and run? I can't swing through these trees like you."

"We cannot go to ground the Gorja hounds will track us and hunt us down. No the treetops are the safest place, the Gorans are strong but their limbs are bulky and short they are not designed to swing through the trees like us Faerians."

"Yeah but I'm not a Faerian. I won't be able to keep up." His eyes were starting to brim with tears. "You better leave me. I will only slow you up."

"I will never leave you, ever, Alfie of the Delaney clan," he said in earnest Unclipping his Lockan and letting it fall loose down his back, the thick plait already bristling with electric energy. "Once I have done this cling tight to my back and hang on for dear life, my Lockan will give me extra strength but you must hold tight, we will be moving at great speed through the branches." With that Risla hauled himself to the very top of the canopy and balanced with his arms outstretched right at the very highest tip of the great tree trying to spot the movement below of his enemies in the darkening light.

For now the paths taken seemed random and aimless. This would not be the case once he sent out the Lockan call. Risla took in a deep breath and rhythmically began to rotate his head as though he was spinning an invisible hula hoop, a great whoosh of air let out each time the thick plait circled above and around him. Below Alfie plugged his ears with his fingers as the ear-piercing sound began to build and boom out into the night sky. Surely now the Gorans and their hounds could also hear the call, the sound so loud it vibrated through the young boy's body, a wave of sound rippling out across the canopy. Alfie anxiously flicked his eyes to the treetop above watching for Risla's feet to appear and praying that below there would not be a Gorja hound snarling and baying at the foot of the trunk homing in on the scent of the human boy caught in limbo between sky and earth. An unearthly screeching seemingly from all around raised up through the trees, the Gorans knew exactly where their prey lay, there was excitable barking of hounds straining at the bit, crashing and ripping through the forest floor.

Scrambling down at a quick pace Risla appeared, ordering Alfie upon his back. The young boy didn't hesitate and instantly they set off at lightning speed, leaping and twisting, running along the branches, oblivious to the snatching twigs and dangers of the fall. Risla was like a man possessed whilst Alfie buried his face swirling upside down images so fast he could barely process their pathway. He had only once before experienced anything like this manic ride, a roller coaster that he'd sworn never to grace again so shaken and scared and completely disorientated he'd been; a definite jelly leg moment. Only that ride didn't have the extra elements like bloodthirsty hounds or grotesque malevolent beings desperate to get their hands on him. Alfie was sweating profusely and the sour bitter taste of vomit was rising in his throat.

"Are they coming Risla?" asked Alfie trying to turn and look behind.

"Do not wriggle you'll knock me off balance. Keep looking ahead, tell me if you see anything, anything at all."

Alfie swallowed back the fear and raised his head above Risla's shoulder to get a clearer view but everything seemed so dark and the speed they travelled made it difficult to focus on any one thing. There seemed to be shadows moving in whatever direction he looked, some kind of lookout he was, thought Alfie to himself. The wind had lifted and was hindering Risla in his selection of route back to safety, and all the while he was trying to hear a return call back from his kinsmen above the noise of his baying enemies, the whole forest was bursting into life, the other residents of the trees also fleeing in panic from the raging Gorans. Birds that had previously settled for the night as the last glimmers of sun dipped into the horizon were now flying aimlessly from their roosts in shear terror and in all directions clattering into the Faerian further disorientating him in his search for a safe path home.

Should he risk sending another call? What if they had not heard the first? If he stopped the delay could give the Gorans a chance to catch up.

All these questions raced in his mind momentarily and Risla lost focus and smashed full on into a sturdy branch knocking Alfie from his back sending him tumbling into the branches below. Alfie instinctively let out a cry of terror as one after the other he bounced from one branch to the next thudding and smashing.

Alfie lashed out, desperate to grab and hold on to something, anything to stop his perilous fall. Suddenly he ploughed into the crook of a great branch landing full on his chest, the impact knocking the breath from his lungs leaving him grasping at his ribcage. The winding felt like he had a tennis ball jammed in his throat whilst his eyes bulged with agony and terror at this lack of oxygen. He turned on to his side and threw up. As disgusting as it seemed the act of vomiting had cleared his airways and he gulped in mouthfuls of fresh, beautiful air. He tried to control his panic by breathing slow and deep, giving himself time to think and regain his logical mind. Looking around he could see no sign of Risla and even more worryingly it appeared Risla wasn't looking for him either.

Where was he? thought Alfie easing himself up into a sitting position trying to look up into the canopy above him. Reluctantly he looked to the ground but fortunately the branches masked his view, if he was honest with himself he was glad, he didn't know how he would cope if his beloved friend was lying broken upon the ground.

From deep within he found the strength to haul himself up and search for his Faerian brother. He climbed with a little anxiety at first but kept talking to himself, reminding himself of what he had so far survived, that this was just one more task to prove himself worthy of the respect of the Faerian clansmen, all the time trying to shut out the noise from the pursuing Gorans.

He after all represented his own family, the Delaneys, like his forefathers before him he had a battle to fight and it was his duty to give his best effort regardless of the outcome.

Softly he whispered Risla's name. He dare not call out any louder, he could hear the hounds in the distance howling and the instruction of the Gorans. They had no doubt that their prey was somewhere up in the trees but as yet they didn't seem certain where. Alfie tried to keep his movements smooth and slow, conscious of the fact that if he let his panic take over he would more than likely bring on an Awakening, the last thing he or Risla needed at this precise minute. Alfie strained his eyes into the inky darkness trying to pick out anything that would lead him to his friend, still calling out his name. A muffled groan floated out on the cool night air. Alfie strained to listen, to track down where it came from, again calling Risla. Again the groan. Alfie spotted a dangling arm. Quickly he picked his way across the roughened branches, desperate to get to Risla before he let out another sound, potentially giving them away.

Gently turning Risla's head towards him, Alfie felt a sticky glutinous substance in the palm of his hand. It was blood; the Faerian had smashed his skull whilst falling through the branches. Not fully conscious Risla groaned with the pain.

"Shush!" whispered Alfie tapping softly against Risla's cheek trying to rouse him. "Please wake up I don't know what to do."

The little boy in him surfacing again, he began to cry, albeit silently, so fearful was he of giving them away to the Gorans down below. Gently cradling and rocking his companion he told himself he needed to man up Risla needed him, he needed to grow a pair and take control. Quickly he tore at the tunic that had been given to him and wrapped a strip around Risla's head like a bandage. Still he couldn't awaken the injured Faerian, and then a brainwave hit him.

Laying Risla back against the tree, he quickly tore at his boot ripping at the lacing, yanking it from his foot. Placing it under the nose of the semi-conscious Faerian, he wafted it from side to side, no reaction, nothing. Alfie sniffed at the boot himself, a faint odour of smelly feet, they were too new and no way as pungent as his beloved grotty trainers that Risla had slung into the river. He quickly plunged his hand right down into the boot rubbing his fingertips across the inner sole, it was slippy with sweat. Carefully retrieving his bounty, he cautiously held his fingers just under his own nose and inhaled.

"Jesus that could wake the dead!" he exclaimed snapping his head back away from this most offensive of smells, his own eyes watering from the vapours. Looking to Risla he cupped the Faerian underneath his chin and proceeded to rub his fingers just under the nose of his unsuspecting friend. The result was instant, Risla's eyes sprung open as he coughed and spluttered frantically scrubbing at his upper lip with his sleeve, tears running down his cheeks and snot oozing from his nostrils.

"What ails me, what ails me?" he demanded as he struggled to get to his feet. Alfie had to practically sit on him to stop him from stumbling off the tree branch.

"Sit still till you get your head together," said Alfie trying not to get the giggles. "And shush up. Man you're gonna give us away."

"What did you do to me?" questioned Risla.

"Nothing mate. You hit your bonce."

Confused Risla shook his head. "I do not believe I possess a bonce."

"Yeah you do, your noggin," tapping Risla on the head.

"My head," snapped Risla. "Can you not speak plain English and not your weird boy language?"

Alfie giggled trying to help haul Risla to his feet.

"You got knocked out so I had to wake you up. We've got to get out of here the Gorans are on to us. Can't you hear them?"

Risla nodded his head in acknowledgement drawing in deep breaths trying to clear his fuzzy mind. Whilst waiting for his double vision to settle he made a plan in his mind, they were hampered by his injuries and Alfie's physical strength. They needed to cause a distraction to give them time to at least reach the river. At this point the birds were still fleeing and were flying past their heads as they stood planning, out of nowhere Risla snatched at one and unbelievably caught it, he beckoned to Alfie to do the same. He was not as successful at his first attempt nor his second, but whether by fluke or judgement he shocked himself as he felt the feathers of a small bird in his hand on his third go.

"What do I do with it?" he asked as the bird frantically flapped its wings in an attempt to get away.

"Hold it, do not let it go. Here, take my binding from my head, coat the bird with the blood."

Alfie stared vacantly at Risla. "Er, come again? Perhaps you better sit down mate. I think you hit your head harder than I thought." He grimaced as Risla scooped the congealed blood from the side of his head and began to smear it over the bird's wings.

"Now copy me," he ordered the boy as he gently laid the bird back along the length of his palm. Taking his index finger he tapped firmly just above the beak and the bird fell limp in his hands.

"God you've killed it!" called out Alfie.

Shaking his head Risla replied, "No I have not, it is merely stunned. Quickly do as I have done, we will need at least five."

Touching the blood made Alfie retch and as for tapping the bird well he didn't trust his clumsy hands not to cause damage to the poor creatures. "I can't do it. What if I hurt it?"

Risla was becoming impatient and his head was pounding. "Look, this must be done. It is our only chance to get away. Hurry with the task."

Alfie could feel his face burning with embarrassment, he felt stupid and redundant. If this had been a game on the Xbox he would have responded as he was expected to without a second thought. *Yes*, he thought to himself, for him to get through this ordeal he needed to persuade his mind that he was just in a game, same as any other game he played at home.

"Here pass me one," he said as he held out his hand. Risla smiled and ruffled the young boy's curly hair.

All five birds lay in a stupor but Risla knew they didn't have long before they came to their senses. Ripping the hood from his tunic Risla proceeded to cover it with his own blood and placed all of the birds inside.

"What are we going to do with them?" asked Alfie peering over Risla's shoulder.

"The scent will draw in the Gorja hounds, as the birds awaken they will fly taking my scent with them. What little sun on the horizon is left will attract the birds in the opposite direction to where we need to go. Hopefully, this will be enough to draw the hounds away and give us a chance to get to the riverside. First we must lower the birds to the ground. Can you hear their thoughts? Do the Gorans know where we are exactly?"

Alfie strained to sift out the random words that were bombarding him, to select only the crucial information he needed.

"They have our scent but it is weak as it is airborne. They lost our ground scent some time ago so they have sent warriors up into the trees and are following the trail of broken twigs. No one as yet has got a good fix on us."

Risla took a hook with a long binding attached to it from his belt. "This will reach part of the way, we will just have to drop the hood and hope for the best, it should jolt the birds back to reality. As I let them go you must cry out as loud as you can and then bury yourself in the foliage. Do you understand? We must bring them to us with sound. They must get to the base of the tree as the birds begin to fly, OK?" Alfie although wide-eyed nodded in acknowledgement and positioned himself ready to wait for the signal from Risla.

The Faerian could hear the nearby sounds as the hounds paced back and forth frustratingly searching for a sign of their quarry, their masters impatiently shouting orders at them. Risla prayed to his ancestors that his plan would be successful as he slowly lowered the precious cargo in his hood. He turned and looked up over his shoulder unable to see Alfie but confident that his young charge was there somewhere amongst the leaves. He softly whistled, at which Alfie let out an ear-piercing scream which took Risla by surprise as he nearly let go of the rope. Quickly gathering his senses he skilfully flicked his wrist as the metal hook slipped free of the fabric and the hood fell the last few feet unaided. Rapidly hauling the hook back to him Risla gave one last look to check that the birds were beginning to rouse as he scampered up into the protection of the trees. As the forest floor below sprung into manic chaos, their enemies had obviously heard the boy's scream and were charging towards the direction of the sound, each one of the Gorans desperate to claim the glory of finding the Chosen One and delivering him to their king.

Risla kept checking to see if the birds were about to take flight, the timing was crucial. As the first hounds broke through the undergrowth, a sliver of light, just the smallest glimmer of hope, remained of the day's last rays of sunshine. If the birds did not take to the air now there would nothing to guide them, their flight would be worthless and aimless. The first two hounds immediately sniffed at the air and simultaneously slammed their snouts into the damp soil, they had found a scent and they were homing in on the blood-covered birds.

FLY, FLY, FLY! screamed Risla in his head as his heart leapt into his mouth. He instinctively grabbed hold of Alfie's hand ready to flee. No matter the outcome of his plan, they could not sit high in the tree awaiting their fate. Just as he felt that they had no choice but to burst into action and make a break for their freedom, the first hound came upon the hood, dribbling and slathering saliva all over it drawing the attention of the second. Both howled out with primal excitement as the Goran warriors called out to each other running through the trees with their flaming torches beckoning for those above to descend.

This was exactly what Risla wanted, their path through the trees to be clear at least for a long enough time to get to the river, which sounded tantalizingly like it was just feet away, so near and yet so far.

He pulled Alfie close to him and whispered into his ear, "Get ready," as he agonizingly watched for the first bird to emerge from the hood. He didn't have long to wait as it flew straight and true stunning the hounds into panic, both of them recoiling with fear at the unexpected appearance of the bird. The second bird was not so lucky as the scent of the blood triggered their animal instincts causing both hounds to leap into the air snatching the unsuspecting bird into cruel vicious snapping jaws. Risla winced and momentarily felt a pang of guilt that was soon replaced by panic at the realization that the other birds might suffer the same fate and his hopes would come crashing down but he need not have worried, they all followed quickly and predictably the hounds took up chase pursued by their masters.

Alfie tugged at Risla's hand impatiently. "Can we go now?"

Risla turned to the boy. "First what conversation do you hear? We must be sure they have all taken the bait."

Alfie just wanted to move, desperate to get away. He had already begun to move across the branches. "Yes I think so. Come on we don't have much time," he said still trying to pull Risla along with him.

The Faerian could see there was no getting through to Alfie he was so scared he couldn't focus, so Risla took the lead. "We must take it slower than before. You will need to follow me closely as it's now so dark. As soon as we get to the river we will climb down and float down to the waterfall, the water will mask our scent." Alfie just nodded his head to let Risla know he had heard what he had said but he was struggling to concentrate. His mind was being bombarded by reams and reams of images, garbled messages, nothing making sense because he didn't want it to. He just wanted to get back to the safety of the Lair, the welcoming smile of Eisiam and the creature comfort of the musty, smokey campfires.

The two companions worked their way laboriously through branches, climbing up and down in a higgledy-piggledy fashion. It was muscle-draining work, trying to haul themselves on to the next branch, not like before when Risla had sprung from one to another with such agility, now he had to steady himself every so often, his injured head affecting his balance, whilst all the time trying to listen out for both his kinsmen and his enemies.

He was confused. Why had there been no return call, no whoop of battle cry? For all intents and purposes his Lockan song had fallen on deaf ears. He slapped himself across the cheeks to snap himself out of this negative frame of mind. Alfie, who was now trailing a little, saw that his friend's energy was waning. He urged himself on and pushed his shoulder up into Risla's armpit.

"Let me help you, we can't have far to go now surely. I can hear the sound of the river." And sure enough a few more paces and the dark inky river with slivers of sliver moonlight dancing across the bubbling surface of the water came into view. Alfie let out a sigh of relief. "We did it!" he said punching the air triumphantly.

Risla smiled wistfully at the young boy, they still had the river to survive yet. Celebrations would have to wait, he thought to himself. Alfie was all ready to launch his body down the roughened bark of the tree, eager to scamper to the riverbank.

"Wait," ordered Risla abruptly. "Tell me what words do you hear?"

Shocked Alfie replied, "Why does it matter, we made it to the river? Stop wasting time. Jeez anyone would think you like being stuck up this bloody tree."

Risla turned the boy to him. "Once we leave the safety of the tree for open ground we will be exposed. I must be sure that the Gorans took the bait, so tell me what do you hear?"

There was a moment's silence then Alfie replied, "They still follow the trail of the birds although they are become tired from the chase."

Risla interrupted. "Do you hear their king?"

Alfie was becoming impatient. "God I don't know, they all sound the same to me. How am I supposed to know?"

Risla tightened his grip. "Think back to when you first saw the image of Traska and the tone of his voice when we sat above the canopy. Can you hear him now amongst his warriors?"

Alfie sat down and placed his hands either side of his face, straining to try and separate the various tones of gruff rasping voices. "No I do not hear him."

"Are you absolutely sure?" came the reply.

"No, I do not hear his voice."

Then out of nowhere came a deep booming voice. "Of course the boy doesn't hear me Risla but you already knew that when you spotted me in the shadows."

Alfie stumbled and lost his footing, dragging his face against the unforgiving bark. It felt like he had taken three layers of skin off. "Risla, it is Traska!"

A slow clap was heard, still coming from out of the darkened forest. "Well done young boy, it is an honour that you know my dulcet tones." The voice was sarcastic and menacing. Alfie was shaking with fear, trying to train his eyes to see into the darkness down below.

Risla stood up tall and demanded, "Come from out of the shadows, or do you cower like the coward that you are, hiding like a frightened child amongst the bushes?"

Alfie tugged at Risla. "Don't wind him up mate."

Risla placed his finger to Alfie's lips. "Shush little man. I need to know where he is in relation to the river."

The baffled boy replied, "Oh..." Then ten seconds later asked, "What difference does that make?"

Risla was moving slowly and softly, peering from behind the branches, trying to locate the King of the Gorans in the undergrowth below. "Because if he is in front of us we will not be able to get to the river as he will be blocking our way."

There was a pause. "What if he is behind us then?"

The Faerian froze as he spotted the merest glimmer of Traska's body armour caught out by the glowing moonlight. Gently he turned Alfie's chin and in the softest of whispers he said, "See," pointing down into foliage of the briars and bushes on the forest floor. "Good he is behind us."

Alfie still couldn't be sure he and Risla were even looking in the same direction. "Why is it good?" he questioned in all innocence.

"Because," said Risla. "We would not be able to do this!" Snatching hold of Alfie by the scruff of his tunic and dragging him at great speed along the straight long length of a seriously thick branch Risla cried, "JUMP!"

The two companions were free-falling through the air, hurtling towards the dark swirling waters below, the roar of the furious Goran king ringing in their ears, spreading through the forest summoning his men and hounds back to him. Risla should have known Traska would not fall for the decoy trick. He sucked in his breath and held it.

The Faerian hit the water first groaning as the impact vibrated through his injured head, quickly followed by the screaming, terrified Alfie, as he slammed into the freezing icy water. Breaking the surface like a missile he coughed and spluttered so hard he thought he might bring up his lungs.

"You... You..." he couldn't get his words out. "You bloody maniac! You could've killed me!"

Risla grabbed hold of the angry young boy under his arms and swam strongly towards a loose log, snatching hold of it and slamming the boy on the top of it, hauling himself up straight after. Both lay heaving vital oxygen into their shocked bodies, neither one wanting nor were able to speak as the makeshift boat ambled its way down the river, it was a welcome respite.

Several minutes went by. "Did we get away?" asked Alfie in a soft childlike voice as he raised himself up and straddled the log.

"For the moment but Traska will soon gather his forces. He knows we must get to the waterfall."

"How does he know of the waterfall?" asked Alfie spinning around to face Risla.

"He knows of it but not of its secrets. He would not normally come anywhere near it but you are a prize worth taking the risk for."

Alfie was puzzled. "But why? Why am I so valuable to them? I'm just a boy."

"No my friend you are more than that, you are the key to the two worlds. The knowledge given to you holds many secrets. If that got into the wrong hands, the consequences would not only affect my world but that of your mother and father, your entire race." Alfie felt a shudder tickle down his back as he surveyed the riverbank on watch for any sign of the Gorans. "Get some rest it will take us awhile for the river to carry us down, I shall keep a watch," said Risla patting Alfie on the back.

"But what about the Gorans? What if they come?"

Risla smiled to reassure the young boy. "Do not worry. Even if they do their arrows will be out of range as long as we stay in the middle of the river and they most certainly will not venture into the water, so please do not work yourself up."

Reluctantly Alfie laid himself along the log allowing his hand to trail in the cold water, sneakily looking out of the side of his eye across the water to the bank but even so it was solid black over there, a whole army of Gorans could be in hiding and he wouldn't have known until they chose to light up their torches. He shivered a little as his wet clothing stuck to him. Risla wrung the water from his Lockan the weight of the wet plait pulling on his tender scalp. He winced as the congealed blood pulled against his flesh. He also attempted to clean some of the dried blood from his face and contemplated how he would be received by Arksanza and Seraphina. In his time he had made some questionable decisions but they had always been put down to the passion and folly of youth. Somehow he knew that he would be given no quarter, his youth was no excuse for this monumental disaster. He surely couldn't expect that Alfie would keep their dangerous interlude with the Gorans and their bloodthirsty hounds to himself and there was the Lockan call for help, although it seemed as though it had fallen on deaf ears. Someone somewhere along the riverbank would have heard it, word would get back to the Elders at the Set, Risla knew he must face up to his shortcomings and accept the punishment.

He lay back on the log staring straight up at the night sky, all those millions of twinkling stars pinging one after the other distracting him from the impending hostile reception. The gentle lilt of the log on the gliding river lulled him softly towards a desperate need for sleep. He could feel a heaviness seep its way up his body from his feet into his calf and thigh muscles, a slowing of his chest heaving up and down, a more relaxed tension in his lungs, the sounds around him fluffy and muffled as he drifted down into the welcoming warmth of slumber. Suddenly there was a slicing cut of the air and Risla was instantly snatched back into the world of reality. He knew that sound, it was an arrow and it was extremely close by, then a second, then a third but where were they coming from? He quickly strained his eyes to check their position on the water, they had not drifted.

"Alfie are you OK?" No reply. Risla reached out for the boy's leg tugging at it whilst still trying to gauge where the danger came from. More and more arrows rained down on them plunging into the dark inky water. Again he yanked more frantically. "Alfie, Alfie wake from your slumber." Risla could hear the boy yawn and stir.

"What's up?" he asked with a croaky throat, wobbling as he remembered he was balanced precariously on the log. A whoosh passed his ear. "What the hell?"

"Lay flat as possible to the log, they are shooting arrows at us."

There were more and more arrows getting closer and closer.

"Who is? The Gorans? I thought you said they couldn't reach from the riverbank." No reply. "Risla you said…"

"I know what I said. They must be using hucks."

"Risla, English. My English! What's a huck?"

"A boat. I think you call them canoes. A flat boat, yes?"

"Oh bloody marvellous! When is this gonna end? How far have we got to go?"

Risla stood up to survey the skyline looking for familiar shapes, in particular he was trying to spot a single lone tall tree. Just as the Moon came out from behind the clouds he spotted it.

"There, that is our destination. We do not have far to go."

"Yeah, but are they gonna get to us before we can get to the bank?"

"I truly cannot say. I cannot see the Gorans on the water but there must a good number of them judging by the arrows coming…" Risla didn't finish his sentence but let out a yell as an arrow slammed into his thigh. Dropping to his knee he clasped at the muscle and tried to ease out the head but it was stuck firm.

Alfie had scrambled up the log to aid his friend and in the broken moonlight could see the foot long shaft of the arrow protruding from Risla's thigh. His friend grimaced as Alfie tried to touch the weapon.

"What shall I do?" he asked.

Risla took a deep breath in, still ducking at the noise of the constant barrage of arrows flying through the air so dangerously close to them.

"I cannot remove the head but we must snap off the shaft, it will hinder me once we get to the bank. You must do this for me." Even in the dark Risla knew that Alfie's face would be one of astonishment. "It is simple little man, just snap the wood like you would a twig as close to the wound as possible."

"But, but…" Alfie began to stutter as he rubbed Risla's warm blood down his leggings from his hands. Didn't Risla remember that Alfie had big issues with blood and stuff? He could already feel his face flushing with sweat and his palms become clammy. "Ooh god," he said reaching down the length, taking it equally in his hands trying to judge how much strength he needed to snap it. "Ready?" he called out.

"No. Wait!" ordered Risla.

"Jesus, you scared the crap out of me! Do want to do this or not?"

"Yes," said Risla getting snappy. "Let me place this in my mouth first." In the dark Alfie could just make out movements as Risla appeared to undo his Lockan letting it fall and hold the bone toggle to his mouth. "The bone will help me with the pain."

"Are you gonna eat it?"

A short sharp answer came. "No, of course not. I will place it between my teeth in order that I do not call out with pain and give us away, the Goran have exceptional hearing."

"OK well stop yacking and let's get this over with," said Alfie scooping a handful of freezing cold water on to his face snapping him back from the brink of a faint. "One, two." There was a crack and a deep straining groan from Risla. Alfie threw the offending shaft into the river and flopped on to the log hastily washing his hands and attempting to dry them on his clothes.

"Stop splashing in the water, they will hear," hissed Risla.

"I'm not. Look here are my hands, nowhere near the water."

Still they could hear the splashing.

"It must be you. Stop panicking about the blood," said Risla.

"Look here matey, they're my bloody hands and I'm telling you they ain't in the water."

"Shush," whispered Risla completely convinced that the Gorans must be extremely near.

With the splashing getting louder and more frantic Risla pulled Alfie up the log closer to him. Both of them were straining to see out into the uninviting darkness as the slapping of an object on the water's surface drew nearer and nearer. Then suddenly out of nowhere an object hit Alfie full in the face. He yelled out in terror clasping at his face sure that he had been struck by an arrow, rocking the log nearly upending both himself and Risla into the water. Seconds later another missile landed this time hitting Risla in the stomach and winding him. More and more came, one after the other until one actually fell into Alfie's lap as he crouched low. He squealed somewhat girly-like as he recognized the object.

"It's a fish," he shouted. "It's a bloody great fish," as another slapped him across the head. "Christ if the Gorans don't kill us the bloody fish will," he said as he rubbed his head.

Then a voice so familiar and so welcome came into his head. *No the fish will not kill you.* It was Seraphina. *Lay down on the log and I will call upon the river sprites, the fish will protect you.*

Alfie motioned to Risla to lay down as yet another arrow slammed into the bark of the log inches from Alfie's hand, it vibrated with such viciousness the Gorans must surely be getting closer.

"How are fish going to protect us?" he asked Risla who was preoccupied with the thought of the reception he would receive from Seraphina somewhere on the riverbank.

A great whooshing noise surrounded them as a funnel of water like a tornado whipped up in front of the log and danced its way towards them bending forward to swallow them up Alfie couldn't help himself as he let out a fearful yell.

"We're gonna drown!" He could feel his heart pounding against his chest as his fingernails dug deeply into the bark gripping on for dear life as he watched in terror as the strange sparkling watery monster surged towards them. Risla instinctively laid himself across the boy protecting him from what was to come, both of them sure that these were their last moments awaiting the huge tunnel of water to come crashing down as it raged above their heads.

Risla gripped tightly to the boy. "I'm sorry, so sorry," he whispered into Alfie's ear.

Nothing happened, no slamming pounding water it just hovered above them whirling round under the log and over the top of them in a continual circle the full length of the log, a protective watery tube. Alfie lifted his face to look up, he could see hundreds and hundreds of fish all contained in the tube all forcing their bodies out of the water in unison to act as a shield from the arrows throwing themselves up and over back into the water to repeat this cycle, the momentum driving the log and its precious cargo closer to the shore. They swam so fast it was hard to keep track, even the fish that had been struck could not fall free such was the force of the tunnel, their lost blood falling as soft raindrops on to Risla and Alfie below.

The Gorans were surely gaining on them now as more and more of the crimson droplets pelted the two passengers. Then abruptly they were thrown forward as the log rammed headlong into the bank and the structure of the watery tunnel was lost, fish and water cascading down on to Risla and Alfie who lay floundering in the mud amongst the dead and flapping fish mound, both coughing and spluttering as unseen hands grabbed them hauling them back up the bank.

An order was shouted out. "Send forward the warriors!" Alfie tried to wipe the mud from his eyes to see the flaming arrows of the Faerian warriors ascend into the dark driving back the Gorans. Flaming missiles in their hundreds cascaded, no match for the motley crew of Gorans.

A gentle hand, cleaning away the filth from his face, offered a tankard of drinking water.

"Wash out your mouth before you drink." It was Seraphina. Alfie threw his arms around her knocking her from her feet. "Gracious boy," she said hugging him back whilst trying to disentangle herself. She pulled both herself and Alfie to their feet throwing a cape around the shivering human child as Risla stood straight in front of her his mouth open as if to speak. "You would be ill advised to speak to me at this moment. Tend to your wounds. Come Alfie let's get you to the safety of the Set," and with that she strode off with a dumbfounded boy staring back at his friend hunched over with his head in his hands, wondering what was to become of him.

Doppelgänger – Chapter 7

Try as he might Alfie could not shake off the feelings of guilt, insidious nagging pangs jumped into his mind without warning.

Dare he say it, he was enjoying himself. The danger, the new world experience, everything about his current existence was so far removed from his normal relatively mundane life at home back with his family. And yet he could feel a tug at his heartstrings, a tug he had tried so hard to erase as quickly as it had appeared but always the image of his mother's face haunting him and questioning him. The feelings were growing stronger at each passing day and always the same question called out to him. Why was he doing this to his family? How could he put them through such pain? They surely must be beside themselves with worry at his disappearance.

He was deep in contemplation so much so that he was not aware that Lolah and Eisiam had joined him sitting under the branches of the great willow shielding him from the view of the world or so he thought.

"Why so sad?" a soft gentle feminine voice asked and he felt the gliding touch of her hand upon his along with the reassuring nose nudge of his furry friend Lolah.

Alfie jolted at the touch completely caught unawares, quickly rubbing at his eyes less they gave him away, boys don't cry ringing in his head.

He forced a smile. "Oh I'm OK." He tried to shrug off the heavy weight of shame that he felt for his own selfishness. Lolah plonked her sizeable head upon his outstretched legs letting out a deep sigh as she eyed him suspiciously with her warm chocolate brown eyes. He ruffled her floppy fringe, flicking the strands of hair between his fingers, almost trying to use the hair as a shield to fend off the questioning expression of the dog's face.

It was all too much for him to bear he simply burst into tears, a gravely sob forcing its way out of his throat as he threw up his hands to cover his eyes.

Eisiam instantly sprung to his side. "What is it? What is it that ails you my friend?" Lolah whined and pushed herself closer to her small human friend. Alfie sat with head still bent, his whole body shaking with the trauma and confusion he felt. He couldn't get a single word past his lips, his jaw muscles clamping tight shut preventing him from forming a spoken word, only howls and sobs. Continual tears rolled down his cheeks, his hands wringing at his stomach through his tunic, he just wanted this gnawing pain to go away. Eisiam tried to gently but persuasively lift his face to make him look at her, softly wiping away the boundless drops of distress pouring from his tear ducts with her fingertips and gown.

"Please my dearest friend, speak to me of your pain," she implored, firmly holding his jaw in her hands tilting his face towards her.

"It's my mother. What am I doing to her?" He jumped to his feet wringing his hands with anguish. "She must be beside herself. Not just her, all of them." He took another gulping of air deep in his throat, pulling at his dark curly hair and screwing up his face with anger.

Eisiam jumped to her feet. "Stop it you'll hurt yourself" she cried grabbing at the distressed boy's hands. "This is no good you must return to the fold of your family, I will speak with Arksanza."

Throwing himself away from the petite Faerian and crouching on his haunches, his head hanging in shame he said, "But that's it I don't wanna go home I love being here. I ain't never had such a good time even though it has scared the bejesus out of me. I just don't know what to do. Please tell me Eisiam what should I do?"

"Lolah go fetch Seraphina and Arksanza, they are down by the well," she said hugging Alfie tight to her, instinctively patting his back as she had done her younger siblings when they were infants to calm them.

"Eisiam, I cannot leave there is too much resting on me. I have no choice, my path is set and you know it. I just wanna do what's right for everyone but how can I do that?" again the tears began to fall from both the boy and the Faerian.

"I simply do not know in my heart how best to help you my friend," whispered Eisiam stroking Alfie's curly hair.

"I do," said a calm but resolute voice. It was Arksanza with Seraphina following quickly behind.

Pulling both youngsters to their feet and throwing her cloak around them both she whispered, "Come." Seraphina guided them with her hands gently but firmly between their shoulder blades, Eisiam stumbled as she tried to turn to question Arksanza.

"How? How will you help him?"

Seraphina tugged at her young charge. "Eisiam remember your place. Do not speak to My Lord with such a tone." Eisiam's cheeks flushed pink as she straightened herself up, Alfie squeezed her hand reassuringly.

Arksanza appearing to have forgiven Eisiam's outburst motioned, "Come we must go to the Book Room," as he strode ahead of the group. "Ancient Magiks is what is required."

Even Seraphina looked intrigued as they stepped up the pace eager to get to the room, both Alfie and Eisiam exchanging glances. This is exactly what Alfie was talking about, all the intrigue, the excitement of the unknown, the giddy sense of danger, everything he tried hard not to like but couldn't help himself, like an addict craving an adrenaline rush, all the while knowing the potential threat to his life as he had already experienced at the Listening Tree. He felt shameful for feeling this way but it didn't stop him stepping over the threshold of the Book Room, the vines rustling and quivering as if to greet him.

The rest of the group were greeted by Exsarmon and his aides who were busy going about the care of the vines and the Ulla.

"Greetings My Lord," said Exsarmon sweeping down low with his arm, Arksanza dismissing the pomp and ceremony with a wave of his hand. "And how may we be of assistance?" he enquired curious as to why Arksanza was attempting to light the blossom urn.

"I have need of word with Betina. Please go about your business, do not let us keep you from your important work." Exsarmon looked bemused as he surveyed the huddled group.

"Come Alfie sit beside me, whilst we wait for her majesty to grace us with her presence," said Arksanza rolling his eyes to the ceiling. He wafted the sweet-smelling smoke towards the entrance of Queen Betina's chamber.

"Will the keepers come today?" asked Alfie sheepishly looking at Eisiam. She was completely uninterested naïve to his intention. Seraphina however was not and decided to have a little fun with him.

"No there is no need of them today, this is not a ceremony but they are as you say 'fit' are they not?" she joked, laughing deep from her belly as Alfie went all shades of pink as his face flushed hot.

"Jeez, I was just asking cos..." he stammered, getting extremely fidgety.

"I know exactly," replied Seraphina tapping the side of her head smiling from ear to ear.

He still hadn't got it straight in his head that his thoughts weren't always his own but he had to agree they were fit if not a little freaky with the no mouth thing, his brothers would definitely agree. "Fit birds," they would say.

Alfie was distracted from his thoughts by a shuffling, dragging noise coming from above. Betina was about to make her entrance as she hauled her plump undulating body along the channel leaving a slimy silver trail behind her. She had two smaller worker worms with her wriggling alongside her, nipping away at the muddy debris that was picked up by her oozing fleshy skirt as she swept along. She simply couldn't abide 'bits' as she called them and so insisted on her 'hand maidens' to be with her at all times to keep her free from the offending granules of mud and vine bark remnants.

Arksanza felt sorry for the two minions. Betina was an extremely demanding mistress and a greedy one at that, the more she smelt the sweet blossom smoke the more she oozed mucus like a salivating dog awaiting his dinner, almost overwhelming her much smaller assistants as they fought their way through the slime river.

"Ah, our Queen Betina blesses us with her presence," blurted out Exsarmon from the back of the room. "Shall I feed you the blossoms oh knowledgeable one?"

Arksanza tutted whilst Alfie whispered to Eisiam, "What a butt kisser."

A booming voice came from the queen. "It is rude is it not in your world to whisper Alfie of the Delaney clan?"

Seraphina shook her head, whilst Arksanza relieved Exsarmon of the blossoms. "I shall feed the Queen of the Ulla, if she so wishes," said the Elder tipping his head towards her.

"Do you perhaps have about your person those delicious sugary treats that you have secured from the human world? Such a delight to the palate. Far more pleasing than pretty flower blossoms don't you agree Arksanza?"

His head dropped slightly and through gritted teeth he smiled, "But of course Queen Betina would you care for one?" He knew that there would be a price to pay to get her to help with the information he needed.

She lay herself across the entrance to the chamber with her head looking down at them. "Er maybe one or two," she answered as Arksanza climbed the rickety ladder left by the team of Faerian gardeners in charge of the vines to reach them. He placed the sweet objects of her desire where she could devour them, her minions dismissed momentarily; she wasn't sharing any of this syrupy sweet loveliness.

Moments went past as she slurped on the sweet lost in her own world, temporarily forgetting her company until Arksanza eventually coughed loudly snapping her back into the presence of the group before her just in time to stop Alfie falling into a fit of uncontrollable giggles closely followed by Eisiam.

"Now what is it that causes you to summon me from my slumber Arksanza?"

Lowering his voice Arksanza said, "We have need of your ancient knowledge, in particular the old ancient Magiks." Looking around into the dark shadows of the room, the vines quivered in reaction to his requested to Betina.

She straightened up her voice becoming stern. "For what purpose do you require this? Many centuries have passed since such knowledge has been used. I am not sure that my memories will be accurate, perhaps a sugary gift will improve it." She did not look down but kept her eye turned to watch the hand of Arksanza enter inside his cloak, her dribbling mouth giving away her greed. He knew she would make him jump through hoops; nothing was ever easy or straightforward with Betina. "The Magiks you speak of, for what purpose is it?"

Arksanza paused and then in a deep husky voice let loose one word. "Doppelgänger."

Seraphina let out a gasp, the vines jumped into frenzied activity and Alfie felt jumpy and nervous as the energy of the vines surged through his blood.

Eisiam clutched at Seraphina's hand. "What is doppelgä…?" She didn't finish her word as Seraphina clapped her fingers across the young Faerian's mouth staring at her, imploring her not to utter another word. Out of nowhere reams and reams of worms appeared through the gnawed out wormholes, spilling out in such numbers that they fell over each other, off the ledges, building into undulating piles at the base of the great vine wall. Leaves and petals from the still raging vines fell from a height filling the air with debris.

Then completely without warning Queen Betina dropped from the ledge, her swollen slimy body bouncing hard into the muddy ground below, her mucus coating splattering all over and around the gathered Faerians. In any other given situation Alfie would normally have been rolling around clutching his sides, laughing his guts up at the sight of the portly, overindulged, fat, slimy Queen Betina bouncing around like a space hopper but the panic he could feel from the vines overrode his natural instinct.

Betina was the queen of this worm den and much like a queen bee releases hormones she had unwillingly released her sense of fear throughout her entire den. Alfie was by now nearly knee-high in worms as they fought and wiggled to swarm protectively around their queen, passing her across the top of themselves to the centre of the Book Room.

Exsarmon who had been eavesdropping shouted out, "What is happening? What have you done Arksanza?"

"Close up the chamber doors and stop crying out like a frightened creature," ordered Arksanza.

Exsarmon looked like he wanted to argue but Queen Betina intervened. "Do as you're instructed!" she bellowed.

Betina and Arksanza played a game with each other, she would abuse her power and he would pamper to her whims, both trying to get one up on the other like a mental game of chess but there was no malice or wickedness intended by either party, there was a mutual respect so she knew if Arksanza was asking of such powerful Magiks, then there was a very good reason. By now the Ulla worms had ferried their queen gently to the very centre of the room, placing her down they quickly cleared a perfect circle around her.

She summoned the link worms forward each joining to the suckers down the side of her voluptuous body and then in turn linking to their fellow Ulla until a connective maze of wriggling creatures filled the floor space forcing the remaining Faerians and Alfie back against the wall.

"What are they doing?" whispered Alfie to Eisiam.

She shook her head. "I'm not sure. I have never seen such behaviour in the Ulla before. They usually link up in the vine chamber where you first met Queen Betina."

"The secrets of the ancient Magiks are buried deep within Mother Earth, the Ulla will absorb the knowledge from the soil so it is best for Betina to be in contact directly with the earth," said Seraphina holding Alfie close to her. As she did so the Ulla began to, what Alfie could only describe as, fizzle and splutter like a firework attempting to ignite itself, as one flushed into life so did its partner and the next one until the entire maze of worms lit up white and bright all leading back to Queen Betina who let out a gasp as the energy surged into her body. Alfie turned his face into Seraphina's body, he couldn't help but feel that the whole thing looked painful and tortuous as Queen Betina seemed to shudder as each wave of light travelled down the line through her followers to be absorbed by her.

Seraphina tipped his chin up. "It's OK little one she does not feel any pain. She is trying to search out the information that Arksanza requires. Do you remember the day the Ulla accepted you? There was no pain when you felt the surge of the vines and the Ulla in your veins and Queen Betina is far more experienced than you in such matters. She just needs to concentrate hard. It will drain her of a lot of energy. No doubt she will require sustenance from Arksanza's sweet treats," she chuckled and winked at the young boy. Seraphina loved the compassionate side of Alfie's nature even as a very young child he showed a real need to be kind to everything around him. He couldn't bear to see a creature harmed whether it be worms caught up in a jar by his brothers or even wasps lured into jam traps. He had suffered plenty of stings from the ungrateful insects liberating them to their freedom. But she was also troubled this new existence he had been plunged into would cause him to be in many dangerous situations, many times where he would have to choose to harm someone else to protect the ones he loved. Would he have it in him she wondered.

He had already shown a deep loyalty to Risla who by all rights should have been banished from their Set to live alone in isolation, removed of his Lockan, never to look upon another Faerian face for his remaining days in this worldly existence.

Alfie's fierce defence and threats to leave had surely influenced the Elders in their decisions regarding Risla's punishment for his blatant disregard for the safety of Alfie and indeed the entire Set.

His angry bright red face, oblivious of pomp and ceremony, had been a shocking sight as he'd burst into the closed off meeting. Not even Risla's parents had been allowed to attend to hear the fate of their son. Showing a total disregard for rank and position Alfie had fought and stood Risla's corner. All the while the Faerian on trial had attempted to calm his young friend, pleading with him just to let it go.

"No. No I won't," Alfie had raged, pacing up and down like a caged animal, working himself up into a frenzy, threatening that they would never see him again if he took himself back to his family, all of which had to be taken seriously by the Faerian Elders all sitting in judgement.

They sat in astonishment at this young boy slammed his fist upon the great wooden table, demanding they listen, such angry tears pouring down his face, finally ramming home his point by having a near full-on Awakening there in the centre of the Elders' Assembly Hall, ripping open his tunic to display the now glowing talisman forever burned on to his chest and for the first time showing some ability to control the growing force within him, a demonstration almost of what they could be gambling to lose.

Alfie didn't completely get his way. Risla still had to be seen to be having a penance put upon him, he had to lose some of his status and was demoted to work upon the land and give up his weapons of warriorhood, an act which greatly stung his heart. He had known no other path since being a child, the House of Aspenola were known for their tradition of warriors, some of whom had fought side by side with descendants of Alfie's. The Delaney clan in the great battles of time gone by, had trained and tutored Risla from such a young age, how was he to adapt to holding tools fit for no more than tending the soil? But deep in his heart he knew he must make the best of this bad situation and be grateful he had not been banished to a soulless life away from his family, friends and Alfie.

The crackling of the energy source travelling along the long links of Ulla snapped Seraphina's interest back into the room.

Arksanza lent forward to whisper, "I believe she has retrieved what we require."

Queen Betina vomited forward a white milky discharge from her mouth into a carved wooden bowl held close to her by one of the vine keepers. "Take the gift of knowledge and prepare it for reading," ordered Betina. "Now place me back within my chambers, I am most tired. But be warned Arksanza, the Magiks you dabble with are not simple or trustworthy. Think long and hard before you perform it there is much at risk should your doppelgänger be discovered." A gasp of almost silent air passed around the few who had been allowed to remain. Alfie thought the whole thing seemed gross.

Exsarmon who stood wringing his hands in silence unwilling to be the first to speak, stepped forward taking the bowl with the mucous and poured its contents out on to a stone slab that had been heating in the fire, it fizzed and spat as the contents connected with the scolding hot surface. He spread the fluid out with a gold metal stake almost like a pancake covering the entire surface, hot air flopped out from underneath as the thickening mixture changed from liquid to solid.

"Words are forming My Lord," called out Exsarmon. "They must be for your eyes only come sit," and he patted the ground beside him. Arksanza did as he was bid and placed himself down upon the ground staring intently as the instructions for the Magiks appeared before him.

As Exsarmon lifted himself up to walk away he gave one last instruction, "Remember it well My Lord, for mistakes will be costly. Burn the words into your mind like your life depends on it and most importantly honour the doppelgänger when its service is done."

Without taking his eyes from the developing spell Arksanza answered, "I will."

They all left the Book Room with great haste not really knowing where they were going just following Arksanza's orders,

Lolah bounding around excitedly barking, sensing something in the air.

"Hush furry one," called Seraphina. "We do not need to draw attention," she said as she attempted to pacify the animal.

"We must get word to Solgiven to meet us at the mud pits, also Moondavna and her sisters but quickly the sun is soon to set," said Arksanza to Seraphina.

"I will go My Lord." It was Risla.

Seraphina let out a mocking laugh. "I do not think so!"

Risla ignored her reaction and strode forward. "Please My Lord. Am I not the fastest here amongst us? Am I not built to fly through the trees? Allow me this chance to make amends."

Seraphina tugged at his arm. "You have proven yourself to be nothing more than a glory hunter no matter the cost," she hissed into his face.

"Enough!" shouted Arksanza. "We have neither the time nor I the energy to listen to your squabbles. Risla do my bidding. Tell Solgiven it is of great importance that he attend me immediately." And in a flash the athletic Faerian disappeared into the trees. Turning to Seraphina who stood shaking her head he explained his actions. "I do not speak against you lightly my dearest. I truly believe you have the boy's best interest at heart and love him as any mother would love a child, however this love is not objective so you must stand down and listen to me. Risla does not wish a hair upon the boy's head harmed, he has much to learn and great wisdom to gain from the likes of you and I. Allow him this chance to redeem himself. We were young once were we not?" he said stroking his hand down her face. "Youth can be a curse as well as a blessing and it is up to us ancients to teach the young, yes?"

She turned on her heels. "I will fetch the triplets," and she vanished into the undergrowth.

"Shall I go after her?" asked Eisiam.

"No, it will do her good to calm down," replied Arksanza. "Come we need to prepare Alfie for the Magiks. Hurry we must get to the pits."

Alfie felt a little nervous. He had already worked out for himself that he was to play a part in the Magiks. He just hoped it wouldn't involve pain, blood or blood, or more blood, or blood of any kind.

The mud pit was quite unassuming. It could easily have been missed if you didn't know what you were looking for. It probably covered the same area as Alfie's trampoline back home and was shaped a bit like a kidney. There was a pungent odour, a deep earthy smell wafting around their feet as the mud plopped and bubbled.

"Is it hot?" asked Alfie reaching to scoop out a handful of glorious chocolate coloured mud, his hand quickly slapped away from the surface.

It was Moondavna. She yanked Alfie back from the edge of the pit obviously uncomfortable with his close proximity to the ever so inviting pool, as inviting as a whole load of mud could be to teenage boy.

"You must not make contact with the mud until we have prepared the Magiks," said Arksanza.

"OK you only had to say," he answered quickly eyeing up the three vine keepers still looking as fit as he remembered them. They had changed their outfits. Gone were the flowing gowns to be replaced by tight-fitting leggings and short cropped leather tunics, much more warrior-like than ladylike, thought Alfie to himself.

Their Lockans were tied up tight into a high bun on their heads, each having a different weapon or tool strapped to their thigh. Alfie couldn't quite recognize what each object was apart from the blade Moondavna had. He recognized that knife from the ceremony when he had rather embarrassingly believed the Faerians and Queen Betina were going to sacrifice him. Somehow he knew that the blade would put in another appearance but he just concentrated on the objects carried by Annaluna and Scalia.

"Eisiam, what do the vine keepers carry?" asked Alfie in his most 'I'm not bothered but really I am' voice.

She pondered for a second and then replied, "To be sure I am not but you do remember the blade. As for the other two, I have no knowledge."

"They are a bolange made from solid silver and a sceptre hook; common instruments used in the Magiks' creation of a doppelgänger," a stranger's voice stated. Alfie was almost fearful to turn around and see where this booming masculine voice came from.

Arksanza let out a yelp of delight. "Solgiven my dear friend come greet me." The two Faerians clasped each other's forearms and pulled their chests together laughing as they did so, the power of the stranger unbalancing Arksanza. "Be gentle with me for I am not as young as I once was." Quickly straightening up his comrade Solgiven turned his attention to the boy.

Alfie didn't know if it was his imagination but the ground seem to shudder as this huge man mountain stepped towards him. He was probably the same height as Risla but was a solid wall of muscle. Like Seraphina he too bore the signs of battle up his arms and thighs. He had a nasty-looking scar that ran from his temple, partially across his eye and down on to his cheek. The eyeball itself looked milky and flat but all that did not detract from the fact that his right ear was missing.

Alfie could feel himself staring and he tried so hard not to. He could feel his jaw hanging loosely open, a trait his mother did her best to try and avert many a time whilst out shopping or talking to a neighbour, he just couldn't help himself. The attention did not go unnoticed by Solgiven.

"So this is the one they speak of." The tone of his voice vibrated through Alfie's chest.

Oh god, don't let me crap my pants, thought Alfie to himself as the striking warrior loomed over him.

"And what will I be addressing you as My Young Lord?" said Solgiven lowering himself down on one knee bringing him face to face with the bemused young boy.

Alfie took a big swallow which he was convinced everyone heard. "Alfie, Alfie Diamond," he gulped completely transfixed on the fish-like eye, trying to keep his inquisitive poking finger stuck to his side and not giving in to the need to test the squelchy texture of the eyeball.

Seraphina looked on in horror, the same look his mother would give him, a 'DON'T YOU DARE!' look.

She quickly moved to the boy's side wrapping her arms around him effectively strapping his arms down. "His full title is Alfie Diamond of the Delaney clan," she gasped out relieved that she had taken evasive action.

Solgiven pinched the boy's cheeks in his vice-like fingers, not painfully just firmly as he studied his human face. "Er you have green eyes, they seem familiar to me."

Seraphina threw Arksanza a look. "Come Solgiven you have already established the Magiks we require your assistance with, let me explain in full what your task will be. We do not have long before the sunset," he said helping his friend back upright, he steered the warrior Faerian towards the pool of mud.

Seraphina's look of panic didn't go unnoticed by Eisiam or Risla. Turning to her brother Eisiam whispered, "What was that all about?"

Shaking his head Risla replied, "I am not sure little one but it would be unwise to ask, Seraphina is not in the best of moods."

"Now," clapped Arksanza, "we are here to perform a complicated form of ancient Magiks, each of you has a task and each must complete it entirely as I ask for it to be done, are we clear?" In unison everyone replied "Yes".

"Risla take this urn and attach it to the rope, throw it strongly into the centre of the mud pit and draw it back quickly. Repeat this process until you have sufficient mud to cover us all, face and body, but do not touch the surface with any of your skin, this is most important. Do you fully understand?"

Already tying the rope to the urn Risla answered, "Yes My Lord, I do." The mud was thick and heavy and it seemed to fight back against Risla's efforts, relentlessly sucking down the vessel but he was determined to fulfil his task, he was desperate to make amends with Seraphina even though the rope was beginning to burn his hands. He hauled load after load until a sizeable mound grew at his feet.

"Firstly, everyone present must cover their face, arms and legs. No area of flesh should be exposed. But not you Alfie. Come closer. I need a cutting of your hair, a drop of your blood and I want you to spit here into my hands into this small handful of mud." Alfie looked confused. Spitting, his mother would cuff him across the ears if she caught him spitting.

"Moondavna the blade please." She stepped forward and clasped Alfie by the wrist, he screwed up his eyes and winced but she only poked the end of his thumb with the sharp point of the knife and squeezed the blood allowing it to drop into the collection of hair and spit.

"Seraphina summon up an Orb, using these contents. Send it to the centre of the pit." As he passed the mashed up items of Alfie's hair, spit and blood, she instantly began to mumble her spell intently concentrating on the manifestation of the Orb. It quickly took on momentum and began, slowly at first, spinning and hovering above Seraphina's hands. She directed it by gliding her hands in a waving motion until it came to a gentle rest just above the surface of the bubbling mud.

"It is ready My Lord," called out Seraphina to Arksanza.

"Good, good," came the reply. "Now Solgiven draw your solar blade and catch the rays of the sun upon it."

The Faerian warrior did as he was bid angling the sharp metal of his curved sword. Alfie could see an intricate carving along the tempered steel as the twisting and turning made the light dance along its length. Alfie could see the strong warrior straining to contain the power of the sun, his athletic frame trembling.

"Arksanza, how long must I hold it?" he shouted to the Elder above the crackling and spluttering of the humming sword.

"Not long. Everyone gather close. Once the Orb enters the mud and is absorbed Alfie you step into the pit, remove your tunic and boots."

Alfie did not look best pleased at the prospect. "How deep is it? What if I sink?" he called out as he removed his footwear.

He wasn't sure which bothered him most, the possibility of being sucked down to his death beneath the oozing slimy gunge or revealing his less than trim rounded belly to his gathered audience.

"Listen carefully Alfie, you must enter the mud and for a count of ten remain submerged. This is vitally important. You must give the spell time to work with the Orb and your body. I shall call out the enchantment and then Moondavna, Annaluna and Scalia will join you. They will pull you quickly to the surface. Moondavna will guard your soul and the two remaining sisters, your physical body. Ignore any light flashing and do not under any circumstances look back once you climb from the pit. Seraphina will guide you to the trees where you will wait until this Magiks is done. Be brave and confident that we will keep you safe," said Arksanza as he led the boy to the edge holding his hand whilst he lowered himself in. The mud was surprisingly warm as it slipped up his thighs and then hips and belly as he sunk deeper and deeper. Aware that he couldn't feel the bottom, only the tugging of the mud, becoming almost vice-like with a determination not to release the boy, a flutter of panic flickered inside his stomach as he looked up at Eisiam standing on the bank as the level of the mud grew closer to his mouth. He inhaled a deep breath in preparation to drop beneath the surface but the constriction of mud around his ribcage was stifling. His primal instinct for self-preservation caused him to attempt to flay his arms but they were stuck tight to his side as though he was strapped into a straightjacket.

Seraphina's voice came into his head, *Do not fight it be calm my boy.* The mud was now up to his nostrils, his mouth clamped tight shut as he prepared himself to dip below. Risla held on tight to Eisiam as together they watched the last glimpses of his curls get swallowed up by the mud, Eisiam hearing the pounding of her brother's heart in his chest.

"Now Seraphina release the Orb from your control. We must all be ready to enter the pit if Alfie needs our assistance but not before the power of the solar blade, the Orb and the enchantment have become one. Your essence must not combine with Alfie's whilst I carry out the Magiks or the doppelgänger will be flawed and there will be a real chance the spirits of the underworld will come to claim Alfie's soul. As I speak I feel them gathering, hoping that they will get a chance to snatch him away from us. We must be alert and ready for any eventually. The mud we have daubed upon our bodies will protect us should we have to enter the pit but it is imperative that Alfie and his doppelgänger never come face to face less they be lost to the underworld to wander for eternity neither dead or alive."

"Limbo," whispered Eisiam under her breath. An uneasy silence fell over the group as they watched two more bubbles pop to the surface then no more.

"Solgiven, the blade. Release its energy across the surface now." A bolt like lightning swept across the surface exploding into action as it collided with the Orb sending the mud bubbling like soup in a cauldron and the force of the combination throwing Solgiven off his feet. Arksanza had to shout out the spell in a language never heard before not even by Seraphina. Three times it had to be repeated. It seemed like an eternity to Risla that his young friend had been below the surface as the gathering wind caused havoc to the trees. Thrashing branches and leaves flew through the air. Something magical was definitely taking place as the ground beneath their feet began to rumble. All the while each being present did not falter and stared intently waiting for Alfie to break the surface, not least Arksanza who had a look of concern upon his ageing face.

"He should be back to the surface by now. Something is not as it should be." Moondavna drove straight in with her blade drawn followed closely by her sisters also brandishing their weapons. "Scalia use the sceptre hook to seek him out," shouted out Arksanza. "The rest of you be prepared. As soon as they break through pull Alfie to the bank."

All hell broke loose as the vine keepers thrashed and lunged as if in battle with an unseen enemy; it was the mud. Eisiam stared in horror as the mud took on the form of a being, faceless but large and strong, snatching and grabbing into the mud, ripping at it, searching for the boy, letting out an ungodly scream of frustration as each shovel-like handful of mud proved to be fruitless. It was a race against time. Who would find the prize first; the vine keepers or the ravenous spirits possessing the mud? Annaluna launched herself on to the back of the mud creature, desperate to distract it whilst her sisters searched, sending a barrage of blows down on the back of its skull with her trusted bolange. The creature screeching with rage and reaching around the back of its neck grabbed her by her hair and unceremoniously slung her across the pit and into the trees that surrounded it. Eisiam and Risla immediately rushed to her aid as she lay groaning clutching at her arm. Risla was no expert but even he could see it was broken as he tried to comfort the struggling vine keeper.

"Get Seraphina," ordered Risla to his little sister but as she tried to jump to her feet Annaluna grabbed her wrist shaking her head.

"Carry me to an open space." Even though they could not see her speak her words they could still hear her insistence. Risla did as he was bid scooping her up and turning to survey the ground. Annaluna pointed and he quickly obliged, all the while aware of the battle raging in the pit, it seemed that by now only he and his sister and the stricken Annaluna were left on the bank.

He was desperate to get to the pit but he knew he could not leave his sister in charge of the injured vine keeper, she was scared and completely out of her depth.

Annaluna called his name. "Risla the Nature will heal me go join the fight to reclaim Alfie of the Delaney clan. Your sister has hidden strengths, I trust her to give me aid. Go!"

Risla turned to look at his sister as she nervously whispered, "Do as she tells you." He was gone in a flash.

Annaluna looked at the girl gently placing her hand on hers. "Lay my arm out straight placing the wound against the earth." Eisiam hesitated as she softly picked up the arm supporting it from beneath. Annaluna winced.

"Sorry, I know it hurts," comforted the young Faerian.

"Do not worry yourself all will be well. Now scoop some soil especially the peat and let it run the length of the wound."

Eisiam seemed puzzled. "Will it not infect the wound? I'm not sure that I should do this."

Annaluna chuckled. "You forget I am born of the vines, my blood is directly of the Nature and Nature does not harm its own. Please do my bidding."

Reluctantly Eisiam did as she was told. No sooner had the soil landed on the blood and protruding bone there was an immediate reaction. Hundreds of tiny little roots and shoots appeared out of nowhere, wriggling into spontaneous life, all meshing together tightening and binding the damaged arm. A pale yellow fluid oozing from the ripped skin spilled out of the wound on to the ground and evaporated into the air. Eisiam not could believe her eyes, the broken arm was repairing right there, right in front of her, the injury disappearing like it had never happened. She took hold of Annaluna's arm running her fingers over the surface of the skin twisting and turning it in total disbelief.

"Can I have my arm back now? There is a battle still to win." At which she jumped to her feet hauling up Eisiam, stripping her Lockan loose and took off running, her Lockan blazing a trail of electricity behind her.

All Eisiam could see was total carnage in the pit, mud-covered bodies camouflaging who was who, arms and legs thrashing around in the chaos, Annaluna slashing at the mud creature with the scolding power of her Lockan, each contact causing it to yell out with excruciating pain. Scalia surfaced dragging something behind her, her energy spent she called out to Eisiam.

"Come to my aid, hurry." Without thinking Eisiam scrambled into the pit up to her knees lurching forward against the weight of the mud, desperate to get to Scalia and whatever she was hauling from the pit. She had hooked something with her sceptre her muscles straining as she pulled with all her might. At first Eisiam couldn't see what or who it was then she spotted the familiar curly hair although clogged and caked with mud. It was Alfie. Her heart skipped a beat as she lunged at him grabbing him under the shoulders whilst Scalia relentlessly wrenched with both hands on her sceptre which she had somehow hooked into the leather belt on Alfie's leggings. Both Faerians found strength from somewhere and dragged him up on to the bank, both collapsing with the immense effort. Eisiam coughed and spluttered almost vomiting as the mud she had swallowed cleared her airway. Scalia let out a high-pitched call to her sisters and they in turn called out to Arksanza, Solgiven, Risla and Seraphina that the boy was safe but the mud creature was not so keen to give up. A lunging great arm formed and darted across the pit straight for the stricken boy, snatching at his leg, launching him high up into the air. Eisiam screamed, she was nearly hysterical whilst the unconscious boy dangled like a rag doll. Out of nowhere Seraphina sprung forward.

"Be gone creature," she called as she threw a white powder into its gaping mouth. It recoiled on itself screaming and writhing as it collapsed in on its body releasing the human boy who was now free-falling. Bounding three paces across the floor Solgiven launched himself into the air and at full stretch caught Alfie in his arms, both of them ending up in crumpled pile amongst the bushes. The mud creature's essence left the physical structure of the mud and the spirits of the underworld returned to their eternal perdition. An eerie calm fell over the scene, the surface of the pit, smooth like freshly poured chocolate, glistened silkiness that showed no sign of the previous madness.

Seraphina smeared the mud away from Alfie's eyes as he coughed and tried to blow the debris from his nostrils. "Didn't the spell work?"

"Hush child do not try to talk. You have probably gulped down a lot of mud."

As she proceeded to attempt to clean him up before dressing him, she glanced across his head directly at Arksanza her eyes questioning. Was the boy right had they failed? She could feel an anger welling up inside her. They had put her charge at risk all for nothing. They had nearly lost the boy to the underworld just for the Magiks to have been unsuccessful; Queen Betina must have got it wrong. Seraphina was lost in her thoughts as she picked at the litter of leaf mulch adhering itself to Alfie's wild curly hair, the drying mud not easily relinquishing the rubbish. He yelped as she tugged at the annoying bits.

"Oh ease up you nearly pulled me bloody hair out!" He rubbed at the patch she had been so intent on clearing.

Arksanza could see her annoyance and was just about to approach her when Solgiven called out, "My Lord," an indicated that Arksanza should turn around. In doing so he was met with a shocking but equally welcome sight. There in the middle of the pit was a small dome-like object.

"Seraphina take the boy into the woods." She was about to argue but his abrupt tone made her realize what was happening. "I said take him now."

She scooped him up as he wriggled. "I ain't a baby I have legs don't you know."

"Just for once in your life can you please be unquestioning and do as you are told."

He felt well and truly put in his place. "OK. You only had to ask bossy knickers."

Risla bit on his lip, there was the little rogue he loved and knew.

Eisiam in the meantime was too busy staring in astonishment as the dome had now raised further out of the mud as though a child was hiding under a chocolate-coloured sheet and was moving up into a standing position on a bed, the folds of mud being sucked in tight to reveal a human form, clear as day; head, shoulders, torso, it just kept coming.

"Hurry Seraphina the boy must not come into contact with the doppelgänger," said Moondavna as she helped push the boy through the trees stopping him from turning his head back to see what all the fuss was about.

As the mud drained from its features Risla and Eisiam recognized the face appearing before them. Eisiam gasped and Risla stepped closer.

"How can this be?" he questioned out loud.

"It is Magiks," replied Solgiven as he bent down to retrieve his sword wiping the mud from it along his arm. "It is a doppelgänger. Alfie's doppelgänger."

The newly created creature walked across the surface of the pit on to dry land. It turned and studied all of the faces before him and then selected Arksanza. The doppelgänger looked like a mud carving of Alfie, solid, an exact replica.

"We must prepare the doppelgänger for its task. Quickly Eisiam fetch some clean water we must clean it down. Solgiven send for your most trusted warriors, we need an escort for a perilous duty. Be sure they wear human clothing and only those who have previously interacted with the human world. We cannot do anything to draw attention, the boy, the doppelgänger must be the focus."

Deep into the woods Alfie was still arguing about why he couldn't see the doppelgänger. What was the big deal and what were they going to do with it? Moondavna had a less than sympathetic attitude towards the boy.

"Do you not realize the trouble that has been taken today to achieve an answer to your desires, to allow you to remain amongst us in such a way that you would make you feel happy?" Alfie felt a little freaked out at this point. It was very disconcerting to be basically told off by a blank-faced, mouthless, irate vine keeper.

It was like being told off by his mother. He could see her head bobbing with frustration, his mother's hands gesticulating but he would always manage to zone out on the words, a more soothing drone replaced the spoken, harsh vocabulary, but a telling off from a vine keeper was a completely different kettle of fish.

No matter how hard he tried the piercing words bombarded his mind, her eyes full of expression portraying her anger all the while her lower chin, like a blank canvas waiting to be finished, jutted forward with annoyance. Seraphina hugged him to her, still wiping at his face with the edge of her gown.

"Alfie I know this all seems strange but it is for the best. There are reasons why you and your doppelgänger cannot come face to face; it is to protect you and in fact the doppelgänger. Were he to make eye contact directly with you he would become aware."

Alfie looked puzzled. "Aware of what?" he asked.

"His own self and worst of all he would seek out your soul to become complete. For now he is content as a shell of yourself with very basic functions, enough at least to fool your family for a time."

Alfie pulled away from the Faerian. "What do you mean fool my family?" he demanded. "What's my family got to do with this?" his face fixed in anger.

"Hush child." Seraphina tried to pacify the boy but he brushed away her hands.

"What's bloody going on, how are my family involved?" Two of the vine keepers and Eisiam gathered closer. Risla tried to prevent Alfie from returning back to the mud pool.

"Please little man listen to Seraphina, let her explain," he pleaded.

Alfie stared at Risla and then back at Seraphina and Eisiam. His young Faerian friend softly smiled and gestured for him to sit upon a broken-down tree stump. Reluctantly he scuffed his feet into the mud and pondered for a second then approached the makeshift seat.

"Go on then tell me," he said not raising his head or making eye contact just resting his chin on his palm.

Seraphina brushed down her gown and then circled the boy. "In order for us to keep the pretence that you have been missing for three nights, Arksanza came up with the conjuring of a doppelgänger, your doppelgänger, Alfie of the Delaney clan. It would not be feasible to believe that your parents would not have caused a countrywide search for you and in doing so would have brought humans deep into our realm. However they are not the only ones concerned for your position. As you know by now the Gorans have had strong belief of your existence for the longest time, your first Awakening would have definitely alerted them and Arksanza believes your family are under constant surveillance. The creatures of the Gorans cannot enter the house but there is nothing to stop them flying over in hopes of a glimpse of you. The purpose of the doppelgänger is to firstly trick your family into believing that they have found you and secondly to throw off the Gorans. At least until we have had a chance to get you to a place of safety and until we can call a Gathering of the Clans." She turned and looked expectantly at the young boy.

"My head hurts. This too much stuff. How's it gonna help my mum? When they find the doppel what's it called, you said it can't talk or do anything, that's gonna well screw with her head."

Seraphina knelt down in front of the boy. "Some of what you say is true but it is a good thing that it cannot make speech for then we would all be given away. Solgiven and his warriors will take the doppelgänger deliberately to a place that it can be found, they will shout and holler to bring the searchers and your family to the clearing. Elancie the dream maker will enchant them. They will believe that you are found, gravely ill but not close to death. To all present you, that is your doppelgänger, will be in a deep sleep from the cold and even the doctors at the hospital will be of the same belief, that you have somehow survived the cold nights and they will tell your mother and father that your body needs time to recover and it will do this by sleep."

Alfie shook his head. "I have seen many things in the last few days that I would never have believed existed but this is all too messed up. How can my own family not know that that thing isn't me? It's just a load of bull…" He stopped himself from finishing his words as he could see the look of hurt on Seraphina's face.

"Even now do you truly believe that I do not speak the truth?" she questioned.

Moondavna stepped forward. "If the precious brat does not want to believe then leave him to his own defence we have other causes to fight."

Seraphina lunged at the vine keeper, a bolt of pure power surging from her palm knocking Moondavna from her feet. "Your ignorance astounds me. Silence your tongue or I shall do it myself." Moondavna looked as if she was about to spring to her feet as Annaluna stepped over her.

"Be silent sister," pushing her sibling back to the ground turning to Seraphina and bowing her head. "Sincere apologies, my sister forgets herself. Perhaps the fight at the mud pool has left her with battle rage."

Scalia appeared from the undergrowth. "If the boy does not understand show him. Show him with an Orb, he can see for himself. Is that not the best way?" Seraphina considered it for a moment and then sprung into action gathering what was needed for the visionary Orb to be formed.

"As before, watch do not touch and give no commands they shall come only from me," she looked directly at Moondavna. Unplaiting her Lockan and shaking it free Seraphina summoned up the power of the earth, her long locks fizzing with energy and sparking light. The spinning Orb whipped up the dusty ground along with small twigs and leaves causing the expectant audience to shield their eyes. Singing out a gentle humming the Orb bounced along Seraphina's hands and then elevated and hovered above the circle formed by the beings below. Just then Arksanza burst through the bushes shocked to see the silver blue spinning Orb. He stopped in his tracks.

Risla motioned to him to sit next to him on the ground and quietly whispered, "We are going to watch them deliver the doppelgänger," and smiled with anticipation his eyes glinting with excitement. Arksanza wasn't sure why this was happening but knew better than to disturb Seraphina whilst she carried out her Magiks. She was oblivious to his arrival and continued to mutter under her breath, encouraging the Orb to spread out wider as the first swirling trails of smoke began to form a moving picture in its centre, the force created by the revolving Orb causing her hair to whip wildly like frenzied serpents attempting to wrench themselves free of their tether.

Alfie screwed up his eyes tightly straining to see what was before him. He could see figures picking their way through the briars and undergrowth carrying the doppelgänger on a stretcher-like board. He recognized one as Solgiven but that was not difficult, he cut a unique figure. As for the others they were strangers to him but they all seemed to be kitted out in nerdy rambler's clothing, they certainly didn't have any of their tattoos on display and most seemed to have their prized Lockans safely tucked up under woolly hats. They all appeared to be homing in on the same area; a lone figure greeted them and pointed to a slight clearing amongst the trees. Already Alfie could see the dancing flickers of the torches of the other search parties through the trees, the humans were getting close.

The images were so clear Alfie almost forgot that he wasn't actually physically present at the site. He picked out Elancie who was busy directing the party of Faerians, showing them where to lay the doppelgänger and redress it in the original clothes that Alfie was found in, including his tatty old trainers!

Alfie quickly threw a glance at Risla, he grinned. "I retrieved them from the river," he proudly announced to everyone. Eisiam rolled her eyes.

Alfie's attention was quickly snapped back to the events going on in the clearing, someone was shouting, "Over here, over here quickly!" It was Solgiven his voice booming and loud. A flurry of activity kicked into action, people bursting through from all over, people he recognized; his family. There in front of his very eyes, his brothers and sisters fighting their way through the barriers of the trees, stumbling over exposed roots all desperate to get to their baby brother's side. Charlie threw himself to the ground landing on his knees beside the doppelgänger.

"It's OK Alfie we found you, we are all here mate," grabbing at his little brother's hand. The rigid frozen fingers caused Charlie to stare anxiously up at the group of would-be rescuers, the band of Faerians, they all returned the gaze of concern but for different reasons. Elancie stepped forward and knelt beside Charlie placing his hand upon his shoulder, his voice soft and lilting.

"Your brother has come to no harm but the cold is taking a hold on his body, you must remain calm for the sake of your family. Your voice should be a source of solace in this time ahead, now call for your healers and be away from this place with the boy." Charlie stared blankly ahead as Elancie stepped back into the group.

Seconds later he was snapped back into reality by the howling of his youngest sister Tallulah. "Is he dead? Is he dead?" she demanded, her eyes wide like saucers as she studied the lifeless body, ashen skin and inky blue lips. Alfie's heart began to pound in his chest. He wanted to run screaming through the woods "It's OK, I'm here. Look, see, I'm safe", the sound of his sister's cries raking across his heart. His eyes welled up as he continued to watch the scene before him unfold. Charlie standing now trying to console his siblings, shouted out to his father.

"Dad this way! Bring the doctor." A moment's scuffling then no sooner had the words left Charlie's lips, his father arrived accompanied by a search and rescue team, who instantly sprang into action unpacking their kit bags, wrapping the doppelgänger in survival blankets, one setting up an IV drip whilst another listened to his heart. All the time Alfie could see Elancie circling the group.

"What is Elancie doing?" whispered Alfie to Eisiam as the Faerian continued to follow his path, a slight subtle movement of his hand giving away him sprinkling some kind of powder.

"I not sure but I believe he is enforcing the Magiks, the illusion. The doppelgänger can be very believable but only with the strength of Magiks behind it. Elancie will have to stay close to it whilst we try to keep the pretence up." Alfie's attention was caught by the movement of someone with a hood over their head fighting through the team assembled around the doppelgänger, one of them snatching at the hood to reveal a cascade of dark curls tumbling down their back, he instantly knew.

"Let me through." They struggled with the medics as they attempted to block their way. "Let me through I'm his mother!"

"Nellie, let them do their work." Alfie's father tried to hug her to him but she pushed him away.

"I want to see my son," she cried as she dipped below the arm of the policeman who was standing in front of the doppelgänger.

She sidestepped the next one and then seized hold of the arm of the doctor. "Is my son going to live?" she demanded.

"Please let us do our work. I will explain everything once we are on the move. We must get him to hospital quickly," replied the medic as he tried to peel back her vice-like grip from his sleeve. Again she shouted gripping his chin this time, dragging his eyes around to meet hers.

"Nellie!" came a shout, more forcefully this time. It was Mark clamping her arms down and physically lifting her from her feet. "For Christ's sake woman, let the man do his job."

Alfie's eyebrows arched. "Oh no, he didn't," he muttered under his breath.

"What? What is the matter?" asked Eisiam.

Alfie's eyes were glued to his parents awaiting the inevitable. "She's surely going to punch him. He called her 'woman'. He did, he called her 'woman.'"

Risla and Eisiam looked perplexed. "Is she not a woman then?" asked a confused Risla. Eisiam nodded.

"Yes of course she is but some women don't like to be called 'woman' by a man. Don't ask me why I'm just a boy. I really do not understand how they work."

"How who work?" asked Eisiam.

"Oh bloody women," Alfie snapped, fidgeting and strain to see the action before him. She instantly jumped to her feet and stomped off to sit next to Moondavna. "What? What did I say?" said Alfie to Risla, who equally looked blank-faced,

"I believe," said Arksanza. "That the female of any species will have an equal reaction to a disrespectful tone used by their counterpart, in this case you Alfie!" The young boy turned to look at Eisiam who steadfastly refused to make eye contact with him. He let out a sigh refocusing on his mother and father, expecting his father to be nursing his chin but to his surprise he wasn't, he was cradling Nellie into his chest her gut-wrenching sobs echoing through the woods. She clung on to him for dear life as the rest of the family escorted the doppelgänger to the waiting ambulance further down the track.

"Come on let's get him to hospital, they will patch him up in no time, soon be on his feet," he said tipping her chin up and softly kissing her on the tip of her nose, her salty tears dispersing on his lips.

She looked up at him appreciating his attempts to lighten the situation. "OK let me just pick up Alfie's T-shirt, it's one of his favourites. Mind you it won't be wearable now it's been cut to shreds." She wiped her eyes with the sleeve of her jumper and bent down to scoop up the tattered remnants of his top discarded by the doctor. She attempted to reassemble it to vaguely look like a complete item but it had been distorted by the force of tearing and cutting the pattern no longer lined up. She held it up to her nose to absorb the smell of her son, much as she had done with all of her children, it was something she did to comfort herself when they had gone away on school trips or she had had to travel down to her mother's when she became ill, a warm maternal feeling would spread over her body giving her a sense of peace. She inhaled deep waiting for that musky, slightly grubby, teenage boy bouquet to slam to the back of her nostrils but nothing; no stale greasy mitts rubbed down the front of the T-shirt, no sugary waft of Coca-Cola, no peanut butter and jam with a hint of salt and vinegar crisps, absolutely nothing but dank earth. Twisting and turning the fabric she sniffed to no avail.

"Er missus, we be on our way now." It was Solgiven, he approached Nellie. She grabbed at his hand.

"Oh my god, yes of course. I, we cannot thank you enough; all of you," as she turned to the rest of the Faerian party, all of them nodding acknowledgement but all equally eager to be on their way. She gripped Solgiven's hand liked her life depended on it and pulled him to her embracing him, forgetting the normal personal boundaries, so grateful was she to them all. The huge hulking great man, awkward and straight-backed, did not quite know how to react to this tiny emotional woman squeezing him with vigour, the remaining Faerians already vanishing into the night.

A voice in the distance shouted out. "Nellie, Nellie come on. We have to leave now if you want to ride in the ambulance. Come on." She dismissed it momentarily.

"Thank you for bringing my son back to me," she said softly, her dark eyes welling up as she gave Solgiven an intense stare, it unnerved him.

He tried to act nonchalantly. "Ah missus we didn't bring him anywhere we were just lucky enough to find him is all," he said still trying to wiggle his hand free. Again the voice in the background called her. "Sounds like they are wanting you missus." He tipped his head in the direction of the voice.

She turned her back on him and held the T-shirt once again to her face. "Something is not right, something feels wrong. This does not smell like my boy!" Nellie slammed the garment down on to the ground. Everyone back in the clearing watching through the Orb let out a gasp as they saw Solgiven struggle to pacify Alfie's mother.

Seraphina felt a sense of foreboding welling in the pit of her stomach just as Elancie burst through the trees.

"We may have a problem!" he spluttered breathless from his run.

"I know I have seen for myself," replied Seraphina. Arksanza now joined the two Faerians as they huddled in deep conversation. Alfie was not sure which drama to watch, his mother or the gathered group before him. Solgiven's raised voice drew him momentarily back to the scene through the Orb.

"Please missus calm yourself, you have had a shock. You really should be getting along to the hospital to be with your boy." Again the voice from the trees called out summoning her.

"Bloody hell, I will follow with the kids just go!" she roared back at the trees her face twisted with anger.

"I really think you need to go missus, you're his mother," pleaded Solgiven, panic-stricken as he watched the neon blue lights from the ambulance fade into the night.

By this time Nellie was pacing back and forth ranting to herself "Something is not right", over and over.

"Missus you're just stressed. Let me take you to your children they can take you to the hospital but we must go now or they will leave without you." He firmly grabbed her arm pushing her through the undergrowth catching her when she stumbled almost lifting her from her feet, so determined was he to hand over his burden, calling out to the remaining family, "Your mother here she is," as he lunged forward towards the cars, physically handing her over to Charlie. "She probably wants to be seeing a healer young 'un, she has got herself into a pretty state."

Jodie wrapped a blanket around her mother. "Mum you've got to calm down, come on let's get after Dad the ambulance has already left."

Charlie shook Solgiven's hand. "Thanks mate sorry about Mum she has been so distressed these last few days." The huge Faerian just nodded in acknowledgement watching as Jodie led her mother to the back of the car. As Nellie bent to slide into the back seat, she turned and looked at Solgiven as he walked away into the night.

"Where are you from? What is that accent?" she called out after him, his shoulders hunched he ignored her and kept walking.

"Mum! What does it matter? Jesus, just be grateful they found Alfie," snapped Jodie, as she slammed the door and jumped into the driver's seat.

The clearing soon emptied and was silent once more. Seraphina unceremoniously collapsed the Orb and snatched up Alfie.

"Come we must be back to the Lair, it is not safe to stay here. The commotions here tonight will have drawn attention, there could be silver ravens roosting nearby and if that be the case the Gorans will not be far behind us." Alfie watched the last silvery remnants of the Orb disappear into the damp evening air as Arksanza and Elancie headed off to the hospital.

"Why aren't they coming with us?" he asked Seraphina.

"Elancie needs Arksanza to help him with the doppelgänger. It would appear that your mother will be more difficult to keep under the spell of the Magiks. She is questioning, her motherly instinct is telling her that all is not well and it would seem that this occurring has awakened latent gifts within her. For now Arksanza and Elancie must stay close to the doppelgänger, their combined power will enhance the Magiks to give us more time."

Slightly out of breath with the pace of the walking Alfie asked, "Why do we need more time?"

"Come little one I will explain later. I am sure that your stomach is crying out for food, when we get back we can have supper."

Risla patted Alfie on the back. "Yes supper that does sound good and maybe you can tell me tales of more delicious treats from the human world," he winked at Seraphina.

Alfie knew that they were trying to distract him but he was too drained and tired to argue for once so he just went along with them, his mind hurting with the strain of all that had happened that night in the clearing.

As he walked back to the Lair he mulled over questions. He got the distinct idea that his mother had a part to play in this saga even if she herself was not yet aware of it. He let out a sigh to attempt to remove his thoughts.

"What is the matter little man?" questioned Risla.

"Oh nothing, I'm just so tried and I need to go to sleep."

Risla hugged his friend to reassure the young boy. "Soon be back and you can cuddle up to Lolah. She does make a mighty fine bed does she not?"

Alfie responded with a soft half smile and concentrated on his feet, one step at a time, carrying him closer to the blissful release of sleep.

A Lost Girl Found – Chapter 8

As Solgiven crashed his way through the trees away from Alfie's mother and her questions, feelings of agitation and annoyance flooded his body. He pulled off the human coat he had worn screwing it up in to a ball lobbing it into the woods.

"That not be an experience I wish to repeat," he muttered to himself, dragging his woollen cap from his head to let loose his hair. He raked his fingers through the strands of sweat-soaked Lockan, giving his scalp a good scratch with his nails, so taken aback by his body's physical reaction to the events just passed. His adrenaline surged through his veins, muscles twitched causing his whole body to tremor. He had three images burnt into his mind Alfie, Alfie's mother and his own beloved daughter Misa. The connection between all three; dark curly hair and unforgettable vibrant green eyes. He had felt a feeling of familiarity when he had first met Alfie at the mud pool but now after having come face to face with Nellie, he could no longer deny his thoughts. Even in the dark of the clearing with just the light of the torches, Nellie's intense staring emerald green eyes could clearly be seen; the same eyes that looked back at him when he faced his daughter and the boy the Faerians called the Redeemer, Alfie of the Delaney clan. The same clan all three blatantly belonged to. His realization hit with such force that he buckled and dropped to his knees as his stomach churned over grinding and knotting tight as he fought not to throw up. Beads of sweat burst forth from his forehead trickling down and stinging his eyes. He rolled over on to his back, his hot fiery breath billowing into the cold night air pouring from his lungs as he tried to suck back in as much oxygen to recover his senses. So desperate not believe his own mind but knowing the inevitable truth, his darling daughter Misa was a Delaney, no three people could have been more identical. He let out a cry so primal, like the sound of a wounded animal. The day he had hoped would never come had found its way to him, here as he lay staring up at the stars so silent, so oblivious to his pain. His panicked breathing slowed and softened, his eyes rolled back in their sockets, he allowed himself to drift off and take solace in his memories, as his heavily burdened body melted into the mulch of fallen leaves and earth.

Solgiven couldn't exactly remember what had drawn him to the clearing that day, as he sat and watched his beloved daughter gather up the apples and berries she had accidentally tipped from her basket.

"Oh I am so bumbling," she exclaimed in annoyance. He smiled and pulled himself up bounding over to help her, playfully tugging at her long dark curly hair, twisting it around his finger.

"Like infant piggy tails it be."

She tutted. "Even my hair cannot behave itself," she cried flicking her father's hand away.

That day so long ago, that dark curly hair was what had drawn him to her, mistakenly thinking her to be a creature of the forest. He had almost plunged his hunting spear into his quarry only to pull back milliseconds away from the softly cooing infant child smiling and excitedly waving her arms reaching up like she wanted to be picked up not at all deterred by his craggy appearance.

He had nervously crouched down, this was a human child so it followed that there would be a mother somewhere nearby. The child continued to babble entertaining itself flicking at the blades of grass that cushioned it and had acted as camouflage from him when he had first entered the clearing.

He couldn't remember how long he had sat low into the undergrowth awaiting the appearance of the child's mother. He listened intently for snapping twigs, or the swooshing of fern being parted, all the while the child was quite content chitter-chattering to itself completely unfazed by its surroundings.

The skyline was beginning to darken. Something was not right; no mother would leave a child for a time in such a place all alone. He stood up to his full height, his muscles aching from the cramped position he had sat in, shaking the pooled blood from his feet to flow freely once again around his body, behind him the child began to whimper. Still no one came as the child's distress became more apparent. There was only one thing to do. Solgiven picked up the child and bundled it up in his tunic, its fingers cold but clinging to his huge hand trying to gnaw on his knuckle with two tiny teeth. He chuckled until the infant really chomped down and he let out a yelp scaring the infant into a full-blown scream.

"Shush, shush, little one." The child went into a rage of ear-piercing shrieks as he bounced it from arm to arm. "Hush, hush," but to no avail, the tiny little face was all screwed up and red with its clenched fists thrashing the air.

Solgiven was overwhelmed. He put the baby down on to the ground amongst a small pile of leaves, scuttling back to the cover of the undergrowth muttering, "Please little one stop crying." Holding his hands over his ears he flicked his eyes back and forth over the woodland. *If that child's mother be near, she surely can hear this ruckus, it's enough to wake the Green Man*, he thought to himself. The crying infant calmed itself as the cries became less urgent, dampening down to a whimper whilst rubbing at its eyes and yawning. Solgiven was surprised at how large this tiny child could make its mouth. "That's it little one you best be going to sleep." He remained sitting in the bush for a good five minutes. *After all that yelling no one is coming?* he thought to himself. Just as he tipped forward to get to his feet, he heard a snap and then another. Quickly he ducked as low as he could, someone was coming. He tried to adjust his eyes to the night but it was difficult to see more than a few feet and he dare not light his torch and give himself away, still the footsteps got closer. He looked to the Moon but it was mostly obscured by cloud, it just needed to move over a little with the wind, just enough to illuminate the wood. Nearer and nearer, snapping and crunching, Solgiven's senses were all primed ready to react to this human coming closer and closer. Then he heard a snort like an animal investigating the soil, followed by scraping sounds, claws on roots and earth and a foul stench on the wind. This was no human it was an animal and an animal of the worst kind, a Gorja hound.

Without even thinking Solgiven leapt from his hiding place, throwing himself at the creature which was no more than three feet away from the now dozing child. The stunned hound fell winded to the floor as Solgiven swooped down snatching up the child, bundling it up into his tunic leaping and bounding through the trees.

He knew their only chance was to get higher up away from the snapping jaws of the angry hound, it was so close he could almost feel its hot putrid breath. Any other time he would have swung away through the branches with ease eluding his pursuer, but not now, not with a small baby, each landing platform had to be stable, he couldn't fumble about with such a precious cargo or worse still pick a rotten branch.

He could feel his energy sapping already, he had spent too long out in the night air. His restorer and life-giving friend, the Sun had long gone from his skin and to add to his problems he knew his solar blade would be of no use for the same reasons. He should have been tucked up deep in slumber long before the Sun dipped below the horizon and his prized solar blade mounted in the embers of the fire, glowing and recharging but he just could not bring himself to abandon the lone child.

His only option was to hope the hound was rogue and alone, that a pack was not nearby, he must face it and outwit it. Firstly he stripped off his tunic looking down at the sleeping child in his arms; he could scarcely believe that it hadn't woken.

"Don't worry little one we be making it back safely," he whispered as he package up the child securely into the tunic, then slinging the arms of the garment over the branches, he knotted them as tightly as he could, the bundle gently swung in the wind like a hammock.

Quickly Solgiven sussed out the best position to come upon the Gorja hound. He must kill it swiftly and silently lest the hound alert others. His natural hunter instinct kicked in as he surveyed the branches, testing them for their strength and solidness, lifting his solar blade to his lips, he kissed it for good luck. "Do not let me down now," he whispered as he laid the blade on to a thick swollen limb of wood. The blade began to glow, spluttering as he willed it to give him enough power to work through the thickness of the branch. The subdued light gave away his position as the hound, foaming at the mouth, snarled and jumped at the foot of the tree, once again manically biting at the trunk. Solgiven so concerned the child would awaken from the racket from the Gorja hound decided his trusted blade was spent, it had no sharpened edge. Its power came from the Sun and the white burning embers of fire. Fully powered it would have cut through the hound like butter but now at best he would be lucky to get close enough to clunk it on the head. No he had to be more intelligent than that, the hound's weakness was its pitiful eyesight but its sense of smell made up for the lack of vision.

Solgiven quickly rubbed the moss from the bark of the tree on to his arms and face, all over his exposed skin attempting to mask his own sweaty body. He needed vital seconds to get down from the tree and position himself with his makeshift spear to hopefully attack the hound's weakest spot, his underbelly.

Slowly slinking down and around the other side of the tree, Solgiven managed to silently drop to the ground, the hound's attention drawn to the bundle hanging high above, as he took in a deep breath and prepared himself for what was to come. Solgiven knew the beast was at least twice his weight and its powerful jaws had the ability to crush his skull. Somehow he had to get to the underbelly, so he did the unthinkable and laid himself out flat upon the ground and proceeded to bang and crash and holler.

"Here, over here you stupid beast!" The hound turned into the air sniffing at the breeze, its hackles raising its head low and stalking as a deep growl rumbled through its chest, saliva oozing from its jaw, its paws armed with razor-sharp claws padding closer and closer. Solgiven prayed his strength would hold out just that little bit longer as an uneasy stand-off developed, the hound wary of the branch in his prey's hand and Solgiven unable to move closer in order to maintain his attacking position.

He goaded the animal, "Come on, come on." The animal slapped at him, keeping itself just out of reach trying to nip at the Faerian. Solgiven had no choice but to try and tempt the hound by perilously allowing his forearm to wave right under its nose. It took the bait and snapped shut its jaws upon Solgiven's arm. He let out a blood-curdling scream as the savage canines sunk deep like burning, searing pokers into the flesh and muscle as the animal tried to tug him over. It took all his strength to stab his feet deep into the soil to stop the hound flipping him over on to his front where it would surely sink its teeth into his skull and brain. He momentarily had to let go of his weapon as he reached for the animal's eye and gouged it with his thumb, plunging it as deeply as he could. The animal trying to shake himself free yelping with pain, released the arm. Solgiven seized his chance as the animal now stood directly over him, he plunged the makeshift spear deep into its belly, forcing it back as far as it could go, hoping the branch would not snap. The creature let out a single yelp and slumped lifeless on to Solgiven as warm blood drained down the branch on to his hands. The dead weight of the Gorja hound knocked the wind from him as he struggled to wriggle out from under the foul-smelling beast, his energy draining by the second. All he could think of was to get himself and the baby back to the safety of the Lair. His last memory of that night was of stumbling into the hut of Seraphina thrusting the baby into her arms and waking the following day with the glare of the full sun shining on his bare chest. This memory and that of the defeated Gorja hound's lifeless body crushing his ribcage snapped Solgiven back to the here and now, back to the present day, he instinctively patted his chest as he fell out of his dreamlike state.

Once again he was desperate to get to the Lair but this time for different reasons, he knew there would be answers, explanations and one person who could set him right, Seraphina. She knew everything about everyone and for the longest time she had tried to persuade him the human child he had named Misa should be returned to her clan. He had steadfastly refused. Why should he? They obviously did not care for the child they had so callously abandoned. He had saved her life and struggled by himself to raise an infant, something he was definitely not a natural at but he somehow muddled through. He watched with great pride over the years as she grew to be a strong, healthy, kind young woman. He had moved them both out of the main Sets in the Lair, to keep prying eyes from his business. They had lived in a small dwelling independent from the other Faerians, coming and going as they pleased, with very few visitors for the first few years. Misa's curly hair and eye colour made her stand out from her companions and the fact that she did not have the delicate fluttery wings of a Faerian infant was a problem. Solgiven got around this by strapping her to his back when he had to venture out but once all the little ones in the Lair shed their wings his life became easier. With her wild curls tamed, pulled taut into a plait, she nearly disappeared into the background dressed as a Faerian and schooled in their ways, she could easily pass as one of his own.

As she grew older she pestered Solgiven to have her body adorned with the clan tattoos, he was keen that she should have floral patterns across her shoulders depicting her free spirit and love of nature. He sneakily shadowed in two separate hollows one on each shoulder blade that gave the illusion that she once had tiny buds from which her Faerian wings had grown as an infant, good enough to fool a passer-by if her tunic slipped and peace of mind for Solgiven.

Now as Solgiven drew closer to the Lair, he dragged his legs like they were made of lead. Instead of turning off the path to go straight back to his dwelling which would have been the sensible thing to do, he was set on confronting Seraphina. How dare she keep this knowledge from him? All along she had known the secret of Misa and yet she never saw fit to tell him. No doubt Arksanza knew. Why was he, the child's father, the last to find out?

Seraphina's voice popped into his head. *Best you be returning to your daughter and your bed.* He was shocked, she had not used mind voice for years upon him. He had no way of knowing if she had read his thoughts but she had definitely not communicated with him this way for the longest time and she had steadfastly blocked him from hers.

He was incensed and outraged, his bellowing voice raging into the night. "Come out and face me, cowardly one," he demanded.

Her voice appeared again in his head. *Hush less you awaken the entire Lair. Return to your Set, I will speak with you at daybreak. Quieten yourself or I shall have no choice but send the warriors.* He pounded the ground with his fists cursing with vengeful anger. Seraphina had no other means to shut him up so she ordered in her warriors. Normally they would have been fearful of Solgiven's strength and reputation but they took comfort in the fact that he would have been severely drained by his unscheduled prolonged stay out in the night air, still they were shocked to see the warrior they all so admired reduced to an incoherent babbling wreck.

"My Lord our Lady Seraphina requests that we escort you to your dwelling."

"Does she indeed?" he mocked spitting the words from his mouth.

"Please My Lord, allow us to assist you, you are in a sorry state of weakness," said Teverie, the lead guard leaning down to place his hand under Solgiven's heavy un cooperative arms, fuelled only with lactic acid rendering them useless to him.

The fallen warrior let out a yell of anguish and frustration. "I be fully aware of that fact," he shouted trying to stagger to his feet shoving the warrior away from him. "I be capable of assisting myself, stand out of my way," he barked at the warriors.

"I am sorry My Lord but we must be carrying out our lady's order," Teverie replied ducking as Solgiven swung out his huge arm and clenched fist, wildly twisting, attempting to make contact with one of them .but to no avail as they flailed about like sails in the wind.

They were all too nimble and sidestepped every attempt by Solgiven, each one reluctant to lay hands upon him. To them he was a legend, a warrior of great feats, they were taking far too long to bring this act of madness to an end. Suddenly Seraphina burst through them grabbing Solgiven by his Lockan, sweeping away his legs and slamming him to the ground, knocking the breath from him. With her mouth close to his ear quiet but breathy, she tugged tightly at his hair.

"Regain your senses and hold your tongue," she snarled at him. He wriggled and tried to turn his face to her but she had a tight grip and held his arm up into his back.

"You knew! You knew all along!" he shouted at her.

Using all her strength she pulled him around pinching his cheeks. "There is your daughter Misa, see how she watches you scramble amongst the dirt like a swine, fighting your kinsmen. Find your dignity and get to your feet warrior!" she hissed at him as he locked eyes with his beloved child. Her eyes were wide as saucers, questioning yet fearful to step forward to her father's aid.

This scene before her was so unexpected, so confusing. Why by the gods of the two worlds would her friend and guardian wish to so unceremoniously dump her father, Solgiven, to the ground? He beckoned her to him allowing her to help take his weight as they both struggled to heave his body upright, she pushed away Seraphina's hand.

"I have him. My father do not trouble yourself further," she glared insolently, something she would never have dreamt of doing before but her anger got the better of her as she struggled, her small frame inadequate to support this huge great lump of a man weakened and mentally shattered. He stared intensely at her watching the same flash of anger dance across her eyes, the same he had seen in Alfie's mother. There was no doubting it they were one and the same, although Nellie's human ageing had drawn some of the freshness of youth from her skin and her dark wild hair had the odd flicker of silvery grey. Misa had been given the gift of Magiks' not eternal youth but nevertheless prolonged life and slowing down of her human heritage, she looked twenty years younger but he wasn't sure of their true connection, he just knew that the outcome would not be good. He felt his heart judder and an overwhelming sense of sadness engulfed him. This was the beginning of the end, the day he had chosen to push away to the back of his mind. He hugged his beloved child to him desperately trying to bury the building howl deep within his stomach, the sour tears brimming ready to burst forth. Surrendering to Seraphina's warriors was his only option he just could not muster one single ounce of strength and Misa though strong in spirit could not be expected to drag his depleted body back to their dwelling. He turned to Seraphina.

"Your warriors may take me now witch," he told her. His words rasping with hatred, though silent to the others, clawed their way into her soul, she physically shuddered such was the effect of the poisoned tongue lashing her mind's eye. To think once she had loved the Faerian known as Solgiven, the bravest warrior known to the great clans. That they had been bound and promised seem to have disappeared from his memory as he glared like a wounded animal before its hunter, defiant and distraught at the same time.

"Assist My Lord Solgiven to his dwelling. Be sure to position him for the morning sun," she ordered as she reached to pick up Solgiven's solar blade from the ground. Misa immediately snatched it from her, struggling with its weight.

"I will take that," she snarled at Seraphina.

Ignoring the young Faerian's tone she said, "Set a strong fire to build up the white embers..." But before she could pass the words from her lips Misa spun on her heels.

"I know best how to deal with my father's blade. Have I not done this for him most of my life?" she snorted with temper and stomped off after the warriors struggling to carry Solgiven. A wry smile spread across Solgiven's lips as he listened to his daughter's scathing words. She may not have been born of his blood but had great strength of mind and a sense of loyalty, a sense he hoped she would still have once the truth was revealed to her.

Seraphina stared after them as they disappeared into the night. With her blood boiling and her teeth grinding she lashed out with her wooden staff battering a tree to vent her anger, the front of her shins aching and bruised. Solgiven's calf muscles were solid like tree trunks. It was no mean feat to clatter them when she took his legs from under him. Yes she had known the truth there was no denying that but she had also begged Solgiven to return the human child once Arksanza had revealed Misa's identity to her. The scriptures of the Great Oracle told of many legends and particularly of a human clan, the Delaney clan. The Geminis were to play a huge part in the future of the survival of the Faerians and in their ever-escalating battles with the Gorans. For centuries an uneasy stalemate existed between the warring factions neither gaining much on the other, that is until the emergence of Triamena, daughter of Traska, King of the Gorans. All Gorans had the capacity for immense evil but she was a whole new level, even amongst her own kind she was hated. Ambitious and greedily hungry for power, desperate to achieve the power of day walking, she would relentlessly seek out the Geminis and the boy child born of one. In just one short day Solgiven had come into contact with all three precious elements of the Trinity of Delaney without even realizing it, what would Triamena or her father Traska have given to have been in that enviable position?

Triamena would have been cackling with delight if she had just witnessed the scene between the two Faerians, the disintegration of their bond would have given her great pleasure and no doubt a sense of false achievement. Peering into the shadows Seraphina pulled up her hood not completely certain that some minion of the Gorans wasn't sitting in the inky blackness silently watching, waiting to report back. Shaking her head and breathing in she was deeply annoyed with herself for being so ridiculous, she was in the Lair the safest place she could be, for now at least. Shuddering as the damp night air crept across her exposed arms, she walked off wearily to her own dwelling emotionally drained, contemplating what the morning mist would bring forth. Life as she knew it would never be the same. All she could pray for now was that Solgiven would have relinquished some of his anger during his night-time slumber and that by some miracle he would be willing to listen, she didn't hold out much hope for that.

Triamena Demon Princess – Chapter 9

What was there to say about Triamena? Evil, evil, evil. Born evil and would probably leave this plain for the next life evil. Her whole existence was consumed by jealousy and an overwhelming desire for power; her only ally her nursemaid Clarimun and her long since passed grandmother Katchatrua.

The elderly matriarch positively encouraged her malevolent granddaughter to strive for greatness amongst the Goran tribes, she nurtured her physical prowess. Her fighting skills were honed by only the best warriors all under the guidance of her doting grandmother pushing her to her limits. She herself had once been the Queen of the Gorans. She ruled during the Black Years as they were known, her torturous nature and bloodlust earned the Gorans the fearsome reputation that prevailed for centuries to come. Rumours abounded that she had dispatched her husband the rightful king to snatch the crown and power from his family stealing away their birthright and rewriting history, changing the fortunes of one to eliminate the other. Her belief that her weak husband Hurran would bring down the might of the Gorans and his attempts to call all the clans and tribes to a great gathering of peaceful talks with the Faerian nations pushed her to take drastic action; she dabbled in the Dark Arts of Medulla. From this practise she devised a spell and potion to poison Hurran sending him to a place of madness in his mind. Katchatrua controlled him like a puppet, manipulating his rulership, convincing him to pass his crown to her whilst he recovered from his illness. A female had never before ruled over the Gorans, they were seen as the weaker sex but Katchatrua was the exception, she towered above her siblings, her athletic physique, aggressive nature and determination to rebuild the Goran clans made the warrior nation accepting of her as their pretender Queen. In the coming days as Hurran wasted away, she took the finest warrior Corzon as her consort, resulting in the birth of her only offspring, Traska, a male child to carry on her legacy. Long after Hurran's funeral fires disintegrated into the sky, huddled groups whispered in dark corners and shadows passing gossip from one to another.

"Murderous she be."

"Hush lest we be heard."

"Lose your head you will be doing if such talk was passed to the Queen."

"Some say she be a witch of the Medulla."

"Shush do not let such thoughts pass over your lips." Common enough comments made on a regular basis by frightened and scared individuals.

Katchatrua was equally aware of how she was viewed by her clansmen but she cared not and in fact she positively thrived on the fear she generated, this same fear she wanted her granddaughter to perpetuate so once again the Gorans would become the ultimate warrior clan.

Traska was deemed a living legend amongst his own kind recording many successes in battle against the Faerians, infiltrating the human world but his mother Katchatrua did not believe him to be worthy of succession. When her health began to fail her, ironically due to the poisoned Waters of Aslanda she purposely drank on a daily basis as a young queen, Traska ordered the council to consider he be made king even though his mother had not passed from this world to the next, announcing her as not fit to rule. He had forcibly taken the Medallion of Kingship from her publicly intentionally humiliating her, aware of the underground support for his mother, he needed to drain the strength from her to show his clan that she was no longer a force to be reckoned with, no longer a symbol of the barbaric awesome power accredited to the Goran clans. The medallion would normally only be recovered from the smoking charred remains of the funeral stack, a shining metallic disc with a ruby stone in the centre, buried beneath the blackened bones and charcoaled hazel branches. Traska had spared his mother's life, an act he would later come to regret, as long as she relinquished her right to reign and publicly showed him support. On the Moon rise of that last night for her as queen, Katchatrua had snatched the small bottle she kept tied on a skinny leather thong from her neck, biting off the cork top and tipping the last few droplets into her dry parched lips as she had done so for many hundreds of years. Triamena clinging to her skirt howled like a caged animal.

"Be silent, this is not the behaviour of a warrior princess," she snapped slapping the young Goran across the cheek. "Clarimun take hold of her see she does not follow, her tears will be her downfall, install some discipline into her," she growled as she shuffled forward with her staff to go and attend her son soon to be king. She spat the water from her mouth, "What is the point of this liquid there be nothing left for me now?" she muttered to herself as she threw the hazy glass bottle to the ground crushing it with her foot as she set off, wincing momentarily as the tiny shards pierced her leather moccasin, the pain reminding her she still had a task to carry out before she left this world for the next. The water could no longer help in fact it winged her more speedily now to her eventual death, the same waters that had made her abnormally strong and muscular, toweringly tall with aggression overflowing, force-fed to her by her father as a child till she became entrapped by its addiction. He had not the blessing of sons; five separate wives had all borne him female infants, by the seventh he decided that she Katchatrua would be like no other Goran female. The waters would help achieve his ambitions for his daughter. She would carry his ancestral name to greatness.

He schooled her as he would have done his firstborn son and she excelled to rise above all warriors. For many years she flourished, healing quickly when injured in battle, abounding with energy and vitality but always a lurking spitefulness and seeping need to inflict pain and suffering on anyone or anything that got in her way. Her notoriety spread through the clans even far from the boundaries of their homeland to reach the ears of their mortal enemies, the Faerians.

As age took hold her bones began to soften, a sign that she had partaken of the waters too frequently. Fractures in her legs and spine reduced her to a hunched up wizened old hag aged long before her time, her darkened leathery skin ill-fitting hanging from her skeletal frame, able only to walk with the aid of a staff, no longer commanding the presence she once had. Her physical body may have worn down but her razor-sharp mind was still intact and now plotting, she threw herself into her granddaughter Triamena. The child had inherited her grandmother's physique naturally, tall and willowy with lean muscular arms and legs. She had twice the strength of her male counterparts and regularly overpowered her father in play fights but it all too soon became apparent that she was a danger to herself and others. She had to push the boundaries, always attempting to impress her father desperate for his approval but as time passed he became more and more concerned by her antics during her training, several sparring partners had been injured and maimed by his wild feral offspring, she developed a taste for blood, choosing a particularly gruesome method of celebrating victory; biting off her opponent's ear and wearing them strapped to her belt on a leather thong, the macabre dried up body parts dangling in the breeze from her hips clattering as they jangled against each other. Purposely she shook her hips like a manic belly dancer just to send chills through the younger Gorans and keep her minions firmly in their place. It wouldn't be the first time she had relinquished an ear from its owner just because she felt like it. Katchatrua positively encouraged such behaviour and would frequently stitch the trophies to her granddaughter's belt for her, cackling with pride as her beloved Triamena swirled about the place. Her many scars from sword slashes were her pride she didn't see them as disfigurements quite the reverse, they were her badges of honour and a sign to others that she had no fear.

Only Katchatrua and Clarimun seemed to have any control over this wayward creature bubbling over with vengeance, fighting back against a father who made her feel second best to his new bastard son Ivandor, his new heir to what should have been her kingdom. Everything she had been existing for, living and breathing for, was slowly slipping away from her as her half-brother grew, her father's interest stolen from her by that sniffling brat. Her outbursts became frequent, more violent and challenging. She pushed Traska, questioning his authority much to the delight of her grandmother.

Triamena was everything Katchatrua could no longer be and she would become only more powerful as she studied the Dark Arts of Medulla, a form of forbidden Magiks supposedly eradicated hundreds of years before Triamena was born. During her lifetime Katchatrua had revived this ancient art setting up a network of supporters, all sworn to secrecy at the threat of death should they give away the widespread covens.

Only female Gorans were initiated into the black arts and from the moment the infants were born as soon as they were introduced to their mother's breast so too did they nurture on Waters of Aslanda. A whole new species of Amazonian-like Goran females soon rose up above their clansmen, a ready-made army bred to serve just one, Triamena the apple of her grandmother's eye. The thought of Triamena witnessing her put through the degrading ceremony to remove her of her medallion caused her to steel her resolve, even though Traska had ensured his mother would not be able to seek the comfort of the roaring fire, her frozen body trembling from the cold, he hoped it would be perceived as fear by the onlookers. This was a ceremony devised to cause her the most humiliation, as she stood not allowed to sit, the plunging temperatures of the dark night rapidly plummeted. As the full moon took her place in the velvet black sky high above, Katchatrua's shivering muscles caused her to tremor, resting only on her staff for support, her breathing was laboured and heavy, silvery white puffs of mist passing from her lips into the night air. Orders were barked at her to bow to her new King, unassisted, stumbling forward as her weakened body vibrated with the effort, she was aware that she had allies amongst the gathered crowds but catching their eyes dared them to stay put not to react to this ridiculous façade concocted by the King and not reveal themselves, imploring them to cheer along with the greater masses so as to keep themselves secret. She knew there was a purpose to Traska's elaborate ceremony; he wanted to attempt to flush out his mother's supporters, the supposed Dark Arts devotees. He watched the faces before him scanning for any signs of dissent to towards him but it was to no avail, he saw nothing. As he stepped towards his mother unceremoniously snatching at the plaited binding holding the medallion around her neck, he sliced it free with his knife caring not if he manhandled her staring intensely into her eyes.

"Thank you Mother, a gift greatly received," he snarled, her eyes did not flicker.

"A gift that is not given nor deserved, it shall be a curse upon you."

His bony knuckles struck her cheekbone with such venom but still she did not react as her head snapped back with the force of the blow as gasps surrounded them and an awkward silence fell upon the gathering. Traska was visibly shaken more like the victim than the perpetrator.

"You forget the tradition son of mine, you must take a lock of my hair to bind with yours for your reign to begin," she hissed after him. Traska stopped short contemplating his thoughts for a second, then turned on his heels at speed back to his mother grabbing at her thinning wisps of hair literally wrenching it from its roots, Katchatrua eyes watered but still she made no sound. He so wanted to strike her down but fully aware of all eyes upon him, he lunged back to the fire and holding aloft the straggly strand of white hair threw it into the flames.

"I have spared my mother death so see this act as a sacrifice to the Gods of Fire in place of her physical body, I pray this will appease them and my reign will be true and strong." The shrivelling strands quickly melted away to nothing and the faint stench of burnt hair stunk in his nostrils as he breathed deep from temper. "Prepare this," as he threw the medallion to the Chief Elder of the Council slumping into his huge carved wooden throne. "Get this gone into the fire also, order my carpenters to sculpt a new throne worthy of Traska Tivalleon, Son of Hurran, new King of the Goran clans." His announcement caused confusion and panic amongst the servants, warriors and members of the council.

"My Lord, the throne has a history of your ancestors, all the great kings before you as well as your mother the queen, please reconsider My Lord." The councillor did not stand a chance as Traska rose up skilfully drawing his sword and sliced the Goran's head clean from his shoulders all in one motion.

"A new King rises today, my word be law, let this be a sign to those who wish to cross me," he called bending and picking up the head holding it aloft showing the crowd.

A nervous cheer came forth from the warriors. "Honour the King, honour Traska," they shouted as he wiped the blood from his sword across his thigh.

"Get this ceremony to a finish," he ordered.

Katchatrua was almost impressed with the barbaric beheading. "Foolish one you do not know what you had and have let slip from your grasp," as she too sniffed in the odour of her own burning hair.

Even when the medallion was placed around his neck he scarcely paid it attention so intent was he on picking up something from the crowd, his young son pulling at the disc pulled him back to reality.

"Father let me be seeing," he cried snatching at the piece of jewellery. Traska turned his attention back to Ivandor laughing.

"Do not pull so young one lest you snap it from me," the young Goran twisted it so the moonlight caught the ruby causing shards of red light to bounce around.

"Can I wear it My Lord?" The new king laughed out loud encouraging his warriors to follow suit looking to them for approval.

"Yes one day when you are King my son."

Under her breath Katchatrua muttered, "A day you will never see bastard child."

Traska raised his head. "Did you speak Mother?" he asked.

"No My Lord, I merely wish to be taken back to my quarters the events of the night drain me." She spat out the words keeping her head bowed so that he could not see the anger in her eyes.

"Yes, but first you may kiss the hand of your new King." He held out his arm waiting for her to shuffle forward surveying the crowd before him as they cheered for him and badgered his mother.

"Remove the hag from the King's presence," they roared. Katchatrua paid no attention she took compensation from the fact that her face carved upon the throne bothered him so that he couldn't bring himself to rest upon it and from his announcement of his entitlement through Hurran Tivalleon. Little did he know of her dalliance with the fine specimen of Goran warrior that was Corzon, she was his only link to the crown and the medallion not his so-called long past father Hurran. This fact she would take to her deathbed to protect the rights of Triamena. Her father Traska was a bastard as was his own son Ivandor, there was no pure claim to the throne, they were all diluted down would-be contenders with Katchatrua being the only living soul to know the truth of it.

Away in the darkened cavern of Katchatrua's quarters Triamena lay grinding her teeth bundled up in her maid's skirt as Clarimun tried to cover her charge's ears fully aware that she could hear the baying crowd mocking her beloved grandmother, the smell of the campfire wafting up the corridor.

"I shall gut every one of them, how dare they treat her so, they shall rue the day. I will dance upon my father's skull happily for what he has done, you mark my words," her talon-like nails digging deep into Clarimun's arm. She winced but let Triamena vent her anger.

"I know blessed one they shall all pay, I believe you when you say so."

Realizing what she had done Triamena released her maid's arm. "Look how I have hurt you, you who have been like a mother. I am sorry, so sorry. See how they have goaded me." With that she set off down the cavern passageway screaming with raw anger.

"Triamena stop, come back. Your grandmother forbids you. Come back my love." The slightly rotund Goran was no physical match for Triamena the athletic youngster had already bounded off and out of the cavern heading straight for the flaming torches and the gathering. Seeing her grandmother kneeling before her father, her darkened silhouette against the burning oranges and reds of the dancing flames, her anger rushed to her head as she let out a blood-curdling scream and launched herself at Traska, completely caught off guard. Chaos broke out as the raging Triamena soared through the air, from nowhere a tall Goran female stepped forward between Triamena and her father blocking her assault and slamming her to the floor alongside her grandmother.

Triamena enraged sprung to her feet. "Stand aside lest you wish to be cast down."

The tall female lent forward. "Show your King your loyalty My Lady," she whispered into her ear.

Triamena spat on to the floor, "That is what I be thinking of loyalty." Katchatrua let out a groan distracting her granddaughter. "What is it? What ails you?" she asked as she bent down to her stricken grandmother.

"Take me to my quarters child," and then whispering under her breath said, "She I one of us." Triamena turned to look at the would-be bodyguard, a knowing look spread across her face as she stepped forward to assist the younger Goran in helping her grandmother to her feet.

"You will have your time young one but today is not your day," she uttered gently stroking the elderly Goran's face.

"I will show loyalty," called out Triamena as she placed her grandmother securely with the tall female Goran, stepping forward staring straight into the eyes of the King, her glare unnerving him as she switched her gaze to the medallion as he presented his hand. She bowed her head lowering her lips and then at the last minute grabbed at his little finger biting it clean off, pulling her knife from her belt backing up whilst waving it in the face of anyone who dared to come at her.

An ear-piercing scream filled the air as the king snatched his hand into his stomach dropping to his knees, staring in disbelief as Triamena scooped up her grandmother into her arms, stomping off in the direction of the cavern and a pale-faced Clarimun who had witnessed the whole event from the shadows, turning only to spit his bloodied finger out on to the mud. Katchatrua glanced over her granddaughter's shoulder at her shocked son writhing in pain knowing there was nothing he could do. He had already shown a disregard for the Goran laws and traditions by taking the medallion in such a manner, the Elders had shown a certain amount of resistance to his proposal, only his insistence that war could come to them with such a weak leader had persuaded them to agree. Traska now had no way of punishing Triamena without risking the wrath of the council and now even more so he needed them on his side as the young challenger to his reign disappeared from his sight.

Back inside the safety of the cavern Triamena, gently laid her grandmother upon rugs. "Clarimun fetch My Lady her waters."

Shaking her head Katchatrua called Clarimun back, "No there is no need, they do not bring me relief anymore. Come both of you sit before me, we have much to discuss and little time left to us."

For the first time in her life Clarimun saw a frightened vulnerable child before her, Triamena seemed to diminish, physically shrinking in on herself. Clarimun had seen many tears before from her charge, mostly anger and frustration fuelled them but these were different, the acceptance that her grandmother was not long for this world painfully dawning on her.

She clasped Katchatrua's hand to her cheek. "Do not speak so you're Katchatrua the Invincible, death is a weakness you will not accept."

Speaking firmly the elder matriarch said, "I did not raise you to have sentiment, gather yourself and your senses. Listen closely, they will come for me no doubt but you must gone, gone from this place." Triamena tried to intervene but Katchatrua raised her hand. "Hush," she ordered. "Traska cannot allow me to survive not after the events passed, he will be on a mission to take my life and that of yours. This cannot be allowed you must leave with Clarimun and Salsea, she is the one who prevented you from having your head removed like the councillor, and you will go into exile with them both. Salsea will school you as I have done, the other dark devotees will join you and your skills in the Dark Arts of Medulla will grow as you learn from each one of them. This is what they were bred for, to serve you and protect you. One more thing, you must keep your temper in check and not harm a single one of them, they will die for you so show them the respect they deserve. My enemies are your enemies keep that always in mind. Finally, Clarimun gather together my hair into a switch, cut it and then plait into Triamena's." Clarimun scraped the sparse hair together sadness growing at the fact that she would never again comb through the once splendid thick lustre of dark hair from her Queen's head, biting on her lip to hold back tears, bunching it together and then cutting through to remove it from Katchatrua turning to blend it and plait into Triamena's own hair.

"Now it is done always keep the hair safe, never cut it, never remove it until the day that you be in need of it," said Katchatrua.

Triamena looked dumbstruck. "How will I know when that will be if you are not with me? I am too young to be alone you still have much to teach me, I cannot leave you." Throwing herself upon her grandmother she cried, "Please, I do not wish to run I will fight my father."

Katchatrua chuckled. "Believe you I do my beloved child but there be a time to stand and fight and a time to be gone, you must be gone. Look Salsea comes for you. Before you follow Salsea from this land there is one more task to be fulfilled, your half-brother stands in the way of your destiny; eliminate him." Triamena smiled sadistically her sadness momentarily forgotten.

"Whilst your father and his warriors come to dispatch you and your grandmother Ivandor will be vulnerable then we will strike. His mother is pathetic and weak she will be no match for us. Come we must hurry I see the warriors already gathering with Traska as they plot."

Clarimun pulled Triamena up from her knees. "Come my child do as you are bid," as Salsea knelt before her Queen.

"It has been an honour to serve you all these years my Queen," Salsea said as she lent forward and kissed the forehead of Katchatrua placing a small vial into her hand. "Let not those scoundrels take you My Lady, this will hasten you from this plain on to the next, wait for me there until my time is done."

Triamena screamed out, "No, no you cannot do this. It is not fitting for a Queen, let go of me Clarimun." Struggling to release herself as her grandmother tipped the bottle to her lips, Triamena broke free to slap the bottle from her grandmother's frail hand, but it was to no avail Katchatrua lay silent, her chest no longer heaving with rattled breath, her eyes empty of life and her jaw tipped slightly open as though she was about to speak her last words but no words came, she was gone from this world, her spirit whisked away, the shell of her once magnificently strong body now a mere skeletal frame lost amongst the rugs. Triamena called her grandmother's name over and over each time her voice becoming cracked and weaker till she could not form the sounds, shaking from head to toe as adrenaline and shock set in.

Salsea reached gently to take her arm. "My Lady we must leave our need is urgent."

Triamena turned on her pummelling her chest with her fists with fury. "You did this, you did this, it should not have been this way," she sobbed, foam spitting from her mouth as she yelled at Salsea, her eyes wild with anger.

Snatching Triamena's wrists she cried, "What would you have me do, leave my Queen here for the blade of your father? That I would not be willing to do, he would dishonour her and not send her into the arms of the Gods of Fire, that is what you must now do, use this anger, let it give you strength."

Triamena softened her resistance and slowed her sobbing. "I do not think I can be doing that, I do not have the will," she whispered afraid to turn and look at her now silent grandmother.

"Yes, yes you do because you bear the blood of Katchatrua, you live, breathe and honour her in everything you do from this day on. Now you must complete this task as she would have wished with the courage of the true warrior princess that you are." Handing her a flaming torch and oil Salsea said, "Say a prayer to honour your grandmother, pour the oil."

"And let this be done," said Clarimun holding on to her young charge with tears slowly rolling down her cheeks.

Triamena joined them both at the entrance calling back up the passageway as the dark void now filled with dancing light and flickering flames as the fire claimed her grandmother.

"Goodbye my beloved Katchatrua, I will avenge you and carry your name forever." Taking her knife she sliced across the fleshy part of her thumb drawing blood allowing it to drip as she squeezed and paced backwards across the threshold of the cavern, repeating this act twice. "No clansman may cross here now without the Curse of Katchatrua falling upon them, let them die a long and torturous death without honour and may they spread their plague to their male offspring down their line for centuries to come," muttering the final part of her spell she stroked her newly plaited hair.

"Come Triamena we must be gone the light of the fire will draw attention and I fear your father will not be far behind."

Striding out into the inky darkness a new resolve came over Triamena. "Now for the sickly brat," she ordered. "The river sprites await him."

Clan Gathering – A Traitor Amongst Us – Chapter 10

For a far as the eye could see there were bobbing faces, scuttling to get closer to the action. Free-flowing hair intermingled with tightly braided Lockans, vibrant colours of clothing all combined to give a rainbow effect, silk banners hypnotically swaying in the breeze, each with its own totem depicting the hundreds of clans gathered and waiting in anticipation for one small boy.

In unison they turned and faced him, Alfie Diamond, the rustling sound of their garments rushing forward like an unseen wave. Naïvely he too turned his body to seek out what the massive crowd were staring at only to see Risla who stood at his side sniggering.

"They look to you little man," he said as he manoeuvred Alfie's shoulders round to the front again.

He let out a gasp. "All of these people are here because of me?" he stammered. Lolah licked his hand reassuringly as he felt his knees buckle under him. He had gone from one extreme to another, all this time since he had been found in the snow by Seraphina and the others, many measures had been taken to keep him a secret, to hide his identity and yet it seemed the world and his wife knew of him. Thousands upon thousands of eyes were upon him, smiling and chattering to their neighbour pointing excitedly at the young human.

Solgiven gripped him firmly. "Steel yourself boy, are you not the legend they talk of over campfires?"

A crushing weight upon his shoulders, he carried the hopes of each individual standing before him they believed him to be a saving grace come to free them from their battles with the Gorans, to once and for all put them in their place.

"Address them, they be eager to hear your voice," prompted Solgiven.

Seraphina slipped in beside the boy and Solgiven. "Let the boy be, he need not speak out today, there is much to prepare him for." She stared intently daring Solgiven with her eyes to speak against her.

Arksanza sensing the hostility between the pair stepped forward with his arms raised. "Let the festivities begin for tomorrow's dawn will bring forth battle plans and a new beginning for the Faerian race," he called nodding at an archer warrior, signalling him to let loose his flaming arrow. It soared high into the sky almost disappearing from sight to return back to the ground and the huge waiting bonfire positioned on the hill overlooking the valley. A huge cheer rose up as the dried branches and tinder sparked into flaming life and the presence of Alfie was temporarily forgotten, there was nothing better than a party as far as the Faerians were concerned. Fireworks soared into the air whilst rhythmic drums thundered around the gathering, campfires sparkled dotted spasmodically amongst the revellers as the dusk took hold. Alfie slipped back into the shadows somewhat relieved at his temporary reprieve as the sound of merriment filled the dusky night-time air. He shuddered at the thought that so many hopes rested upon his shoulders. A slight feeling of nausea rolled over his stomach, pinching his skin on his wrist he questioned still whether he slumbered in some fantastical dream but no, the nipping searing pain was truly real as was the situation he found himself in.

A tugging at his hand dragged him back into his reality, it was Eisiam. "Come let us dance and be merry." She giggled as she guided him forward to a clearing, encouraging him to sway to the rhythm of the drums.

She was one reason he could push aside his doubts and worries, her enigmatic smile and self-assured confidence for one so young caused his heart to flip as her gentle touch upon his hand made him weak at the knees. If his best mate Harry Wilsbury could see him now he would wet his pants, such a sight he would be, clumsy-footed, doe-eyed, love drunk, softie.

His natural shyness diminished each passing day that he spent with his Faerian cousins. He didn't worry about opinions on his clothing or wild curly 'girly' hair, his paunchy little stomach or whether or not the 'in' crowd didn't want him as part of their dining group in the lunch hall and for once it was a release to uncover his head and proudly display his dark ringlets in all their glory such was the attention they were grabbing as inquisitive fingers gently played and twisted them inspiring conversations of envy and desire to have curls.

This kind of dumbfounded Alfie. *Did the Faerians not realize how cool their Lockans were?* he thought to himself. To have such a deadly weapon, it was awe-inspiring. *Oh to have such power*, he thought forgetting completely his own newly discovered powers. He knew exactly who would feel the lash of his electrifying hair across their backside if he had a beautiful plaited Lockan; Tommy Saunders, school bully, total pain up the arse and all round loser.

"Hey you Dumpy Diamond where's my lunch money today?" Tommy's grating Scottish accent popped into Alfie's head. It wasn't so much that Alfie was scared of Tommy more like he was scared of his own reaction. Deep down he knew that there was the potential for him to loose it, 'hulk out' as his brothers and sisters called it. Tallulah in particular loved to push his buttons and see how far she could carry him towards a 'Hulk'. Timing was always essential and so far she had managed to avoid a battering but only by the skin of her teeth. Tommy Saunders would definitely have come off the worse there was no doubting that so the best plan of action was to avoid the conflict. Tommy as annoying and obnoxious as he was didn't deserve to be on the end of Alfie's rage because when he went, he went big time, like a raging bull.

He had plagued Alfie for the last two years of his last school just before the family had moved to his grandmother's house. On a daily basis Alfie had to run a gauntlet, planning routes around the school grounds designed to avoid Tommy and his posse but somehow he always seemed two steps ahead and would appear like magic out of nowhere. At one point Alfie did consider that maybe Tommy had an underground system of tunnels directly beneath the school and somehow had implanted a tracking device upon his person, so at all times Tommy Saunders knew exactly where Alfie Diamond was. *Perhaps a little paranoid*, Alfie thought grinning to himself. Maybe he watched too many movies and this fired up his overactive imagination.

"What do you smile about little man?" quizzed Risla as he hauled his young companion up on to his shoulders; he could see the interested parties were becoming more and more intrusive with their hair twiddling.

Alfie was quite relieved as the joy of pulling and pinging the curls was beginning to lose its appeal at least to him, he wasn't quite sure that he liked his hair being compared to piggy tails which caused much giggling amongst the younger Faerians and Eisiam it would seem was not very keen on the attention the Faerian females were lavishing on him either shooing them away.

"If I didn't know better my young friend I would be believing that my younger sibling has taken a shine to you," Risla said as he watched his sister get hot and bothered, chasing off the giggling cooing group.

Alfie could feel his face burning hot with embarrassment, relieved the darkened night would not reveal his scarlet colour but equally tickled by the butterflies flitting in his stomach as he stared down from Risla's shoulders at the flustered face of Eisiam scolding the would-be suitors or so she thought.

Secretly pleased at his tall gangly friend's comment he could just about hold his air of cool aloofness. "Oh really? I hadn't noticed." Risla burst out laughing dropping his cargo gently to the ground.

"Of course that be the case," he said ruffling Alfie's curly locks as he bounded off into the crowds clapping his hands and punching his arms into the air to the beat of the music.

Alfie stood a little away from the festive throng leaning against a tree content to watch protected by the shade of the hanging tree branches. It felt good to watch them all enjoy themselves even Arksanza was attempting to throw some shapes, the flickering of the campfires bouncing off smiling carefree faces.

Alfie let out a sigh of contentment and yawned. "Best you make the most of this night false hope-giver," came a tight grip on his arm and a hissed whisper in his ear, hot and breathy. He froze to the spot unable to speak too scared to even attempt to turn and see who spoke the chilling warning. He swallowed hard as the hairs on his forearm stood on end, the grip released and he could no longer feel the energy of the hidden would-be assailant.

Out of nowhere Seraphina burst through the mob of bodies her Lockan buzzing neon blue with electric energy, her staff drawn followed closely by Arksanza both breathless with adrenaline-fuelled panic.

"What happened?" demanded Seraphina pulling the boy close, patting and checking him all over roughly in her eagerness to be reassured he had come to no harm. Lolah broke through the undergrowth her hackles raised as she sniffed the ground around the base of the tree growling low in her throat.

"The hound has a scent," said Arksanza he signalled to two warriors to follow him.

"Wait My Lord a trap could be set for you," urged Seraphina.

"I do not believe so, the point was to make us aware that Alfie is not safe even amongst us. Did you see anything?" he turned and asked the shocked boy.

"No nothing, just a hand on my arm, the voice was low. I couldn't say if it was male or female but something makes me think it was female. I don't know why but it just felt like it." Arksanza quickly skipped through after Lolah her manic sniffing at the disturbed soil loud and gusty as she weaved in and out amongst the trees closely followed by the Faerian warriors, weapons at the ready. They took a few more paces into the wood and abruptly came to stop even Lolah sat on her haunches.

"What is it? Why do you not follow?" called Arksanza trying to keep pace.

"My Lord the hound has lost the scent and there are no tracks to trace either, it is as though they be vanished into thin air." Arksanza stopped where his warriors and Lolah stood initially puzzled then a look of knowing spread across his face as he bent to stoop and kneel on the ground.

"What do you see My Lord Arksanza?" asked the warrior as he rushed to assist the Elder to his feet cupping him under the elbow.

"Back to camp everyone this not be the place to be lingering," he shouted as he held an object up into the night sky towards the moon, the glint of silver shards flashing as he twirled the feather between his fingers, Seraphina let out a gasp.

"What? What is it? What is going on?" demanded Alfie.

"Take Alfie back to the Elders' tent, Lolah is to be with him at all times," ordered Arksanza. "Send word to Risla and Eisiam also, they are to be at his side from this point on, am I deadly clear on this matter." The warriors both nodded in acknowledgement as they hooked Alfie up under each armpit, his feet barely touching the floor as Lolah used her huge hairy bulk to best use causing the still partying revellers to part with her booming deep bark and bustling backside swinging from side to side, clearing a pathway straight through to the Elders' encampment where Alfie was unceremoniously dumped upon a pile of rugs and then promptly sat upon by an overly protective Lolah. Alfie tried to manoeuvre his hairy companion but she stubbornly refused to budge.

"Jesus girl you are bloody heavy," he said as he lay back accepting she would not be moved and he would just have to put up with a dead leg until someone saw fit to release him.

"Do not swear Alfie Diamond, you are in a place of respect." It was Seraphina.

"Looks like a tatty old tent to me," he argued. "Can you get this bloody dog off me?" She threw him a look. "Sorry. Please would you ask Lolah to remove herself from my leg before I develop gangrene?"

"Sarcasm does not become you and anyway if you would not be wandering maybe she would not feel the need to treat you as a mischievous pup. Lolah lay down." Instantly the dog jumped up licked Alfie's face and ambled over to Seraphina and lay at her feet.

"Jeez thanks Lolah just what I needed," as he scrubbed at his face with his sleeve.

"What words were spoken to you?" Seraphina asked.

Alfie thought for a minute and tried to ignore the knot in his stomach. "Something about making the best or the most of the night, I can't remember exactly and then she called me a name, false hope-giver, whatever that means," he said shrugging his shoulders. "How did you know where I was anyway?"

Sitting herself down before him she patted him on his lap. "Have you not learnt anything these past few days?" a wry smile passing across her face.

"Well shit, sorry loads of stuff. It's making me head hurt." Yawning he laid back on the warm and inviting furs. Seraphina lay next to him and stroked his curls off his face whilst Lolah snuggled herself the other side of him. He patted her belly and she grunted in appreciation.

"I will always have the ability to feel your fear, it is something that I have been able to do since your birth and all those years that have passed. Like the time you had a tooth removed because you fell out of the tree you were told to not climb, or the time you broke your wrists trying to ride your bike down the slide, or the time you hit your thumb with a metal lump on a wooden stick."

Alfie giggled. "You mean a hammer."

Seraphina giggled too. "I am not familiar with all human words, apart from swear words, which you seem to have rather a lot of in your vocabulary."

Alfie looked puzzled. "How do you know they are swear words if you don't use them?"

Still twirling his curls around her finger she answered, "Because I judged your mother's reaction and worked out that they be words your mother didn't approve of and then one day I heard your father tell you that if you spoke another swear word out loud you would have to look after the dishwasher for a week all by yourself and as you're a lazy creature by nature that seemed to work for a while."

He looked indignant. "I'm not lazy." She looked at him sideways. "Well maybe a bit cos it's boring," he admitted.

"The effort you put into getting out of a job is astounding. Why don't you be just getting on with it boy?" she tickled him sending him into proper belly laughs, squealing with delight as Lolah bounded about pouncing and barking. A curtain of animal hide that divided the tent into two suddenly swished back, an extremely wizened face with a long white wispy beard appeared through it making both of them jump.

Seraphina instantly sprung to her feet. "Apologies My Lord, we were not being aware of your presence, I trust we not be disturbing you." From behind her she could hear muffled sniggers.

"Is that the boy?" a gnarled bony finger pointed at him.

"Yes My Lord," said Seraphina bowing low as the hunched over elderly gentleman shuffled towards Alfie, who by now was stuffing his mouth with the corner of the rug as tears of merriment rolled down his cheeks. He stooped down to scrutinize the boy before him, prodded at his wild untamed hair.

He tutted. "Feed him something before he devours the entire pile of furs."

Alfie spat out the corner from his mouth as the Elder silently disappeared back behind the curtain. Seraphina spun on her heels and placed her finger firmly to her lips.

Shush, she said without a word passing her lips, he heard it loud and strong in his mind and decided he best behave himself from this point. She sat back down beside him and winked.

The mood quickly changed as Alfie said, "What did she mean?" Seraphina paused she knew exactly what he was talking about.

"Are you sure it was a female?"

He considered for a minute. "Yes."

Seraphina let out a sigh. "There are signs that it could well have been Triamena, Princess of the Gorans. Her father is Traska, you remember him from your vision in the Listening Tree." Just as she said this Risla and Eisiam fell through the entrance to the tent both flustered and stirred up.

"Is he safe?" they both demanded.

"Yes. Yes, hush your noise both. Sit," and she pointed to the rugs next to Alfie and Lolah. "As I was saying you remember Traska from your adventure in the Listening Tree," she threw a look at Risla who immediately sunk low into the rugs and furs.

"Yeah," said Alfie. "He was well weird and a proper nasty piece of work," he added.

"Triamena is a thousand times more deadly and far more dangerous than her father, Traska. For the longest time we believed her to be dead murdered by her own father but our allies found this not to be true, she had in fact disappeared with a coven of witches who practise the Dark Arts of Medulla. It be believed they have taught her well and she has thrived amongst them to become one of their most highly skilled governing witches but time has not tempered her evil streak. She be hell-bent on revenge on her father and gaining the ultimate goal, to be a day walker." All three sat mouths wide open not a sound coming from any one of them. "It is said that the Dark Arts could conjure a spell so powerful that the mistress of that spell would have the ability to shape shift."

"Cool," gasped Alfie and Risla nodded in agreement.

Opinionated as ever Eisiam snapped, "No it is not cool. It means whoever has that power could be amongst us and we would have no clue. Isn't that right?" she said looking to Seraphina for confirmation. Risla screwed up his face mocking his sister's intelligent thoughts.

"Yes Eisiam you are partly correct. As far as we be knowing only animals can be replicated, thank the gods of the two worlds. The spell is not strong enough to be able change to human or Faerian form. However, Arksanza is of the belief that it may well have been Triamena who ambushed you Alfie. The feathers he found were that of a silver raven and he be thinking she must have shape-shifted into one in order to fly in and out undetected, it would explain the sudden disappearance of her scent and tracks."

Eisiam let out a gasp of horror and launched herself at Alfie. "Oh my poor friend you must have been so fearful such a terrifying thing to happen." Overcome with embarrassment, Alfie wasn't sure whether to take advantage and hug the object of his affections back or wriggle free, man up and be blasé about the whole affair, he opted for the latter.

"Oh it wasn't really that bad just made me jump is all." He was very careful not to make eye contact with either Seraphina or Risla, as he hopped up on to his feet and wiped his sweating brow with the back of his hand. "Cor blimey it's hot in here," he commented blowing out his cheeks and almost tripping over Lolah who lay oblivious to the whole charade. Risla purposely did not speak but stared at the back of Alfie's head as he suddenly developed an interest in the ink drawings on the taut stretched tent walls. "They're good," he said all the time knowing his lanky friend was waiting and willing him to turn around. Seraphina was also enjoying the little pantomime Alfie had put on for them, she could have at any time broken the stalemate with just one word but she chose not to. All the time the skin on Alfie's face grew redder and redder flushing down his neck making his green eyes really ping against the scarlet background. Just as he thought he could take no more and would blurt out, "OK you win, yes I do fancy her," Eisiam came to his rescue.

"Shall I prepare some food? I am sure Alfie be in need of something after such an ordeal."

Risla burst out laughing. "I am sure he is in need sister of mine." Even Seraphina had to pretend she was blowing her nose to contain her giggles.

Alfie threw himself on to the rugs. "Yes I am feeling weak I would really love some food," he gushed as he planted his face into the fur wishing the ground would open up and swallow him.

He lay there for what seemed like an eternity waiting for the tent to clear, Eisiam off searching for food and Risla having drifted off into a snooze. Alfie could hear his bubbling snorts and snores so he quietly turned himself over, stretched and sneakily peeked to see if Seraphina had also left the tent too. She was bending over the entrance to the tent and he could hear her muttering.

"Yes I am still here," she called out without turning round.

Alfie propped himself up on his elbows. "What are you doing?" he asked.

"A moment let me finish," she replied back. Standing up and rubbing her hands together, "There that be done," she said as she turned back to face him. He looked quizzical. "A spell, to be precise a protection spell, salt across the threshold and boundaries of this tent, no being may cross with evil intent, an unseen force will keep you safe as long as you stay inside."

Alfie chucked himself back with annoyance, "Bloody great, a prisoner again."

Seraphina let loose her hair pulling it all around to the front and began combing the long locks with her fingers. "Better a prisoner here than with the Gorans or worse Triamena herself."

Alfie pondered for a minute. "Seraphina am I really in that much danger?" He stared intently as she turned towards him.

"I cannot lie little one, yes." She saw his face drop and rushed across to him grabbing his hands. "Also know that we are all here to protect you, even now Arksanza and the Elders make plans to keep you and your family safe."

He shook his hands free. "My family? What have they got to do with this? You said the doppelgänger would be a distraction and that would be enough to keep the Gorans busy."

She hesitated. "It would seem that the doppelgänger has not fooled your mother. On a daily basis she grows stronger in her belief that the creature she sees laying before her is not her son, you."

Alfie's eyes widened. "What does this all mean, has she told anyone?"

Shaking her head Seraphina said, "No but Elancie has got word to us that your mother's doubts are weakening the spell cast over your family and the people caring for your doppelgänger. If it becomes much more broken down the illusion will be shattered, the condition of the doppelgänger deteriorates on a daily basis." Alfie was beginning to become agitated pacing up and down not sure whether to get angry with his mother or pleased that she had sensed from the beginning something was not right and recognized the doppelgänger to be the fake that it was.

Alfie's breathing began to rasp as he struggled to get air into his lungs, his heartbeat boomed in his ears and the talisman on his chest began to throb and glow, he clasped at it, panic-stricken, imploring Seraphina to help him but she just stood in front of him. Only her voice in his head made him stand still.

Be calm, be calm this is a gift not a curse, slow your breathing, slow your breathing, but he could still feel the rising tide of panic within him. "Alfie!" she shouted this time out loud. "You must learn to master your gift, follow my voice. Breathe in, breathe out, breathe in, breath out." She nodded in approval as he tried to obey her voice. "Again. Breathe in, breathe out. Good you gain back the force, see," and pointed to his chest. The talisman was still glowing but was stable not spluttering like a dodgy gas burner, he was aware of his pulse in his ears softer and regular.

"Now I want you to try something for…" He started to shake his head in refusal, his heart rate skipping up a beat. "No. No, calm remember," she softly said lowering her hands, he took a deep breath.

"OK, I will try."

She smiled at him. "The Awakening is a force for good when you be mastering it. You can protect yourself and others, it will act as a shield, you can also be using it as a weapon and use it to manipulate objects safely without putting yourself in harm's way." Alfie listened intently to his teacher. "Now, do you see that stool? I want you to focus on the talisman in your chest, picture it coming to life slowly lighting up, a tiny star upon your chest building its brightness as you fire up its power, really focus on the stool and the energy building with in you, imagine there is a silver string connected from your talisman to the stool and you be transferring the power from you down that sliver thread."

Alfie's brow screwed up with the effort. "Er I can't do it."

Seraphina walked across to stand behind him she placed her hand on his shoulder, he instantly felt calmer. "Now clear your mind think only of the stool, if it be helping close your eyes and picture the stool off the ground hanging free." Some minutes passed and the stool began to nudge at first then bounce across the floor. "Good keep your thoughts on the stool." She could hear his breathing now soft and regular as the stool slowly lifted from the floor. "Look," she whispered softly. Alfie gently opened his eyes adjusting to the dimly-lit tent. To his amazement the stool was there right before him levitating, a little unsteady, but nevertheless definitely off the ground. He gasped and the stool went crashing to the floor narrowly missing a slumbering Lolah and the equally unresponsive Risla loudly snoring away. "Some guard you make," tutted Seraphina to herself nudging the sleeping, lanky Faerian. "Make yourself useful up and away outside, guard the tent!" she ordered Risla.

"God did I really do it? It wasn't any of your Magiks was it, it really was me!"

Seraphina laughed. "Yes it be all you little man."

He squealed with delight, "Yes I have super powers! Let me do it again, again," bouncing about like a playful puppy.

Seraphina placed her hand upon his shoulder. "You are right you must be practising but this gift not be just for parlour tricks, your powers will one day become immense and you may well have to take a life to save a life, such is the responsibility you will have to bear." She could see by his face that this a was not something he had thought of or considered, even though he had seen for himself the after-effects of his first Awakening in the clearing and yet he could not quantify the abilities he would possess and how he would need to mature quickly to learn how to handle them.

A sense of heavy responsibility bore down on Seraphina. She had hoped for more time to teach and hone his skills but time was one thing they did not have. Somehow she would have to awaken his deep primal need to protect his family and his

195

Faerian comrades by dragging him, kicking and screaming if necessary, to a place deeply buried in his inner soul. He would need to tap into the essence of his ancestors those who had passed before him and she was the person to help him.

Looking at his upturned hands, Alfie slowly turned them examining them closely. "What is it that you look upon my child?" the colour of his previous sense of joy and excitement at his stool trick draining from his face as his ashen, concerned expression fixed on Seraphina.

"You said I could kill with this gift. How is it a gift to take a life?"

The tall beautiful Faerian looked troubled. "No one be setting out to take such actions but you have to be remembering the Gorans have no peace to them, they thrive off the fear that be walking before them, they deem it dishonourable to die in the comfort of a bed, only by violence of the sword is their way and they will stop at nothing to gain the knowledge of Magiks to help them day walk, they will think nothing of smiting down your family to get to you, you hold the key to their desires."

Alfie tutted. "What's the big deal about day walking? Wouldn't it be easier to fight them during daylight anyway instead of skulking about in the night?"

Seraphina was becoming agitated with the boy. "There is no easy anything with the Gorans, they always be plotting if they walk upon sun-warmed soil then they be taking over the human race completely. Everything that is evil or bad in your world is governed by the Goran race, they influence the most infamous gangs, drug pushers, criminal warlords and only because they themselves cannot achieve ultimate control hindered by their need to return to their dens as the morning sun rises. Your world would be changed forever and the human race would be cast into a pit of slavery, as they once so nearly were. It was not for nothing that your ancestors aligned with the Faerians, in return for their loyalty a few select predecessors of yours were granted the gifts that you be training to bring to your full potential, these gifts enhanced by the union of your great-grandmother and one of our Faerian heroes, Kairon." Alfie's ears picked up as he scuttled over to Seraphina and sat cross-legged on the rugs patting the space next to him inviting her to sit and continue her story. Before walking over to her young charge, Seraphina silently slipped up to the opening of the tent and peered through the chink in the flapping animal fur. She could see the warriors standing a little away from the tent, their silhouettes enhanced by the golden orange flames of the campfire as Risla waved his arms about as he enthusiastically recounted an adventure, the noise of the party having softened to a chilled afterglow. Sure that no one could hear her conversation she turned and sat down by the boy, who eagerly stared at her with eyes full of anticipation.

"Firstly, what I am to tell you must be kept between us. Do not be telling another soul." She hesitated as though she was considering backtracking, her hands wringing with agitation as she furtively glanced back at the opening.

Alfie encouraged her. "There is no one there. You were going to tell me about my great-grand mother, I can't remember her name, my mum did tell me once."

Seraphina pulled him closer to her and lowered her voice. "Her name was Branna, Branna Deidra Delaney and a very brave woman she was. Generations of men in your bloodline passed on the Awakening to their firstborn sons." Alfie went to interrupt. "But!" she put her finger across his mouth. "I know what you be saying let me just finish my words. Branna was the first in the line that the Awakening didn't pass to a boy child. A boy child was born and he was the eldest but by the time he was five of your human years it became apparent that he had no gifts and for a while the whole family were shunned by their clan for fear they had been cursed. None of the elders from either race could work out what had gone wrong until one morning your great-grandmother's father ran from their dwelling carrying the body of a limp boy ashen and lifeless, screaming for the elders and their healers. There was nothing they could do for the child he had passed in his sleep. So distressed were the entire family all wailing and crying, inconsolable, and amidst all this pain

Branna took on an Awakening completely catching everyone off guard. All that time she had kept secret that she had been having visions, hearing voices, knowing what the people around her were thinking, always trying to keep her emotions in check but the day her brother had been taken by the angels she could not contain herself any longer, the pain was too much to bear as a fearsome and ferocious power grew within her. All around her the force whipped up everything in its path, chaos broke out as everyone tried to take cover from the flying debris whilst those who had been thrown from their feet sat stunned and dismayed staring at the small girl in the centre of the vortex screaming from the very depth of her core, foaming at the mouth with pure rage that her sweet and fragile brother Aedan had been taken from her."

Alfie let out a gasp. "So she had known that she had the gift all along?"

Seraphina nodded in agreement. "Yes and because Aedan had been so sickly Branna felt she couldn't add to his anguish at not having been bestowed with the Awakening by letting her family know she be having the gift, so she kept it from them and protected her brother at all costs. Some say she knew he was not long for this world and that is why the spirits did not see fit to pass on the gift; they knew he would not see his eleventh year."

Alfie hung his head in his hands. "That's so sad. How would Branna have known about his illness?"

Seraphina took hold of his hand. "Simply because she could feel it in him, she might not have understood the illness but she could sense it. When she watched him play with animals, their reaction to the boy, his life essence was dull and low, the creatures seemed to want to just sit and comfort him and calmed their boisterous behaviour around him, he was a gentle soul." Alfie sat for a while as he let his thoughts mull in and out of his mind.

"So what happened when they all realized Branna had kept the secret?" he asked.

Seraphina let out a sigh. "To say they were not best pleased would be an understatement, for after all the family had suffered as a consequence. Their kinfolk had huddled in corners whispering, they were shunned from many a gathering all the time Branna knowing she could put a stop to it but she refused to her brother Aedan was more important, once it was out she was sent away."

Alfie jumped to his feet. "Why?" he demanded dragging himself back down to the rugs.

"Hush boy child, she was sent to a Faerian camp away in the Emerald Isle."

Still fluffed up with indignant attitude Alfie chipped in, "You mean Ireland." Seraphina tutted.

"Yes but it was known to us as the Emerald Isle then and still is now," she said eyeing him up daring him to interrupt. "Anyway," she continued, "her training had been held up on account of the fact no one knew she was the Gifted One. There was much catching up to do plus the Elders had no real idea of her abilities as she was the first girl to be blessed, it was here at the encampment that she met Kairon."

"Ugh, this isn't gonna be some mushy love story is it?" Seraphina giggled.

"On the contrary Alfie Diamond, they hated each other at first. They had a fierce competitive battle between them, each wanting to be outdoing the other, Arksanza said."

Grabbing on to Seraphina's arm Alfie cried, "Arksanza! Was he about when this all kicked off?"

"Yes of course, we Faerians do not age as you humans. He would have been a younger soul then but he was already schooled in many Magiks and rising rapidly in character and knowledge of the old ways."

"Wow," said Alfie. "You learn something new every day. Fancy that! Arksanza knew my great-grandmother!"

Clapping her hands softly together still wary of eavesdroppers Seraphina said, "We have got off track here, now be listening to me. As I said Branna and Kairon hated each other but as time went by Kairon developed a keen respect for your great-grandmother. She excelled in everything she be put to task on, her fighting skills were far superior than those who were born to be warriors, her Magiks grew in strength and the gift of the Awakening in her was never before seen so strong in one so young. She lapped up whatever the Elders threw at her, no matter how they pushed she refused to break. It was this strength of spirit that turned Kairon's eye, he no longer saw her as a freak of nature. He gave her his loyalty and support and she eventually in return did the same for him. They were inseparable much to the concern of the Elders, a relationship such as theirs was never before heard of let alone accepted." Once they had both learned as much as they could, they were returned back to our lands under orders to join the forces in separate camps but this they could not do so drawn were they to each other".

Alfie got fidgety. "You're not gonna start talking about the 'birds and the bees' are you, cos I really don't need to hear it thank you very much. Jeez this is my great-grandmother we are talking about."

Ruffling his hair she smiled. "I will be skipping to the point I am trying to make, as a result of their…"

Alfie blurted out, "Relationship!"

"OK relationship, your great-grandmother gave birth to a female baby, half human half Faerian. Nobody knew if such a child could survive or what the consequences would be as a result of the two races mixing. The child was kept a secret from both the Faerian and human clans for fear that the Gorans would get word of her existence, so just a small select group knew, sworn to protect the child with their lives."

Alfie looked puzzled. "If that was my great-grandmother's baby then the baby must be my grandmother Maggie." He turned to face Seraphina and waited for her response.

"Magdalene not Maggie she was called Magdalene until she got older and rejected her Faerian heritage then she renamed herself Maggie."

"Whoa up there! What do you mean reject? What was there to reject, power, knowledge, kick-ass ninja fighting skills?" Seraphina interrupted him by placing her finger upon his lips, something that was becoming a habit. He didn't know if he just waffled on too much or if she just liked the instant effect it had upon him, raising her eyebrows as if to reinforce her need for him to be silent.

"Her powers cost her, her mother, what child wouldn't be running away from such a trauma?" Alfie's jaw dropped. It was obvious to Seraphina that none of this family history had been passed on and having spent a long time shadowing Maggie and her family she was hardly surprised, so many dark secrets, so much time covering tracks, she doubted even if Nellie had any real knowledge as she certainly didn't know she was a twin, a Gemini, as was written in the Book of Oracles.

Branna had known what fate awaited her family and particularly her daughter Magdalene, she gained knowledge from The Book of Oracles after Betina had hinted at something sinister in her daughter's future.

The only way to find out the truth was to break into the closely guarded Book Tower and read the ancient manuscripts for herself. Kairon accompanied her with their girl child strapped to her mother, he felt sure that Branna would not be able to decipher the time old language and that even he might struggle with it.

Kairon was a trusted warrior and easily passed through the vaulted gate room at the entrance to the Book Tower, he wasn't even given a second look but Branna's access to the tower was not so easy, she had to scale the tall stone column hauling herself and her child up using a rope thrown down by Kairon. He did his best to pull from the other end of the rope as Branna grew tired with such an effort, her feet slipping and her hands burning from the rough fibres of the rope, his newborn child safely strapped to her mother's back snoozed blissfully unaware of the perilous drop beneath. Kairon had not been keen for this course of action but Branna wouldn't settle and he knew she was stubborn enough to try by herself anyway. The words of Betina had really struck a chord particularly the fact that Betina had said Magdalene's destiny lay in the hands of her mother.

Branna called up to Kairon, "Wait let me catch my breath." Resting her forehead against the damp cold stone, she heaved in breath, desperate to replenish her oxygen-starved muscles to give her the strength to make the final few hauls to the safety of the tower window.

"This be madness let me lower you."

But Branna growled at him through gritted teeth, "Don't you dare, I'm coming now," as she summoned an inner strength and planted her feet firmly, yanking hard on the rope and with every bit of strength hauled herself upwards with renewed determination. Kairon muttered to himself and did as he was told, he knew better than to argue, she was determined to get to the top. Just a few more wrenches and he was able to grab her under the arms and haul her back on top of him, them both falling to the book tower floor. All the time Magdalene was sweetly unaware of the adventure she had just been a part of as her parents both anxiously checked to see if she had been harmed in any way. Kairon unstrapped his daughter and gently lay her upon his cloak as he and Branna proceeded to the book altar.

Branna stood motionless as she looked in awe at the magical hand-carved stone altar illuminated by a single shaft of moonlight sliding through the opening they had all just fallen through, she could just make out images of Faerians, participants in battle scenes, faces carved with exquisite details, a story depicted in stone.

Her fingertips following the grooves where centuries before a craftsman with a chisel had applied his skill.

Kairon tugged at her sleeve. "Come we not be having much time, look there is the Book of Oracles," he said as he stepped up on to the pedestal of the altar, his hand reaching out to touch the wizened leather binding.

She pushed his hand away. "No let me get a feel for the history of this treasure before we expose the writings."

She stepped next to him and taking a deep breath placed her flat hand upon the carved front of the book, instantly she felt an energy like no other surging through her body. Her head filled with images, faces, places, sounds of battle, babies crying, laughter and merriment of a great feast, all whooshing around her mind, getting faster and faster making her feel dizzy as the power of the book overtook her, voices one after another babbling as they merged together till nothing made sense. She shuddered and jolted as though slammed about by unseen forces, her hand still firmly fixed to the Oracle. Kairon could see she was struggling with the Magiks, it was too much for her to handle, she seemed completely lost to it so he did the only thing he could and with all his might snatched her hand away, both of them being hurdled across the room slamming into the wall.

At this point Seraphina stopped her tale and looked at Alfie. "No questions?" she asked as he sat absolutely absorbed hanging on her every word. He merely shook his head and motioned for her to continue. She took a sip of water and then recommenced her story.

Having checked that Branna had not sustained any injuries and having brushed them both down, Kairon slipped quietly to the chamber door convinced that someone would have heard all the commotion, easing the heavy iron latch back slowly so as not to make a sound, he put his shoulder into the solid oak door and eased it back, the corridor was pitch black and empty much to his relief. Turning back to Branna he was about to suggest they abandon their mission, when to his surprise as he turned, she was already perched on the ledge with Magdalene strapped to her poised to drop below the thick stone sill.

"What be happening, what of the book? Where are you going?" He had so many questions as he scampered over to her.

"I do not have use for the book, I have seen what I need to know," her voice empty of emotion and with that she descended from his sight. He almost felt like leaping out after her, firstly out of sheer temper that she could be so dismissive of this great book, this fount of knowledge that had guided his race for centuries and secondly he couldn't judge her state of mind whilst she free-fell rapidly down to the ground stopping only inches from the solid packed mud with his precious daughter strapped to her back. In his riled state he just about remembered he had been seen coming in and must be seen leaving. Trying to gather himself he checked his rapid breathing and slowed his pace. Wiping the beads of sweat from his forehead and face down the sleeve of his tunic he barely acknowledged the warriors at the entrance as he stomped past only to issue an order.

"When the dawn breaks send out a party to clear the briars and shrubs from the tower, I want those walls to be free of foliage and whilst you be at it iron bars to be fixed to the openings, call in the blacksmith be sure he not be alone in the Oracle Room, I want a guard on him at all times until his quest is complete."

The warriors looked a little perturbed but called out in unison, "Yes My Lord."

Kairon raced ahead but Branna nor his daughter were to be seen, he couldn't call out their names, so frustrated, he worked his way back to the Set to catch up with her. Little did he know that that would be the last time he would set eyes upon his beloved Branna and their daughter.

Alfie let out a huge gasp. "What? What did you just say?" he demanded. "What do you mean the last time?"

"Hush little one, hush."

He shoved her hand away from his mouth. "No I won't bloody hush. What do you mean last time?"

Seraphina jumped to her feet to once again check the entrance. "If you don't calm down I will not be continuing with the tale," she said throwing him the sternest of looks.

"Jeez, OK I will be quiet," he hissed through gritted teeth muttering swear words under his breath.

She ignored them and returned to her seat next to him, "Now," she began. "This next bit is very important. This part shaped the destiny and history of your family so no interruptions or questions."

"But," he blurted out. Seraphina raised her eyebrows and her Lockan buzzed with life. *Shit*, thought Alfie to himself as she slapped him across the knee. "What? I didn't say anything!"

"You didn't need to be saying the cuss out loud did you petulant boy." He could see that Seraphina was becoming very irritated by his behaviour.

"OK I will sit here and shut my cake hole, please continue." She rolled her eyes and gathered her thoughts.

Branna had stolen away into the night in the opposite direction from the Set, her destination; back to her non- human roots far from the dangers of the Faerian enemies or even the Faerians themselves. She knew that there was only one place to take her baby daughter, only one person who could be trusted. Her journey to the Emerald Isle would be long and fraught with danger but she had no choice, she had seen the Oracle's story and her daughter's destiny and that of her grandchildren and great-grandchildren. She would sacrifice everything to keep them all safe even if she had to pay the ultimate price, her own life. Alfie again stifled a thought as Seraphina paused in anticipation of the youngster with his demanding questions; silence, he was learning.

Thomas Tobias Trendall was that person, the man who had helped to raise Branna and her siblings whilst their father was away trading, or so she thought. Really he was fighting in battle side by side with the Faerians, raging against the Gorans and Thomas had been assigned the task of keeping the children safe and protecting particularly her brother Aedan, who at the time was believed to be the chosen one. Even as a young child Branna remembered Thomas had been elderly, with greying hair at the sides and very little on top, the sparse thin lengths tightly plaited down his back and his unruly eyebrows bushy and abundant over his weathered brow giving him the appearance of a bald owl, his large brown eyes peeping from beneath the shelf of bristled hair.

Alfie sat up, something had taken his interest. Seraphina continued on with the tale puzzled by the boy's sudden fidgety behaviour like he was waiting for something. He looked at her to continue which she did, filling in details about the would-be bodyguard, Thomas Tobias Trendall, describing his build and large arthritic hands that had carved many wooden toys for the children to keep them entertained whilst their father was away. Still Alfie waited, then suddenly there it was the thing he had been waiting for, the words barely out Seraphina's mouth, "And he had a crescent-shaped scar across his right cheek."

Alfie punched the air. "Yes I know him, I know him! Old Tom. Old Tom, Grandma Maggie's gardener!" A wry smile spread across Seraphina's face as the young boy suddenly realized what he had said. He was talking about a man he had known all his life and yet Seraphina was describing him as a carer to his own great-grandmother.

"Jeez how ancient is the old boy?" She laughed and told him not to be disrespectful. "But seriously how can this be?" The Faerian began to explain when Alfie butted in, "You know what don't even bother, nothing surprises me anymore with you lot. What is he a Faerian, human with gifts, or a bit of both?" he asked hunching his shoulders in mocked amazement.

"My dear boy he is none of those, he comes from a race known as the Sentinels. They live even longer than us Faerians and are assigned to one family down the centuries until their protection is no longer needed."

Alfie paused for a minute. "What happens to the Sentinel, or sorry Old Tom, if that family has no use for him anymore?"

Quite matter-of-factly she replied, "They disintegrate," with no expression or emotion.

"I'm sorry. Did you say they disintegrate?" he said in an annoyed manner.

"Yes, like a puff of beautiful lilac sparkling smoke," she replied still with no concern for her use of speech and with a deadpan look on her face.

"Are you winding me up cos I don't think it's funny," he tutted as he grumpily sat with his arms folded scowling at her. "So you're saying Old Tom could in theory just disappear, just like that, right in front of my eyes if my family no longer need protection. Well that seems like a bum deal to me. So it's thanks for your long service Tom but we don't need you anymore old fella so off you toddle and go evaporate quietly in a corner." He almost spat the words out so angry was he at the injustice of it all.

Seraphina waited patiently for him to finish his rant. "Be you quite done with your tempered words little man?" He just screwed his face up and looked the other way picking at the hardened callous skin on the palm of his hand, rewards of his hard labour climbing the Listening Tree. "We Faerians revere the Sentinels and the service they provide, when their task is complete, their reward is their release from this world." She bent down to come eye to eye with a still disgruntled Alfie. "They are not punished by the process of disintegration, they are set free and move on to another plane, where they are become young, unburdened by the weight of responsibility, no longer in a state of readiness for whatever may come to their charge. There in the new world they can be childlike, carefree, a complete freedom and peace is their reward, and also know they do not be forced to take the route of disintegration, they be choosing it at a time for themselves. Now do you understand better? We are not a callous race."

"I really don't know how my brain hasn't popped trying to keep up with you lot and your ways. One minute you're telling me that only the firstborn son receives the gift, then you're telling me that Branna inherited because her brother Aedan was deemed to be sickly by the Spirits of the Ancients, then I'm sitting here thinking, well I'm not the firstborn son or even the firstborn child, I'm the sixth so how the hell did I get chucked in the pot? And if indeed Branna was the Chosen One how come Old Tom is still about now even today because without knowing the ending to Branna's story I have enough sense to know she would have died of old age if she had been able to get there so how is it he is still around? You're going to tell me something that will turn everything on its heels aren't you?" He flopped back on the rugs and tried to focus on the one lone star he could see through a tiny hole in the canvas roof.

"I am sorry that this be such a strain for you little man, you were not born into this knowledge, there is so much to tell you and I have to decide which be necessary for you to develop your skills and give you a bigger picture to maybe help you understand your gifts better. You are correct in your belief that it is all very complicated. Thomas, Old Tom as you call him, could not choose to end his existence in this world because he had knowledge of Branna's hidden secret. He had sensed and witnessed her changes keeping this to himself. He chose to merely observe, to see how things panned out. As time passed he knew Aedan would not linger long in this life, cradling him on the night he passed till his last breath left his weakened fragile body." Alfie felt a lump grow in his throat and his eyes burned with tears tilting on the brim of his lashes. He coughed to force the emotion away.

Seraphina rubbed his hand gently. "You are a sensitive little soul," she whispered.

"Oh I just got something in my eye but it's gone now. Carry on," he bluffed.

"You know that Old Tom is not so much there to protect you as the rest of your family. You be having an advantage over them, they are completely unaware of the dangers they face or what lurks at the bottom of the garden."

Wiping at his eyes with his sleeve he replied, "Tallulah would crap her pants if she heard about the Gorans, let alone see one or any of their minions. She's scared of her own shadow." He giggled, a proper belly laugh, as he remembered some of the tricks he and his brothers had pulled on her, scaring her so bad she had to sleep in her mum and dad's room for nearly six weeks and of course he took great pleasure in reminding her on a daily basis what a baby she was. Alfie could feel Seraphina staring at him. "Maybe it wasn't that funny," he added trying to redeem himself.

"It is getting late and I need to finish this tale. Branna sought out Thomas to give shelter and protection to baby daughter Magdalene. He had removed himself from the community after the death of Aedan as many believed that he had failed the family, some believed that Aedan had been poisoned and others that he had had a hand in the death of the young boy. Branna knew all of this was not true and she stayed loyal to Thomas often wondering why he had never chosen to take his chance to move on to the next world, but as she made her way through forest and rugged terrain on her journey to the Emerald Isle, crossing the sea in the smallest passenger boat, the cruel waves pounding the tiny wooden structure relentlessly, she suddenly knew why. He had known that one day she would seek him out to once again perform his Sentinel duty and take care of her most precious little daughter, Magdalene. As she placed the tiny bundle into his arms neither one speaking, she kissed her baby for the last time never once looking back as she strode over to his dilapidated barn entering for a few minutes to emerge on the back of a white stallion with weapons strapped to her back and thighs. His abiding last vision was of the strong determined dark-haired human, powering the stallion saddle free, clinging to his rippled white mane, surging on into an unknown destiny, her steely gaze fixed firmly ahead even though she could feel her heart shatter into a thousand pieces, she never once faltered or was tempted to turn for one last look upon her beloved family."

Alfie was hesitant to put into words his next question. He was half hoping he wouldn't need to and that Seraphina would read his mind and just tell him. She sat looking at the ground tracing the pattern woven into the rug with her finger patiently waiting for him to spit it out, this he supposed was what growing up was all about, dealing with things that you would rather went away for someone else to handle.

He sighed. "What happened to my Great-grandmother Branna?" he stuttered and fluffed his words as shockingly he spotted a single solitarily tear slide down her cheek. "How did she never see her child again?"

Sniffing and then drawing in a deep breath to collect her thoughts Seraphina continued. "She did a very brave but very dangerous thing, an act that saw her treated as a legend amongst the Faerian race. I'm surprised you didn't hear some of the gatherers describe you as the great-grandson of Branna the Brave Heart."

Alfie sheepishly looked at her. "I heard something but I wished in my head they would all shut up, it got so loud and confusing I got scared. Was that bad to do that?"

She ruffled his hair. "No not at all. Did the noise stop?"

"Yes," he said looking surprised.

"Well that shows you be beginning to understand your gifts, you managed to control them so that be a good thing." He smiled at his achievement temporarily forgetting what was to come next. "Now let me be getting this next part out quickly and without interruption, if you be having questions ask me after I be finished," she paused waiting for him to acknowledge her. "Branna purposely rode to the encampment of the secretive Medulla Witches of the Dark Arts. After climbing down from her horse she untied her talisman and bound it into the stallion's mane stroking his neck she whispered 'Return to your master' and slapped across the horse's rump sending him on his way. She strode into the camp bold as brass and demanded to speak with their shaman, Tilka. They instantly pounced upon her, bound her and dragged her to a pit and unceremoniously threw her in." Alfie inhaled a breath but resisted the urge to speak.

Seraphina continued, "She gave them just enough information to make them think she was of importance but did not tell them exactly who she was, she refused to speak again until she was presented to the shaman and her inner circle. They beat her viciously but still she refused any more confession, so she got what she wanted and was hauled from the pit and dragged through the encampment like a trophy with the witches spitting and kicking her, cackling and screaming in her face until they reached a wooden hall, which was surrounded by flaming torches flaring up into the night sky. From this point only the two witches dragging her were allowed to enter, throwing her around like a rag doll but still she kept her silence till they eventually slung her forward into a semicircle of carved chairs, 13 in all. Momentarily she heard shuffling all around her and as she raised her head she could see through the less swollen eye, hooded figures taking their seats with the centre one empty."

Alfie let out sigh. "Did they beat her?" Seraphina shushed him. He could see this was an emotional thing for her to tell him so he let her continue.

"They demanded she tell them who she was, nodding to the guards to punch and kick her each time she refused to answer. All she would say was that she would only speak to the shaman." At this point Alfie held his head in his hands almost wanting to cover his ears but he knew he couldn't. "A stalemate be occurring, Branna not giving in to the beatings and the witches not able to extract anything from her. 'Enough,' came a voice from behind the central chair, it was the shaman, Tilka. 'This one be tricky, you waste your efforts,' she said as she sat upon her seat letting the hood fall from her head and face. At this point Branna raised her head to look at her foe, in the dim light she could make out this tiny wizened creature not all what Branna had imagined. 'You look upon me with surprise stranger. What did you expect to see?' as she transformed into a huge silver raven, then a snarling wolf and then back to a raven taking flight and landing immediately in front of Branna grabbing her arm with its cruel claws wrenching her up to get a closer look. 'What are you? You dress as a Faerian but you do not have the features of one,' pecking at her dark wavy hair that had fallen from her plait.

'I am human,' spat out Branna. A huge cackle rang out around the circle.

'She be a pathetic human,' called out the shaman who had now returned to her normal state. 'And what does a human want with me?' she laughed as they all did.

'I have come to tell you of my child,' again they laughed.

'What makes you think we need to know of your pathetic human child?'

Branna began to laugh unnerving the audience around her. She received a slap to her face.

'Be silent,' said the guard as blood and teeth spewed from her mouth. Tilka pointed her bony finger at the guard as she stood over Branna and then whipped her hand back to the wall sending the guard flying back into the structure with an unseen force leaving her winded and lying upon the ground groaning.

'Let her speak of this child,' called out one of the other elders in the circle.

'I am human, my child is not; her father is Faerian,' all of the witches gasped.

Tilka slumped herself in her chair. 'What interest is it to us of your filthy breeding?' and then your great-grandmother, Branna, quoted a script from the Medulla Dark Arts.

'And low a child of exception shall grow from the seeds of two worlds and she shall spawn a race of warriors destined to end the Goran kings, they shall be but dust upon the scorched earth never to rise again burned forever from the land.'

They all gasped and began jumping from their seats wailing, 'It is as was told in the scriptures. We should seek out this child and destroy her. It was wrong to have kept this secret to ourselves we must send many servants to discover her.'

Tilka sat silent in amongst the chaos. 'How do you know of these writings? You have not seen such things.'

By now your great-grandmother was standing her hands still behind her back. 'I have seen the like in the Book of Oracles.'

Another gasped, 'She knows of the Oracle she must know its location.'

'Silence!' bellowed Tilka. 'She is human and cannot possibly read the scriptures, only the Faerian elders can carry out such a task. She has been sent here to trick us.'

Again Branna laughed, almost manically, most of the witches cowered as the ground began to shake some tried to get to the heavy oak doors but she flicked her head. A wooden bolster slammed across the two sealing them from inside.

'She has powers, she has powers!' they screeched.

By now Branna had worked her hands free from the bindings and raised her arms above her head all around her she generated a powerful wind whipping up everyone and everything."

Alfie wrung his hands as his palms became sweaty and his heart rate began to elevate. "Remember your training Alfie slow breaths," prompted Seraphina. She could see the young boy becoming agitated, he just nodded as he wanted her to finish her tale, whatever the ending he knew it was going to be traumatic.

Branna called upon every skill she had learnt, her connection to Mother Earth, her control of the elements, all drawn up from the soil beneath her feet; her vengeance and need to protect her family and bloodline. She trembled with the power surging through her body fighting to keep it contained until the time was right. This was more than an Awakening, this was a vortex of immense power with only one outcome. She had orchestrated this situation to ensure that the only ones with knowledge of her daughter would not set foot outside the hall. They would die, as would she, with the knowledge of Magdalene's existence left only to the Oracle. With one last push she raged against them, a pure white blast of energy booming out from her core disintegrating bodies, solid wood, flattening the structure like it was made of paper. All that was seen from outside was a blinding white light which lingered for a minute then disappeared as quickly as it had formed. What had happened to the inhabitants? There was no sign of any of them, they had been wiped from this earth forever just as Branna had intended, she had bought her family some safety for a few years more and prevented the Gorans and the Witches of the Medulla claiming her daughter.

For a moment there was silence neither one speaking then Alfie jumped up and hugged Seraphina as tightly as he could, she squeezed him back just as hard trying to stop her own tears falling.

"Seraphina if everyone died how do you know all this stuff?" he stared up at her face, she sighed fearful that he might ask this question.

"How I have watched over you and your mother and her Gemini is how I watched over Branna. I was with her until the very end. I could not bear to watch her carry out her plan so I left moments before she caused the explosion. She had told me all she had seen in her vision in the Oracle room, how her entire family were in peril in fact how the human race would have been if they had taken Magdalene and her Gemini twins. They could change the course of history, so I could do nothing to prevent her from completing her task, she had no choice.

Only I and Arksanza knew where Magdalene was. We even kept it a secret from Kairon because his heart would cause him to seek her out. For many years she grew safely and carefree passed off as the granddaughter of an elderly fisherman until her gifts began to emerge. Then she was brought to England, sent to a school on the moors far from the cities where the Gorans' familiars could spy easily. Thomas schooled her in her skills but she rejected them and kept them hidden. Her heritage had cost her her mother and her father. She felt like a freak and didn't fit in. She absolutely wanted nothing to do with Magiks. Through the years she became more and more reclusive marrying your grandfather and settling down to have her children. For a time she was very happy, content you could even say, that is until the night I showed you in the vision Orb and her baby daughter Mimi or Misa as you now know her, was snatched from her arms lost to her forever."

"What I don't understand is if Maggie had such powerful gifts that the Gorans would seek her out, then why didn't she save herself from the cancer that eventually killed her?" questioned Alfie.

"You forget Alfie she was half human and she chose to ignore the Faerian side of her heritage, she froze out her healing abilities because she be sick of this other world. Thomas said that she never recovered from the stealing of Mimi. She roamed the forest at night calling out to her lost daughter leaving Nellie in his care, month after month and year after year. Nellie knew very little off her mother's attention as she was passed between her father and Thomas, then suddenly she stopped looking and went on to have your aunts and uncles. Thomas felt like she convinced herself that Mimi never existed, the only reminder was your mother, Nellie."

Alfie sighed. "Is that why they were so strained with each other?"

Seraphina nodded. "Yes you noticed then, I was not sure if you were aware."

Alfie let out a forced laugh. "God yeah, they use to fight like cat and dog, Dad was always acting like a referee. To be honest

I don't think Mum liked going back to the house much, if she could put it off she would have but when Grandma Maggie got ill she wanted to help her. Do you think my mother remembers anything of her sister Mimi?"

Seraphina straightened her clothing and began combing out her hair. "You know little man I believe she is unsettled because feelings and memories are beginning to come back but I am not sure she can make sense of it all at the moment. She be very confused and I am sure that is why the doppelgänger bothers her, she can sense what it really be but is not yet able to unravel what is really going on. Mark my words when this adventure, shall we call it," she paused to smile, "is over, she will be better able to understand her past."

Alfie yawned and scratched his head. "Can I go outside yet? It sounds like things have settled. It's bloody stuffy in here, I can feel a nosebleed coming on and I need to stretch my legs."

Seraphina laughed at his reasoning. "You can be pinching your nose if needs be and if your legs be that stiff then jump on the spot that should get the blood following. You will not be going anywhere until the sun comes up. Are we clear?"

Alfie threw himself back on the rugs resigned to the fact that she would not back down. "Shitty, bum, arse."

Seraphina did her best to stifle her giggles and lay down beside him. "Hush now, get some sleep," she whispered tucking a fur around him. He listened to the sound of distant chatter outside, the cracking of the embers on the waning fire, the odd cough from the warriors outside the entrance and the contented snoring of Lolah who hadn't moved position all night even though she was meant to be on guard. He smiled to himself watching the stars sparkle in the night sky through the torn hole in the canvas. He heard the lone hoot of an owl no doubt hunting the night creatures and slowly and gently he faded into sleep.

It felt like only moments since he had drifted off but he was awoken by angry raised voices outside, he instinctively felt for Seraphina but she was gone, her spot cold, he could also hear Lolah barking agitatedly. He quickly jumped to his feet and peeked out of the opening, Seraphina and Solgiven were arguing and Lolah was bounding around in circles. They were drawing the attention of many others who were also emerging from their sleep, confused and puzzled at the commotion.

"What is going on?" shouted Alfie trying to get between them. Seraphina told him to stand back and go to the tent and that it was nothing for him to worry about. Solgiven however wanted the boy to stay.

"No let him be, he needs to hear what your meddling has done." Lolah was now jumping up at Solgiven seeing him as the aggressor, pushing against him with her huge paws and warning him with her bark.

"Lolah come here," shouted Alfie. Much to his surprise she did as she was told, stood at his side all be it growling low in her throat. "Now what the bloody hell is going on?" the young boy demanded of them both. Solgiven loomed over Alfie and blurted out so much stuff the boy could not make head nor tail of it. "Jesus mate, slow down. You're talking too quickly."

He looked to Seraphina who seemed equally as shocked at this barrage of abuse from the warrior, and was also becoming painfully aware of the gathering bystanders.

"Let us take this discussion inside," she suggested and pointed to the tent.

"No!" he boomed. "Let's not. Let every soul hear what you have done."

Seraphina's face grew red with rage as she began to stride with anger towards Solgiven, his face grimaced with defiance preparing himself for her attack but before they could come to blows the young boy stood between the two and placing his hands upon each chest zapped them both with a blast of energy sending them both tumbling back like leaves caught in the wind. Gasps came from the crowd as they scuttled to get out of the way while Alfie stood with a look off sheer annoyance and surprise at his own strength.

Solgiven groaned and rolled about whilst Seraphina rearranged her hair and brushed down her clothes, at this point

Alfie awaited either one to initiate their Lockan as he suddenly snapped back to reality.

Nervous and jittery he shouted, "You gave me no choice, I couldn't let you come to blows, you're supposed to be the grown-ups here!" He jumped out of his skin as Risla placed a hand upon his shoulder. "Shitting hell you scared the crap out me!" he yelled. "I thought you were a warrior come to arrest me."

Risla smiled. "I see you have been practising your skills," he said as he watched Eisiam help Seraphina to her feet.

"Oh god I'm in deep…"

Arksanza interrupted. "No my young friend you did what you have been training to do, by the looks of things you have taken on new skills." He signalled to Seraphina and Solgiven to follow him into the great tent extremely angry with both of them. Alfie scuttled along with his companions but Arksanza put his hand up signalling he did not wish them to follow and then unceremoniously swished shut the opening. Risla grabbed hold of Eisiam's hand and whispered to Alfie to follow. His sister protested trying to free herself.

"Oh shut up goody two-shoes you be wanting to hear what is going on as much as I be, quit wrestling."

Alfie hushed them up. "Shussssh!" he hissed with his finger to his mouth as he placed his face as close to the fabric as he could without touching it. He beckoned for them to come closer his eyes wide with surprise, his face intrigued. Eisiam who was standing with her arms stubbornly folded across her chest inched forwarded slightly as Risla let out a gasp, she couldn't resist and launched herself with a ballet-like leap towards the huddled boys.

"Oh now you want to know!" said Risla sarcastically. Alfie was straining to pick out the words as Risla started to giggle. "Alfie what are you doing? Use your noggin, that is the right word is it not?" as he gently tapped his human friend's head with his knuckle. "You have the power of mind reading, your ears do not need to be straining so hard, unlike me and Eisiam," as he pushed against the tent.

"No I think they will block me, they have done that before."

Risla waggled his finger in front of Alfie's face. "No you be wrong in this circumstance, they be bellowing not paying attention to anything but each other."

Eisiam stood between the two of them. "It be wrong for Alfie to use his gift in such a way, it is only meant for the need for information from our enemies."

Risla huffed. "Only you would be coming up with such an opinion." They squared up to each other.

"Christ Almighty! What is the matter with everyone today? All you Faerians seem to want to do is bloody fight each other," he exclaimed as he wriggled between the siblings. Alfie got clobbered at least twice by Eisiam jumping at her brother to reach his 'stupid face' as she put it.

Then Alfie suddenly froze. "OMG!" he pronounced. "They use to be an item."

Risla looked confused. "An item of what?"

Eisiam giggled a nervous giggle. "Together as one," she announced.

"Who?" said Risla.

"Those two," said Alfie.

"What two?" demanded the lanky Faerian.

"Seraphina and Solgiven," blurted out Eisiam.

In unison Alfie and Risla cried, "How do you know?" They both swarmed around her.

"I can just tell, there is a lot of passion between them, it be a fine line between love and hate."

Both Alfie and Risla had jammed their ears with their fingers and Alfie walked around in circles saying, "La, la, la. I don't want to hear it."

Risla caught hold of his sister's arm. "You be making it up," he insisted. "I have known them many years longer than you. How would I not have seen for myself?"

Eisiam laughed. "Because you be a stupid boy and can't see beyond the end of your nose." All this speculation was getting them no nearer to why Solgiven had ranted at Seraphina. What caused such a public outburst and why had Seraphina not been able to contain her anger?

Alfie motioned them to sit beside him and lined up they all silently listened. Arksanza was reprimanding them both, it seemed equally were each responsible. He brought up their past lives how they once had been so close, Alfie and Risla both squirming at this fact with Eisiam tutting. He told them they should put their differences aside and work together, something Solgiven just could not do after all it was she who rejected him. Seraphina's training and her calling had meant more to her than their relationship, Solgiven couldn't accept that she wanted to concentrate on her Magiks. He mistakenly felt that after his accident in the human world his scars repulsed her, never mind the fact that she had saved his life using the skills he once mocked. Even Faerians were not invincible; 50,000 volts was not a joking matter and she had use all her skills to bring him back from the brink but his melted skin and damage to his face was beyond her. This history between them was played out like a film in Alfie's head as he relayed the tale back to his two comrades nestled either side of him.

That day had taught her a harsh lesson. She and Solgiven had travelled the wrong path, they had been seduced by the lure of the human world, the bright lights, the bohemian attitude of a gang of young humans they had become acquainted with, one in particular, Jack Mansey. He had turned Seraphina's attention she had felt an instant attraction to him, his wild untamed spirit drawing her in like a moth to the flame. Solgiven was acutely aware of the growing feelings she had for Jack and he wasn't about to let his promised one slip through his fingers for a human boy.

Jealousy had clouded Solgiven's rational mind and he took Jack's challenge to do a dare to prove his courage. Jack ran the dodgem cars on the fair, he took care of the mechanics and if it broke down he repaired it. When all the lads got drunk they would play a game of chicken. Who would hang off the wire caging above the cars for the longest time before the rerouted electric current with no earth switched back on and the full volts kicked in? Jack held the record. Of course he did. He knew exactly how long it took before the current would travel through at life-threatening speeds, always triumphantly dropping to the ground with his handsome smile flicking across his face with seconds to spare but always the winner as a group of hysterical teenage girls swarmed around him like he was a gladiator returning from the arena of death, a hero. It didn't go unnoticed how Seraphina's eyes glistened with admiration for this athletic human even though she kept her relief to herself that he was unharmed. A stupid need to prove himself ruled that day as Solgiven was insistent that he could beat the great Jack. Seraphina had tried her best to persuade him not to take part; that they didn't need to draw attention to themselves. He stubbornly wouldn't listen, even snarling at her that she had no faith in him because she was smitten by the human. She had stormed off refusing to watch or take part in any of it and hadn't managed to get to the field boundaries before a huge explosion lit up the sky; the screams were blood-curdling. She instantly knew in her gut something had gone wrong and ran to the dodgems to find every one of the gang had scattered leaving Solgiven for dead, just a few humans standing around helpless to do anything for the stricken Faerian as he laid lifeless upon the ground.

As Seraphina threw herself to the ground trying to detect the beat of his heart in his huge chest, she was overwhelmed with the smell of burning skin, catching in her throat making her want to throw up. She peeled back the melted fabric off his clothing from his torso, his skin puckered and bubbling. She remembered screaming for water to try and cool the angry surface, his hair sheared off from the side of his head and his eye closed and swollen where the track of the electricity had found its path up the side of his body. She pounded his chest with her fist. Nothing, no response. Again she beat down hard with all her might ignoring the bystanders telling her it was no good he was gone. A third time; still nothing. Then she did the only thing left to her; Magjiks. Caring not who was there she held her hands over his heart and muttered an undecipherable language drawing up the energy from her body until she was roaring out the spell as physically as loud as she could, her power source rising from the earth until the crescendo of noise boomed through her hands into his chest slamming into his still motionless heart, stinging it back to life as he let out a gasp and dragged in a breath of oxygen screaming out in agony at the pain of his burns and panic that he couldn't see from his eye. She quickly dragged him to a sitting position cursing his weight as she hauled him forward with all her strength.

"You must get to your feet and we must be away to the Set," she ordered him. Solgiven although nearly delirious with the pain tried his best to rise up leaning heavily upon her but only succeeded in taking a few steps before crashing to the ground again. Seraphina felt desperate, they were in a dangerous predicament, the night sky had blackened as the sun had set; the best time for Gorans to be on the prowl and she did not know how badly injured her impetuous jealous friend was. Her resilience was beginning to wane when assistance came from the last person she would expect, Jack. He stepped out of the shadows.

At this point Eisiam broke the silence. "I knew he would come back, how romantic."

Risla did a fake gag. "So he should. He be causing the trouble." Alfie scowled at the pair of them.

Seraphina was not sure how much she could trust Jack but he was her only means of getting Solgiven back to the safety of the Set where she could get help for Solgiven's injuries. Jack had wasted no time in fetching a tractor with a trailer, between them both they hauled the hulking great Faerian on to it and Jack awaited directions. Seraphina was in a dilemma. How much could she trust Jack with? How close could she take him to her people? What if he gave them away?

As if he could read her mind Jack placed a hand on her shoulder. "I have known for a while you weren't from these parts. My Nanna was a gypsy card reader, she told me stories about a clan of, well fairies she called them. I know you're one of them. I don't want to harm you and anyway my Nanna said I would curse the family if I didn't help you in your hour of need. Seems to me this is that time." Seraphina didn't know whether to cry or laugh and threw her arms around their saviour, she was just grateful that he was there to help. Eisiam threw her brother a look, Alfie ignored it.

Solgiven awoke in his hut having no idea how he got there or how long he had been there. Still painful but not excruciating, the sensation of pain had dulled a little, his burns were covered with herbs that cooled and soothed. His hand wandered up to his face. He could feel his eyelid was open but he could not see out of his eye just shades of light.

"How long have I been here?" Seraphina who had been sleeping on a rug on the floor awoke and stretched.

"Seven settings of the sun," she mumbled pouring water into a bowl so he could sip some. She was exhausted both physically and mentally, she stared at him.

"What do you look upon? Am I that unsightly?"

She looked away. "No I marvel at the damage not being more, even the fact that you be alive." Her tone was cold.

"Who knows of this?" he questioned.

"Arksanza and the Elders."

He sighed. "What reception awaits me, am I to be banished?"

She let out a disgruntled laugh. "Yourself is all you be caring about, never mind the trouble you have brought upon me."

He tried to heave himself up on to his elbows. "I shall carry the blame you need not be implicated, it was my fault after all."

She tutted and turned away to look through the window. "You do not know the risk I be taking to get you back here. The human Jack had to assist me."

Solgiven interrupted. "Him."

She flew around at him her face inches from his. "Yes Jack. Jack the one you be so jealous of that you cause this," pointing at his burned chest.

He looked away from her. "That puny human."

She grabbed his face. "That puny human helped me save your life. That puny human hauled your carcass for over a mile through the undergrowth and that puny human swore to me he would never reveal us." She shoved his face away from her, he winced with the pain.

"I'm sorry, truly I be sorry for the sorrow. I did not think. I should have known he was not a threat to me."

She strode towards the entrance. "You be your own worst enemy, now you will have an altered life, your destiny has been changed and I shall no longer play a part of it. To save your dying body Arksanza and the Elders performed a ceremony over your body. To prevent your bones from crumbling further they have aligned your physical form with the Sun, it will give you energy as long as you have the solar blade with you. It will conduct the energy from the rays to power your body, when the Sun's sister rides into the sky, the Moon shall take your powers and only her servants Annaluna and Moondavna will guard you while you sleep. This will be your fate choose what you wish to do with it," and with that she was gone.

All three youngsters sat in silence for a good long time as they absorbed the story laid out before them.

Risla was the first to speak. "Well that truly be a tale and some. All this time not knowing their story. It certainly puts some things into place that I didn't understand before."

Eisiam looked sad. "Why are you upset?" asked Alfie.

She shook her head. "I just feel that they lost a lot along their journey and they obviously never got back their love."

Alfie sighed. "Yeah I know but that's life, you can't always be in charge. I mean look at me. I never thought I would be sitting outside a tent in another race's encampment, with ugly Gorans with beast-like hounds trying to find me, whilst I'm zapping people right left and centre with my new super powers." Eisiam smiled. "Anyway we are still none the wiser as to what they are arguing about." And then whether by coincidence or on purpose, they heard Arksanza call them.

"You three outside come in here." All three stood motionless and silent. "I know you be there." Risla started pushing Alfie first who in turn pushed Risla back and then pushed his sister who then pushed Alfie till they all eventually fell in a pile through the entrance.

Ignoring them brushing themselves down, Arksanza announced that Misa had left the camp. Alfie screwed up his eyes which was immediately spotted by Seraphina.

"Tell me what do you feel? Is it likely she has left?" This sudden questioning caught him off guard and panicking he stuttered over his words.

Solgiven boomed. "See he has no knowledge of Misa."

Arksanza said, "Give the boy a chance. Stop pressuring him."

Seraphina pulled him closer to her. "Remember how we spoke of trusting yourself, let your mind roam free things will come to you easier."

Eisiam whispered to Risla, "I do not be believing Misa would leave the encampment not while there is much concern for all our safety or after the incident with Triamena."

Solgiven spun on his heels. "What incident with Triamena?" hissed Solgiven.

Arksanza grabbed Solgiven's arm. "You were recovering from the traumas of the day, deep in sleep. There was no need to waken you, it was dealt with." Arksanza was desperately trying to play down the incident.

"If Triamena set foot near this camp it not be nothing. How you be knowing she was here? Did you see her?" he implored looking to each of them.

"It was me," said Alfie. "She spoke to me, I did not see her face but I now know it was her."

Seraphina looked puzzled. "You were not so sure before, how you be knowing now?" she asked.

"She has continued to speak in my mind, I have been blocking her. She tries to taunt me but I have not been listening so she flows in and out." Seraphina was obviously proud of her pupil but distressed that he had been subjected to Triamena's evil thoughts, he had done well to learn so quickly how to defend himself from both physical and magical threats.

"You could be mistaken, it may not be her."

Arksanza put his hand up in front of Solgiven's face as he twirled the silver feather. "She left this behind," he said as Solgiven snatched it from him, his face completely overcome with horror.

"She has the power to transform?" he questioned Arksanza who now was sitting on a stack of cut wood with his head in his hands.

"I believe she does but I not be knowing how far her capabilities take her, whether she has mastered the transformation spells completely. It could just be creatures of the forest or maybe even," he paused almost scared to say it, "one of our own kind." Eisiam let out a gasp making Alfie shudder as once again the voice began to build in his head.

"Be she talking to you now?" asked Risla. At that point Lolah came bounding up to the boy with a rag in her mouth at first wanting to play tug with him, growling playfully.

"Give it to me Lolah," he ordered making the huge dog sit. He flicked the slobber from the fabric twisting and turning it trying to recognize it.

Solgiven snatched it from him. "That's Misa's headscarf she uses it to cover her hair."

Arksanza bent in front of the dog. "Clever girl where did you find it?" he asked tickling her muzzle.

"Wait!" shouted Solgiven. "There is blood," his fingers tacky from the substance. "I knew she would not leave the camp without telling me. She never leaves before I awaken. She always polishes up my solar blade." He began pacing up and down. "What has become of her?" his voice straining with emotion, his eyes pleading with Alfie's wanting to ask the boy if Triamena had her but petrified with fear, not wanting to hear the words so not capable of speech. His eyes flicked like a madman from each of the faces in front of him, each one feeling his pain.

Seraphina placed her hand upon his but he snatched it away. "This is your doing. By speaking of Misa and her heritage, you have released her secret. Spies are everywhere, you gave her away," he raged at the Faerian.

Risla and Eisiam were speechless, stunned at this new information but still not fully aware of what Misa's secret was. They looked to Arksanza who brushed them off with a look.

"Do not be asking me now," he said as he pulled Alfie to him. "Now my young friend, are you still hearing her? Are there any images? Whose eyes do you see through? Quickly Solgiven, the scarf."

Alfie felt reluctant at first to hold the material now that he knew it had blood on it but Seraphina assured him it would the best way to connect with Misa. Alfie closed his eyes and let the voice come through. It was like turning on a tap, thunderous and roaring at first blasting his senses, causing confusion. Seraphina held his hands to help steady him whilst he tried to gain control again and clean up the message.

"She keeps saying a rhyme over and over."

"What? What is it?" asked Arksanza.

"'There be three, soon to be two, now I be flying, coming for you.' She just keeps saying it. What does it mean?"

Arksanza and Seraphina locked eyes. "I believe she speaks of the Trinity of Delaney; you, your mother and your mother's sister, Misa."

Again loud gasps came from Risla and Eisiam and not a glimpse of shock from Solgiven. The two siblings sat huddled whispering, "Today be a day of much surprises sister of mine." She nodded and wondered how much of this was a shock to Alfie. He was pale and focused but he didn't look like he was being given information for the first time. Risla who had known of the Geminis hadn't worked out that Misa was the stolen child from the Orb vision, suddenly pieced it all together. "Oh the Gorans must have abandoned the baby and somehow she came into the care of Solgiven, is that why he kept her away from the Set all that time till she grew older?"

Solgiven butted in. "No I did not be knowing who she be. I wanted to keep her safe as she was a human. I grew to love her like my own, my only fear was that her human mother might come to reclaim her, that be the only reason I hid her away, I couldn't bear to let her go," his voice cracking with lump in his throat.

Seraphina stepped towards him. "I'm sorry, none of this should have happened. We tried our best to keep Misa safe after the Goran minions abandoned her and left her for dead. We knew that you could not be told the truth but the best way to protect her was to keep her amongst us and who better than you our most loyal warrior."

He interrupted. "Well your plan failed, they have found her out and I have failed her. They took her from under our noses whilst you were so busy protecting the boy."

Arksanza stood up. "You are right. We were fooled into letting our guard down so focused on keeping Alfie safe not realizing the real intent of Triamena. For tonight at least he not be the target, Misa was."

Eisiam coughed and cleared her throat. "I do not wish to speak out of turn but I know Misa well she would not willingly leave her..." she stuttered a little, "Father's side. She always made sure she be there for his awakening with food and water and his solar blade to hand. Something or someone must have made her leave their dwelling."

Solgiven strode over. "She speaks the truth. Misa is very much a creature of habit."

Arksanza thought for a moment and then turned to Alfie. "Have you managed to connect with Misa? She may be able to give us a clue to her surroundings." Alfie shook his head overwhelmed by this responsibility.

Solgiven knelt before him softening his voice. "Please Alfie Diamond of the Delaney clan, be trying again, you be our only means of rescuing her." Alfie studied the scarred face and milky eye. He could see the pain of the great warrior, he also remembered Misa was in fact his aunt, his mother's sister, so he nodded in agreement and focused as Seraphina held the scarf to his face.

"Inhale the smells, nature is your champion let it help you." Silence fell upon the place as the young boy began to work his Magiks.

Triumphantly he announced, "The blood is not Misa's. I see a Faerian warrior upon the ground his head split open, he is lifeless, she took his form. Triamena took his form." Then Alfie paused he seemed confused. "The warrior is showing Triamena to your dwelling. He leads her through a way away from the campfires, away from the light. Everyone has run to the other side of the encampment, the warriors, all of you,

Lolah you are running to me, to the tent. She hands him a pouch, he seems pleased with it, whatever is inside it chinks. As he turns to leave she strikes him sending him and his treasure to the floor. Misa heard the noise outside and comes to investigate. Triamena in the form of the warrior hides in the shadows observing Misa as she finds the warrior with his head wound. She tries to bandage it but before she can raise the alarm Triamena has used all her power to change into a powerful bird with talons as sharp as knives that clamp on to Misa's shoulders, so deeply she faints with the pain and the bird carries her away." Then he paused again everyone hanging on his words.

"What? What's wrong?" asked Solgiven clasping his hand. Alfie wince as the huge man didn't realize his own strength.

"Give the boy some space to breathe," said Arksanza.

"I cannot see anything more. There is just darkness and a damp smell. I cannot hear anything or see anything."

Solgiven's eyes were now like saucers with fear. "What does that mean, what does that mean?" he cried shaking Alfie by the shoulders. Eisiam clung to her brother, her fingers growing numb with the tension as she gripped the front of his tunic, her heart pounding in her chest whilst Seraphina grappled with Solgiven, attempting to release the boy from the huge man's grip.

"Calm yourself let the boy do his work," she said as she snatched away his arms and threw him to the ground, turning and pulling away the scarf from the panic-stricken boy. Seraphina took hold of the scarf and inhaled deeply. "She be unconscious, the soil tells her story now. She be in a tunnel, no lights, it is pitch black, she sleeps bound and tied." Solgiven let out a groan of anguish. "And yet she is not alone, someone tends her wounds."

Arksanza spoke softly, "It be dark Seraphina how be you knowing this? How could anyone see in the dark to help her?" Then Alfie cut in full of enthusiasm.

"There are glow-worms loads and loads, they gather. I can see her face she looks like she is sleeping and I can see someone else in their glow, it's not clear. A hand washing away the blood from her wounds, there is a stream that runs through," then Alfie drew in a deep breath.

"What do you see?" demanded Solgiven.

Alfie looked at Arksanza and then said, "A Goran!" Eisiam buried her head in her brother's chest, Lolah whined, Solgiven pounded the ground with his fist.

"Calm down," ordered Seraphina. "Alfie what does he look like?"

Alfie was puzzled. "A bloody Goran same as all the others, ugly and smells weird."

"What do you mean smells weird?"

Alfie thought for a minute. "If I didn't know better I'd say he had been poking through my Grandma Maggie's perfume box."

Arksanza and Seraphina's eyes lit up and in unison they both said, "What is the smell?"

He screwed up his face in thought. "Well it's kinda, er, sort of flowery. Er, I'd say lavender." They both screeched with delight and hugged the boy.

Solgiven stood with his mouth open. "By the gods of the two worlds what has affected you so? My daughter be missing and you act as if it is time for celebration. I have had enough, I be going to find her myself."

"No, listen. The Goran with Misa is no ordinary foot soldier, he is from the Halenska family line. They are our sworn allies and spy for us at great risk to themselves and their families. They do have all the physical characteristics of the Gorans but they do not drink from the Waters of Aslanda and do not have any of the evilness their kinsmen thrive off. Can you see any markings upon his hands Alfie? I know it is dark but try," said Arksanza.

Immediately the boy answered. "Yes a star and something that glints with the hue from the glow-worms in the centre." Again there came a triumphant punch into the air.

"Manutik. How by the two gods be that happening?" Even Solgiven's spirit lifted at this news. "He will do everything in his power to help Misa escape, so we have one advantage. We just be needing to get to them as quickly as possible," said

Arksanza. "Does Manutik have mind speech?" asked Arksanza to Seraphina.

"No, I'm afraid not but we can get word to them that we know of their predicament and that we speed to assist them." Seraphina strode towards the entrance and stepped outside momentarily coming back with a black raven perched upon her hand. "Now my feathered friend this will not hurt you but will be protecting you from the others." She took a pouch from her gown and tipped a fine sparkling powder into her upturned hand, she gathered some with her fingertips and began to let the shiny dust fall all over the bird's feathers, back and forth she went until the once black bird shimmered in the light of their torch, flicking and flapping away the excess powder from its wings and squawking.

Alfie was unnerved by the racket the bird was making, he had never been keen on them and certainly hadn't been this close to one. He stepped back a little putting Risla between himself and the feathered messenger.

Arksanza scribbled something down on to a small piece of parchment and then proceeded to tie it with a strand of his own hair to the skeletal leg of the bird, round and round he wrapped it to keep the message safe in place.

"One more thing," said Seraphina as she pricked the tip of her finger with her knife and let a tiny drop of blood slip into the eyes of the raven. Its transformation was complete, silver with burning red eyes. "Now friend fly, use your brothers and sisters to aid you on your journey, they will help you find Manutik. Give him this message but do not linger in the land of the silver raven it will not take them long to realize you are not of their clan." The bird seemed to look directly into Alfie's eyes.

"Ugh what's it looking at me for? Gives me the heebie-jeebies." His mind flooded with the images from the Alfred Hitchcock film 'The Birds'.

Risla started giggling. "What? Are you afraid of the little bird?" he mocked bending down closer to Alfie's face who by now was beginning to jig from one foot to the other convinced the bird was going to launch its talons straight at his face and eyes. Lolah kept half hopping half standing on her hind legs trying to sniff the bird only to inhale the dust from its wings sending her into a sneezing frenzy. "Serves you right Lolah, you shouldn't be so nosey," Risla said as a slime-sloppy ball of saliva projected from her mouth as she let out another sneeze all over Risla's face and tunic. Arksanza grew increasingly agitated at the lack of appreciation for the seriousness off the situation.

"Gather your thoughts!" he snapped holding out his arm for the bird to hop to the end of his finger and take flight leaving a trailing shimmer of silver particles in its wake. "May the gods of the two worlds protect you," muttered Arksanza under his breath.

"Now," called Seraphina. "We must find the traitor and see if he be alone or a member of a party of bandits." They all set off in the direction of Solgiven's dwelling nipping around and behind the tents and hurriedly assembled shelters so as not to draw attention to themselves or give away their destination.

"We have no idea if we be watched. We must assume the worst, that Triamena has spies amongst us," said Solgiven. "Check the trees for silver ravens, their calls will be silenced lest they give themselves away but I be feeling sure they are there." Arksanza nodded in agreement and called one of his Arrow Warriors to escort them.

"Shoot to kill," he whispered to the archer pointing up into the canopy above. No sooner had the words passed his lips as two whooshing arrows shot passed Alfie's head making him drop to the ground.

"Bloody hell you nutter!" he called as he clasped his hands over his ears checking they were still there.

Thud, thud. Two silver ravens landed at his feet. Eisiam gasped and quickly flicked her eyes over the branches straining to see any further birds. Lolah bounded about flicking the birds into the air with her muzzle as though she had rendered the feathered spies dead herself as Seraphina grabbed them away, wrenching the arrows from their lifeless bodies, wiping the blood from the tip against the soil before handing them back to the archer.

Before long they came across the slumped body on the ground, a pool of congealed blood oozing from the wound, a dark crimson gash from the top of the skull across and down to the right ear. Alfie felt woozy at the sight remained standing, a bit back from the group. Solgiven hauled the body over so the face could be seen.

"Remensa!" called out Seraphina.

Arksanza studied the face. "I do not recognize him."

"He is not of our Set. He comes from the Upper Northern Clans." Solgiven rolled the body once more again to expose shining gold coins caught under his body.

Picking them up Solgiven turned to Seraphina, "He trained with us when we be much younger, do you recall?"

She turned away from the warrior. "Yes. That is how he came to know your marks upon your dwelling, you never be changing them since that time." Solgiven threw down the coins angry at himself and at Seraphina for making the point.

Arksanza quickly stepped in to cool the atmosphere. "Do we be thinking he carried this task out by himself?" He looked to Solgiven who was watching Risla tiptoe around the area.

Somewhat distracted by the gangly Faerian he answered, "I'm not sure My Lord." Screwing up his face he boomed, "What you be doing boy?" making both Eisiam and Alfie jump.

Risla held up his hand. "Stand still everyone do not be moving. Seraphina grab hold of Lolah." Solgiven looked incensed as it dawned on Seraphina what the boy was doing.

"He's tracking!" she muttered under her breath struggling to keep a noisy wriggling dog still, Lolah's huge great paws would disintegrate any clues.

Risla jumped across an area to examine the low hanging branches. Some were freshly snapped off and the ground beneath showed partial footprints and a dragging mark in the soil surrounded by huge bird prints. He bent down to sniff at a damp patch that had left the ground slack and clay-like, as he did so a glint in the undergrowth caught his eye. Risla rummaged and tugged at a leather strap, eventually it gave way and he came tumbling back into the opening hold a ceramic flask high, triumphantly in his hands. Alfie hauled his friend up to his feet as Risla proudly announced his findings.

"There be only one traitor here. See the same shaped foot with a half moon missing where the big toe should be." He held up his hand as Solgiven went to speak, he wanted to make the most of this moment of glory. "See it is repeated all over, the only other one except the bird, which means Triamena never stepped from the grass and that she hid over here in the bushes whilst she awaited Misa," he paused dramatically; Eisiam tutted. "Gold was not the only reward Remensa was expecting," he revealed as he untied the binding around the top of the flask. He let them smell it.

Seraphina instantly recognized the metallic earthy odour. "The Waters of Aslanda," she said as the others all inhaled the vapours of the liquid. She immediately tipped the contents away after they had all taken turns to smell it.

"Remensa must have bargained with Triamena for gold and the waters. He must not have trusted her because see here, some was tipped on to the ground, probably where she let him taste it to confirm it was as expected," said Risla hunched over the damp patch. "The only other tracks are those of Triamena when she transformed and the dragging marks are from Misa's heels when she was grabbed by the huge bird."

"Good Risla, your father has taught you well. At least we do not need to waste time searching the camp for others. I think it is safe to say Remensa worked alone."

"Why do you think he be needing the waters?" asked Eisiam.

"There could be many reasons but he probably mistakenly believed that somehow he would gain more strength and earn the respect of his kinsmen in the Ceremony of the Dordan clans." Alfie looked puzzled none of this made any sense to him. Arksanza pulled him aside. "I believe in your human world you have such a thing as the Highland Games, it be originating in a place known as Scotland."

Alfie nodded in acknowledgement. "I don't know much but I have heard of it. What's it got to do with Remensa?"

"Our clans come together, mostly the younger male Faerians but occasionally also an exceptional female," he threw his eyes over towards Seraphina and winked at Alfie.

"I bet she won," whispered Alfie.

Arksanza stooped lower. "Yes she did and she be defeating the great Solgiven." Alfie stifled a giggle as the great warrior was only an arm's length away from him.

"I gave her the victory," protested Solgiven.

"Of course you did," called back Seraphina busily packing up a sack.

"For Remensa to win over all others would be a great honour for him and his clan, his name would have been placed in the Book of Oracles for centuries of Faerians to know of him and his greatness."

Alfie paused before responding, "Is it really worth dying for just to get a mention in a book? So what? He might have been a good fighter or chopper of logs or whatever it is they do, but really to sell Misa out to Triamena just to get bigger muscles, it just doesn't make sense."

Arksanza was shocked at Alfie's indifference to their rituals and ways. "I do not think you have considered the importance of our beliefs. We are not like you humans. Our world respects nature, we value the…"

He was interrupted mid flow. "My Lord I do not believe Alfie wishes to offend, I think the point that he be making is that there is much more to this than first meets the eye. One dose of the waters would not have made any difference to Remensa's physical or mental state, he would have needed to be exposed over some considerable length. No I believe this to be part of a bigger plan, maybe Remensa wished to be part of the Goran underworld, maybe he barters the waters with the Goran overlords, maybe he passes information to Triamena regarding her father's dealings, after all Traska believes her to be long dead and she will still be hell-bent on revenging her grandmother," Seraphina paused to allow Arksanza time to absorb her thoughts.

"Yes I believe you to be correct. I have no doubt she concealed her identity to Remensa. It would have been foolhardy to have done anything less. He surely would not have known he was dealing directly with Triamena."

He walked over to Alfie who was sitting on a pile of firewood. "Apologies young sir," he smiled at the boy. "I jumped to a conclusion and forget that you are young and do not understand all of our ways yet."

He ruffled the wild curly hair of the youngster as Alfie proclaimed to the group, "And I don't think I bleedin' well ever will either!" They all laughed out loud, even frosty, hostile Solgiven. It was a relief from the tension even if only temporary for now.

"Alfie are you still sensing Misa? Have their circumstances changed yet or do you feel as though they remain prisoners?"

He pondered for a minute. "I think so yes but Misa does not feel the pain as much and she is chatting. She seems quite comfortable with Manutik."

Seraphina nodded. "She probably has not set eyes upon him yet and no doubt he keeps outside of the range of the glow-worms."

"Why would he do that?" questioned Eisiam.

"Manutik knows his appearance will disturb her so I believe he will try to gain her confidence before revealing himself. Misa has probably got more reason than most due to her father's calling, his role as terminator of the Gorans has exposed her to the most evil of their clan but she does have good judgement and I believe she will look beyond his skin, if she is given time to listen to his soul," said Arksanza.

Alfie looked thoughtful. "Would I be able to influence her? Maybe somehow I could give a message, a sign that Manutik means her no harm, in fact the opposite."

Seraphina smiled at her young charge. "It be good that you are beginning to recognize your strengths and gifts but at this moment in time we be having no way to tell if any of Misa's latent powers have been triggered, we could be doing more harm than good. No, myself and Risla will try to trace their position whilst you remain here in the safety of the camp."

Solgiven attempted to argue. "That boy should not be going to my daughter's rescue, that be my purpose," he said pointing at

Risla who tried his best to look tall and strong whilst holding his knees tight together lest anyone else could hear them knocking.

"No," ordered Arksanza. "Have you not taken note of the inkiness falling from the sky, your saviour the sun is leaving us, darkness falls upon us swiftly."

Again Solgiven protested. "I can summon my protectors their Moon powers will revive me enough to carry out the rescue of my daughter Misa. Moondavna and Annaluna are sworn to me are they not?"

Arksanza tired of the huge warrior's arguing. "Warrior take hold of yourself, your senses leave you as does the energy the queen of the skies gives you. You would be a hindrance and could well cost Misa her life. You do not think as a rational being and therefore I forbid you to go." An awkward silence fell across the gathering, no one knew quite how to break it. Solgiven's heart pounded with rage and could be heard thumping in his chest, or so Alfie felt. He wasn't sure if it was genuinely that loud or he was using his gifts but judging by Eisiam's expression they all could possibly hear it such was the anger burning inside the great warrior. He stormed off through the trees, crashing and tearing at the undergrowth back in the direction of his dwelling to take his position ready for the morning sun, bellowing and roaring with exasperation.

"Better he gets it out of his system, else his night-time recovery will be no benefit to him at all," whispered Seraphina.

"Now," Arksanza clapped his hands. "Risla gather your weapons and some provisions, also take these herbs they will hopefully be preventing infection in Misa's wounds. Seraphina do you have your trusted staff and your senses about you? Take no risks and be successful with your mission we must be recovering the Gemini and be returning her to safety." Alfie felt a little peculiar at the use of the word Gemini, even now things felt surreal. The woman they were to rescue was his mother's long-lost sister that Nellie knew nothing of, his aunt and him her nephew, the great Alfie Diamond of the Delaney clan, it was mind-boggling.

He wasn't clear how any of his family would react once the truth came out but one thing was for sure, none of their lives would ever be the same again and for his part Alfie couldn't help but feel guilty. Lolah nudged him with her muzzle and licked his hand with her huge pink tongue as if to reassure him.

"Silly dog you know nothing of my worries," he said as he tickled her head with his fingers. She screwed up her face with appreciation and then rolled over on to her back so that he could scratch her belly, her legs rotating as though she was riding an upside down bike. He laughed as she grunted in sheer bliss but the moment was short-lived as a Faerian warrior came bursting through the trees breathless and exhausted collapsing at the feet of Eisiam.

She let out a shrill cry in shock scaring the life out of Alfie and setting Lolah off barking. She must have been distracted by the belly tickle as she never heard the warrior coming. The Faerians instantly jumped into defence mode pulling Alfie in close behind them in anticipation of an attack.

"My Lord," the stranger put up his palm whilst heaving in breath deeply. "I be alone. No one follows." Again he sucked in oxygen as Arksanza dropped his weapon and attempted to help lift the stricken Faerian into a sitting position.

"Eisiam fetch the poor soul some water." Risla also took hold of him under the arms and hauled him across the ground to rest against a tree.

"Take your time, recover yourself. Here sip slowly," he said as he held the animal hide of water to the shattered Faerian's mouth. Lolah sniffed at the stranger but he did not seem worried by the huge dog as he gulped at the soothing liquid coating his parched throat. "Slow down you'll be sick. Slower my friend," said Risla pulling the water away from the overeager warrior.

Everyone gathered around him waiting in anticipation for him to speak. "My name is Weslan and I am sent by Elancie of the Truth Makers clan."

Arksanza let out a sigh of frustration. "Continue Weslan although I fear I already be knowing your message."

"Elancie has instructed me to tell you, the Gemini is aware. Her fellow humans believe her mind to be sick and she presently is under their medicines. The doppelgänger rapidly disintegrates from inside. Elancie fears that once the Gemini regains consciousness all will be lost."

Alfie let out a howl of distress. "This is all my fault. I have got to get to my mother, this has gone on long enough." He grabbed at Arksanza. "You cannot stop me," he challenged his eyes burning with determination and his chest beginning to glow as the ground beneath them shuddered and rumbled.

"Calm yourself, we shall attend your mother but first you must calm down."

Seraphina stepped forward and placed her hands upon his shoulders. "I shall travel with you," she said.

"No, we must stay true to the plan. Now more than ever we must regain Misa. Forces are afoot here and it is time for Alfie's family to be told the truth. Travel with Risla and bring her back, also Manutik, his knowledge of the Harpy Caverns will be invaluable." Seraphina didn't even both to argue she knew in her heart he spoke the truth.

Both she and Risla gathered up their supplies and with one last look, she mind spoke to Alfie. *Trust your instincts little one and listen to Arksanza, he will keep you safe.* With that they disappeared into the night, his stomach flipped as Eisiam slipped her hand into his and squeezed reassuringly.

"Weslan you have carried out your task, now do this one last thing. Go to the barracks and assemble a team, 12 at most. Be sure to included at least two truth makers, Elancie will require their help. Send them to the hospital to the doppelgänger, we shall already be there. Make sure they dress as humans and be sure to provide them with a Barracness toad. We cannot be sure if the Gorans have infiltrated the grounds." He then started to gather up a few essentials they would need not least garments to help them fit in to their surroundings.

"What's one of them toady things?" whispered Alfie to Eisiam.

"They are very sensitive to the odour of the Gorans. If one has passed by or is near they become immobile and lie flat on their backs, we sometimes use them in tunnels to check for traps. I think Arksanza will not be sure of the people at our destination. Gorans can be very deceptive and in their bid to seek out your family they will be no doubt all the more determined. As it is night-time we must be extra vigilant because they will be at an advantage, they have better night vision than us hence the need for the toads." She carried on packing the items set aside by Arksanza as he gave final orders to Weslan.

"Once the team have been sent on their way please go to the dwelling of Solgiven. There you will find Moondavna and Annaluna. Tell them of the circumstances and tell them to ensure they get Solgiven to the house of Magdalene Delaney and to await us there." Alfie's stomach flipped at the mention of his grandmother's house.

Alfie didn't want to question Arksanza any further but an uneasy feeling crept over him. He did his best to move the feeling on, concentrating on the impending meeting with his mother and the rest of his family. So many questions. How would they react? Would they be pleased he wasn't lying in that hospital bed close to death? Would it be relief or anger that greeted him? Charlie would probably want to batter the shit out of him after he had hugged him in his bear-like grip but mostly it was his mother's reaction that worried him the most.

From the sounds of things she was not coping well. He truly felt sorry for that. He hung on to the fact that once everything had been explained they might understand; maybe, hopefully, probably not. His heart was heavy.

The Tale Unravels – Chapter 11

Neon flashing blue lights and wailing sirens signalled they had arrived at the back entrance to the hospital. An old sense of familiarity rippled over Alfie as he surveyed his surroundings. People huddled in dark corners having a sneaky cigarette, automatic doors whooshing open as patients and visitors passed within range, ambulances sweeping up to offload their cargo, the industrious clanging and scuttling of wide heavy rear doors as trolley legs dropped to the textured dark tarmac to be trundled along into the blinding white light of the A & E corridors. Controlled but loud confident voices calling vital readings, temperature charts, one medic aloft above his patient, rhythmically pumping the chest, whilst his colleagues raced them both down the passageway, out of sight like competitors in a madcap trolley race. Babies crying, people arguing, some laughing, others just passing the day as they dropped the stub of their cigarette, grinding it into the ground with the toe of their shoe and scuttling back into the entrance as security guards fumbled and struggled with a drunk who without warning vomited the entire contents of his stomach down the front of the guard's trousers and shoes, colourful words invaded the air as Alfie whispered "Gross".

This organized bedlam fazed Eisiam. Her eyes were wide and glassy, the manic noises battering her senses, fuzzing up her thoughts as she stood mouth agape unable to decide what she should be doing. Quickening shallow breaths left her light-headed as panic began to set in, all this was new to her she had certainly never been so close to the human world. Arksanza gripped her under the elbow and guided her towards an abandoned wheelchair.

"There now that's better," he said as a bemused Eisiam tried to stand back up. Alfie realizing what the elder Faerian was doing joined in.

"No. No sit. Your ankle will only get worse if you try and walk on it," he stared intently willing her with his eyes to just abide by his instruction, wishing she had the power of mind speak, that would have made things a lot easier.

A look of knowing spread across her face as she realized what was going on. "OOH!" she cried out. "Yes it does hurt," she said leaning forward to soothe her injured ankle. Alfie stifled a giggle at her appalling ham acting although her ashen grey face from her near faint made the situation all the more believable.

He turned her towards the entrance whispering under his breath, "Let's hope there are no Gorans around to witness that." He smiled looking to Arksanza awaiting his instruction. The Elder seem to be watching for something.

"Let us just walk slowly I am mindful that we cannot dally, I be waiting for a sign," he muttered as he lent his hand upon the handle of the wheelchair turning his face both left and right, they were all three on the lookout although two of them didn't have a clue what for.

"Who are we waiting for, is it Elancie?" asked Alfie.

"No, he will not be able to leave the doppelgänger's side. Our fates hang perilously in the hands of the two gods. I am hoping Weslan will appear at any moment with aid for Elancie, he must be exhausted with the strain on his Magiks all this time." Alfie continued to scan the faces of the people looking back over his shoulder towards the scrubland they had stumbled through when he became aware that one of the security guards was beginning to give them some attention. Maybe it was their furtive behaviour or maybe he thought the Faerians looked strange in their 'blend into the background' clothing which actually was anything but. Arksanza had adorned himself with a Jimi Hendrix T-shirt and bell-bottom jeans finished off with cherry red Dr Martens, not the normal attire of an elderly gentleman nearly hitting 90 in human years. Thankfully his spindly Lockan was neatly tucked up under his Bay City Rollers cap. As for Eisiam she had selected a more modest outfit and mostly resembled a school librarian but for the shiny thigh-high patent leather lace-up boots which thankfully were mostly covered as she was sitting in the wheelchair so she drew less attention than her Elder.

Alfie's mind boggled. *Where the bloody hell did they get these clothes from and how had he not managed to spot them until the last minute as they were about to enter the hospital?* he thought to himself.

The security guard was making steps towards the misfit group, eyeing them up and down suspiciously. "Been to a fancy dress or summat?" he grunted as he circled the group. Arksanza's face was a picture, his expression blank and puzzled at the question.

"No sir these be my normal garments." Alfie wanted the ground to open up and swallow him as Eisiam then joined in.

"Look!" she smiled as she hiked up her skirt to reveal the magnificent boots in all their glory. "Be they not most glorious?" she asked buffing up the shiny surface with her sleeve beaming proudly, the guard almost choked on his chewing gum as Alfie hurriedly dragged her long skirt back over her knees.

"Your ankle isn't going to get better by showing the people your boots," he said as he tucked the material tight under her legs in case the urge to flash the boots again came over Eisiam.

"And what about you then, what you come as?" questioned the guard nodding his head towards Alfie who by now was becoming hot and sweaty under the collar desperate to remove himself and his companions from the intense scrutiny of the guard. Stuttering he looked himself up and down realizing he had the clothing of an office tea boy who's Great-Aunty Louie had knitted him a tank top to keep his chest warm albeit a couple of inches too short in the body.

Alfie sighed and then answered, "I'm their carer," as he released the brake on the wheelchair. "Now which way is it to X-ray?" The guard was about to question Alfie further when the crackle of his radio kicked in, it was the other guard telling him to come round to the side entrance that he was needed to help with an abusive patient. Alfie was relieved as he watched the guard go sprinting off, he had felt his heart rate build up and he was fearful that his talisman would begin to glow but he was also aware of another sense, the image of his mother popping into his head. "Oh my god it's my mother. That's who they were talking about, the patient that is kicking off. Crap!"

Arksanza grabbed the boy. "Are you sure? Tell me what you be seeing."

Alfie paused for a minute. "Yes I see her she has a hospital gown on and she is trying to get into a room but they won't let her. Shit my father is there, he is pleading with her but she won't listen. Oh no!"

Eisiam jumped from her seat. "What? What is it?" He turned and looked her straight in the eyes his face drained of colour.

"She is about to have an Awakening!"

Arksanza gasped. "What makes you think such a thing be happening to her?"

Grabbing his hair in his hands he blurted out, "I can feel it in her body, it is building. A real rage is about to erupt. I have got to get to her!"

Without a second thought he took off running in the same direction as the guard with Arksanza and Eisiam in hot pursuit shouting his name. "Alfie you cannot do this the shock would kill your mother. Stop. Stop!" But his rational head had long gone, his Awakening taking over his body. Voices just became a blur, his feet pounding on the lino floor as at each turn of this labyrinth of corridors he grew faster and faster desperate to get to his mother leaving the Faerians far behind focusing only on the image of his mother, Nellie.

He began to hear shouting, raised voices, he must be near. He heard a woman's shrill tone demanding to see inside the room. The blood was pulsing through his veins, pounding away in his head as he grew breathless with his physical effort. Just one more push as the stabbing pain of a stitch in his side kicked in and his lungs shrivelled and dried in his chest wall, an acid acrid taste on his tongue, as his body began to tremble from head to foot, his jelly-weakened legs unable to carry him a step more.

Somewhere, somewhere deep inside he must find the energy he desperately wanted to get to his mother, to tell her it would be OK, that she was right, that it wasn't her son lying in the bed, that she had been right all along. He hauled himself up and began to run again towards the voices, not far now just around the corner one more push. Then out of nowhere he was slammed into the wall of the corridor, the wind completely knocked out of him, his ribs burning and his body sapped of energy.

Through blurred eyes he could just make out a figure as he felt himself being hauled across the floor by his legs into a side room. If this was the Gorans he was done for, he had nothing left to give, he was completely at their mercy, defenceless, not even able to stir up an Awakening. He had let them down, his mother, his family, the Faerians, everyone. Slipping in and out of consciousness, aware only of faint mumblings, his brain battled to make sense of his surroundings; he thought he heard Eisiam. It took every ounce of strength to force his eyes open, the figures smokey, black and grey, blurred and intermittent, his legs felt heavy, even to think about wriggling his toes hurt. A face formed in front of him through the blur as first he tried to steal himself, after all this could be the enemy. He urged, no ordered his body to react. A gentle hand upon his shoulder soothing and passive, his brain was confused. This was not the action of a Goran captor, as the face became clearer the old familiar features of his friend Eisiam filled his vision.

"Hello you. What happened to me?"

She put her fingers to her lips, "Shush." He tried to push up with his arms to get himself into a better position but something heavy lay across him, was preventing him from moving. Still groggy he looked down. There laid across his lap was a person. He looked up at Eisiam and the others in the room; Weslan, Arksanza, Elancie, other warriors he presumed Faerian. Still confused he looked down again at the stranger but this was no stranger. His eyes shot up at Eisiam her beautiful face smiling but her lilac eyes brimming with tears. He inched his hand out from underneath his thigh and gently pushed away the dark curls that shrouded the pale face with tiny freckles sprinkled across the bridge of the nose. Many a time he had counted those freckles, he knew their pattern off by heart. His fingers traced the soft tickly eyebrows across the forehead stopping at the tiny scar on the left-hand side, he let his palm hover over the eyelashes remembering the butterfly kisses his mother used to tickle his cheek with when he was little, she fluttered them to distract him when he had to have jabs or got himself in a paddy.

It was her laying in his arms, his Mother. He hugged her tight to him sobbing liked he had never sobbed before, his chest hurting from the pain of his joy as his fat salty tears fell on to her face, snorting and blubbing but not caring who saw or heard.

"Oh Mum. Oh Mum," he repeated over and over. "Is it really her?" he questioned.

"Yes it really be her," said Arksanza kneeling before Alfie, still holding her tight to his chest inhaling her mum smell, her almond shampoo hair, her perfume, the only thing missing was her dramatic eyeliner and customary 'Hot Plum' pink lips.

"Is she OK? Why isn't she awake, what's the matter with her?" She slept deeply upon her son's lap, her breathing soft, rhythmic, peaceful.

"She be fine, just sleeping. I gave her a tincture. We had to stop the Awakening and calm her. There be no telling if the Gorans would be about. She will not sleep much longer and then we must reveal the truth to her and the rest of your family about the doppelgänger."

Alfie felt sick to his stomach. None of this was going to be easy and he really had no way of knowing how anyone would react, least of all his mother, to the news that she had a long-lost sister.

"Is there any news of Misa? I haven't heard anything from Seraphina. Mind you I have been a bit preoccupied and by the way who took me out?" He looked around the room. Weslan sheepishly raised his hand. "Well you certainly stopped me in my tracks," he smiled at the warrior. "I reckon the England rugby team should signed you up," he giggled. Weslan looked confused. "I will explain it another time," said Alfie.

"Seraphina and Risla were successful they have recovered Misa and Manutik. They travel to meet with Solgiven. We shall all meet up at the house of Magdalene Delaney, however Seraphina is concerned that the rescue of Misa be a little too easy so she takes measures to ensure that they are not followed. They do not take a direct route back to the house and she has requested that we send archers ahead to seek out the silver ravens, the last time scouts were sent out the house was surrounded."

Alfie looked surprised. "Have you been watching the house?" At that moment Nellie began to stir, she stretched out, her eyes flickering and adjusting to the light as she began to focus on the face in front of her, she let out a soft breath as she rubbed at eyelashes.

"My boy, I know it is you." She gently stroked his face with her fingertips, again the tears flowed as they embraced.

"I'm sorry Mum so sorry for all this trouble," blurted Alfie. She hushed her son and then turned to look at the strangers.

"Who are your friends?" she asked as she studied the Faerians. Alfie helped his mother to her feet, she was a little unsteady. "Whoa, I feel like I have had a good night out but don't remember the night," she smiled as they both giggled.

Arksanza stepped forward. "My name is Arksanza Arrusan of the Fronan clan," sweeping low to greet Nellie. She smiled and considered whether she should curtsey, so regal was the greeting from the elderly gentleman. "And I am afraid it be my doing that you have a swimming head."

Nellie turned to Alfie. "Did he clobber me?" she asked winking to ease her son's obvious anxiety.

"Mum!" Alfie's face went crimson. Blustering, he tried to steer his mother around the room, shaking strangers hands but comforted by warm greeting smiles. Eisiam giggled causing Nellie to turn and look at her.

"And who might this be?" a gleam in her eye as she questioned her son taking in the natural beauty of the pale-skinned Faerian. "Gosh you have beautiful eyes and your hair is so soft, are you Alfie's friend as well?" Alfie spluttered and coughed tongue-tied, racked with acute embarrassment as his mother twirled the pale strands of hair around her fingers.

"I be Eisiam," she paused and considered for a moment nodding. "Yes I am honoured to be a friend to your son, Alfie Diamond of the Delaney clan." Nellie was taken aback by the full title bestowed upon her son and drew in breath.

"Delaney, that's a name I haven't heard in a while." Alfie sighed, all this time he had spent with the Faerians he had grown comfortable with the reverence that seemed to surround him but now watching his mother's reaction it felt well kind of geeky, his brothers were going to rip it out of him mercilessly. Alfie could feel things already beginning to unravel as he watched Eisiam study his mother's face. She seemed a little too attentive taking in all the information in front of her, her eyes moving up and down, across and sideways, her hand reaching up to pat the curly hair, delighting in it springing back to shape. This strange behaviour had not gone unnoticed by Arksanza whose once smiling face now looked grim, concerned.

Before either one could say anything the words began to fall out from Eisiam's lips. "You look just like…" Everything seemed to fall into slow motion as Alfie tried to kick-start his frozen brain into action whilst Arksanza reached out for Eisiam's arm.

"ME!" shouted Alfie. "ME!" His outburst causing both his mother and Eisiam to jump.

"Jesus boy you scared the bejesus out of me," she cried slapping him playfully across his shoulder.

"Yes I was going to say that," said a puzzled looking Eisiam. Arksanza slumped against the wall he could tell the next few hours were going to be fraught, so much to tell Nellie and so little time. He winked at Alfie but Alfie did not wink back, this whole situation could easily blow up in his face if it wasn't handled right. He knew he needed to double think, even triple think, everything he did or said. If he had allowed his brain 30 seconds longer before reacting, he would have realized Eisiam was not going to give the secret of Misa away to his mother.

Obviously they were twins, but Misa had been protected for many years by the Faerian Magiks and she didn't look a day over 20, his mother had not been so fortunate. Every day she would stand in front of the mirror stretching and pulling her face slapping on expensive creams and potions that had no telltale price labels on.

"Oh that was only a couple of quid," she would mutter to Alfie's father but went mental when the cat knocked her precious jar out of the window sending it tumbling and smashing into the paved path below. Mark had never seen her move so fast, bombing down the stairs with an old jam jar swiped from the shelf in the garage and teaspoon in the other hand. Possessed wouldn't describe her accurately but she scooped that cream like she was digging up gold dust. How were they going to deliver the news to his mother, his entire family? It really didn't bear thinking about. How could he soften the blow? Should he just shut up and let Arksanza do all the talking? Should he take the lead? After all if nothing else the last few weeks had toughened him up, drawing out a hidden maturity that he and certainly his family would never have expected. Whilst all these thoughts bounced around his head, he became aware that Arksanza and a few of the group had left the room, leaving just two Faerian guards. He quickly flicked his eyes across at his mother and Eisiam who were chatting away like long-lost friends both sat cross-legged on the floor whilst Nellie scalp plaited the younger female's hair.

Bizarre, he thought to himself and silently slipped out through the heavy fire door looking both left then right. The corridor was empty, this felt strange with no people about. A sense of uneasiness fell about him, something didn't feel right. Instinctively he felt like he should walk left, the sound of his shoes scuffing and squeaking slightly, sticking to the shiny plastic-looking lino. He wished he had his slippers on, they would have slipped silently over the irritating and unforgiving floor. His ears pricked and alert to the sound of someone approaching, he kept walking, his breath shallow almost as though the sound of air being swallowed up by his lungs would give him away, his head tucked down deep into his chest shielding his face. Closer and closer just around the bend. Alfie felt his heart skip a beat, his whole body on high alert, adrenaline flooding his veins in preparation for flight or fight, flight or fight, flight or fight. He decided to stand his ground and took on the stance of a ninja warrior.

"No. No that looks ridiculous." Then he tried leaning against the wall looking cool and casual adjusting his clothes nervously, all the time his heart thumping matching the sounds of the approaching footsteps.

In his head he could hear his big brother Charlie telling him, "Act like a nutjob. Swing your arms wildly, that will scare off the school bully." Standing smack bang in the middle of the corridor, he proceeded to windmill his arms and grimace, more with the effort than anything else, although the image of his scrunched up face red and sweating would have at least confused, if not scared off, a would-be attacker. Unfortunately the swinging and the physical effort which Alfie was not yet accustomed to made him pass the loudest fart he had ever done in his life, he quite shocked himself and immediately stopped moving. A slow creeping odour began to invade his nostrils; it absolutely stank, catching in his throat.

"Bloody hell!" he called out temporarily forgetting about the ominous footsteps approaching. He could hear coughing and spluttering from around the corner, maybe his insidious but toxic bottom burp, as his grandmother use to call it, had done in the assailant. Alfie could hear muttering, extremely irritated, angry mutterings, perhaps this was another skill he didn't know he had. 'Death by Fart'. He felt rather proud of himself as he edged towards the round metal trim of the corner of the wall. Still he could hear spluttering as the full force of the offensive smell hit its target.

"By the two gods what be that stench?" Alfie's eyes widened with shock, he knew that voice it was Risla. Like an overexcited puppy he gambled around the corner straight into Risla who was temporarily blinded with tears from the overpowering stink. Both went crashing to the floor.

"Risla, Risla! What you doing here? I thought you were with Seraphina."

Clearing his throat Risla replied, "Indeed I was but she sent me to help escort your family back to Magdalene's house. More be the point, why be you wandering alone? Where be Arksanza? Do you have a toad with you?"

Alfie jumped up and hauled Risla up. "Jeez one question at a time. I snuck out of the room. I left my mother with your sister; they are getting on like a house on fire." Risla looked puzzled.

Rummaging in his pocket he hauled a fat squelchy toad from it. Seemingly not bothered about having been unceremoniously squashed into the dark confines of said pocket it blinked its amber eyes and its aubergine coloured tongue slid across the surface of its eyeballs clearing away any lint from the fabric, fixing its stare on Alfie.

"God what's it looking at me for? Eww, slimy bloody thing gives me the creeps."

Risla laughed. "It probably be thinking you be ugly as well." He shoved his hand towards Alfie. "Here, you be holding the toad whilst I find it some food."

Alfie recoiled, "Get lost, I'm not touching that thing!" holding his hands high up on to his chest.

"I cannot be putting the creature upon the floor. You must keep it safe whilst I go outside to fetch some earthworms. I will not be long," he said as he plonked the toad on top of Alfie's clenched fists. "Do not let it fall," he instructed as he turned on his heels in search of a doorway to the outside.

"You said I shouldn't be out here alone," he half whispered half shouted after the Faerian.

A faint voice came back. "You're not alone, you have the toad." Alfie could swear he heard Risla giggling as he disappeared out of sight.

The toad however did not seem the least bit perturbed as it inched its way up from the back of Alfie's hand to perch triumphantly upon his shoulder. Alfie strained to glance at the toad out of the side of his eye, just in case it decided to try and lick his eyeball if he turned his head to face it. Alfie made a forced retching noise as he wiped his hands down the front of his top to attempt to clean off the glutinous slime from his hands.

"I'm going to bloody well kill that Risla," he muttered under his breath. The toad just croaked as if agreeing with Alfie, whilst he became more and more anxious. Risla seemed to be taking an eternity. Alfie was in two minds. Should he continue on his original quest to find Arksanza or go back to his mother before the feel-good factor of the tincture she had been given began to wear off and she would then start to remember the whole reason why she became a patient and not a visitor, the doppelgänger. He hopped from one foot to the other undecided.

"What do you think I should do Mr Toad?" turning his head to speak to his new warty friend. To his shock the toad was gone, missing from his shoulder, as he patted his shoulder blade in case the toad had gone walkabout he heard a splat. Looking down at his feet the toad lay flat on his back, his legs all rigid not moving but very softly breathing, Alfie could see his little belly gently rise up and down. "Oh crap. Did I drop you or did you fall off?" He prodded it with his foot trying to nudge it back into consciousness, nothing, no response, and then he noticed a blue tinge begin to slowly spread across the toad's stomach. Crouching down he looked puzzled and prodded it with his finger. "What is going on?" he murmured. He suddenly became aware of running feet, very fast running feet slapping against the lino. Alfie's body became taut as he strained to hear beyond the feet, subtly underneath there was a sound of scuttling and whipping, like rope flicking against the walls and floor. Out of nowhere Risla came sprinting at full pelt a look of extreme anxiety across his face. He stooped to pick up the toad in one swift movement and snatched Alfie by the arm.

"RUN!" Alfie didn't even hesitate or attempt to ask questions as it suddenly dawned on him why the toad had reacted the way it had, there were Gorans around, probably very nearby judging by Risla's reaction. They backtracked on the way Alfie had come, all the time Alfie running but turning to see if the Gorans had come into view.

"Stop looking just run," ordered Risla. "Where is the room your mother and Eisiam are in?" he asked breathless from his exertion.

Alfie looked startled. "We can't lead them there."

Risla dropped back a bit. "We have to because they be searching all the rooms and if we don't warn Eisiam she will not be prepared so where they be?" He allowed Alfie to edge ahead but in the panic Alfie forgot the room number and all the doors looked the same, white upon white, he started to flip out.

"I can't bloody remember!" he called back. Risla pulled him to a stop. "What you doing you nutter? Let go!" he screamed struggling to wriggle free.

Again Risla tugged at him. "Be calming yourself. Now use your gifts to sense your mother's presence, a few deep breaths be helping. I saw the Gorans but I believe they did not see me so we may have a little time, now concentrate." All the time his panic-stricken eyes focusing on the end of the corridor. Wiping sweat from his forehead to stop the stinging salty balls from blurring his vision, Risla began to hop from one foot to the other. Still listening Risla silently urged Alfie to hurry the hell up, his thoughts suddenly pinging into Alfie's mind. *The vines be upon us we must run.*

Alfie grabbed at Risla's face. "What vines are you going on about?" he stared sternly at his companion.

"Ugh we not be having time for this, concentrate on your mother and don't be reading my thoughts!" he cried pulling himself away

"I bloody didn't they just got there all by themselves," shouted Alfie. "Am I right in thinking that these aren't the good kind of vines like the book room ones, judging by your fear?"

Risla was incensed. "I not be afraid, I have no fear for anyone or anything." Alfie gave him a wry smile, but he too now could hear the whiplash of the vines getting closer and closer. "They have our scent!" exclaimed Risla as he spotted a janitor's bucket and mop. Without a second thought he upended it tipping the strong-smelling disinfectant-laced water across the corridor and precariously slapped the stringy head of the mop up the walls and over the ceiling. "That should be foxing them for a while," he said as the intensely strong medically clean aroma wafted towards Alfie. It gave him a temporary clarity as the sharp freshness stung his nostrils, grabbing his hair he tried to focus on his mother. His thoughts fought him, distracted by the blue hue of the toad becoming almost indigo and the fizzing sound of Risla's Lockan. He wanted to scream with temper but knew he couldn't in case the Gorans were close enough to hear. Judging by the state of the toad they seem to be gaining on them, it was now so rigid it looked like rigor mortis had set in, then suddenly a number popped into his head.

"213, 213!" he screeched excitedly as they both began to search the doors. They were miles off; the numbers were only in the hundreds. "Shit I must have got it wrong, how can I be this far out?"

Risla grabbed his shirt. "Come on it must be the next one round hurry." Alfie could hear the sound of voices and urgent, but not yet running, feet hitting the floor all coming from the same direction just around from where they had come. The human and the Faerian stared wide-eyed at each other, without a word between them they took off counting down the rooms. 201 on the right, 202 on the left, 203 on the right, 204 on the left. Quicker now, jumping up a few till they hit 211, 212 and bursting through 213 to be greeted by surprised faces at their abrupt entrance.

A breathless Risla called out, "Gorans and poisoned vines," while shutting the door so softly both leaning with their backs against it, heavily panting.

"What colour is the toad?" said Alfie as he and Risla fumbled to turn it over on to its back. A deep purple presented itself.

Risla hissed to everyone in the room, "SILENCE!" Eisiam immediately pulled Nellie to her feet and pulled her to the corner of the room whilst the warriors tipped over the bed to act as a makeshift barrier for them. Dragging down Alfie's mother Eisiam put her finger to her lips, for once in her life Nellie didn't argue. Time stood still in the room as they all listened in anticipation for noises outside the room, every Faerian with their Lockans primed and ready to go if needed.

"Be sure to direct your Awakening outside this room if we be needing it. Be you thinking you can do that?" whispered Risla. Alfie just nodded, his eyes closed tight and he took a deep gulp as he swallowed hard. "Only forward not around," mouthed Risla as Alfie read his thoughts.

"I know, I bloody I know," hissed Alfie. He flicked his eyes across to his mother, she seemed hypnotized by Eisiam's Lockan hovering above their heads like it was being blown about by a gentle summer breeze, snaking back and forth, the crackling white sparks spitting in readiness.

He heard Eisiam whisper, "Do not touch it Nellie." His Mother just nodded and tucked herself deep into the mattress and bedding that had cascaded on to the floor. It seemed like an eternity as they listened to the low voices the other side of the door, the scratching of the probing vines slithering up down and around the corridor. They were definitely Gorans, Alfie recognized the language. They appeared to be arguing. He could feel his talisman begin to fire up, the energy within him begin to rise, pins and needles tingle in his hands and his mouth became dry. He was glad Eisiam was covering his mother he didn't want her to see the glowing fire-like light beaming from under his shirt, she would definitely have freaked out. Still the toad remained purple, he could hear them brush against the door. Alfie felt as though he would pass out as the metal handle began to tip down slowly, beads of sweat slipping down the side of his face as he struggled to contain the energy of his Awakening. It took the strength of both he and Risla using all their might to hold the door in place, the other warriors tiptoeing across to join them, praying that the Gorans could be fooled into thinking the door was locked. Then suddenly there was shouting, the handle snapped back up and the sound of footsteps running away from the door was heard. Alfie slid silently to the floor looking up at Risla who held the rapidly returning to normal toad in his hand, the colour fading and the creature jerking back to lift as blood filled its stiffened legs and body.

"I could bloody kiss that toad," said Alfie. Risla grinned and held the warty creature to his lips. "I said could but I won't," he said as he screwed up his face as the toad woofed down a big fat juice worm, his reward for his services.

Risla sat down beside his friend. "What be making them leave? I felt sure we were about to be battling them."

"Arksanza, he sent Weslan to cause a diversion. He sensed the danger we were in and mind spoke to me. We must wait here until he sends for us."

Risla patted Alfie upon the shoulder. "Good job little man, good job. Anyone be having any food?" he stared around the room as he rubbed his belly. Alfie just smiled and allowed his body to return to its normal state.

His attention switched to his mother who was whimpering beneath the covers. Eisiam appeared over the top of the upturned bed her face full of alarm.

"Alfie the tincture be wearing off, come comfort your mother," she called. Nellie sat with her heavy head in her hands groaning as though she was suffering a hangover.

"What's happened to me, where am I?" She started to lift her head, her eyes bloodshot and heavy lidded, screwing them up to try and focus on her son. Suddenly she shoved Eisiam away, backing herself into the corner. Eisiam ended up in a heap with Alfie rushing to help her.

"Are you OK?" he asked looking at her lip which was cut where she had fallen face first on the hard unforgiving floor.

"I am fine. Attend to your mother." She wiped the blood with her sleeve.

Alfie was angry. "Mum what did you do that for?" Nellie had pulled herself up tight into a ball, her knees under her chin.

"Get away from me you vile creature, you're not my son."

Alfie knelt before her. "It's me look," he said as he tried to easy her hands free from her face. She slapped out at him his cheek stinging, he grabbed at her wrists to stop her doing it again. "Mum." Much firmer now he said, "I am Alfie." But Nellie wasn't having any of it.

"You're not you're all lying to me, my son died in the woods. That thing they brought back is not my son. You are not my son!" she roared causing Risla to bound over.

"Shut her up! She be bringing back the Gorans."

Alfie took umbrage. "Don't tell my mother to shut up," he called as he squared up to Risla, all 6ft 6 of him. Risla tried to turn Nellie towards him to explain what was happening to try and calm her but she just flipped out and Alfie's anger took the better of him as his talisman began to glow. "Get your hands off my mother," he growled. Eisiam could see no good would come of this altercation both of them were going to come to blows if she didn't intervene. She quickly thought of a Magiks Arksanza had practised with her, a binding spell was what she required. She snatched hold of both Risla and Alfie's wrists and muttered the spell under her breath. Both found their hands bound as though they were in prayer, struggled to free themselves.

"Eisiam what have you done?" demanded Risla, as did Alfie. They could see nothing but neither could they pull themselves loose.

"You be leaving me with no choice, so pathetic are you being. You be bickering like Faerian babies, this fighting does your mother no good. The only way to resolve this is to be showing Nellie the truth." Both Risla and Alfie gasped in unison.

"Arksanza said we must wait for him to send for us when it is safe," said Alfie.

"I do not be caring, he is not here with us and in this situation. I care only about your mother's welfare. She will alert the Gorans if we do not give her proof that you be who you say you be." Alfie knew deep in his heart that Eisiam was right.

"You mean go to show her the doppelgänger?" Eisiam busied herself preparing Nellie. She pushed her hair away from her face and spoke to her softly, gently stroking her hand.

"Would you like me to be showing you something that be making you understand all of this mess?" Nellie looked up and stared at the beautiful lilac eyes, she lifted her hand to softly touch Eisiam's swollen lip, making the young Faerian flinch.

"I did that didn't I? I'm sorry." Eisiam looked up at her brother and Alfie, they both looked sheepish, she flicked her finger and both their hands fell free. Shaking them to get rid of the sensation of pins and needles and wriggling them to get blood back into them Risla proceeded to attempt to argue with Eisiam.

"Were we not told to wait, maybe we should be doing as we be ordered?"

Tutting Eisiam merely replied, "Since when did you ever do as you be told?" Alfie stepped forward towards his mother but Eisiam placed herself between them calmly placing her hand on his shoulder. "It be best if you hold back from your mother until we have got her to the room. Please try to understand she will best deal with this situation if we can keep her calm." Alfie's face looked so sad Eisiam felt awful. "It will all work out in the end but we must be taking things slowly." Alfie nodded and turned away to stand at the back of the room out of his mother's view his eyes heavy with tears about to brim over. What had he done to his mother? She looked so pale and confused, her face drawn and gaunt. He agreed with Eisiam that his mother should see him and the doppelgänger together only then would she be able to believe her own eyes, there was only one thing to do.

He sent a message that they were coming. Arksanza argued at first, even refusing to give Alfie the room number, but so insistent was Alfie that he would search anyway. Arksanza gave in. He didn't want them wandering around aimlessly and potentially straight into the arms of the Gorans or their minions.

"You must be making a pact that you will not be looking at the doppelgänger. Your energy and presence in the room will revitalize it and it most likely will attempt to seek you out. Under no circumstances must you make eye contact, do you promise me that sincerely Alfie Diamond of the Delaney clan? Eisiam must bind your eyes tightly and Risla will guide you. What be your mother's condition, are you truly sure this be the only way to reveal the truth?" Alfie explained how he had tried to reason with his mother but she refused to accept that Alfie spoke the truth, from the day they had taken the doppelgänger she had sensed something was not right. Arksanza believed her latent gifts were probably stirring but she did not have the skills to decipher her feelings, that and a combination of lack of sleep and anxiety had pushed her to the brink of madness, her family not trusting her instinct pushed her over the edge.

They were all under the spell of Elancie and the Magiks. For all intents and purposes, their family member was lying grievously ill in a hospital bed, their mother's breakdown kind of half expected. This last year had been traumatic to say the least, the loss of her mother, Georgie's friend being attacked, the house move to a house she felt no peace in. Alfie's father Mark thought he was doing the right thing when he agreed to have his wife admitted as an inpatient for treatment for post-traumatic stress. The hospital had agreed to keep her on a ward nearby so that the family could switch between Nellie and the doppelgänger. Disturbingly, Nellie spent most of her time in some other place in her head and had been barely responsive, not because she had been given high doses of medication but her doctors felt this was a side effect of her stressed out body. She almost needed to shut down to recover.

Risla stepped out into the corridor first, his precious toad in hand, it just sat upon his palm casually taking in the light of the bare walkway. Risla was confident at least for now there were no enemies within the immediate area, he indicated for the others to follow. Eisiam led Nellie out by her hand. Alfie stayed a little behind so as not to disturb her. He felt so bad having to hide from his own mother but it was the safest way to get her to the doppelgänger without causing a scene. Having already torn a strip from her skirt Eisiam passed back the make-do blindfold for him to tie around his eyes once they got to the room. She had made him swear not to be tempted to look upon the doppelgänger. He was beginning to get annoyed with everyone who kept reminding him, "Don't look it in the eye." Of course he wasn't going to do that, he knew the consequences, the fearful images of the mud pit on the day the doppelgänger was created still caused him to break out in a cold clammy sweat.

Such things were made of dreams or more accurately nightmares. That had been one time he had seriously thought, *That's it I'm off home, no more mud beasts for me.* If the truth be known he was scared witless that day, the closest he had ever come to actually vomiting over himself with the surge of paralysing fear rising up from his stomach, barely able to believe the images before his eyes. He had quickly learned in this short time that if a Faerian Elder told you a tale of jeopardy involving your safety then you would be best advised to listen and take it seriously; being lost to the dark spirits of the underworld was one thing not on his bucket list. There definitely would be no chance of him even attempting to sneak a look at his doppelgänger.

Alfie gripped tightly to the binding his knuckles white with the tension until they came within a foot of the door. Risla slipped inside as Weslan took the fabric from Alfie and securely knotted it at the back of the young boy's head careful not to catch the curls.

"I would be suggesting your eyes be shut tight as well," he whispered into his ear, pulling the hood from the back of his tunic to hang low over his face disguising his bound eyes.

"Christ why doesn't anyone think I can actually not be tempted to look at the bloody doppelgänger?"

Weslan steered him through the door his voice low and soft. "Be knowing Alfie Diamond, the spirits will know you are close, they will sense you through the doppelgänger. Do not listen to their voices for sure they will try to trick you." Alfie's stomach was in knots, an acid acrid taste in his mouth and the smell of decay and death with the overly sickly odour of disinfectant filled his nostrils. Picking at the edges of the fabric he peeled it down enough to shield his nose from the throat-catching stench. He was aware of others in the room, he could hear murmured conversations, the familiar tones of Arksanza and to his utter relief Seraphina mind spoke to him.

My boy do not be speaking aloud, your family are all present in this room, your binding and clothing will keep them from realizing you are amongst them. Listen only to my voice and instruction, nod if you be hearing me clearly. Alfie tipped his head forward slowly, he strained to hear his family speaking, it seemed like an eternity since he had heard their spoken words. He could pick out his sisters, Charlie was standing very close. Someone brushed against him to reach past for his mother's arm, he guessed it would be his dad as he heard her begin to cry, his father trying to reassure her but also trying to prepare her for the worst.

"Our boy isn't doing so well Nellie but I'm glad you came to see him."

Soft gentle crying surrounded Alfie. God this was the hardest thing he had ever had to do, he just wanted to pull back the hood, rip off the binding and scream from the top of his lungs, "It's me, I'm here."

Seraphina sensing his anguish moved silently across the room and placed a reassuring hand upon his shoulder. *Steel yourself my young friend soon all the truth will made known but we must be guided by Arksanza, there be a right way to do this, patience my young friend.* She looked across to Arksanza and Eisiam as they leant over the doppelgänger, machines monitoring its condition, beeping and alarms going off, scuttling nurses and doctors at a loss do anything more. It was futile, the body laid before them all looked all but dead, greyish white waxy skin, bubbles of perspiration glinting under the unforgiving harsh white light of the room, a rasping laboured sound of ever-decreasing breath, each one causing his brothers and sisters to hold their own whilst they willed their little brother to take another. Alfie really couldn't stand it anymore, his body trembling as he fought to control his Awakening, the hood over his face making him sweat, adding to the sense of panic. Now voices, new voices he had never heard before filtered into his mind. His head began to swim, he could feel himself swaying, the rasping gravelly voices urging him to give in, surrender to his urge, telling him the doppelgänger was his brother, telling him he should protect it, the others in the room were all traitors sent to trick him, all the time his heart thumping louder and louder, blood racing through his body, his fists clenched to try and stem the building rage. A symphony of noise and confusion in his head, while in the room the machines were all going off now, the doppelgänger growling and fitting, foam splurting from its mouth Arksanza shouting above it all, ordering Elancie to end it now. *They're going to kill it, don't let them kill it!* said the voices in his head. Ripping his hood from his head and clawing at the binding covering his eyes, a primal scream surged from his stomach as the blinding light seem to scold his eyes. For seconds the whole room stood still as he adjusted his eyesight the first face he came upon, his father's, then panic ensued.

"What the bloody hell is going on?" shouted Mark, as Faerian warriors grabbed and restrained Alfie's family and the medical staff, Arksanza now bellowing as Alfie stood frozen stunned at his father's horrified face, his sisters crying whilst his brothers struggled to free themselves. It was a chaotic room full of pandemonium, no one really knowing what was happening. Still a war went on in Alfie's head the voices telling him to turn and greet his doppelgänger, other voices telling him to keep his back turned.

"Do not make eye contact, avert your face, do not listen to the spirits of the underworld." Elancie ran amongst them all like a berserk child throwing dust up into the air chanting. Seraphina grabbed him, pulling him to the floor and covering both hers and his nose and mouth with her cape protecting them from the dust. Out of the corner of his eye Alfie could see that the Faerians all followed suit, grappling his family members to the ground protecting them with their capes from the effect of the dust. The doctors nurses exposed, some of them already dropping to their knees slumping in a heap, overcome by the Magiks cast by Elancie, Alfie trying to call out to his Father and siblings not to fight back that they would come to no harm..

Seraphina pulled out her knife. "Give me your hand," she ordered Alfie. "I need your blood." He was still shell-shocked and confused. *She means to trick you, to kill you. Fight her, fight her.* His eyes flitted back and forth, he could see her speak but the voices in his head grew louder and louder overwhelming him. He did not know what to believe and this unnatural urge to turn to face his doppelgänger was growing like he had unseen hands upon him clawing at him, twisting his body. His muscles trembled with the exertion of fighting back, his neck wrenching to turn his head, the sound of the doppelgänger roaring at him like it was demanding his attention.

"The doppelgänger is aware, it knows you are here," shouted Arksanza as the doppelgänger sat bolt upright causing Eisiam and Alfie's sisters to scream as the creature held out its arms towards Alfie. *See your brother knows you greet him*, said the insidious voices torturing him, his Father and family in an absolute state of confusion looking at the doppelgänger and then back to Alfie, then back to the doppelgänger. In amongst all this madness Nellie had somehow slipped away from Eisiam who was now more concerned for Alfie. Nellie had made her way around the outside of the room avoiding the chaos in the centre to stand directly before the creature.

As she rolled down her scarf from her face, she leant forward and hissed at it, "Leave my son alone, he doesn't belong to you." It chilled her to the bone this perfect replica of her son, like he was carved from alabaster, still spitting and screeching indignantly at the presence of Alfie. Deep within her she felt a rising sense of unexplainable strength and anger, she now knew in her heart for sure that this creature was a pretender and her beloved son stood at the end of the room. As though it knew who she was it began to mimic faces, faces Alfie made as a child at her. She could not be swayed, her guilt at not having believed Alfie drove her on. Snatching Eisiam's knife from the floor, she launched herself upon the bed, sitting astride the doppelgänger she plunged it deep in to its chest. A blood-curdling scream filled the air as it slapped at Nellie flaying its arms about her head, trying to knock her from the bed, scratching at her face. There was no blood only white ooze that had fooled the medical staff for so long under Elancie's Magiks. She was shocked. How was she to kill this thing if it did not bleed? And if anything it seemed to becoming stronger with each stab of the blade. Alfie could hear his mother but not see her; he desperately wanted to help her.

"Give me your hand, this will save your mother and save you," bellowed Seraphina. She snatched up his hand flipped it over to expose his palm and without any hesitation she drew the sharp blade across it. Alfie winced as the stinging burning sensation drew across his hand but he didn't struggle even though the spirits of the underworld were bombarding him, it took every ounce of strength to resist them whilst Seraphina laid the blade across his palm. "Close your hand around it. Good, now be opening it." She lifted it up coated in bright red blood. "Elancie be you ready with the casting spell?"

"Yes milady." Then Seraphina turned her attention to Nellie still battling with the doppelgänger.

"Nellie of the Delaney clan hear my roar warrior," she cried as she launched the knife covered in Alfie's blood at the back of Nellie who turning with ninja-like skills caught the knife by the butt and plunged it straight into the heart of the doppelgänger. An eerie silence fell upon the room as the once pale creature began to turn a deep red as the blood from Alfie filled its veins. Shuddering as the veins flowed crimson Nellie was confused. What had she done? It didn't look like it was dying more the opposite, like it was stealing life back. Mark snatched her down albeit on wobbly legs as his senses began to return.

"The blood that gave you life takes back that life, away with you back to Mother Earth." Elancie drew out a sword and in one swift move chopped the head from the doppelgänger, it had barely hit the floor before the remaining torso began to disintegrate, bubbling and dissolving like acid melting through flesh.

Arksanza quickly wrapped the head in his cape, "We must be returning this to the mud pit to complete the spell, the rest must be burned by fire. Weslan that be your task."

Alfie whispered in a dry hoarse voice, "Can I turn around now?"

Seraphina kissed him on his forehead. "Yes I believe you can." He pulled the remaining binding from his neck and wrapped it around his hand slowly turning to face his stunned family.

"I…" That was all he managed to get out before the tears fell and his family all launched themselves at him, tears of joy all around, gasps of disbelief, pokes and prods.

"Where's your belly gone?"

"Where's his tatty shorts?"

"What no tomato sauce down yer front?"

There was laughter and then more tears as the Faerians stood back for a moment before Alfie jumped into host mode introducing everyone, handshakes and greetings passed between the two races, Risla showing Tallulah his Barracness toad. Alfie was shocked normally she would have screamed the place down and run a mile but she was obviously taken by the tall gangly Faerian, Alfie just smiled as she cooed over the toad like it was a cute little kitten. Arksanza and Seraphina greeted his parents as Nellie thanked them for keeping him safe.

"We still not be safe Nellie Diamond. In fact we must be away to the House of Magdalene Delaney as quickly as possible. The Gorans will soon be upon us."

Nellie could see her other children looking confused, "Grandma Maggie's."

"Oh," came in unison.

"Is everyone recovered from the dust?" called out Elancie as he helped up anyone looking groggy.

"We must be on the move." Arksanza passed over the bundled up head of the doppelgänger and the remains from the bed and sheet to Weslan and his warriors. "Make haste my friend the sooner this be done the better. Remember the head be to the pit and the rest be burnt until there are just cinders." Weslan bowed and walked towards Alfie.

"If I never be seeing you again it has been an honour to be in the company of Alfie Diamond of the Delaney clan. I shall be having many tales to be telling my sons."

"And your daughters," piped up Jodie. He turned smiled, bowed to her and with that they were gone.

Seraphina scanned the room, checking the state of each person, assessing them for the next stage of their journey, all of them full of questions but having to put on hold any replies. This was not the time or the place.

Arksanza was also making plans. "Will Manutik be at the house? We will need his knowledge of the Harpy Caverns," he asked Seraphina.

Alfie's ears pricked up at the mention of Manutik's name. "So the rescue was successful then?" he questioned Seraphina.

"Yes," and before Alfie could even ask. "Yes Misa will be being at the house, the whole family must be evacuated together." Alfie's heart sank the thought of this dirty little secret unnerved him. In the background he could hear his sister Tallulah saying something about a pretty blue colour. He looked around to see where Risla was, he was attempting to pick up some of the knocked about furniture.

"Isn't it pretty? Look I think it likes me, look," she said shoving the toad at Jodie and Mollie.

"Let me…" Alfie cried snatching the toad away from her.

"Oh rude, Risla said I could hold it!"

"Risla!" shouted Alfie. "Your toad!" he said holding it up in the air for all to see as the stiffening toad was overcome with paralysis and its skin burst out in a vivid indigo colour. Seraphina gasped and ran to the window forcing it open, her Lockan already fizzing with life. Arksanza placed his hand upon the closed door; a cold blank expression came over his face as he focused.

"They are not outside but they not be far."

Alfie and Eisiam shouted, "What do you want us to do?"

Seraphina began snatching at the sheets, "Check the cupboards, we need more to reach the ground," hurling a pile at Risla. "Bind them together to make a rope, ensure they be tightly knotted." At which Risla whipped out his knife and began shredding the sheets into lengths.

Alfie's father stepped forward. "What can we do to help?" he asked Arksanza.

"Gather the furniture and build a barricade that should give us some more time but please be doing it quickly but quietly, the Gorans do not yet know for sure which room we be in." He then turned to Elancie. "Can you be working your Magiks once more my friend?" Elancie nodded and gathered everything into a small sack. Arksanza placed his hand upon Elancie's shoulder. "We be needing an illusion from the other side of the door, it will be taking time to get everyone out through the window and down to the ground, the longer we can keep the Gorans from discovering us the better."

Alfie lunged at Elancie. "You cannot go outside the door they will find and kill you!"

Tallulah gasped. "Who will? Who are the Gorans?" she demanded her eyes large and full of fear.

Alfie corrected himself and mind spoke to Arksanza, *You do realize it is a death sentence that awaits Elancie.*

Arksanza ignored the boy. "As soon as you are able slip away and meet up with us at the Lair. May the gods of the two worlds shine fortune upon you." The two Faerians hugged and Elancie edged carefully through the door mindful of the stack of furniture precariously balanced against it. "Quickly," ordered Arksanza, "finish the barricade," as he rushed to the open window. "Risla you go down first check out the area and keep the sheeting stable. Come everyone line up." Seraphina finished securing one end to a solid concrete pillar in the middle of the room and flung the other end to Risla who perched on the edge of the window frame in readiness to begin his descent. Alfie took his sister Tallulah's hand and led her to the opening, they both watched Risla descend quickly and expertly. Alfie knew of all of them Tallulah would struggle with the height. He hoped to persuade her to remain calm without having to scare her down with tales of horror about the Gorans but before he had a chance to speak she was scraping up her hair into a bun, tucking her phone safely into her bra and calling down to Risla in the most sickly-sweet girly voice.

"You will catch me if I fall won't you Risla?" a beaming Risla below eagerly nodded. Alfie rolled his eyes at his father who winked and two seconds later she was over the edge and gone. Her sisters quickly followed and one after the other they all quickly but quietly descended to the ground unharmed. The last to leave was Seraphina she untied the sheet pulled up the length throwing it all into a pile.

"What's she doing?" asked Charlie. "How's she gonna get down now, silly mare?" as he watched the athletic Faerian woman slip along the sill, slide the window down gently closing it and then stand calves together, arms out, head tilted and draw in a deep breath as she launched herself off twisting and spinning several times like an Olympic high diver before securely landing her feet.

Alfie beamed with pride. "Silly mare eh?" he said nudging Charlie in the back.

"Wow, what a woman!" he muttered back to his little brother as Em slapped him across his shoulder.

"Of course I could have done it like that, I just didn't want to put you guys under pressure," said their dad. They all groaned and Arksanza patted Mark on the back.

"Another time my friend maybe."

Nellie gathered her family together. "We must do exactly what Seraphina, Risla and Arksanza ask us to do. They kept Alfie safe and I believe that they wish to do the same for us, so no more messing this isn't a game." She looked to her youngest son. "I don't know how or why you are involved in all this but I do see that you trust your friends so lead the way Alfie." Seraphina smiled at her young charge her heart felt it would burst with pride, how he had grown in maturity in such a short time, shown

267

a willingness to take responsibility. She knew one day he would prove himself worthy of the title 'The Redeemer'.

Arksanza called them to come close. "Firstly we must be keeping to the shadows until we reach the vehicles, we must then travel to the house of Magdalene Delaney. Upon our arrival I wish everyone to linger outside to act as though you be joyous at the return of Alfie, be sure to call his name loudly in celebration." They all looked dumbfounded, all except Alfie. He already knew that the silver ravens, ready and waiting to spy, would be there at the house although he hadn't yet worked out why Arksanza was so keen to flaunt their presence but that was the least of his worries. His main concern was Misa. How on earth was this going to turn out? He kept flicking sneaky looks at his mother and picking at the skin around his thumb, his nervousness getting the better of him.

They had snaked their way around to the minivan dipping in and out of the bushes, only moving in small groups where they couldn't avoid the lights of the car park all the time, Arksanza and Seraphina holding back to make sure they were not followed. Once everyone had safely made it they quickly got into the van and flicked over the engine. It spluttered and coughed. Again Mark flicked it over but it steadfastly refused to kick into life.

"You didn't leave the lights on again did you?" called out Nellie.

"NO!" came the sharp reply.

"Well what is it then?" called Charlie. Again the engine rumbled and juddered.

"I don't bloody know, I'm not a mechanic. It probably got damp and the plugs need warming, it's been sitting here all day."

Seraphina jumped out. "Where be the plug thing that needs heat?" she demanded growing tired of the delay. Mark looked at her through the windscreen hands on her hips.

Risla leaned forward and whispered in his ear, "You best be telling her, save yourself a whole lot of trouble." He slipped back into the safety of the relative darkness of the rear seats away from Seraphina's glare. Mark gulped and leant forward to pop the bonnet.

"Show Seraphina where the plugs are Georgie." Georgie had been settling himself for a nice chat with Alfie about what the bloody hell he had been doing all these days whilst his family thought he was on his last legs.

"But I was going to talk to Tiny Pickled Onion."

His father sighed, "That can wait go and show her. Hurry up she looks like she is getting impatient." Alfie grinned at his brother.

"Is she some kind of lady wrestler? She's not going to choke slam me on the roof of the van or something is she?"

Eisiam spoke gently. "She merely wishes to help so please be pointing out the piece of this contraption that appears to be failing." Georgie was mesmerized by her soft voice and serene expression staring at her doe-eyed. Suddenly he received a quick swift kick to his butt. It was Alfie.

"Get out then, we will be here all night." Georgie jumped to his feet and scuttled around the front, there was a lot of muttering then suddenly the van sparked into life. Everyone cheered as Georgie slammed shut the bonnet triumphantly and he and Seraphina reclaimed their seats.

"Well I never, how did you do that?" exclaimed Mark.

"She put her hand over it and heated up the plugs, glowing they were, like magic."

"It was magic," whispered Alfie under his breath.

"Now are we all present and correct?" called back Mark.

"No, Charlie's gone for a wee in the bushes," shouted back Mollie.

"Oh Jesus Christ how long has he been?"

"A couple of minutes. He shouldn't be much longer," came the reply. Everyone got fidgety. Arksanza got out and softly called Charlie hoping he wasn't too far from the van and could hear him.

There was a lot of shaking of trees and a muffled voice, "Two seconds."

Seraphina was by now becoming very agitated. "We must be on the move lest the Gorans begin to search outside. To be

269

sure they will have discovered the room. Elancie's Magiks cannot prevail much longer." Alfie felt her anxiety she was sensing the closeness of the Goran warriors, they really couldn't be that far.

Alfie leaned out the door. "Charlie move your bloody arse."

His mother gave him a look and then she leant out and shouted, "If you are on your phone I will slap you and flush the damn thing down the loo." Turning to Eisiam and Em, "The boy is obsessed with some stupid game, he never tires of it, drives me up the bloody wall."

Mollie started flapping her hands and stuttering. "What is it are you choking?" said Jodie.

"No, no look!" thrusting the toad in her sister's face.

"Erk don't do that, its slimy foot nearly went in my mouth!"

"Look. Look Risla!" as she practical threw the poor toad at him.

He instantly spun around looking through the windscreen and hissed at Mark, "Turn off the lights," as the once again rigid toad alerted them to the Gorans. A deathly silence fell over the van; they all froze into their positions. Seraphina strained to see into the darkness ahead of them, she could just make out the form of a person but could not be sure if it was a Goran. Alfie concentrated to try and pick up any conversation that might be passing between the warriors but it was just a jumble of mixed words from lots of voices, people in nearby cars, visitors in the hospital, even his family sitting in the car, his dad in particular massively stressing out in his head. Alfie placed his hand upon his dad's shoulder.

"Keep calm we will get through this, just listen to Arksanza."

A wry smile spread across his dad's face. "Seems that a lot of changes are coming our way lad."

"Yes indeed Pops you don't know the half of it." Alfie noticed Seraphina walk across the front of the van and then disappear into the darkness. "Arksanza where has Seraphina gone?"

"What do you mean gone?" he called back from around the back. "By the two gods, your brother surely be pushing my patience. Charlie return immediately or we be leaving without you," he yelled, as Alfie approached him. Again he asked, "Where has she gone?"

Alfie shook his head. "I don't know I thought you told her to go and find Charlie." They both began to call Charlie's name this time with real anxiety, there was no way he could be taking this long especially as he knew they were keen to be on the move. Then the bushes and trees began to rustle and snap before them, they could just make out two figures. Alfie let out a sigh of relief, "Jesus Charlie sometimes you do my head in," as he stepped forward.

Arksanza snatched him back. "Wait," he whispered. Arksanza's Lockan fizzed and popped with energy, the indigo blue hue lighting up the area instantly drawing everyone's attention. "Stay in the van," he ordered, their faces all placed firmly to the glass of the rear window. Still the shaking and rustling of the leaves could be heard. Alfie could feel his heart rate rising. "Concentrate boy what do you feel?"

Alfie was shocked. "Are you really giving me a lesson now?"

"No my boy this is for real. Hone your skills and tell me what you feel they draw near, quickly."

A flash of an image fleetingly zapped into his mind. "I see a Goran not like any I have seen."

"Describe it."

"Much shorter very squat, hairy, beast-like, no piercings, god damn ugly is the one word for it." Arksanza hauled Alfie over to the side of the van as the very same beast stepped into the light dragging with it Charlie, his head in a headlock spluttering unable to speak so tight was the grip of the Goran.

"Charlie!" shouted Alfie as he tried to wriggle free from Arksanza.

"No boy it be holding a blade to his neck hold back," as Risla appeared from out of the van followed by Mark.

"Jesus what the bloody hell is it?" Mollie shouted from inside nearly hysterical. "Is it a Goran?" as she clung to her mother. Eisiam stood by her brother's side both in combat mode both with bad tempered Lockans fired and ready, still Charlie coughed.

"Do something," shouted Jodie. "He's gonna choke to death."

"What is it?" said Alfie.

Arksanza replied, "It be a foot soldier they be very simple in mind but grievously evil in thought, one step up from their Gorja hounds." The creature snarled and snorted at them rocking back and forth taunting them, challenging them to come forward.

A stalemate developed. Arksanza knew it wouldn't be alone they seldom were, normally they came in packs of three, so two more could possibly be lurking close by if the reaction of the toad was anything to go by, not least any others. The commanders of the Gorans would not have sent Durras inside the hospital because of their appearance.

Nellie had now come to the side of Arksanza. "Help my son." But as the words left her mouth a blinding blue light flashed from behind the Durras, a snapping crackle and smell of burning flesh, then a second and third came, so fast, so quick like forked lightning. The Durras staggered forwarded letting go of Charlie as he slumped to the ground. Alfie lunged forward to his brother kicking away the blade whilst Arksanza, Seraphina and Risla finished off the Durras, three final mortal strikes and it was dealt with. Mark rushed to help Alfie drag his brother to the van.

"Get him inside, everyone get inside. There are more coming I can feel it," shouted Alfie almost hysterical with the fear he felt. They flung Charlie unceremoniously into the back of the van with Em and Mollie washing his face off checking for wounds and giving him some water to drink. Mark had already slammed into gear and wheel spun out of the car park as at least 12 Gorans scampered out of the darkness alongside the van clawing at the windows screeching like banshees. A sudden thud and one was on the roof, the younger girls screamed as they were all flung about like rag dolls as Mark swerved from side to side trying to dislodge the unwanted passenger. Suddenly a long pointed blade sliced through the metal of the roof. Again chaos and ear-piercing screams erupted as they all tried to move away from it. The blade disappeared only to reappear somewhere else, one, two, three, four times. Alfie was getting sick of this now. A second Goran launched itself at the speeding vehicle bounding up the bonnet and somehow clinging to the wipers. Mark switched them on as the Goran slid down the front but dug its claws into the grid under the window. It swung back its fist and pounded it hard into the glass a tiny fracture etched its way across the surface, then a second assault and a third.

Mark hollered at the top of his voice, "This glass is coming in. Someone better do something quick." Risla jumped to the front pulled out his knife and timed his swing with that of the Goran attempting to bring down his fists again. Risla punched through the glass shattering it into tiny particles showering Mark in debris.

"Keep going," shouted Risla as he slammed the knife into the hand of the Goran clinging to the front, the creature screeched with the pain and was forced to let go but managing to bring his other hand over to stop himself slipping down and under the wheels. Risla frustrated with anger screamed at the Goran, "By the two gods, die you foul creature!" It just looked back up at him and grinned. Risla's Lockan fired up as he clambered up on to the dash and exited out the window throwing back his head and lashing his Lockan round, whipping the arm of the Goran, slicing it perfectly from the hand. The telltale bumping of the van was a sign that the Goran had gone under the wheels. Risla stood up holding the window frame looking back to see the other Goran but he was too far for him to reach with his Lockan, he slipped back inside to be greeted by Tallulah.

"Oh my god that was so brave," she said as yet another blade sliced into the roof. He yanked her down as the blade missed her by millimetres.

Nellie yelled at her, "Get your hormones in check this is neither the time nor the place." Tallulah flushed red and threw herself to the prickly carpet of the floor.

Alfie could feel his anger rise, "I'm going to do something about this crap." He placed his hand upon the ceiling.

Georgie snatched his hand back. "What you doing you nutter? That thing up there could stab you in the hand!"

Alfie pulled his arm away from his brother, "Let go I can do this!" Georgie went to grab him again but Seraphina held him back.

"Let your brother try."

Georgie just looked at her. "Are you mad? You may be some sort of superhero ninja woman, he's just my little brother."

"Have faith," and then she turned to Alfie. "Controlled and outwards, one hand only." Alfie nodded took a deep breath placed his hand up on the ceiling his arm trembling, his chest glowing, his eyes blazing green and he let his breath out. A boom sounded up and out blasting a hole in the metal sending the Goran screeching, soaring and clutching at its face until he could no longer be seen as the car careered down the road leaving the remaining Gorans for dust.

"Floor it Dad," shouted Charlie whilst everyone else sat staring at Alfie and the glowing talisman in his chest.

"Oh yeah, that's something else I've got tell you about," he smiled sheepishly.

"How far do we be travelling to reach our destination?"

Mark called back, "Not far, ten more minutes at this speed."

Arksanza looked back. "It seems we be clear at the moment perhaps we can be slowing down a little, we do not wish to be attracting the attention of your security forces."

Tallulah giggled. "You mean police." The mood lightened a bit as they all began to wind down still shell-shocked, still reeling from the events just passed but with relief that they had all survived. Nellie looked up through the hole in the roof at the dark sky with sparkling twinkling stars as they rushed closer to home. Home that was a funny word, it didn't feel like home, it never had her whole life and yet she felt that somehow some of its secrets might be opened up to her for the first time ever. She shuddered with anticipation mixed with a little excitement and fear, and pulled her youngest son to her. She ruffled his hair and sniffed his smell deep into her lungs.

"Mum!" protested Alfie. This was her boy, she knew that smell and no one was ever going to take him from her again.

"Whatever happens or is said tonight I want you to know I am very proud of you and we will face this as a family, what will be will be." Alfie hugged his mother still with a nagging uncertainty of how Misa would be received. He looked across to Seraphina as she smiled at him and mind spoke.

Have faith little one, your family's love is strong, your mother is strong, all will be well. He gripped his mother harder as the van came to a stop at the beginning of the long drive down to the house.

Arksanza sat forward as he and Mark surveyed the house, it was dark, a solitary foreboding structure against the night sky.

"The way appears to be clear. Remember when we pull up be as boisterous as you wish to be, we must light up the house quickly. We must be in plain sight of the silver ravens, they be at roost in the trees surrounding the house of Magdalene Delaney."

Tallulah piped up, "Why does he keep calling Grandma's house that Mum?"

Nellie sighed. "There is a lot you do not know about your Grandmother and the fact that her real name was Magdalene is one of them. I only found out purely by chance when I went through some old papers I found in her attic and even then I just thought she had just shortened it to Maggie for ease but I get the feeling there was more to the name change and we shall probably find out the real reason tonight." She looked across to Seraphina who smiled at her reassuringly. Nellie began to mentally prepare herself for whatever came her way. They all got out, Mark ran up the steps and flung open the huge door, he stepped inside and flicked on the hallway lights and the switch to control the security lights outside. The whole house was bathed in a sheet of illuminating white. There could be no mistaking that they were home, even the lanterns that lined the road down to the house pinged out in the dark. Whilst everyone else made a good job of being pleased to be home with their brother, Arksanza and Seraphina surveyed the trees listening for the sound of feather against feather taking flight, the glint of the silver wings making ready to lift off and the giveaway red eyes like rubies in a sea of mottled greens, browns and splayed out branches.

"Let us be away inside and drink to the safe return of Alfie Diamond of the Delaney clan," called out Risla as they made their way up into the house, closing the door behind them to stand silently in the hallway listening to the mass exodus of the silver ravens. For a good minute all they could hear was the rising roaring whoosh and squawks of the leaving birds. They had got what they came for, what they had waited for patiently all these days, taking flight back to their masters the Gorans to deliver their glad tidings, the boy, the family, all under one roof.

Like a game of musical statues, no one dared move, breathe loudly or even flick an eye for minutes after the silence fell outside beyond the barricading front door. The darkness seemed to shrink in on them, stifling and menacing. Nellie couldn't stand it any further, she hated the house in daylight and being inside in pitch-black dampness clinging to her arms did nothing for her mood.

She hissed, "For god's sake can we put the bloody lights on now?" Arksanza stood to her right she could just make out his silhouette against the window as her eyes adjusted.

"Yes but first we must be drawing the awnings."

Alfie was confused. "You mean the curtains."

Mark was getting tetchy. "Does it really matter what they are called? Quickly everyone run to the windows upstairs and down. I presume you believe there might be someone still watching?" as he turned to speak to a faceless Arksanza in the dark.

"Yes indeed there will be, so we must ensure they cannot see inside or the preparations we make, so hurry to cover the windows." Alfie shot off ahead, like he was on a mission.

"What's with him?" whispered Georgie to Charlie.

"Probs looking for food," he chuckled.

Food was the last thing on his mind somewhere in this house was Manutik and more importantly Misa; he needed to find them before his mother who wasn't too far behind him. Each room he came to he flung one curtain across and then the other pulling them tight to obscure any gaps, some rooms had more than one set. Frustrated at the time it was taking, he began to sweat as panic set in.

"Where the bloody hell are they?" he muttered to himself. He decided if he were hiding in this house the round room at the very top would be a good option so he set off in that direction. He could hear his mother speaking with his sisters they seemed pretty close.

He heard one of them say, "Alfie must have done this, look they are drawn and the lights and lamps are on."

He spun on his heels, *Must go faster*, as he found himself at the bottom of the stairs to the round room. He placed his hand against the door and standing on tiptoes reached up to let his fingertips search for the slight indent which sheltered the key. It was thick with dust which made him cough and sneeze as the liberated dust flew into the air. His mother had thought the location of the key was a guarded secret but she didn't allow for six nosey kids hell-bent on finding out the secret of the round room. In actuality when they had stepped softly and quietly into the open door, how their hearts had fallen. It was empty except for a few old tea chests and they were just stuffed with screwed up newspaper.

"Bloody hell what a crock of shit. There's sod all here," stamped Charlie in raging annoyance.

"Don't do that maybe the floor is rotten," Georgie tutted at his brother.

"If you believe that baloney, then you're a few slices short of a loaf." There a was no big secret, no hidden monster and certainly no batty old lady locked away from the world by her family. They all sloped off down the stairs completely defeated and dumbfounded but mostly confused at the insistence of their mother that they were not to go up there.

Now as Alfie strained to discover the key, he slightly unbalanced himself, grabbing hold of the fixed metallic door handle, only it wasn't solid it tipped downwards with his weight, it was unlocked! He gulped and tentatively edged it open desperately trying to stop it from creaking with tiny, tiny movements but it was to no avail. Alfie was convinced the whole house would be alerted to his invasion of the forbidden room, the groans of the door defiantly disobeying him. He decided one quick yank would end the agony but remembered to not let the handle slam into the plastered wall.

He jumped back caught unawares by a huge dark shadow filling the space at the top of the stairs.

A booming voice calling down, "Did I be scaring you?"

"SHUSH!" he hissed recognizing the man mountain above him as Solgiven. "Do you want to let everyone know you are in here? Jesus! And anyway how were you sure I wasn't a Goran or something else, shouting down like that?" he asked as he sprang up the steps three at a time, desperate to silence Solgiven. "Man alive, aren't you capable of whispering?"

Solgiven looked puzzled. "That's what I be doing."

A voice came from the shadows, "The boy does have a point father." It was Misa as she stepped into a shaft of moonlight that sliced across the room, illuminating her face. Alfie stuttered as he realized they were not alone something or someone stood silently in the corner.

Alfie called out, "Manutik?" A soft slow shuffle was heard as he edged out from the protection of the darkness.

Misa skipped passed Alfie and grabbed Manutik's hand. "This is my friend Manutik," she announced protectively. Alfie could just about make out his face and even though he was expecting a gnarled leathery face with a heavy jaw and protruding teeth, he was equally taken aback by the softness of his expressive eyes and his whole demeanour, as though he was willing Alfie to accept him. Alfie instantly reached for his Manutik's hand and pulled him forward to greet him.

"I'm so pleased to meet you. You did a great thing in rescuing Misa, I am sure Seraphina and Arksanza will be as glad as well. What a brave thing you did, isn't it Solgiven?" Alfie was very aware that he was over talking, over gesticulating, with no pause for breath, verging on the point of rambling and he was very uncomfortable with the fact that all three were staring at him with puzzled expressions on their faces. Change the subject he kept thinking. "Anyhow, how did you know it was me?" he turned to Solgiven.

"Simple the stench of your feet, that not be an odour I be forgetting so soon." Alfie hung his head in shame.

Misa tried to lighten the mood. "My father be having an extreme sense of smell on account that he be such a good hunter, I would not be worrying." Alfie smiled at her and yet he was troubled, she didn't give off any indication that she was aware of the impending meeting with her sister Nellie, she seemed too calm.

Alfie turned to Solgiven. "Do you want to help me with covering the windows? Arksanza wants the light blocked out, just in case there are any Gorans outside. I think there are some old blankets in a cupboard downstairs," he nodded his head in the direction of the stairs.

"I could help," offered Misa.

"Nah you're alright, your father can help me, the blankets will no doubt be covered in dust and they're pretty heavy. Come on Solgiven this way," as he attempted to tug the large man. Alfie had barely reached the bottom step before he turned on Solgiven. "She doesn't bloody know!" he shouted furious that Misa was unaware of the situation.

Solgiven fumbled his words, "I, she, doesn't be knowing what?"

Alfie rigid with temper cried, "Stop sodding about! You know exactly what I mean. Why haven't you told her? What if I had said something?"

Solgiven fiddled with his belt. "I would not have let you be saying anything I listened carefully to your speech." Alfie by now was pacing up and down the corridor like a caged tiger.

"Oh what would you have done, flattened me to the ground, broken a couple of ribs or smashed my face into the wooden floor? Very subtle, that wouldn't have looked at all suspicious."

Solgiven tutted. "I be at a loss as to what you wish me to be saying and I detect a tone in your voice which if the truth be known I do not care for." Raving like a proper nutter but in a hissed whispered form Alfie wanted to bellow at Solgiven. Then it suddenly hit him. Solgiven should not have been anywhere near this house, darkness had descended, his energy would have been spent and he surely should have returned to his home to prepare to regenerate himself and his solar blade.

"How is it you are here and where is your blade?" he whispered.

Quickly looking over his shoulder Solgiven replied, "I did not wish to let my only daughter find out the truths of her origins without me by her side. What kind of a father would that make? She will be scared and confused."

Alfie was so angry, "You won't be much use to us or Misa if you pass out and coming crashing to the ground." Solgiven dug about in his tunic and pulled a small pouch, shaking it with a wry smile upon his face. Alfie looked confused.

"Come closer. See," said Solgiven untying the tightly bound pouch, a luminous glow seeping out.

"What is it?" whispered Alfie as his face lit up.

"Moonstones!" announced Solgiven triumphantly.

"What do you do with them eat them?"

Solgiven tutted. "Do not be trying to annoy me, of course not. I hold them and absorb their energy. They have been enchanted by the Moon Maidens but I can only use this one time until I get back to the safety of the Lair." He looked at Alfie as though he had accomplished some great deed which Alfie did not appreciate.

"Why are so pleased with yourself? You're making a dangerous situation all the more difficult and no doubt putting a strain on Misa, she will be worried. You should have told her before now."

"I didn't want to. I don't want her to know."

A small voice came from behind the door. "Know what?" asked Misa staring at them both waiting for an answer.

"Oh nothing my child. Go back up, we will bring the blankets." But she refused to move and now she was joined by Manutik.

"What do you argue about? We could hear the disturbance upstairs."

Alfie glared at Solgiven. "See big gob."

Again Misa questioned them. "I not be the village idiot, I feel something passes between you. There is a hostility, I can sense it."

Solgiven hung his head whilst Alfie frantically sent a message to Seraphina. *It's all hit the fan, you best get up here now.*

She replied with, *Speak plain English boy, I'm busy at this minute, I be laying salt at all the entrance points to this house.*

The salt will have to wait. What's the salt for? Oh I don't care just get up here. He could feel Misa's eyes burn into the back of his head.

Seraphina quickly finished casting the salt and the protective barrier Magiks and then went off in pursuit of Arksanza inside the house. She called out to him and he quickly found her.

"We have a problem Alfie needs us all to join him and the others at the top of the house." Arksanza walked into the kitchen where they had all gathered, half opened packets of biscuits, the butter with the lid off, a block of cheese with crackers strewn about the worktop, the freshly boiled kettle still steaming, with a jar of dried powdered milk and little packets of sugar niftily pinched from the many coffee shops that Nellie had visited all randomly spread about amongst the hungry, thirsty family. They all turned to look at Arksanza in anticipation.

"We must move up to the upper floor, please do not ask questions bring your food with you. Come, follow me." As he walked passed Seraphina he lowered his voice. "Do you be having all that is necessary to create an Orb?"

Solemnly she nodded and then mind spoke to Alfie. *We are coming. Do not put on the lights, until Arksanza has spoken to everyone.*

Alfie at this point was jumping from one foot to the other like a cat on a hot tin roof, still trying to fob Misa off with a story of some kind but she was having none of it, she steadfastly refused to accept that they hadn't been having an argument which she strongly believed involved her somehow. Alfie almost let out a cheer when he heard the first footsteps on the landing below coming closer.

Solgiven also took the chance to sidetrack Misa, "Come we must get the windows covered Arksanza will not be best pleased we have not carried out his orders." She eyed him up and down and then relented allowing him to escort her back up the stairs.

"Leave the lights out till we are told to put them on," called Alfie after them, he waited to greet everyone coming up, he could hear them chatting amongst themselves, as they appeared around the corner.

"Ooh this is all a bit spooky isn't it?" giggled Tallulah as she gripped at her mother's hand. Nellie tried to laugh back but she was nervous as hell, something was coming her way and it was something big, every fibre in her body felt like it was on fire. She knew she needed to prepare herself she just did not know what for. Alfie felt he must prepare them for their first sighting of a Goran up close and personal even if he was friendly.

"There is someone upstairs that I wish you to meet, he is not a Durras or Goran." Arksanza looked panic-stricken but Seraphina stopped him from speaking allowing Alfie to finish what he was saying. "He is very brave and courageous. Please do not judge him by his looks, I truly wish you to welcome him." As he finished Solgiven appeared behind the door.

"Are you ready to come up?" he boomed. They all jumped and clung to each other in awe of the big man in front.

"Seriously, are you sure they aren't all from an American wrestling tag team because I am really having my doubts," said Georgie as he tucked in behind his dad.

Arksanza stepped forward, "Yes my friend, we shall come now," as he led the way. Alfie slipped in behind his mother and pulled her close to him wrapping his arms around her from behind. She patted his hand and tipped her head back on to his chest, she could feel his heart thumping through his chest.

"Don't worry it will all come out in the wash," she said, one of her weird family sayings. Another one was 'no point crying over spilt milk' or 'well I'll go to the foot of our stairs' none of which seemed suitable for this occasion.

"Why isn't the light on? We'll all be tripping over each other," said Mark. "There is someone else in here not just your big mate, who is it?" Tallulah and Jodie let out a nervous squeak, Mollie announced she didn't like it and Em buried her head into Charlie's jumper.

Seraphina spoke to both Alfie and Arksanza. *There be no more point in keeping Misa from Nellie, simply reveal her then I can prepare the Orb and all will be explained. We be fighting a losing battle to keep this painless and easy, it will never be so, best we just get on with it.*

Arksanza asked Solgiven, "Are the windows shielded from the outside world?"

"Yes My Lord."

"Well then Mark you may switch on the lights." A few footsteps and the room was illuminated by a single unshaded bulb creating a small circle of light upon the floor. "Come in closer all of you. Please Misa and Manutik step forward into the centre," he called. As their eyes adjusted Nellie was the first to spot Manutik, Alfie felt his mother's body flinch but she quickly corrected herself and hastily offered her hand.

"You're very welcome in our home Manutik." The rest of her family quickly followed suit, just to close down the slightly awkward silence as they all gathered their thoughts and surprise at their guest. Manutik's broad warm smile put any fears aside and Tallulah and Eisiam were instantly asking questions about his piercings, Tallulah even showing off her tongue to reveal a shiny silver ball in the centre.

"When the bloody hell did you get that?" demanded Mark looking to Nellie to back him up but she was focusing on the small framed female standing behind Manutik. Alfie stayed close to his mother, he could sense her curiosity as she studied the face of the young woman in front of her and soon the rest of the room also became aware, turning their attention from Manutik to Misa.

"What's your name sweetie?" asked Nellie. Alfie felt like his heart hit the floor, a timid voice came forth.

"Misa, Misa daughter of Solgiven."

Always one to speak first and think later Tallulah piped up, "OMG Mum she looks like you, only she doesn't, but also bit like Jodie seeing as Jodie is younger than you. Well she would be wouldn't she because she is your daughter."

Alfie clamped his hand over Tallulah's mouth. "For once stop with the verbal diarrhoea," he whispered into his sister's ear. As the two sisters stared at each other, each one looking for similar if not the same traits, Nellie stepped closer and slowly put her hand up to Misa's covered hair.

"May I?" As she slipped the scarf from her head the long dark curls fell free, the same curls that Nellie and Alfie had, only Nellie's was now peppered a little with singular silver strands. She stared intently into the same green eyes she looked at each morning in her bathroom mirror. Misa placed her fingertips upon Nellie's cheek and pitter-pattered across the line of freckles that sprinkled across the bridge of her nose in exactly the same way hers did.

"Who are you?" asked Charlie unnerved by this stranger's resemblance to his mother and sister and to a point Alfie.

Again she repeated, "I am Misa." Misa turned to her father whose head hung to conceal his face. "Father, who are these people? Why do I look like them?" He could feel his heart crack, as he spoke the words out loud he would have given anything not to ever utter.

"They are your family," he blurted out through tears as she flung herself at him.

"What do you be saying? What do you mean? You be my family, my only family." He sobbed broken and forlorn, his anguish bring a lump to everyone in the room, all except Arksanza who decided to take control of this situation.

Slapping his hands together loudly he called out, "Come everyone sit upon the ground we will use the Magiks of Seraphina, to show you the story of your family. All will be revealed, all of your questions be answered. Nellie and Misa sit together, Solgiven beside your daughter, Alfie by your mother, everyone else behind."

Seraphina began to chant and had gathered the items from her pouch as well as dust from the floor. "This dust holds a story, a story that be hidden for too many years." There was absolute silence, hardly a breath drawn as the miracle of the Orb began to take shape. "No one must stand or touch the Orb." They all silently nodded in a agreement, none of this unexpected for Alfie as he had seen it all before but he watched the faces of his family, of Solgiven, Misa and his mother as the tale unfolded before their eyes, their gasps at the raid of the Goran minions, Maggie trying to fight them off, the agony of a mother her child stolen from her. Both Nellie and Misa sobbed as they watched their fate laid out before them, the sacrifice of their great-grandmother, Branna Deidra Delaney, the passing of the Awakening to Alfie. It was relentless one tragic event after another, scene after scene of their family history all flashing before their eyes, the powers of the Gemini, Nellie and Mimi, as Misa was named before her abduction, the legend of the Trinity of Delaney, Old Tom the eternal guardian and finally, for Nellie at least, the realization that her mother Maggie had indeed loved her but had pined for the lost child, the other half to her twin birth, the identical Nellie a constant daily reminder of the stolen Mimi, she turned to Misa who flung her arms around her.

"You are my sister."

"Yes I am." There was not a dry eye in the house as the Orb began to slow and softly disintegrate disappearing into a powdery fine dust. Seraphina slumped to the ground exhausted at the draining task of holding the Orb stable whilst it gave up its secrets. Misa held Solgiven's hand. "You have been both father and mother to me, nothing be changing that." The huge man looked lost, he smiled softly but inside his heart felt torn, their lives would never be the same. He knew that the little girl he had named Misa that he had kept sheltered from the world would want to explore this whole new world now laid at her feet. Her dormant skills would ignite now that she had the last piece of the puzzle, her Gemini sister, and nephew Alfie a legend in himself. Solgiven believed her simple woodland life would pale into insignificance and now, to rub salt into the wound, she would forever more be exposed to danger, no matter how careful they all were the Gorans would be hell-bent on recovering the Trinity of Delaney for themselves, but his worst fear was the possibility that Triamena would rise up and claim her birthright. He just wanted to snatch up Misa and disappear into the dark night never to be seen again, their fate was now taken from his hands, he was no longer the master of Misa's destiny.

Seraphina mind spoke to him. *You should be proud, you have brought her up well, we may not always be agreeing with each other but she has grown to be a strong woman. I trust we can all work together to get them through the trials they will face over the coming days.* Solgiven smiled at her and tipped his head to her.

Arksanza did not miss the gesture, he gave a sigh of relief, at least the hostility between the two would not be a distraction. Once again clapping his hands together he summoned them all to group together.

"I be realizing some of you here tonight will have seen and heard many strange and wondrous things. That be said we must now focus on the task ahead, the safety of Alfie, his mother and Misa be paramount. To our best ability we must be giving the Gorans the impression that you have all perished in a terrible fire and that their powers have died with them."

"What are you saying, we have to burn the house down?" called out a concerned Mark. The family gasped.

"But this is our home, where will we live?" said a tearful Tallulah.

"What about the cats?" said Mollie.

Arksanza was being bombarded from all sides, Alfie had had enough. "Don't you people realize the danger we are all in? This isn't a game for Christ's sake. Whatever we are told is being done to literally save our lives, so start listening and do as you are instructed." Risla and Eisiam stood behind Alfie in support of their friend as an emotional boy wiped at his eyes with the sleeve of his shirt.

"Well I for one don't care if you burn this place down to the ground, I will be glad to see the back of it," called out Nellie.

"You don't mean that," said Mark.

"Yes I do. This place has brought me nothing but sadness. I obviously have memories which haven't surfaced yet, my mother rambled around here like a lost soul and now I know why," she said looking to Misa. "Even after other siblings were born nothing changed with Maggie. This place has no soul or life about, burning it will put the ghosts to rest, so let's just get on with it." Alfie felt like he wanted to cheer. His mother's support meant the world to him and helped to ease the guilt he felt at bring this all down upon his family.

"Firstly there be many ways into this house though they may not be apparent to us, we must be waiting for Thomas Tobias Trendall. As we speak Weslan is recovering him, he knows the mazes of this house like no one else and he will be helping Seraphina enchant the house and give us protection." Nellie's heart skipped a beat at the mention of her oldest and dearest friend. She looked upon him as a grandfather figure. She had felt sad that he had chosen not to stay on after her mother died although they had seen him on occasional visits, now she understood an intricate web of mistruth, smokescreens and illusion had needed to be created to fool the Gorans. She suspected that Old Tom's presence at the house would have maybe given Alfie and herself away. Maybe even too the Gorans could have known Old Tom as Thomas Tobias Trendall, sentinel and family protector. She pinched the skin on the back of her hand just to make sure she could feel the pain, to check she was awake and not in the twilight world of sleep and dreams. A Hollywood film script is what this story sounded like, almost unbelievable, yet she had seen with her own eyes the fantastical tale through the Orb created by Seraphina and the tales her son had excitedly relayed back to her upon their reunion, the pain of her pinch was real enough. By now everyone had descended downstairs to the kitchen.

"We must gather anything that will burn, furniture, clothing. Tallulah go seek out your pets but no one is to take anything else. We will travel by the tunnels of the Harpy Caverns, they are low and narrow, so we will take only ourselves." Tallulah and Jodie scampered off with a tin of cat food, two cat baskets and a fork. Fortunately for them the cats had not been fed for a couple of days so the gentle tap tapping of the tin sent them scampering from all directions eager to feed. Seconds later an empty clean bowl and contented full cats were scooped up and securely locked into the baskets.

A mysterious tapping noise appeared to be coming from the pantry cupboard. "What is that, listen?" said Mark.

"I think that it be coming from in here," as Risla tapped on the door.

"Don't do that, it could be a Goran or one of those Durras things," said Em. The tap responded.

"I hardly think they would alert us to their presence," said Risla as he edged the door open. The tapping previously muffled now became louder, both Risla and Eisiam knelt down and listened to the sound. "Who's there?" whispered Risla.

"Look," said Arksanza, "there appears to be a secret opening," as he scratched away the packed in soil and dust from the edges with his knife. "Be prepared," he whispered over his shoulder as he began to prise the wooden edge with the tip. Risla grabbed a broom, Eisiam a rolling pin and Em a huge bag of flour she was just barely able to lift above her head.

Risla looked at her with some confusion and Mark said, "What you going to do with that bake them to death?"

"Flour in the eye is very painful actually."

"Hush up you two I can hear a voice."

Softly they heard, "Arksanza, it's me open the trapdoor," with coughing and spluttering and the door slightly lifted but did not give way.

"Quickly Risla push your knife along the edge I will do the same on mine." Both Faerians chipped away as the time old seal began to give way. Suddenly the trapdoor flew open and two muddy, dust covered faces with cobwebs clinging to their hair appeared into the light of the pantry.

"Old Tom!" exclaimed Mark. "What you doing down there my old mate?" he asked as he reached with his hand to help pull up the elderly man. Arksanza was equally shocked to find Elancie and not Weslan with his elderly companion.

DIAMOND BOY IN THE ROUGH

"You made it my friend," he cried and hugged Elancie. Manutik and Misa came into the kitchen, Manutik looked back down the hole where they had come from and sniffed the odour of the tunnel.

"We should be able to use this to gain access to the entrance to the Harpy Caverns."

Old Tom embraced the Goran. "My boy it seems an age since I have seen you how is your father, Nenrin?"

Manutik brushed some of the soil from Old Tom's shoulders, "He fairs well considering his age, we lost my brother Islan. A traitor gave him up to Traska."

Old Tom hung his head with sadness at this news. "These are truly dangerous times my friend." Alfie came into the kitchen; instant joy crossed his face in recognition of the two strangers covered in muck.

"Oh my god Elancie, I'm so pleased you escaped," and he embraced the Faerian. Then he turned to Old Tom. "I know all about you, what you have done for my family, what you did for Branna." He could feel his bottom lip begin to tremble, the old man grabbed him and held him in a headlock and ruffled his hair.

"Less of the slushy stuff young 'un seems you been busy," he said pointing at the axe in his hand. "Does your mother know you got that? She'll be having kittens." Alfie laughed grateful Old Tom had saved him from a blub fest.

"I really don't think she is going to be worried about that after what he has gone through," said Alfie's father.

Arksanza leant forward to close down the trapdoor when Misa said, "Wait I hear something," as she dropped to her knees. "Listen!" Alfie was next to her his head hanging inside straining to hear as Risla hung on to his legs.

"It sounds like a dog." A faint echo vibrated up the tunnel.

"Woof, woof."

Elancie came to the opening. "That damn dog be the death of me, I told her be guarding the entrance."

Alfie popped his head up. "Is it Lolah?" he asked excitedly and then began to call and whistle her, she jubilantly barked back.

"Why does that animal never be doing as she be ordered?"

Alfie chuckled. "Simple she can smell the pancakes we cooked, they are her favourite." Out of the shadows a dirty grey face with a big black nose appeared manically barking at the sight of her friend Alfie. She tried to launch herself up the first few rungs, clambering her huge hairy great feet grasping clumsily and then slipping back down, standing on her hind legs to reach up and lick Alfie's face. "Who's a clever girl," he said as she whined, as each effort to climb the stairs failed.

"Someone will have to go down and lift her up, if she be barking much more like that then the Gorans will definitely find the tunnels."

Misa jumped to her feet. "I will get my father, he be the best person for the job." She was gone and back in seconds. Georgie eyed up Solgiven.

"Will he even fit through the entrance? What if he gets stuck?"

Charlie giggled but instantly stopped when Solgiven turned and said, "I maybe big but I not be deaf. Now make yourselves useful, as I push her up you haul her through the hole." Both boys looked equally chastised and rushed forward to get ready. At first Lolah did not cooperate, she thought it was a game of chase and Solgiven was the least patient person to be dealing with her. They tried to stifle their giggles as they could hear Solgiven cursing the dog, even Misa had tears of laughter running down her cheeks.

"Dad get me a packet of those biscuits," he planned to get Solgiven to tempt her with them. By now the hole was blocked by Alfie, Georgie and Risla who was munching on the biscuits. "Nice are they?" said Alfie sarcastically as the Faerian chomped away in his ear.

"Err most pleasant, sugar is a wondrous thing," said Risla spluttering crumbs over Alfie's face.

Wiping at his cheek with Risla's tunic Alfie said, "Do you think you could give them to the bloody dog then?" Arksanza was now agitated they needed to be getting on with their plans or they would soon lose the cover of night.

"Get that dog up here now, we do not be having time for this charade." One, two, three pulls and one large hairy dog and three boys covered in mud and slobber fell through on to the kitchen floor.

Solgiven emerged looking green in the face, "That creature has a foul problem with its stomach, I doubt the depths of the underworld be having such a stench," and as if to prove a point a loud rumbling fizz of air exited the dog, clearing everyone from the kitchen.

"It must have been all that squeezing," muttered Alfie from beneath his hands. Nellie and Seraphina had now come down to see what the commotion was about. Nellie nearly dropped to her knees in total shock as she set eyes upon the Old English sheepdog. Lolah also stopped in her tracks as she studied the dark-haired woman with her face in her hands sobbing, then she whined and lunged at her excitedly wagging her tailless butt barking like a puppy as Nellie threw her arms around her.

"Oh my baby girl is it really you?" Nellie cried as she ruffled the dog's mane of hair and pulled it free from her eyes, to look at her expression. "Oh my god it really is you!" She looked up at Seraphina.

"She was brought back from the spirit world to protect your son, your bond was so strong, we knew she be instantly attached to Alfie. She found him when he be close to death because of your love for her, we would never have found him in time if it not be for her."

Nellie threw a look at Alfie. "Oh yeah I forgot to tell you about that."

The dog was so excited springing about the room running from person to another lapping up all the attention, sniffing at the cats in their baskets, much to their distain, and then eventually resting at the bottom of the stairs in the hallway.

"I think she remembers this house, she always slept there, as a child I would try and sneak over the top of her and tiptoe to the pantry for a snack. Every time I turned around she would be waiting for a biscuit and scare the life out of me."

Tallulah tickled Lolah's belly whilst she settled for a snooze, "So she really was your dog, not one that looks the same, the real one? That's amazing, the whole thing is amazing!"

Alfie patted the dog on the head, "Now we need to get on with the wood for the fire." Mark couldn't believe the almost cavalier attitude that Alfie and his mother had towards this lovely big old house being burnt to the ground and not to mention the antique furniture that was being quickly disassembled with too much relish for his liking. Alfie could sense his father's anguish. "Dad it's just bricks and mortar nothing is more important than family. I don't want to scare you but those are some crazy creatures out there." He handed his father a lump hammer, which Mark reluctantly took and set about a bookcase. A pile of mangled wood soon rose up in the centre of the front room, Arksanza inspected it and declared it was enough and then ordered them all to go to the entrance of the trapdoor in the kitchen all except Alfie, his mother and Misa, Seraphina also stayed behind as well.

"Why do they have to stay?" asked Mark.

"Do not worry my friend we will follow shortly. Go down into the tunnel, take the cats and Lolah, a strong Magiks needs to be performed and now the Trinity of Delaney is brought together we can accomplish this. Please my friend, follow Manutik and Elancie." The others had all followed Risla.

Old Tom took Mark by the arm, "Come with me, they will be safe and soon with us. Come."

Nellie turned to him, "It's fine go on," she said trying to disguise the excitement she felt growing within her. She had no idea where it came from only that she felt energized and powerful. Arksanza paused for a moment then called all three to stand around the outside of the wood pile.

"As you are a Trinity your powers combined will be so much more. Alfie is aware of some of his skills but you Misa and Nellie do not yet know your capabilities, your powers have been latent. Alfie summon up your talisman and we shall see if this stimulates that of your mother and aunt." He stood before them his shirt pulled open as he began to focus and draw up his energy, his arms out and taut as the talisman in his chest began to glow, both his mother and Misa gasped.

"Do not move from your spot," he ordered them both, the ground began to shake beneath them as the clinking of the glass chandelier in the hallway drew their attention temporarily.

"Focus," shouted Seraphina. Nellie looked at her son, his face so determined as the talisman grew ever brighter and pulsed like it would spring from his chest, his eyes blazing vivid emerald green as were Misa's, the power generated by Alfie now lifting the furniture like an unseen tornado spinning it in a column, growing faster and faster. Seraphina had to shout above the roar, "Keep control Alfie." He didn't answer but she knew he heard as his face stiffened. Nellie began to feel a warm sensation generate in her chest, she felt with her fingers as a form began to move under her hand. She caught her breath shocked to feel such a thing as she looked across to her sister Misa who had the same glowing symbol developing and causing her the same alarm.

"Do not worry it will not harm you. Feel the energy, embrace it, it is part of you, your birthright, now is your time to claim it." Her hair had worked loose as had the other women's, Arksanza's Lockan was primed and ready, on alert as was he, the noise now generated would surely be heard outside the house. Alfie's talisman had never burned so bright it was almost white with its energy as surge after surge raged through his body; it took every ounce of strength to contain a full-on Awakening. Nellie and Misa were both entering a state of power, their natural instincts overtaking them when suddenly Seraphina called out.

"The forces outside are amassing we must be completing this Magiks with haste. If you ever be needing to find strength, now be that time."

Alfie could sense the panic in her voice. "Come on Mum we can do this," he roared inspiring Misa also, then something completely unexpected and never before experienced happened. The talisman in Alfie's chest tore from his skin, the form of a fiery eagle-like bird swooped up and around the column of twisting mangled furniture. For a couple of seconds Alfie lost concentration and some pieces flew out causing them to duck.

"Control it Alfie," roared Arksanza. Alfie quickly regained his composure and stared in awe at the graceful swooping bird soaring above his head, as Misa began to let out a primal powerful scream coming deep from her core as her talisman too burned white hot quickly followed by Nellie as simultaneously, they both released their own fiery creatures. A flaming horse with a whipping mane trailing behind had sprung from Misa and it scorched the ceiling as it made contact and a snarling wolf with slashing claws erupted from Nellie. Seraphina was in total awe of these mythical creatures, she had heard legends of such a thing but never believed she would see it in her lifetime, she mind spoke to all three members of the Trinity. That in itself scared the life out of both Nellie and Misa, to hear a voice that was not their own in their heads. The intense heat set the column alight, a huge sheet of bubbling blue white flame rolled across the ceiling in response to the emotion of fear both women were experiencing. The eagle seemed calmer, more controlled, gliding with ease, consciously targeting and picking out the best spots to set alight with his smouldering wing tips.

These creatures are yours to command, speak to them with your minds. Misa and Nellie you must steel your minds, push fear to the back. See how the talisman of Alfie is focused and direct. The curtains spontaneously burst into flames, paint spitting, blistering and dropping to the floor. *Set your creatures free about this house, they shall not rest until it all burns and lights up the night sky. Come we must be away to the tunnel for our safety.* The screeching talisman animals set about reaching, burning vengeance about the house, the fire roared, screamed and sucked the oxygen from the rooms, each one of them, slashing, melting hot claws into plastered walls, swiping hot fiery wings across the carpets, landings and remaining furniture, stamping flaming hooves into the solid oak beams and wooden floors, the column of twisting fire assisting in causing chaos and destruction, heavy charred black with burning orange centred pillars toppled to the ground smashing and splintering the natural wood floors as Alfie, his mother and aunt all ran to the tunnel with the two Faerians close behind, dropping into the already smoke-filled tunnel as the trapdoor was slammed firmly shut behind.

"What about the talismans, how will they escape?" asked Alfie as he turned to look back up at the wooden slats of the trapdoor.

"Leave them to their business, they be returning to your bodies when their task be done," called Seraphina as she took off ahead. "Come we must make haste."

Above them they could hear the satanic screams of the fire, it sounded like the gates of hell had opened up, with crashing and shattering, popping and ear-piercing booms. They were all breathless but all eager to get distance between them and the fire as they scampered down the dimly-lit tunnel towards the rest of the family and other Faerians, Old Tom standing his arms out waiting to greet Alfie, Nellie and Misa.

"That wasn't so bad then," he said as he wiped the smutty smears from their faces with his jumper sleeve, the tunnel was now rapidly filing with the toxic smouldering smoke, harsh and abrasive on their eyes and throats, Alfie noticed Solgiven clinging to his Moonstone pouch.

"We need to be getting out of here quick march Arksanza," he said nodding his head towards Solgiven, the elderly Faerian acknowledge Alfie.

"Yes I am aware but the tunnel ends here and opens out into the field behind the house and leads into the forest, we will be in the open for about 500 yards."

"What!" came a cry in unison.

"Nobody said anything about being outside with those creatures. Are you mental?" shouted Georgie.

"Would you have come if he had told us?" snapped Mark. "No you bloody wouldn't, so shut up, man up and pin back your lugholes," he instructed looking around at everyone.

Risla whispered to Eisiam, "What be lugholes?" She just look blankly at him and shrugged her shoulders, Alfie was too tired to even raise a giggle.

Arksanza crouched low and slowly crept forward towards the entrance, trying to breathe low so the cold air would not fog up and give him away.

Seraphina also shuffled forward. "Do you see anything My Lord?" she whispered. Without speaking he pointed to the left, she could see a small group their backs to them all facing towards the inferno, he then indicated that another group sat on the right just in front of the entrance into the forest, she looked at him wide-eyed and in her mind said, *What are we to do?*

He smiled, "I am waiting."

She was tired and exhausted and in no mood for games and in annoyance said out loud, "Waiting for what?" As the last word fell from her lips a world-ending boom and massive explosion ripped through the atmosphere sending out a sonic wave of energy and earth tremors, knocking them from their feet and showering them with soil, roots and gritty sediment. The tunnel vibrated in reaction to the gas boiler in the house succumbing to the heat of the raging fire causing a sky-high explosion.

"That be what I was waiting for. Everyone run, run as fast as you can as if your life depends on it. Don't look back, follow Old Tom, he knows the way." Arksanza gave one more check and as he had hoped the Gorans and their Durras ran towards the engulfed house leaving the way clear, if only temporarily. He waved his hand forward and en masse they took off.

Old Tom set a blazing pace holding tightly to Tallulah and Mollie. "Jesus I don't know what vitamin supplements he's on I but want some," Mollie cried amazed at the pace of the old fella. Em and Charlie put their long legs to good use and quickly cleared the ground. Solgiven lumbered along, he wasn't built for speed and in his weakening state was some way behind the main group. He urged Misa to catch up as Seraphina dropped back.

"Misa go ahead stay close to Alfie and Nellie." Misa hesitated but took off once her father waved her on. She ploughed her way through the long grass to quickly come to the entrance where everyone else sat heaving and breathless recovering from their panicked, adrenaline-fuelled run. She threw herself to the ground and lay flat on her back.

"Where is your father?" asked Risla as he stood looking out across the field.

Misa still lying flat pointed loosely, "Over there. Seraphina is with him they not be far behind." Risla strained to see the two silhouettes against the yellow orange backdrop of the fire. Alfie and Arksanza now both came to stand next to Risla.

"I cannot see them, can either of you?" he asked. Arksanza shaded his eyes against the brightness of the fire.

Nervously he said, "No."

Misa jumped up. "They were right behind me. Where they be?" her voice wavering with emotion.

Suddenly Alfie spotted movement. "Look there I see something." Two figures had appeared from out of the tall grass. Alfie tried to mind speak to Seraphina but she was not responding. He glanced quickly at Arksanza, he too could get nothing.

"Something is not right, something has happened."

Misa was beginning to cry, "Do something someone."

"Manutik," shouted Arksanza. "Take everyone down the tunnels to the Lair, alert the warriors and send them prepared to meet us should we be in need of them. Elancie, Risla, Alfie stay here with me."

Nellie instantly protested. "No it's not safe for him here, I will not leave." Alfie shook his head.

"Madam, your son is no longer a child he has proved himself time and time again, it is time to cut him free from your apron strings and let him be a man." Mark gasped. Alfie gasped. All the Diamond children gasped. She was not going to like that.

Strangely she did not burst out with anger or rant at the Faerian who had basically told her to shut up, she merely muttered, "I apologize, I am tired. I know you speak with knowledge. Please just bring him back to us safely," and with that she turned on her heels ready to follow Manutik.

"Jesus Dad, you should have burned the house down before now," said Charlie.

Georgie stood looking up at the sky. "What are you doing?" asked Tallulah.

"Oh just looking for the alien spaceship that came down and swapped the real Mum for this one." He felt a sharp clip around his earhole.

"Shut up you idiot and get moving, you heard your Mother!" barked Mark.

Alfie pointed to the sky. "What is that?"

A miffed Georgie mumbled under his breath, "A spaceship." Three bright lights soared up into the sky leaving a trail like a comets.

"The talismans, they have completed their task and must return to you. Brace yourself Alfie, Misa, Nellie, come quickly stand beside us." The burning lights arced high up into the sky like distress flares illuminating the area below and then with superspeed dropped down flat across the grass field heading straight for them, whooshing rapidly towards them, leaving a burned out trail cut through the field.

"Is this gonna hurt?" shouted Alfie shaking from head to foot.

"That depends on you. How accepting are you of this gift? If you resist it will, my dear boy, be most painful."

"Bloody brilliant, that's me done in then," he said as he screwed up his eyes waiting for the impact. His mother and Misa took a different approach they both calmly stood next to each other holding hands breathing deep and slow, each opening themselves up to receive back their own talisman. The once speeding balls of energy came to a sudden stop inches away from the women and then gently slipped on to the surface of their skin where the birthmarks sat, to melt and combine with the horse and the wolf, just a gasp of surprise and no injuries for Nellie and Misa. Alfie however was not so lucky, he was rigid and fearful, anticipating great pain, and that was exactly what he got as the once elegant and controlled eagle slammed into his body sending him tumbling backwards. He felt like he had been run over by a steam train as he lay groaning looking up at the night sky. He waited patiently for someone to come and assist him up.

"Can I get some help here?" No reply, no friendly hand. He tipped his head forward to look down his body as the others stood in a huddle all looking out into the field, he could just make out their conversation.

"Look along the trail burned out by the eagle, two forms though they seem to be still, not moving. One seems large, the other smaller. Do you think it be them?" said Risla.

Arksanza was not sure and tried to mind speak again to Seraphina, this time she groaned a little. "She be injured it must be them." Risla set off without a second thought even though Arksanza was calling him back, then Elancie was next.

"I see a Gorja hound it stalks them, we have no choice." Elancie was right directly behind the huddled couple was the huge menacing silhouette of a hound. Alfie's heart dropped into his stomach even though he was groggy he staggered to his feet.

Pull yourself together, he told himself and began running, his jelly legs feeling like they could give any minute, then a weak voice appeared in his head.

Use the power of the vines they are in your blood Alfie but you must come quickly. Solgiven is spent and I am too weak to defend us hurry! The sound of her voice spurred him on, a new vitality urging him to run faster soon catching up with Elancie and Risla.

"They have been attacked by the hound." All three now sprinting to the aid of their friends. Alfie got there first and positioned himself between the hound and Seraphina, she was holding her leg. Solgiven was unconscious but there was also another body slumped to the side of them, it was a Gorja hound, motionless, dead.

"He killed it with his bare hands," she said through tears. "We were ambushed we never saw it upon us till it be too late." Elancie dropped down by them and turned Solgiven over.

"Where be his Moonstones?" he asked as Risla and Alfie edged closer to the snarling beast. Seraphina couldn't find them upon his body.

"He must have dropped them." Then Alfie saw a sight he would have given anything not to see, the pouch containing the precious stones was on the floor between the paws of the primed Gorja hound.

"Shit!" Risla tried to taunt the creature to come his way but it seemed to sense the energy from the stones within.

"They come from the Moon and their power source is the Moon. The Gorja is descended from forest wolves they are ruled by the seasons of the Moon. We will not get that creature to leave them willingly, the stones are the only reason they both be alive such is the attraction they have on the hound. Once they are removed it will return its primal attention to the fallen ones, I do not be knowing what to do," admitted Risla.

Elancie called up, "Seraphina is bitten badly. I cannot give treatment here." She groaned. Alfie knew there was only one thing to do; he called upon the earth to help him to summon an Awakening. Small trembles came at first as an energy source entered his feet and tingled up his legs and body into his outstretched hands.

"Risla get behind me," he shouted. "Do not let loose your Lockan the light will be seen for miles." The Gorja stood firmly over the pouch snarling and snapping, white froth dripping from its savage teeth, stamping and standing its ground as Alfie stepped closer.

Arksanza came running forward, "What you be doing with the beast? It looks ready to pounce. Do you be possessed?"

Seraphina called out, "Summon the vines Alfie. You are joined with them and them to you." She gasped as Arksanza applied pressure to her wound whilst Elancie bound it tight, blood oozing through the fabric. The beast sniffed at the air.

"Hey! Hey!" shouted Alfie waving his arms frantically trying to distract the hound, desperately fighting the building panic in his mind as the enraged creature began to edge towards him. Alfie felt sure it was about to spring through the air. He winced when out of nowhere Lolah came flying through the air blindsiding the hound, slamming into its great chest, knocking the wind from it, rendering the hound semi-paralysed for a few seconds whilst it gathered its senses and staggered to its feet. "Risla call off the dog," Alfie shouted.

Risla roared at Lolah, "Come here girl," but she refused so determined to protect Alfie. She circled the stunned and confused hound as it tried to focus upon the dog slashing at her with its claws, tufts of her white and grey fur scattering into the air. She yelped as the razor-like talons raked across her ribs. Alfie was incensed that his beloved friend was injured he tried to focus and remember the feelings he had when he took part in the ceremony in the Book Room. Inhaling a slow deep breath, he asked for their help, his body relaxed as though his very blood were leaving his body to unify with deep buried vines juddering to life beneath his feet. Ripping and tearing soil defiantly the vines burst to the surface, prodding and probing, sensing and scattering ahead of Alfie to explode up and out surrounding the Gorja hound, caging and locking it down in time to stop it going in for a fatal bite to Lolah. It hurled itself at her but to no avail, the rigid solidness of the vines flinging it back like it had been shaken by the scruff of its neck. It was infuriated snapping and biting into the green luscious barbs of the earthy captor; no effect, and one vine was quickly replaced by another, the sour pulp and oozing sap causing it to gag as the bitterness hit the back of its throat.

The hound tried to howl and bark. "We must finish this now before it alerts the Gorans," shouted Risla. Alfie summoned up more vines, they slithered and writhed bubbling like a brook with one mass purpose.

"Silence the beast!" roared Alfie to them and silence it is what they did, overcoming and constricting till its huge bulk disappeared under a tangled ball of crushing power and confusion. Running quickly to Lolah he grabbed her by the scruff and commanded her to come with him, she obediently followed his instruction and ran ahead of him and laid to rest next to Seraphina nuzzling her and whining.

Alfie didn't hang around for the outcome, it was obvious there was no howling, no barking, he didn't need to see the awesome power of the vines he could feel it in his own hands. Turning on his heels, he and Risla returned to Seraphina, Arksanza, Eisiam and Elancie. Alfie tossed the bag of Moonstones to Eisiam she quickly tipped them from the bag into her upturned hand, three of the remaining five stones had lost their glow and a fourth was beginning to dim.

"Quickly place the stones upon Solgiven's heart," shouted Elancie.

Eisiam looked concerned and hesitated, "I believe they should be into his hand," fearful that she was questioning Elancie's judgement.

"In these circumstances we be needing to boost the power and effect quickly and bring the big man to his feet fast. Do you be wishing to haul his carcass back to the Set? Best he be walking out of here under his own power." She wanted to double-check but Arksanza nodded at her to carry out the instruction, so tentatively she did as he was told opening Solgiven's tunic to reveal bare skin. The sight of his scars and rippled, damaged old wounds caused her to pull back her hand.

"Just do Eisiam!" shouted Risla to his sister.

Alfie walked across and softly smiled at his friend. "I will do it if it helps?" She shook her head and threw a look at her brother then gently let the stones sit upon Solgiven's chest. He jolted like he had been hit by a lightning bolt and let out a huge gasp, his eyes wide and panic-stricken as he clawed at his chest. Risla and Alfie jumped upon him to calm him down.

"What be occurring here? Why so much pain?" Eisiam stood in front of him, telling the others to let him go.

"I put the stones upon your chest. Elancie said we must use the power of the waning stones to their best advantage." He stepped forward with agitation as he rubbed his skin to try and sooth it, Eisiam stumbled back slightly flinching as Alfie threw himself between them.

"I took a Gorja hound out, I certainly could handle you big man," said Alfie defiantly into Solgiven's face, who instantly roared with laughter.

"I be very pleased to hear that, I merely wished to thank Eisiam for bringing me back albeit painfully." He winked at the young Faerian maiden. "I know I passed out, I remember telling Seraphina to leave me. Where she be now?" The group huddled around the stricken Seraphina parted, Solgiven's face dropped as he rushed to her side. "What be happening? Why does she not speak?" he cried as he stared horrified at the seeping wound. "What be doing this? Tell me!" he barked.

"A hound that's what. She wouldn't leave and she got bitten, no doubt because she was protecting you." Alfie couldn't help himself as he lunged at the warrior grabbing at his tunic his face distorted by rage. "Why didn't you use the stones? By now you both would have been safely back to the Set." Elancie and Risla tried to pry the angry young man's fingers from the fabric as Alfie's eyes blazed brilliant green.

A soft weak voice entered his mind, *Alfie Diamond of the Delaney clan this not be the way and you be knowing that. Stop this madness at once.* He spun on his heels and looked straight at Seraphina still lying prone on the ground cradled by Arksanza who looked for the first time unsure, weak and frail, at a loss what to do for the best.

"Why aren't you doing anything?" shouted Solgiven as he dropped to his knees next to her on the ground.

"The poison from the bite rapidly attacks her body. We have no medicine, no herbs to heal her, no way of making a potion, her only chance is the Set," said Elancie.

"She is still in there she just spoke to me. We have to try, we cannot let her die, not here, not now," Alfie insisted his eyes filing with angry burning tears, setting off Eisiam, and even Risla sniffed and did a sneaky wipe with the back of his hand. It seemed like time stood still as Arksanza let his head hang in defeat. No one spoke a suffocating silence enveloping them and then suddenly Solgiven scooped her up in huge arms and ran.

"Run!" he shouted, never once looking back to see if they followed. Like a steam locomotive he cut through the grass heading flat out for the entrance in the forest to the tunnels and on to the Harpy Caverns.

"That's why we awakened him in such a manner," said Elancie triumphantly. "He has the power of a demon. See how he covers the ground, Seraphina be like a feather to him. Quickly we must catch up," as he waved them all on. Alfie held back a little to keep pace with Arksanza who was drained and tired, the elderly Faerian stumbling frequently as his exhausted leg muscles felt like they had turned to jelly. Arksanza tried to wave him on but he wasn't having any of it, he called Risla back.

"The longer we are out in the open the more chance one of those freaks is going to see us, give him a backie." Both Risla and Arksanza looked puzzled. "Like you did to me when you found me in the snow. If you can carry me then I'm damn sure you carry a skinny old man, no offence," he patted Arksanza on the back.

"None taken I think," replied Arksanza who secretly could not have felt more relieved, his lungs felt like they were on fire and ready to burst. He happily left his dignity in the field along with the distant amber burning flames, the dead Gorja hound and handful of confused shell-shocked Gorans and their minion Durras. He turned to give one last look as he jumped up upon the younger Faerian's back. "Make haste my young friend," he called out.

"Yeah and don't bloody drop him," said Alfie as they scampered across the remaining distance to the safety of the tunnel entrance to be met by the warriors Manutik had sent back to assist them. Alfie stood looking out as the skeletal frame of his grandmother's once imposing house which shuddered and trembled, giving in to the power and ferocity of the flames, sending scorching embers up into the night sky, hissing and cracking, crashing to the ground. He could feel the heat even now on his face. One more last look and then he turned his back on that episode of his life as he looked to see if Solgiven had disappeared down the tunnel with his precious cargo. Alfie didn't doubt for one minute that Solgiven wouldn't get her there in time, the speed he was travelling at, and deliver her into the hands of the Elders and their healers.

A sense of accomplishment filled Alfie's heart. He was tired, hungry and exhausted. He knew there would questions but he could handle that knowing for now his family were safe, that Seraphina would be safe, that his mother and her sister were reunited and for once his older brothers were in awe of him. He smiled to himself as he stretched out his aching muscles but as he did so a weird feeling crept over him. A cold chill ran through his veins, the hairs on the back of his neck stood up and his stomach flipped over. His brain felt like some was raking through it with a hot knife, like a bony, cruel finger scraped down his spine and then the voice, the hissing, low voice, the cackling, full of vengeance voice he knew, the same voice he had heard at the encampment.

What you be smiling at boy? You can run, run, run but you cannot hide. I have your essence. I hold it in my hands. I be coming for you.

13237055R00180

Printed in Great Britain
by Amazon.co.uk, Ltd.,
Marston Gate.